He's a vampire, a threat to her very life, so why does she want him—need him—so badly?

She felt his breath against her skin as he bent his head to kiss her temple, the wet warmth of his tongue as it teased the curve of her ear. She shivered as he kissed the sensitive skin, tracing the line of her jugular until he stopped and sucked gently, not breaking the skin, not yet, just gliding his tongue in a circle as if marking the spot.

She could feel the smooth brush of his fangs against her neck, the hard length of his cock against her belly. She raised her arms, wrapping them under his shoulders and around his back, pressing herself closer, rubbing herself against his arousal.

Raj chuckled softly. "So eager, little one."

Sarah heard herself moan softly, a sound so full of sensual hunger she couldn't believe it had come from her own throat. Raj responded, growling as he lifted her easily, spinning her around and pinning her against the wall. His hand slipped beneath the silk of her dress, pushing it up her thigh and over her hip. Her arms circling his neck once again, she hooked her bare calf around his hip and urged him closer, wanting to feel him hard and erect. Raj lifted her leg even higher across his back, sliding his hand under her thigh and into the wetness between her legs, pushing aside the soaked triangle of her silken thong.

Sarah cried out as his thick fingers slid easily into her slick folds, penetrating deep inside her, stretching her, preparing her for the full thickness of the cock she could feel growing ever harder, ever longer . . .

Dedicated with love to a most remarkable woman,
my sister Diana

ACKNOWLEDGMENTS

Thanks first of all to Linda Kichline for her patience and skill and everything she does to make it all work. And to Patricia Lazarus for once again producing a gorgeous cover and bringing my words to life so beautifully.

To Steve McHugh and Michelle Muto, two wonderful writers I'm fortunate enough to have as my critique partners. Saying "thank you" doesn't come close to expressing my gratitude for their unflagging support and brilliant input in making this a far better book than it ever would have been without them. But, I'll say it anyway . . . Thank you.

Thanks to John Gorski for his invaluable input on police procedure, as well as all manner of weaponry. If I've made any mistakes or taken any liberties with the facts, it's all on me, never John, who does his darnedest to keep me accurate. To all the members of the OWG who keep spirits high and creative juices flowing even when they're clogged, and to Kelley Armstrong for creating such a great place for writers.

To Adrian Phoenix whose continuing friendship and generous spirit make me believe there might actually exist something called the greater community of writers. To all the bloggers and reviewers out there who continue to spread the word about my vampires, and to all of my readers whose comments and e-mails keep me going by letting me know there are people in the world who love my vamps as much as I do.

Love and thanks to my wonderful husband for putting up with a wife who stays up to all hours of the night writing about vampires and other odd things. And finally, this book is dedicated to my sister Diana whose belief in me has been a constant from the very first word I wrote. No matter what the world throws at me, I know I'm never alone, because Diana's got my back. So, this one's for you, Buddha. I love you.

For contests, teasers and Vampire Vignettes, visit me at:
http://dbreynolds/wordpress.com

Other Books by D. B. Reynolds

Raphael
Jabril
Coming soon
Sophia
Duncan

Rajmund

***

D. B. Reynolds

ImaJinn Books

Rajmund
Published by ImaJinn Books, Inc.

ISBN: 978-1-933417-07-3

10 9 8 7 6 5 4 3 2 1

PUBLISHER'S NOTE:
This book is a work of fiction. Names, characters, places and incidents are products of the author's imagination or are used fictitiously. Any resemblance to actual events or locales or persons, living or dead, is entirely coincidental.

Books are available at quantity discounts when used to promote products or services. For information please write to: Marketing Division, ImaJinn Books, Inc., P.O. Box 74274, Phoenix, AZ 85087, or call toll free 1-877-625-3592.

Cover design by Patricia Lazarus

Cover Photo Credits:
Photo - Yuri Arcur- Dreamstimephotos
Photo - Fotoeye75 - Dreamstimephotos
Photo - Klotz - Dreamstimephotos

ImaJinn Books, Inc.
P.O. Box 74274, Phoenix, AZ 85087
Toll Free: 1-877-625-3592
http://www.imajinnbooks.com

Prologue

Buffalo, New York

It was totally dark. She touched her fingers to her eyes to make sure they were open. They were. But the room was like pitch black, like she couldn't see her freakin' hand in front of her face. Her mom must have pulled the stupid blinds down behind the curtains again to save energy. Regina was all for saving energy, but she wasn't a damn bat either. She sat up with an irritated groan and reached for the small lamp near her bed, nearly falling on her face when it wasn't there. She frowned and felt around blindly with both hands, finally hitting something solid. A small table lamp, but not hers. The first stirrings of unease coiled in her chest as her hand felt its way up the unfamiliar base to an old-fashioned push-button switch. A press of her thumb yielded a dim, yellow light.

She stared, abruptly wide awake. This wasn't her room. The strange lamp should have warned her, but somehow she'd still expected to see her familiar bedroom with the old-timey furniture she'd inherited from her Gramma Lena and the cheesy posters she'd bought with her twenty-first birthday money two years ago, the ones she'd thought were so sophisticated, but turned out to be just weird. But this wasn't her room; it wasn't even her house. So where the hell was she?

She blinked, forcing down her fear and thinking furiously. She'd gone out with friends. Right, okay. Katie's bachelorette party. But after that . . . She'd probably had too much to drink. All the signs were there, the sick stomach, the pounding head. God, had one of her friends dragged her home with them? Had she been that out of it? A wave of guilt swept over her, replacing the fear and tightening her chest with remorse. She could hear her mom's voice lecturing her, saying, "If you can't drive, you catch a cab or go home with one of the girls instead. Just make sure you call me, Regina, so I don't worry." She clutched the rough blanket close against a sudden chill and swung her legs over the side of the bed. Her feet touched a cold, damp floor and she frowned at the sensation. A concrete floor? She looked up. No windows either. Was this a basement? She didn't remember any of her friends having guest rooms in—

It all came rushing back—the lights on the dark street, ice gleaming on the sidewalks. She'd almost fallen. No she *had* fallen. She flushed in embarrassment and remembered a strong hand gripping her arm, keeping her from hitting the ground. She'd glanced up, wanting to thank her rescuer and then—

She jumped as a noise broke the silence, something loud and heavy, a door slamming into a wall. She froze, listening, expecting footsteps.

She heard a soft sob instead, a woman's voice somewhere nearby. She stood, taking a tentative step toward the door which was little more than an outline in the dim light. "Hello," she whispered, wondering if the other person could hear her. She reached for the door knob. "Hello?" she said again, louder this time.

A heavy footstep scuffed in the hallway and she snatched her hand back, holding herself tightly. Her heart was racing suddenly, her breath fast and shallow, making her lightheaded as she strained to hear. A key rattled and the unseen woman began to cry, louder now, pleading. Regina stumbled back onto the bed, pulling her feet up, wrapping her arms around her legs, trying to be small, to be invisible.

The woman began to scream . . .

Chapter One

Sarah Stratton's eyes opened, a scream filling her throat, choking her as she fought it down, as her hand slapped the switch next to her bed. Light flooded the room and she sat up, her gaze taking in every familiar detail. She inhaled, a deep sucking breath that was more of a sob, like in her dream.

"Stop it," she told herself. It had been a dream, a nightmare, nothing more. The darkness, the terror—they weren't real. Not this time. Hot tears flooded her eyes and she dashed them away angrily. Climbing out of bed, she stumbled over to her closet. There was no point in trying to go back to sleep, she had to get up soon anyway. She had two classes to teach and blue books to grade. Might as well get an early start, get in her morning jog, maybe have a real cup of coffee at the local Starbuck's instead of sleeping that extra hour. It wasn't because she was afraid of the dream, afraid the fear would come back, the helplessness—

"Stop it, Sarah," she repeated.

She pulled on her winter jogging clothes with quick, sharp movements—warm leggings, a sweatshirt over a sensible athletic bra. It was nearly spring, but she'd learned the hard way that cold weather lingered here in Buffalo, especially in the mornings. She twisted her long blond hair into a secure ponytail before bending to lace up her shoes. Downstairs, she grabbed her warm windbreaker from the closet and zipped her cell phone and ten dollars into a pocket, adding her keys once she'd locked the front door securely behind her.

She paused for a moment to adjust to the freezing air, noting the slick spots on the short walkway down to the street. The girl in her dream—Regina she'd called herself—had fallen on a walkway much like this one. Sarah shook her head adamantly, refusing the memory. *A dream,* she reminded herself. She did a few warm-ups, leaning against the old wooden railing, stretching her hamstrings. The light was still burning on her landlady's side of their shared porch, but it was too early for even that industrious lady. But not too early for Sarah.

She took the stairs down at a quick jog, stepping to the side and running across the dead grass to avoid the slick pavement. On the street, she settled into her regular pace, legs pumping smoothly, breath easing in and out in a steady rhythm, her body warm despite the icy morning. And finally, she permitted herself to think about the dream and what it might mean.

It had been years since she'd had a nightmare that bad, the kind that brought her awake screaming, that brought back the cold and the damp, the despair . . . the wisp of humid breath over a bare cheek, the heat of a hand as it reached to touch—

Sarah stopped in the middle of the empty street, breathing hard, her heart pounding. She bent over, hands on her knees, each breath a gasp for air.

"Hey, you okay?" She jumped at the man's voice, nearly stumbling as she backed away, eyes wide. He raised his hands, palms out and took a step back. "Sorry. I just thought—"

Sarah forced a smile, trying to look normal, but she could tell by the look on his face that it wasn't working. "No, *I'm* sorry," she said, fighting to even out her breathing. "I didn't hear you coming. Yeah, I'm fine. Bad night last night."

The other jogger nodded, clearly not believing her, but anxious to get away from the crazy lady. "If you're sure—"

"Yeah. Yes." She waved him away. "Thanks for stopping, though. I appreciate it." She began to walk slowly, hands on her hips, cursing her own stupidity. She didn't even look up as the helpful man jogged past, not wanting to see the concern, or the curiosity, on his face.

The dreams, the damn, stupid dreams. Why were they back? And why now?

Chapter Two

Her office was too warm. Coming from California, it was always a surprise to Sarah that people on the east coast kept their rooms so warm. It made her drowsy, which only reminded her she'd gotten up an hour early this morning, and why. She hunched determinedly over her desk at the university, trying to keep her eyes from crossing as she read what passed for freshmen college essays these days. Low music played in the background, a golden oldies station, playing tunes from the sixties and seventies, the songs of another generation that somehow spoke to her soul. But not even the sweet rhythms of Motown could soften her disgust with the essays she was reading. What did they teach these kids in high school anyway? Half of them couldn't spell worth a damn and most of the other half had the vocabulary of a thirteen-year-old. Granted, most of them were only taking her World History class because they had to, but—

A phone rang. She'd already picked up her desk phone's receiver before her brain processed the fact that it was her cell phone ringing instead. She dropped the landline receiver with a disgusted sigh and fished her cell out of her coat pocket where it was thrown over a nearby filing cabinet.

Checking the caller ID, she smiled and flipped it open. "Hi, Cyn."

"You ever wonder what people did before caller ID?" Cyn asked.

"Answered the phone and hoped for the best, I suppose. Why?"

Cyn made a discontented noise. "How's Buffalo?"

"Hmmm. Okay, I guess. But there's this white stuff everywhere. I'm not sure what it is exactly, but it's cold and slippery."

"Sounds intriguing. Except for the cold and slippery part."

"Yeah, well, not really. So, not that I'm complaining—because I'm grading blue books and I'll take any excuse for a break—but why are you awake? The sun is shining, where you are anyway. Shouldn't you be cuddled up next to that gorgeous vampire you're living in sin with?"

Cyn blew out a dismissive breath. "Don't be stodgy, Sarah. You're too young for it. Besides, we did the whole blood exchange thing . . . repeatedly actually. We're mated and that's the vampire equivalent of marriage. When in Rome . . ."

"Okay, *yuck* on the blood thing. I still don't understand how—"

"The *blood thing* is important, Sarah. Especially for a super vamp like Raphael. It marks me as his mate, which is a sort of protection. And it links us in a way . . . I don't know if I can explain it. But it's important."

"All right, I believe you. Changing the subject now. *Please* tell me it's not like eighty degrees in Malibu."

"It's not. It's raining, which means the natives are convinced the end is near and are engaged in ritual auto pileups in an attempt to appease the angry gods."

"I remember it well. So why *are* you awake? It's barely past noon on your coast."

"Shareholder's meeting. I had breakfast afterward with my father and grandmother. Sometimes I don't think we'd recognize each other if not for the family resemblance."

Sarah thought about her own family and forced a polite laugh. Cyn, of course, wasn't fooled.

"Everything all right, Sarah?"

"Sure, why?"

"Oh, man, that was weak. What's going on?"

"No, really. I'm fine. It's probably just this God-awful weather."

"You're the one who wanted to move far away from sunny California."

"Yeah." Sarah sighed deeply and said again, more softly, "Yeah."

"Okay, that's it. We need to get you out of that two-horse town. I think a vacation is definitely in order."

"I can't, Cyn. Even if I had the money, which I don't—"

"I've got—"

"—I can't take the time off. I'm teaching two classes and they've loaded me up with committee work. I'm the new kid, I'm untenured and I'm female, which means I get all the crap assignments, because they know I can't refuse."

"A weekend," Cyn insisted. "The university won't collapse if you take a weekend off. Come on. Somewhere close. What's close to that place? Niagara Falls? Hell, no," she answered herself. "Full of tourists and all that water, which is probably frozen stiff by now. Wait! Where's my head? Manhattan! You're like an hour away by air, and my God, Sarah, the stores!"

"Cyn, I can't. Besides, we'll never get a hotel—"

"Who needs a hotel? My father has a townhouse or a condo or something. It's always empty this time of year. He hates the cold."

"Okay, fine. One weekend, Cyn. That's it."

"What a grouch. Is this what happens when you become a professor? You're not wearing tweed, are you?"

Sarah laughed at last. A real laugh this time, not the forced, polite one from before. "No, no tweed. That stuff itches. I'll figure out which airline to call and—"

"No, I'll make all the arrangements. I don't trust you. Any weekend in particular good for you?"

"No, they're pretty much all the same," Sarah admitted, contemplating her dreary life.

"Well, Jesus, Sarah. No wonder you need a vacation. Okay. Let me talk to Raphael and I'll get back to you. This is going to be fun!"

"If you say so."

"Work on that attitude, girl. I'll call you back."

Sarah pulled the phone away from her ear, feeling abruptly deflated as Cyn disconnected. She could have told Cyn about the dreams. Cyn would have understood, would have tried to help. After all, she was living with a vampire, for God's sake. What was a little telepathic dreaming compared to having your lover suck your blood every night? But Sarah had never told anyone. Not since she'd gotten out of that place.

Maybe Cyn was right. She'd been under a lot of stress with the new job and the move across the country to a city she'd never even visited, except for her job interview. And Buffalo was so different from L.A. or even Berkeley, *especially* Berkeley.

She stared at the backlit screen of her cell phone until it went black, then slid it into her pocket and went back to her blue books. There were pills one could buy over the counter now, sleeping pills that worked as well or better than some prescription meds. Maybe she'd stop at the drug store on her way home. Bad enough that Cynthia would show up looking like a runway model; there was no need for Sarah to look like five months of bad weather. Even if she was living in Buffalo.

Chapter Three

Malibu, California

Raphael stood in front of the full-length mirror, automatically sliding the red length of a silk tie beneath his collar as he watched Cynthia move absently around the room behind him. His Cyn was normally a direct woman, but there were times . . . Usually when she wanted something she knew he would resist. He smiled, meeting her eyes in the mirror as she came up behind him.

"I'll do that," she said, and slipped around in front, taking the tie and running it through her elegant fingers.

He surrendered it willingly, always pleased when she ministered to him, which wasn't often. She was fiercely loyal. She would, and had, killed to defend him and his. But she didn't take to what in his day would have been considered the more womanly chores. He almost laughed out loud at the thought.

She caught the edge of his smile and scowled up at him. "What are you thinking, vampire?"

"Only of how much I enjoy having you fix my tie for me."

She squinted doubtfully. "Uh huh." She finished knotting the silk and reached up to turn his collar down. She had to stand on tiptoes to reach behind his neck and he put his hands on her hips, steadying her and pulling her closer, enjoying the press of her full breasts against his chest. She raised her face to his, and he indulged himself in a long, slow exploration of her delicious mouth, feeling the soft warmth of her breath against his cheek.

His body responded to her as it always did, his cock stirring eagerly, as hungry for the taste of her as if they hadn't just made love less than an hour ago. He slid his hands from her hips to the firm curve of her ass, pulling her close and let her feel his arousal. "Trying to ply me with sex, my Cyn?"

"I don't need to ply you," she murmured against his mouth. "You're already mine."

He smiled. "True enough, *lubimaya*. Why don't you just ask whatever it is?"

She stiffened in his arms and his smile grew.

"Whatever what is?" she demanded.

He laughed out loud, and she drew back enough to slap his chest, immediately smoothing the spot as if afraid she'd hurt him. "Damn vampire."

"Ah, but I am yours, am I not?"

She wrapped both arms around his neck. "I was thinking," she admitted slowly. He gave her a smug smile and she scowled up at him.

"I want go to New York this weekend."

He frowned. "It's snowing there."

"But it's Manhattan—shopping, clubs, museums. What's a little snow?"

He raised one eyebrow and she clicked her tongue in disgust. "Fine. You remember my friend Sarah?"

He hadn't met that many of her friends, but the name . . . "The one in the bar?" he asked, doubtfully.

"That's the one. Something—or someone—is bothering her. I want to know what. She's in Buffalo," she said with a grimace of distaste. "As if that's not enough to get someone down, but I don't think that's it. Or not just that, anyway. I'm going to meet her in Manhattan for the weekend."

"Are you?" She glared up at him and he added, "I cannot let you go to Manhattan alone, my Cyn."

Her glare turned to a look of interest. "My father has a place there. I'm sure—"

"I too have a *place*," he chided her gently. "With far more suitable accommodations than your father's. But it is not a simple matter for me or my mate to travel to another's territory." He drew a long breath, thinking about Cyn's request and how it might serve a purpose of his own. "One weekend, *lubimaya,* no more."

She grinned, standing on tiptoe again to kiss him hard on the mouth. "I love you," she whispered.

"I know," he said smugly.

She slapped his chest again. "Say it."

"You are my heart, my soul, my life."

Her lovely green eyes filled with tears and she coughed to cover her emotion. "Should I talk to Duncan?"

"I will do so. Arrangements will need to be made with Krystof and with Rajmund, who runs the city for him."

His phone rang and he turned to pick it up from the desk. "Duncan," he said, answering. "A few moments, thank you." He hung up. "Do you have plans for the evening?"

"I'm sparring with Elke later, and maybe Mirabelle, and then I need to check on some Internet searches I've got going and send off a few reports. Nothing major."

"I will have Duncan coordinate with you then." She grabbed him when he would have turned away, fisting her fingers in his short hair and pulling his head down for a deep, lingering kiss.

"We could stay in and have wild monkey sex all night instead. It's cold and raining up there."

"He glanced at his watch. "Three hours, my Cyn, and then I will permit you to ply me with sex until morning."

She gave him a wicked look. "You've got a deal."

He took his jacket from the closet and shrugged it over his shoulders, standing still while she smoothed his tie and straightened his lapels. "I do love you, you know," she said.

"And I you, *lubimaya*."

* * * *

Raphael sat at the conference table, watching as Duncan ushered the last of their human guests out of the room. He could feel the surf pounding against the cliff below, vibrating the floor beneath his feet. It was one of the reasons he'd chosen this location to build his home. He loved the ocean, the primal energy, the smell and feel of it, the silver shimmer of the moon on the black water.

"My lord." Duncan closed the door and crossed the room, taking the chair to Raphael's right. "It went well, I thought."

"It did, Duncan. As much as I dislike dealing with humans, this investment is promising." He pushed his chair back and crossed his legs at the knee. "Tell me, is Rajmund still requesting a meeting?"

Duncan showed his puzzlement at the change of subject. "He is, my lord."

"Cynthia wants to visit Manhattan."

Duncan frowned. "It's very cold there this time of year."

Raphael met his lieutenant's eyes and smiled. "My reaction, as well. Unfortunately, Cyn is convinced her friend Sarah is in need . . . of a friend, I suppose one would say."

"I see."

"Make the arrangements, please, Duncan. Check with Cyn on the date and use our people for everything, including Sarah's travel. She is Cyn's friend, not mine. I know very little about her."

"I understand, my lord. What of Krystof?"

"I will contact Krystof, but we both know who the true Master of Manhattan is."

"Shall I call Rajmund, then?"

Raphael nodded. "You know what we want, Duncan."

"My lord." Duncan bowed slightly and left the room.

Raphael stood slowly, stretching to his full height. He hadn't planned a visit to New York so soon, but it might work out for the best. Krystof was declining. That much was obvious. And there was only one vampire among the aging lord's children who had the power to take and hold the territory. It was time for a new order among the Vampire Council of North America, and what better place to start than with an alliance between the two coasts?

Chapter Four

New York, New York - Manhattan

Sarah sat in the big, black SUV and watched the city zoom by outside the tinted windows, feeling like a bit player in some movie with the Secret Service hustling the president around a shadowy foreign capital. She kept waiting for the bad guys to jump out in front of them with guns blazing. Although, come to think of it, she was pretty sure the Secret Service could have taken a few tips from these vampire guys.

There were three SUVs, two of them, one in front and one behind, jammed full of big, no-nonsense vamps. She rode in the middle vehicle with Cyn and Raphael, and Raphael's lieutenant, Duncan. In the front seat were two of the security types, including the mountain Cyn called Juro. He was apparently in charge of the whole thing. All the security vamps were wearing these totally gorgeous charcoal-colored wool suits, which had to be custom-made given the sheer physical size of some of them. And how weird was that? The latest in vampire security attire . . . charcoal wool. Even the lone female among them was wearing one . . . and looked like she could break Sarah in two, which she probably could. Duncan was wearing the same thing, albeit with a different shirt and tie. And, of course, Raphael's outfit probably cost more than three month's worth of Sarah's salary as an assistant professor.

She eyed the vampire lord where he sat on the middle seat in front of her, one arm around Cyn, their heads together as they murmured back and forth. She had to admit she was intimidated by him. He was otherworldly handsome, a masterpiece of sculpture come to life. And although he rarely said anything—at least not in her hearing—when he walked into a room, he was instantly the focus of attention. He was like a massive sun whose gravity pulled everything else—planets, stars, passing meteors—into his orbit just by existing. Except for Cyn. Cyn was never one to hide her light under a bushel, but when she and Raphael were together, they both burned just a little bit brighter.

And as for Sarah, she was pretty sure Raphael wouldn't have noticed her at all if not for Cyn. Not because he was rude or anything, but because she honestly didn't cross his radar. Which was fine with her because in the final analysis, he was one scary guy.

The driver cursed abruptly, slamming on his brakes as the SUV in front of them did the same. Sarah grabbed the strap of her seatbelt. She was the only person wearing one. The vamps probably didn't need them, and neither did Cyn, for that matter, what with Raphael never taking his hands off her. The SUVs took off again, speeding through Manhattan, running signals and cutting off traffic with impunity. She supposed in a city with so many dignitaries, people were used to motorcades like this. There were plenty of blaring horns, but then, when *weren't* there horns honking in New York City? That's probably why it was called the city that never sleeps, who could sleep with all that noise?

She glanced over at Duncan, sitting next to her. He was the most human-seeming of all the vampires, but Cyn had assured her that Duncan was nearly as powerful as Raphael himself. He caught her glance and smiled absently, just as all three SUVs turned into the alley behind Chopin's. The most expensive and trendy club in Manhattan was owned by vampires. Who knew? Although, it actually seemed rather appropriate, given the elite club's usual clientele, which consisted of people famous for nothing but the accident of having been born with lots of money to spend on themselves. Unlike those glittering folk, however, who arrived at the front door in full view of the paparazzi—which was the whole point of going to Chopin's—Raphael and his group had detoured around the block to what was apparently a very private entrance.

Located in an alley, it was hardly a typical alley entrance. A dark gold awning of some plush and glittering material extended above a single door, with a dark blue carpet runner beneath it. And, rather than the glaring motion sensor lights of the other buildings they'd passed, a subdued, gentle glow picked out the gold in the awning and scattered it into the dark alley.

The SUVs pulled to a halt with Raphael's vehicle closest to the entrance. His security personnel debarked first, pouring from the two escort vehicles. Several of the vamps ran off in each direction, obviously to make sure no one was lurking nearby, while the others took up station in a half circle around the SUV. In the front seat, Juro didn't move, other than to raise his wrist to his mouth a couple of times. He had a radio microphone there and Sarah noticed he was wearing an earpiece too, again just like the Secret Service guys. Fascinating.

With no obvious warning, everyone was suddenly in motion. Juro whipped out of the SUV faster than Sarah could follow. The doors opened on the building side of the vehicle and at the same moment, the back door to the club swung outward in welcome. Unlike his security people, Raphael moved unhurriedly, sliding gracefully out of the SUV and holding out a hand to help Cyn—*as if she needed it*, Sarah thought, smiling. Still, it was sweet the way he waited, the way he kissed Cyn's hand and twirled her into the curve of his arm, the two of them laughing. And they certainly made a beautiful couple, Cyn in her figure-hugging black knit dress, those long legs going on forever above a pair of to-die-for stiletto heels, and Raphael with his silk wool sports coat and slacks over a black cashmere turtleneck. Sarah sighed. Ironic, really, that of all their friends it was cynical Cyn who'd fallen for a guy who was obviously a true romantic.

"Yo, Sarah!" Cyn's voice interrupted her musings. "You coming with us?"

Sarah looked up and grinned. Now *that* was the Cyn she knew. "Yeah, yeah." She scooted across the seat, self-consciously tugging the short skirt of her red silk sheath down over her thighs. It was a beautiful dress. She and Cyn had engaged in a little shopping therapy today, wandering all over Manhattan, spending money like they both had it. Cyn had pressed Sarah gently about what was troubling her, but she wasn't the type to push too hard. She had too many issues of her own to dig unwanted into someone else's. Instead, they'd shared a very pleasant afternoon, shopping, drinking coffee, gossiping about mutual friends. By the time they'd returned to the townhouse, Sarah had convinced Cyn she was simply homesick after an unexpectedly long winter in a new city.

Besides, the day had been the best therapy she could have asked for. She'd spent several carefree hours with a good friend in one of the greatest cities in the world, found this beautiful dress at a terrific price and a pair of gorgeous shoes to match, and hadn't once worried about those damn dreams. And now she was about to go dancing at one of the hottest clubs in Manhattan.

But there was *no* way she was going to be able to get out of this stupid truck without flashing everyone in sight.

Cyn strolled back over to the open SUV door. "Come on. I'll block the view."

Sarah laughed, touching the running board briefly before stepping onto the surprisingly deep carpet. *Nice carpet*, she thought. Too nice to be sitting out in this weather. She was wondering if they'd deployed it just for Raphael, when her thoughts stuttered to a halt as every hair on her body suddenly stood on end. Her skin prickled almost painfully as something very like a giant electrostatic charge swept over the entire alley. "What the hell?" she gasped.

Cyn took her arm, unconcerned. "Vamps," she whispered in Sarah's ear. "Too many and too strong in one place. They're like super territorial. This is Rajmund's city—that's RYE-mund, by the way, but they call him Raj, like Roger—anyway, it's his city, but Raphael's the more powerful vampire, which means all the security guys are on edge. They have this instinctive drive to protect their masters. No one's really threatening anyone, but it's an automatic reaction. They all brought their power up at the same time just now, but it'll calm down in a minute."

"Cyn," Raphael's deep voice, smooth as honey, called back to them, and Cyn hustled them forward to where he waited just outside the club door. Patting Sarah's shoulder, Cyn left her to Duncan and stepped up to Raphael, sliding her arm through his and holding her face up for his kiss. His lips lingered over Cyn's mouth before he leaned closer and whispered something in her ear, something that made Cyn respond with a low, sultry laugh that had every male in hearing range turning his head to look.

"This must seem odd to you."

Sarah glanced over at Duncan. "It's kind of like royalty, I guess, huh?"

Duncan nodded. "Just so. Lord Raphael is a visiting prince, or if one is accurate, closer to a king. There are formalities which must be observed, particularly as this is *vampire* royalty. A wrong move could result in . . . considerable violence. Something we all wish to avoid."

"Absolutely," Sarah agreed fervently. She had a feeling any violence would be very bad for a certain assistant professor. Next to her, Duncan smiled, as if aware of her thoughts.

"Once we are seated indoors, everyone will settle."

"Okay."

"Shall we?" He gestured toward the open door where Cyn and Raphael had disappeared along with half of their security people.

Once inside, they moved quickly down a long hallway and through a small anteroom. She could feel the low throb of a drumbeat from a door to their right, which was upholstered in tuck and roll leather. It sounded way too much like a heartbeat to Sarah, but that was probably just her imagination, given present company. The door opened to admit music and laughter, the typical sounds of a club, along with the hum of conversation and the soft chime of crystal. This was, after all, Chopin's, not some neighborhood bar.

Sarah found herself hustled along in the middle of the group, moving not so much under her own direction as carried by the general tide of motion. They passed through another leather upholstered door and into some sort of VIP lounge, with a long bar and a surprisingly empty dance floor. There were a few tables against one wall, but it was mostly low slung, open banquettes of black leather, with chrome and glass coffee tables and the occasional freestanding leather chair. There were candles on the tables, but most of the light came from wall sconces, their light beaming toward a dark ceiling where it bounced back to provide subtle shadows.

As Sarah observed all of this, she noticed that every eye in the place was on *them*. The dance floor was empty because everyone was focused with an almost scary intensity on Raphael. And she noticed something else. A lot of those watching were vampires, their eyes gleaming in the dark room as they followed the powerful vampire lord's progress. Their gazes were a mixture of fear and desire, as if they didn't know whether to run for their lives or to throw themselves at his feet.

A pair of double doors opened briefly on the far wall, admitting a blast of much louder music and raucous noise. And something else. The air pressure dropped sharply, and Sarah would have staggered if Duncan hadn't taken her arm. "What now?" she muttered.

"Rajmund," Duncan said softly.

Chapter Five

Sarah concentrated on breathing as a big vampire headed across the room toward them. He was tall like Raphael, but blond, with close cut hair and clear blue eyes in a face so stereotypically Slavic he defined the word. High, flat cheekbones, slightly narrow eyes, a strong jaw and a beautiful smile filled with white teeth. He was dressed in elegant formalwear, a tuxedo jacket and pants, and a crisply white formal shirt with smooth, flat pleats. But the neck of the shirt was open, the top button undone, and the confining black tie was hanging loosely, as if he'd just whipped it off.

The music was still playing, but what little conversation there had been was now silenced as everyone, human and vampire alike, held their collective breath, waiting to see what would happen next. Sarah looked around quickly, wondering if she should be worried. But Raphael's security seemed unconcerned—or at least no more concerned than they'd been all night—and Cyn was leaning casually against Raphael's side.

She turned her gaze back to the new arrival and realized there were no fangs in that devastating smile. None of the vamps were flashing visible fang. Probably some sort of protocol thing, like not bringing your guns to the peace table.

Raj stopped just short of Raphael's security and gave the massive Juro a grin that managed to be both friendly and challenging at the same time. The pressure against Sarah's chest increased and she began to wonder if she'd survive the greeting portion of the night, much less whatever came after. Juro didn't react, other than to stand aside, while Raj took a single step forward and bowed slightly. "My lord."

"Rajmund," Raphael acknowledged.

Obviously, vampires didn't waste words, Sarah thought, somewhat irritated and wondering how much longer this would take. Her new shoes were spectacular and the four inch heels did wonders for her legs, but they were never intended for standing around like this.

"This way, my lord," Rajmund said easily, as if continuing some silent conversation. And maybe he was. She'd heard rumors of vamp telepathic abilities, but hadn't had a chance to ask Cyn about it. For that matter, she wasn't sure her friend would have told her even if she'd asked. There were some things Cyn volunteered and others, well . . . Sarah could understand that. Cyn's first loyalty was to Raphael, after all.

"And who is this?"

Sarah looked up and found her gaze neatly captured by a pair of icy blue eyes. A frisson of energy sparked as every nerve in her body suddenly woke up and began to hum happily. She forced herself to move, to offer a handshake. She felt the strength of his fingers as they wrapped around hers, dwarfing her hand. He was not just tall, but big. His shoulders, his upper arms and chest were massive, tapering to narrow hips and muscular thighs and . . . oh my. Sarah had always liked big men. Of course, most men were big compared to her, but she liked *big* men, the kind who gave off heat, a coiled energy that warned they could spring into action at any moment. There was an air of contained violence to such men, an alpha male arrogance that said they could meet all comers and take every one of them. *This,* she told herself, *was a vampire.* Suddenly she understood what Cyn had been talking about, what it felt like to have all that power and energy focused on only *you.*

He smiled—a slow, lazy smile that sucked away in a millisecond the little bit of air left in her lungs, leaving her gasping for breath and trying not to show it. Something in his eyes told her he knew it anyway, and she was suddenly struck by vivid images of naked bodies in a darkened room. But, no. He'd leave the lights on, so those icy eyes could drink in every tremor of her body as she writhed. *Jesus, Sarah, get a grip!*

Her eyes flashed to his face, and she realized she'd been staring like an idiot when he said in a rich, unhurried voice, "Rajmund Gregor. Raj, to my friends." His words were deep and resonant, starting way down in his diaphragm and making the long journey up through that wonderful chest to her ears.

His eyes glinted with humor and Sarah bit her lips against the urge to get even closer to him, to feel that big body wrapped . . . What was wrong with her? She swallowed hard and managed a presentable smile. "I'm Cyn's friend, Sarah Stratton," she said, and cursed her pale skin as a blush heated her cheeks.

Raj only laughed cheerfully and placed his huge hand at the small of her back. "Let's get you seated, sweetheart," he said, propelling her across the floor in Raphael's wake. A vamp Sarah didn't recognize went ahead and held yet another door open for them. Juro disappeared inside this new room briefly, then reappeared and nodded.

The room was clearly reserved for very private parties. It was furnished much like the VIP lounge they'd crossed through, but the leather was softer, the tables burnished steel rather than chrome, and the glass tops thicker and polished to a gleaming finish. Raphael and Cyn strolled over to the largest of the banquette-like sofas—an open curve of black leather against the wall, with a low glass coffee table sitting in front of it. They settled next to each other, while Duncan took a leather barrel chair facing Raphael across the table. Sarah sat on the other side of Cyn, studiously ignoring the wicked grin Raj sent her way, promising a dangerous evening ahead. She tucked herself against the soft leather and pretended to care about the décor.

The space was small enough that it felt warm and intimate, rather than isolated—a feeling that was enhanced by the wall of glass facing the VIP lounge. Sarah remembered seeing it as a black, lacquered wall from the lounge side. From in here, however, it was a slightly opaque glass providing a clear view of everything going on in the larger room. Speakers suddenly came to life, bringing in sound, the music and the buzz of voices as the club guests—human and vampire—resumed their interrupted festivities.

A full bar lined one wall and Sarah saw row upon row of the finest labels of various alcoholic beverages, many of which she recognized from her parents' wet bar. Of course, that was long ago, before the dreams . . . and what came afterward. She forced the memory aside, focusing instead on the sterling silver champagne bucket waiting on the polished mahogany counter, with what looked like a nicely chilled bottle of Krug Grande Cuvee. She could already feel the bubbles against her tongue. But, wait. Did vampires drink? Other than blood, that is.

Raj was still standing, one hand resting on the back of the sofa. "We have a full bar here, my lord," Raj said, answering her unvoiced question. "Danny—" He gestured at the vamp who'd opened the door for them. He was tall and slender, smoothly handsome, with a mocha complexion and an elaborate tattoo that wound around his neck before disappearing into his shirt. He nodded when Raj said his name, smiling at her with the assurance of a man who knew women found him attractive.

"Danny," Raj continued, "can get anything you'd like. If it's not in here, we certainly carry it at the main bar. And, of course, there's blood available in whatever form you prefer." He caught Sarah's eye when he said that, holding her gaze for a moment before letting his eyes travel along her body like a warm caress, over her breasts and down her bare legs to her high, high heels and back up again. She shuddered slightly under the impact of his inspection and he smiled confidently. Danny wasn't the only vampire in the room who knew women liked him.

Sarah resisted the urge to tug her skirt down and wondered absently if vampires ran in packs—like all of Raj's vampires were lady killers, while all of Raphael's were the strong, silent type, like he was. Of course, Raphael's people were in hostile territory, so that was probably part of it. But Raj just seemed younger somehow, more carefree. Raphael carried an air of tremendous authority, a confidence that no one would ever dare cross him. She didn't think anyone would ever cross Raj either, but it was because he looked damned dangerous.

She saw Raphael whisper something in Cyn's ear. Her friend sighed in annoyance, but she stood, pulling Sarah up with her. "Come on, Sarah," she said, scooting around the glass table. "We womenfolk have been banished to the bar while the big bads discuss serious business."

Sarah glanced at Raphael, but his attention was on Cyn, his eyes shining silver, his lips curved into a gentle smile. "Thank you, *lubimaya*," he said.

Cyn blew out a dismissive breath, but grinned at him before dragging Sarah over to the bar where a glass of delicious champagne was waiting with her name on it.

* * * *

Raj watched the two women as they crossed the floor and climbed up onto the high bar stools. He had to admit Raphael's woman, Cynthia, was stunning. But she was like an exotic animal, something wild and lovely and totally unpredictable. He had a feeling she'd be a hellion in bed, but a lot of work out of it. Too *much* work for Raj's taste.

Her friend Sarah, on the other hand, was something else. It was obvious she felt outclassed by the strikingly beautiful Cynthia, but that was a shame, because she was a lovely woman in her own right. If she were to walk through the room outside that door, the eye of every vampire would follow each tiny movement of that tight little ass. She was shorter than Cyn, maybe five-foot-four without those heels, but half of that was legs and the rest was all lush curves. She'd covered her breasts with the red silk of her dress, but she filled it out nicely. Nicely enough that he already knew what it would taste like when he put his mouth on those firm nipples he could see pressing against the straining fabric. She scooted back on the bar stool, tossing her long blond hair over one shoulder and crossing her legs with a hiss of smooth skin. Raj felt himself growing hard in anticipation.

"Rajmund."

Raj blinked back into instant attention. "My lord." He sat on the leather sofa, twisting slightly to face the vampire lord. Duncan nudged the low table aside and moved his chair closer, so the three of them could converse.

"You wanted a meeting," Raphael said.

Raj studied him silently for a moment. His next words could very possibly condemn him if Raphael was his enemy. Raj had power, enough to defeat his own master when and if he decided to take that step. But he had no illusions about his ability to defeat Raphael, and he couldn't be certain where the vampire lord stood when it came to his fellow council members. On the other hand, Raj trusted Duncan—insofar as he trusted any vampire who wasn't of his own making. And Duncan had encouraged this conversation.

"You were at the council meeting last fall, my lord," Raj said to Raphael. "You saw that Lord Krystof is . . . not what he once was. He weakens and the entire Northeast weakens with him. Already vampires are siring their own children without permission, building private fiefdoms within the territory."

Raphael frowned. "I hadn't known it was that bad."

"But you knew something was wrong."

"I suspected."

Raj sighed inwardly. Conversation among powerful vampires was like swimming through mud; there was no clear path and too many unseen hazards. Every word became a weapon, and what was left unsaid often conveyed far more than what was said. On the other hand, boldness was a virtue. "Time runs out, my lord. Even for vampires. I need to know if you intend to remain neutral, as you have in the South."

"And why would I not?"

"Because Krystof did you a favor once."

"Did he?"

"Krystof has told me, my lord, of how you arrived in this country, how you came to his court and he permitted you to travel through to the West Coast to establish your own territory."

Raphael's black gaze focused sharply on Raj. He bared his teeth in a slow smile, seeming genuinely amused, but there was nothing friendly about it. "Do you really believe he could have stopped me, Rajmund?"

Raj swallowed his irritation, sorting his own truth from his master's fantasies. "No," he answered evenly. "No, my lord, but Krystof believes it, and he might call upon you if he felt threatened. I wondered if you might have a lingering fondness for him that would respond."

"My interest is in stability. If Krystof is unable to maintain his territory, it endangers us all."

Raj nodded, figuring that was the best answer he was going to get. He was surprised when Raphael kept talking.

"I have long felt there should be more cooperation among the territories," he said calmly, crossing his legs and smoothing away invisible wrinkles. "It occurs to me that you and I have much in common."

"My lord?"

"A certain outlook, Rajmund. A practical approach to doing business." He met Raj's gaze directly. "Should the occasion ever arise, I believe it would benefit us both, and the Vampire population at large, if we were to . . . consult in the future."

Jesus Christ, Raphael was not only giving his tacit approval for Raj to overthrow Krystof, he was proposing a fucking alliance. With Raj ruling the Northeast and Raphael the entire West, they would go a long way toward controlling the Vampire population of North America. The other council lords would scream bloody murder if they knew. The lords *never* cooperated in anything; it made doing business with each other almost impossible. But if he and Raphael—

"What do you think of the South?" Raphael continued casually, as if he hadn't just dropped a political bomb in Raj's lap.

"It's hot and sticky," Raj said, grinning, "But I doubt that's what you had in mind."

Raphael gave a bare smile.

"I was surprised when Anthony seized control," Raj continued, in a more serious vein. "I thought he was content with New Orleans."

"He was," Duncan confirmed. "Jabril let him run New Orleans however he wanted, as long as he paid tribute. But then the hurricane wiped out half of his holdings and more than half of his people."

"That many?" Raj said in surprise.

"At least," Duncan said, nodding. "He's being very cagey about the specific numbers, but it's no secret he wouldn't have gone for the territory otherwise."

Raj frowned thoughtfully. "I don't know Anthony that well, but I wouldn't have judged him to have the juice to hold the territory for long."

Raphael shrugged. "Anthony required certain assistance, particularly with regard to Jabril's rather convoluted finances. One of my own, Jaclyn, is quite skilled in such matters and is remaining in the South for the time being.

Raj kept his expression blank as he glanced between Duncan and Raphael, surprised again by the bluntness of their conversation. Raphael had all but said outright that Anthony was only able to hold his territory because of Raphael's backing. Was this meant to be proof of Raphael's new policy of cooperation?

"As you said, my lord," Raj said finally, nodding at Raphael, "Stability is the goal for all of us. It would be . . . unsettling, to say the least, if the South were to suffer another loss so soon."

"Yes," Raphael agreed, his eyes raised to follow the progress of his mate who had left her perch by the bar and was now returning to the banquette. "*Lubimaya*," he said.

"Time's up, handsome," she responded, taking his hand and pulling him to his feet. "I want to dance." She gestured toward the VIP lounge through the glass wall. The dance floor had filled once again with writhing bodies, some of which were actually dancing.

"My lord," Raj said, standing up next to Raphael. "I can drop the window entirely, if you prefer."

"Perfect," Cynthia decided. "Let's join this party!"

Raj glanced at Raphael who gave a minute shrug and then nodded. Raj signaled over his shoulder to Danny, who reached under the bar and hit the controls, causing the wall of smoky glass to slide down into a pocket beneath the floor.

The music and noise crashed in on them, along with the smell of marijuana, human sweat and cologne. The lounge was in full swing, the humans intoxicated by more than just the free-flowing alcohol. These VIP rooms existed in every one of Raj's clubs for one purpose only, and that was blood. Like the blood houses maintained by Krystof in Buffalo, or by Raphael in L.A., the VIP lounges brought together hungry vampires and their willing human donors who offered blood from the vein in exchange for a mind-blowing sexual experience and the illusion of dancing with death itself. Every human who walked through those double doors signed a legal waiver and release, and the whole thing was captured on security video as proof of willing participation, should it ever come to that. As recently as a hundred years ago, the vampires simply took what they needed. Now, they had lawyers and forms in triplicate, just like everyone else.

By this time of night, or morning, all pretense dropped. Vampire and human were coming together in shadowed corners, on the dance floor, or if a couple preferred privacy, in one of several private rooms in the back. The scent of arousal was everywhere, along with the powerful and seductive influence of several dozen vampires on the hunt. Raj inhaled deeply and cast his eye on sweet, little Sarah.

* * * *

Sarah watched Raphael twirl a laughing Cyn out onto the floor. They disappeared almost instantly in the crowd, as if they'd somehow pulled a curtain of shadow around themselves. She frowned, trying to see, but it was dark out there, the lights seeming to shift almost constantly making it difficult to focus on any one thing. She caught a brief glimpse of a couple on one of the leather couches and blinked in surprise. Maybe there was a good reason the lights were so low. She blushed and looked away quickly, only to find Raj staring at her from across the room. Her eyes widened and her heart raced, and she suddenly felt like a bunny beneath the gaze of something fierce and hungry and fully capable of swallowing her whole.

Raj smiled that slow, lazy grin and started toward her with the loose hipped prowl of a born predator, his eyes, the gleaming blue of a deep glacier, pinning her in place. He held out his hand as he drew closer. "Come, little one. Dance with me."

Every nerve in her body trilled with excitement and screamed, *Yes!* But she scowled at him irritably. *Little one?* Not in *this* lifetime. "My name is Sarah," she corrected firmly.

Raj laughed, warm and sexy and full of intimate knowledge, as if they'd been lovers for years. "Very well," he agreed. He took her hand and pulled her from the high bar stool, an arm circling her waist when she would have stumbled at the sudden movement. "Dance with me, little Sarah," he whispered against her ear.

Sarah shivered involuntarily. She knew she should say, *No.* He was an arrogant bastard who thought that charming grin could get him any woman he wanted. She knew she should thank him nicely, climb back onto that ridiculous bar stool and get drunk on expensive champagne, but before her brain could formulate the words, her body decided for her, leaning into him as he led her toward the other room.

The music changed as they neared the dance floor, becoming soft and sensuous, slow and delicious. Sarah was swept into Raj's embrace, feeling small and delicate against his broad, muscled chest, circled by his strong arms. Even with her heels, she didn't come up to his shoulder, but he didn't slouch like some men did, or pick her up bodily and drag her around the dance floor either. He took the fingers of her right hand, curled them into his left and held them close to his heart, then dropped his other hand low on her back, his fingers drifting a little bit lower still. He exerted the slightest pressure and their bodies were touching, her breasts against his chest, his hips against her belly. Sarah looked up as they moved out among the other couples and met those beautiful blue eyes.

"Put your arm around me, little one," he murmured. "Dance with me."

Sarah narrowed her eyes at the endearment, but slid her left hand over his impossibly broad chest, before letting it curl around his waist.

"There you go." He bent his head closer and began to sway gently to the music. "You smell delicious," he whispered.

She smiled at the blatant double entendre and found herself relaxing, truly relaxing, for the first time in months, maybe even years. She closed her eyes, letting her head rest against his deep chest, letting the flow of his even breathing lull her gently, the steady rhythm of his heart beating beneath her ear.

They moved easily through the densely packed dance floor, circling around until they were nearly hidden in the dark recesses of an empty alcove, the soft velvet of a black curtain against the back wall, drinking in and absorbing the dim light from the crowded lounge.

Sarah felt Raj's hand slide lower until it rested on the swell of her ass, felt his fingers press harder until there wasn't even the smallest space between them. She felt his breath against her skin as he bent his head to kiss her temple, the wet warmth of his tongue as it teased the curve of her ear. She shivered as he kissed the sensitive skin below her ear, tracing the line of her jugular until he stopped and sucked gently, not breaking the skin, just gliding his tongue in a circle as if marking the spot.

She could feel the smooth brush of his fangs against her neck, the hard length of his cock against her belly. She raised her arms, wrapping them under his shoulders and around his back, pressing herself closer, rubbing herself against his arousal. Raj chuckled softly. "So eager, little one."

Sarah heard herself moan softly, a sound so full of sensual hunger she couldn't believe it had come from her own throat. Raj responded, growling as he lifted her easily, spinning her around and pinning her against the wall. His hand slipped beneath the silk of her dress, pushing it up her thigh and over her hip. Her arms circling his neck once again, she hooked her bare leg around his hip and urged him closer, wanting to feel him between her legs. Raj lifted her leg higher across his back, sliding his hand under her thigh and into the wetness between her legs, pushing aside the soaked triangle of her silken thong.

Sarah cried out as his thick fingers slid easily into her slick folds, penetrating deep inside her, stretching her, preparing her for the full thickness of the cock she could feel growing ever harder, ever longer . . .

"Sarah?"

Sarah blinked . . . and froze, suddenly terrified. Wondering where—

"Sarah?" Raj repeated, his fingers lifting her chin gently.

She blushed hotly and stepped back, putting space between them, feeling the heat of her own arousal, the wetness between her legs. Anger flashed through her and she glared up at him.

"Are you all right?" he asked solicitously.

She drew a deep breath, certain he'd done something to her, but he seemed truly concerned, and she didn't want to embarrass herself by accusing him of . . . She swallowed hard, trying desperately to forget the feeling of his mouth, his . . . Oh God, they weren't in some hidden alcove. They were still on the dance floor. Had that all been her head? "It's probably jet lag," she said weakly.

"Come on," he persisted. "I think you need to sit down." He took her hand in his strong fingers, and she felt a renewed flush of desire, remembering exactly what those fingers had felt like between . . . her legs were shaking when Raj lifted her onto the bar stool.

"Here you go," he said, handing her the tall champagne flute. "Take a sip, you'll feel better."

Better? Was he mad? If she felt any better, she'd be a puddle of needy goo on the floor! "Thank you," she said, took a small sip and closed her eyes, feeling the bubbles tickle all the way down her throat.

"Tell me where we were," he murmured against her ear. "What we were doing."

Her eyes shot open and then narrowed suspiciously. "I don't know what you mean."

"Yes, you do." He smiled teasingly. "You whispered my name."

"I did not!"

He laughed, a purely masculine sound, full of confident sexuality. "You've never been to a blood house before, have you?" he asked.

"What's a blood house?"

Raj lifted his chin, gesturing toward the dance floor. "This, sweetheart. Blood and sex for the taking . . . and the giving."

"Oooh," she said and felt her face heating with renewed embarrassment. "I didn't know. I'm sorry, I—"

"Don't apologize," he said cheerfully. "I quite enjoyed it."

She looked up at him quickly, wondering what—

"Nothing happened, Sarah. You just sort of drifted away while we were dancing. I'd be insulted—" He lowered his voice. "—but since you were dreaming about me . . ."

Sarah gave him a disgusted look.

"You know," Raj continued, his amusement obvious, "I get to Buffalo every once in a while. Maybe we'll meet again."

"Maybe not."

"Ah, now. Stranger things have happened."

"Not to me," she muttered. She flashed suddenly on her dreams of tormented women and shuddered, knowing that wasn't quite true.

Raj frowned and moved closer, putting one of his huge hands on her arm. "Are you cold, sweetheart?"

She felt inexplicable tears pressing against the back of her eyes and lowered her head so he wouldn't see, focusing on the glass of champagne she was still holding. "I'm fine," she lied. "Just tired. I'm not usually up this late. I live a very boring life in Buffalo."

"We'll have to change that then, won't we?"

Sarah took another sip of her now warm champagne and wondered what it was she really wanted. Back in Buffalo, all she'd wanted was for things to return to the way they were, the way they'd been before the dreams came back. But now . . . She heard Cyn and Raphael returning from the dance floor, heard them laughing with each other as they settled back onto the banquette. And she felt the solid presence of Raj standing next to her, the comfort of having a protector, even for a short time, someone who stood between her and the rest of the cold world.

And suddenly she wasn't sure what she wanted at all.

* * * *

The next night, Sarah opened the door of the big SUV and jumped out, walking around the back where one of Raphael's vamps was waiting with her small rolling suitcase and the hanging bag with the new red dress in it. She took the bag and draped it over her arm, running a hand down the nylon cover as if stroking the dress beneath it. She glanced at Cyn who was waiting to say good-bye. "I'll probably never wear this again," she said wistfully.

"There's always the faculty Christmas party."

"My colleagues would have apoplexy, and their wives would be convinced I'm trying to steal their pale, chubby husbands away from them."

Cyn laughed. "Sounds like a lovely bunch. I'll have to visit sometime."

Sarah added her own laughter. "You'd die of boredom before you ever got out of the airport." She looked up and met her friend's green eyes. "Thanks, Cyn. I had a great time."

Cyn studied her for a minute. "You call me, Sarah. If you need anything, you call me, okay? Even if it's just a friendly voice."

"I will." She hugged Cyn, then grabbed the handle of her overnight case. "I gotta get going or I'll miss my flight."

"Take care." Cyn kissed her cheek before walking back around and sliding into the SUV. Sarah stopped to wave awkwardly around her baggage and saw Raphael's arm circle Cyn's shoulder and pull her close, as if even that few minutes apart had been too much.

She stood and watched until they were gone, then trudged into the terminal as the automatic doors whisked open in front of her. She had a life waiting for her back in Buffalo. Maybe not the one she would have chosen, maybe not even the one she'd planned when she took the job there. But at least they didn't lock her up at night. Not yet, anyway.

Chapter Six

"So what'd he say?"

Raj rested his elbows on the rooftop railing, ignoring the question to gaze moodily at the busy Manhattan street thirty-five stories below. He leaned forward and stared intently, thinking he'd seen a woman in a red dress. He laughed at himself. Sarah Stratton was long gone, back to her books and her classrooms. She'd been right about one thing. He'd probably never see her again. Which would be a shame, he decided and immediately wondered why he'd thought that.

"Raj?"

He turned a cool look on his persistent club manager. "How's the new club doing, Santos?"

"Great. We're picking up all the overflow from Chopin's, plus even more with the new location. But we gotta talk about this other thing, Raj."

"You want to talk to someone, get a therapist."

"Damnit, I thought—" Santos's next words were cut off as Raj grabbed him by the throat and lifted him off his feet.

"Do we have a problem, Santos?"

Santos tried to answer but could only gurgle wordlessly. Raj opened his hand and let him fall to the ground, where he remained, crouched on all fours and coughing furiously.

"Forgive me, Master," Santos finally choked out.

Raj gave him a dismissive glance. "Get the fuck out of my sight."

Santos started to stand, but one look at Raj had him crawling the several feet to the stairway door before dragging himself up to stumble down the stairs.

Raj scowled, listening to the metallic racket of the vamp's footsteps fade away. He returned to his perusal of the street below with a disgusted curse. "I hate that fucking vampire shit," he said.

"But you do it so well." The woman's voice was laced with amusement. She strolled out of the shadows to lean over the rail, joining him in his contemplation of the faraway traffic. "He was only asking the question we all want answered, you know. It's been two nights since Raphael left and you still haven't said a word. We're curious."

"You too, Em?"

Raj's lieutenant shrugged. "Me especially."

Raj sighed. "You're all so eager, maybe one of you should take on Krystof instead."

Emelie laughed. It was a low, sensuous sound. "He'd eat me alive. You're the only one, Raj, and we all know it." She glanced over and away before reversing to brace her back against the cold metal.

"What if I don't do it?" Raj asked quietly. "What if I decide not to get rid of the old man?"

She gave another graceful shrug. "I'm yours, Raj, body and soul. You made me, you own me. My loyalty is yours whether you stick with what you've got or take on Krystof and the whole Northeast." She paused to lean closer. "But I'm also your friend. And as a friend, I need to understand what's going on so I know whether or not to be worried. You and I both know that Krystof can't last much longer. If you don't take him out, someone else will, and then we'll have a fight on our hands because whoever it is will want this city for himself. Krystof might be content to fester in Buffalo, but no one else will be."

Raj studied the beautiful woman who'd somehow had the strength to become his lieutenant in the dog-eat-dog world of vampire politics. She'd meant what she'd said about being his friend, and her loyalty touched him somewhere he didn't want to admit to. "You know," he said. "Raphael told me right out that he thought Krystof had lost it. So did Duncan."

Emelie's face showed her surprise. "I thought those guys played it closer to the vest."

"Yeah. It gets better. He offered me an alliance once I take the territory."

"Excuse me?"

Raj laughed. "That was pretty much my reaction, too. He wasn't that blunt, of course, but the meaning was pretty damn clear."

Em absorbed this new information. "Well," she said finally. "You *are* the obvious choice. I mean, if he thinks Krystof needs to go, you're stronger than anyone out there, and you know the territory."

"Yeah," Raj sighed. "And I'm sure as hell not going to stand back and let someone else move in on us, so I guess—" His cell phone rang, playing a distinctive tune that could only mean one thing. "Fuck," he swore and yanked the phone out of his pocket.

"My lord," he answered.

"Rajmund," his Sire, the Vampire Lord Krystof, said silkily. "How did the visit go?"

"Quite well, my lord."

"Excellent. You can tell me all about it when you get here."

"My lord?"

"Something's come up, Rajmund. I'll need you in Buffalo for a time."

Raj frowned, wondering what the old man was up to. Krystof had given Raj the rich territory around New York City for a reason. It kept him happy—and far away from Buffalo. Sure, the old man was curious about Raphael's visit, but they could have handled that on the phone. So why was he being called back now?

"Something, my lord?" he asked.

"Something rather ugly."

"What does that—"

"You'll find out when you get here."

Raj was tempted to ask what kind of trouble could possibly have come up in fucking Buffalo that the old man's usual flunkies couldn't handle. But that flirted too closely with rebellion, and he wasn't ready to show his hand yet. "Very well, my lord," he ground out through clenched teeth. "I can fly at first dusk tomorrow—"

"Fly tonight, Rajmund."

"My lord—"

"You have a private jet." Krystof's voice turned petulant. "Use it. I'll see you an hour after sunset tomorrow, and I'll expect a full report on your visitor." The old man hung up.

"Fuck!"

Emelie just looked at him. Her vampire hearing would have given her both sides of the conversation, enough to understand Raj's anger. "We're going to Buffalo?"

"Not we. I need you here; I don't trust anyone but my own, and besides, I don't want Krystof knowing about you yet, not officially. He might be senile, but he's not blind."

"You can't go there alone, Raj. At least take a few of the guards with—"

"I *am* capable of defending myself, Emelie. Besides, I'm not supposed to *have* guards."

"He's got to know you're making your own. His spies—"

"His spies can report anything they want, but if I show up surrounded by my own children, he'll have to do something about it. I'm not ready to push him yet. I'll go alone. Call the airport and get the jet prepped." He calculated the remaining hours of darkness and swore softly. Damn that old man. "And tell them I'm on my way."

Chapter Seven

It was cold. So cold. Regina shivered in her thin jacket, wishing she'd worried more about staying warm when she'd dressed for Katie's bachelorette party and less about looking good. *Note to self: next time you get kidnapped, wear a decent coat.* Her desperate chuckle became a sob of terror as the heavy metal door clanged open once more, sending tremors through the concrete floor. She pushed herself back against the wall, feeling the hard chill of the metal bed frame low against her back. She'd heard someone crying again last night. A cell door had clanged open and she'd been so grateful it wasn't her they were coming for, so desperately glad she wasn't the one crying, begging.

She jumped at the sound of metal on metal, close in the darkness. Her door opened and dim light fell in from the corridor, piercingly bright to her eyes which had grown used to the near total darkness of her cell. A man filled the narrow doorway, a dark silhouette with wide shoulders and a square head, eyes gleaming in the faint light. She scrambled off the bed and into a corner, tucking her knees to her chest, her whole body shaking with the force of her pounding heart. She clamped her lips tight, refusing to make a sound.

"I know you're there, little girl. You can't hide from me."

A cry of dismay escaped her lips and she heard herself sobbing just like the others, pleading. "No, please," she whispered, staring up at him. "Not me."

Her protests crumbled as he drew closer, as his eyes bored into hers, clouding her mind with something sticky and warm. The light from the hallway faded until there was nothing but his eyes, *his* will, *his* desire. He reached for her, and somewhere deep inside she screamed.

* * * *

Sarah rolled out of bed, not even stopping to turn on the lights in a blind dash for the bathroom. She fell to her knees and threw up, her stomach heaving uncontrollably as she gripped the sides of the toilet bowl, gasping for breath.

Tears rolled down her cheeks and she begged silently, *Not again. Please, God, not again.*

She huddled on the floor next to the cold porcelain, her stomach empty, her throat burning. Repulsed by the smell, she slammed the seat down, reached up and flushed. Pushing back against the wall, she levered herself up to sit on the closed lid and turned on the water in the sink, splashing her overheated face, ignoring the water that spilled over the sides and onto the linoleum tiles. She grabbed a towel from the rack and covered her face, leaning forward until her forehead touched her knees.

It was all so familiar, the isolation, the cold, every heartbeat like a bass drum against her rib cage, every breath as loud as a bellows in the dead silence of her captivity. Theresa Bracco, the teenager from West L.A., and Julie Seaborn, a mother of two from Hollywood . . . and the others, the nameless others who'd haunted her dreams. The ones she'd tried to ignore. She remembered them all.

And she remembered what had happened when she went to her parents for help.

The institution they'd sent her to was more of a boarding school than an asylum—except for the locks on the doors. She'd been fifteen years old when she walked through those doors, and she hadn't walked out again until her eighteenth birthday when, as an adult under California law, she'd fled her parents' tender care and reinvented herself. A new name, a new city, a new life. College, graduate school, a job. Just like everyone else. No one knew who she really was. No one. Not even her good friend Cyn knew the truth about Sarah Stratton. There was nothing to distinguish her from the millions of people who went to the office or to school, who worked hard and slept safe in their beds every night. And that was just the way Sarah wanted it.

But now the dreams were back, and with them had come the memories of all the women who'd cried in her nightmares and now lurked like ghosts, half-seen in the corners of her mind.

She stood and opened the mirrored cabinet, taking out her toothbrush and toothpaste with quick, determined movements. She couldn't do this again, she decided firmly. She *wouldn't* do it again. This wasn't some docudrama on television. This was her *life*. The years of working two jobs to put herself through college and graduate school, piecing herself together from scratch, from nothing. Helpless, frustrated tears filled her eyes. She let them come until she was nearly choking on toothpaste. She spit sloppily into the sink and rinsed her mouth, then forced herself upright. She gazed into the mirror, seeing the pink and gold reflection of sunrise just visible between the slats of her mini-blinds. And she couldn't help wondering if Regina was looking at the same sunrise, if that damp basement had a window somewhere, a taunting shred of freedom for her and the others. The ones she could hear crying in the dark.

Chapter Eight

Raj made a sharp turn down the alley without slowing, feeling the rear end of his big BMW sedan fishtailing slightly on the slippery pavement. It was that time of year in Buffalo when the weather couldn't decide if it was winter or spring, when one day could bring a last ditch snowstorm and the next a quick melt that might freeze overnight into slick ice. It was one of the reasons he hated this town. Too cold, too wet, too windy. And too goddamn dead, even for a vampire.

He punched the remote attached to the car's visor as soon as he made the turn. By the time he reached the garage, the door was fully open, and he slid the big sedan into the narrow space, closing the door behind him before he'd even turned off the engine. He was cutting it too damn close and knew it. He should have stayed put at the airport, but he hated sleeping in a public place, even a well-guarded one. He never felt really safe unless he was behind his own door, with his own security. He'd known too many vampires who had trusted others and were no longer around to bemoan their foolishness.

The garage was mostly dark inside, but that was no problem. Vampires could see as well in dark as light, maybe even better. In the dark, one saw only what was necessary. By lamplight, one could be distracted by beauty or whimsy.

Feeling poetic, tonight, Raj?

He grunted at his own idle thoughts. It was more morning than night by now. He had only moments to get inside or he'd be sleeping on the garage floor next to his car, and there was nothing poetic about that.

The interior door closed behind him with a heavy thud, locks sliding home automatically. He walked directly to the security panel, rearming it with his thumbprint and a six digit code.

His Buffalo lair was in a small warehouse, fifty feet on a side and nearly three stories high, echoing in its emptiness and lit only by the green glow of the alarm panel's LED. This was his private place, a place even Krystof didn't know about. Raj might hate this city, but he came here far more often than the vampire lord was aware. He crossed the bare concrete floor to a short stairway running down below ground level. Ten steps, a turn and five more steps and there was another heavy door, another security panel. A different six digit code and the door cracked opened with a rush of warmer air.

Raj shouldered the vault-like hatch open, letting its own weight swing it shut behind him. There was light here, a dim, golden glow that rose up automatically to touch the otherwise dark furnishings and bring out the ruby depths of a burgundy carpet. The room was spacious, covering two thirds the square footage of the warehouse above. A huge custom-made bed dominated to the left, linens neatly tucked in by Raj himself the last time he spent the night here. To each side of the bed was a table of dark mahogany, and against the wall, a suede headboard the color of old blood. A matching sofa and two black leather chairs were situated to the right, next to a fully-stocked wet bar. Contrary to legend, vampires could both eat and drink, although they gained no nutrition from it and the food had little taste. Booze, on the other hand, tasted every bit as good as it always had. It might not have the same kick, but for a man born and raised in Poland, the taste of vodka was as natural as breathing. Which was another thing the legends got wrong; Raj was as alive and breathing as any human walking the streets in daylight. With a few very useful enhancements.

He would have enjoyed a shot of ice-cold vodka right about now. Unfortunately, getting to the small airport outside Manhattan had taken longer than it should have, and despite the short flight, the sun was already bursting over the horizon. He could feel the urgency of the coming day in every cell of his body. Eventually he would succumb to its effect—the legends got that part right—but he was old enough and strong enough to resist the fall into unconsciousness for a while. He deliberately took his time, checking the security panel and entering a final code to lock down both the warehouse above and this room. He was kicking off his boots when daylight finally began to suck away his awareness. With his last threads of consciousness, he stumbled to the bed, ripped off the rest of his clothes and pulled back the covers. The last thing he felt was the slide of crisp, clean sheets against his bare skin.

Chapter Nine

Sarah nodded her thanks to the barista as she grabbed her latte and eased her way through the caffeine starved morning crowd back outside the café. The cold air hit her like a wall after the heat inside, and she shivered slightly, pulling her coat closed with one hand, being careful not to spill the hot drink. The weather had been nice enough recently that the café had resurrected the umbrella tables from winter storage, and she dropped onto one of the cold, metal chairs, thankful for the heavy wool of her coat. She pulled out her copy of the local newspaper, The Buffalo News. It wasn't the New York Times, but if one wanted local news, this was the newspaper of record. And what Sarah was looking for was very much local news.

She sipped her drink and flipped open the paper, nearly choking when she saw the front page. She snapped the newspaper closed and sat back in her chair. Deliberately lifting her cup, she took a sip, and then another, watching the cars drive by on Elmwood, watching mothers with their babies in giant strollers maneuver through the door of the café to congregate in a far corner inside and trade stories of dirty diapers and sleepless nights. Her eyes wandered to a park across the street, where a swing set waited forlornly, its seats hanging empty on their heavy chains, one of them a baby's seat, its safety enclosure tilting unevenly, the chain kinked somewhere above.

The cold spring air stung her lungs as she drew a deep breath and put her cup down on the table, resting her hand on the folded paper for a moment, her eyes closed in resignation. She sighed and opened both her eyes and the paper.

The story was on the front page below the fold, along with a black and white photo of a pretty girl with curly black hair, a thin face and the smile of a child who knew she was loved. Sarah stared at that smile and wondered what it looked like by now.

Patricia Beverly Cowens, called Trish, the article said, eighteen and a first year student at the university. She'd attended a party on Sunday night, two nights ago, and hadn't been seen since. Sarah frowned and thought back. Her first dream had been nearly a week ago, long before Trish disappeared. She'd never known for sure, but she'd always believed her dreams happened in real time. And now, reading about Trish Cowens, she was sure of it. In her dream last night, Regina had— Sarah didn't even know what to call it. How do you describe being in someone else's head, someone else's nightmare? Regina had *remembered* hearing her abductor bring in someone new, a new victim, on what could easily have been Sunday.

Sarah fisted her hands against the desire to pound the table. If he had taken Trish, did that mean it was already too late for Regina?

Please, she begged any gods who might be listening. *Please don't let Regina be dead.*

She closed her eyes against a nearly overwhelming despair. *I can't do this,* she thought desperately. *Not again.* But she had to, didn't she? Because there was no one else. Feeling fate laughing over her shoulder, she picked up the paper again.

The Police Commissioner himself had presided over the press conference, which struck her as odd until she read further and discovered who Trish's father was. William Cowens, self-made billionaire, friend to presidents and movie stars. In a perverted way, she thought bitterly, it was lucky Trish was the latest victim. Not for Trish, of course, but for the others because Trish's father had the influence to make things happen. Sarah continued reading. As usual, the police were very circumspect in what information they released. Sarah had hoped for some mention of Regina, some confirmation that there were other women missing. But it wasn't there. So, maybe this was an isolated case. Maybe someone had kidnapped Trish for ransom, or even that hefty reward her daddy was offering. Maybe Sarah herself was seeing serial killers where they didn't exist and Regina was just a figment of her imagination, a function of too much stress and too little sleep. It was possible, wasn't it? She sighed. What did it mean when she didn't even believe her own rationalizations anymore?

She skimmed through the rest of the article, stuttering to a halt when she saw the name of Cowens's spokesman. She stared at the words, unable to believe what she was seeing. What were the chances? she wondered. Edward Blackwood. One of the few people who could connect Sarah Stratton to a young teenager from California, and he was here in Buffalo.

Not that Blackwood's presence was surprising, given William Cowens's net worth. Blackwood was a prodigious fund-raiser for Humanity Realized, which was the institute he'd founded for the announced purpose of facilitating the "achievement of full human potential," whatever the hell that was. He'd been interested in Sarah once upon a time, had offered her parents a full college scholarship in exchange for her cooperation. Unfortunately for him, her parents didn't want his money. What they wanted, and what no one, not even Humanity Realized, could give them, was a normal daughter, one who didn't channel traumatized women in her sleep. Sarah only knew she didn't want to be anybody's lab rat, especially not Edward Blackwood's. And now he was here, just as her dreams were starting again.

His participation in the case vastly complicated Sarah's life. If she'd been wary of getting involved before, his presence clinched it. She wanted no part of him or the tabloids that reported on his every movement. She would have laughed if it hadn't been so tragic. The one person guaranteed to believe her dreams, and he was the one man she wanted nothing to do with.

She stood abruptly, throwing her half-full latte into the trash container and the paper after it. She strode down the sidewalk toward her office, determination in every step. She had a class to teach, a life to live. The police were investigating. They didn't need Sarah and her dreams.

* * * *

The faculty parking lot was only half full that afternoon as Sarah headed back to her car, deftly sidestepping the puddle of ice melt she'd somehow managed to park right next to. The day's early promise of sunshine had come through, and even now the air felt almost warm. She lifted her face to the weak sunlight and wished she could just take off, maybe drive into the countryside, stop for a sandwich and sit at a picnic table, enjoying this first real sign of spring because she was pretty sure it wouldn't last. There were apparently no halfways in this part of the country—you were either freezing your ass off or melting into a big, steaming puddle.

Stop complaining, Stratton. You have a job, don't you? Sometimes she felt guilty about that. So many of her friends from grad school were struggling to make a go of it, people with families and obligations, while she had snagged a tenure track position at a decent university. Jobs like this were hard to find anymore, but even so, she sometimes wondered what she was doing here. It wasn't that she didn't enjoy teaching. She did, although she knew most of her students viewed her classes as a necessary evil, something to fill out a breadth requirement on their way to whatever career they'd chosen—law school for too many of them. Like the world needed a whole new batch of lawyers every year. And it wasn't that she didn't enjoy the research part of it. She loved history, loved discovering obscure bits of knowledge about people and events long past. What she didn't enjoy was doing the kind of research that would gain her tenure—the footnotes and the literature reviews, the presentations and the conferences, with their incumbent glad-handing and ass-kissing. And academic politics were a world all to themselves—backbiting elevated to the finest of arts.

She crossed the boundary between the walkway and the parking lot, her brain registering the change in texture beneath the soles of her sturdy, flat-heeled boots. She remembered her red dress from the weekend, with the skinny little high heels that Raj had so openly admired. *When the hell did I start wearing sturdy boots?* she wondered with a sigh. Probably the first time she'd fallen on her ass in the wet snow. But whenever it was, spring was here and it was time to stop. Tomorrow, she was wearing her heels again.

"Good afternoon, Professor Stratton!"

Sarah jolted out of her thoughts and turned with a smile for her best, and perhaps only, friend on campus. "And a fine afternoon to you as well, Professor Hoffman. You're far away from your usual haunts."

Linda Hoffman had a temporary appointment in Art History, courtesy of her husband Sam who was something of a star in the Art Department.

"That's because I'm looking for you. You're coming to Sam's birthday on Thursday night, right? And don't give me any excuses about work," she added, anticipating Sarah's response. The break starts Friday, so I expect you to show up and get drunk like the rest of us."

"Linda, I really—"

"And bring a date."

"Right. Where do I find one of those again?"

"Foolish girl. It would help if you'd say 'yes' once in awhile. Look at you. I *know* you get offers. In fact, my cousin Tony was asking about you a couple weeks ago, after my mother's birthday party." Seeing the look on Sarah's face, she rushed ahead, saying, "Don't worry. I didn't give him your number. Even I know he's not your type, although, come to think of it, I'm not sure exactly what your type is. But," she added, the gleam of gossip in her eye, "speaking of Tony, did you hear about Trish Cowens?"

Sarah's stomach knotted, and she forced herself to exhale and fake a frown of confusion. "Trish Cowens?"

"You've got to pull your nose out of the books once in a while, girl. Patricia Cowens, the daughter of *William* Cowens? You know, the bazillionaire who invented . . ." Linda waved her hand in the air. "Something or other, I don't know. But that's not the story. She's a student here at the university, and she's gone missing. Her daddy's whipping the local police into a frenzy trying to find her."

"That's awful," Sarah said in a low voice. She was having trouble focusing on the here and now. Her mind kept wanting to replace the smiling picture of Trish Cowens with the terrifying images from her dreams.

Linda sobered immediately, as if aware she'd been gushing over someone else's tragedy. "Of course, it is. Tony says they're working night and day—"

"Wait," Sarah interrupted. "What does your cousin have to do with this?"

"Oh," Linda said, scrunching her face in thought. "Tony's a cop. I thought you knew that. A detective actually. He and his partner . . ." Linda paused, eyeing her speculatively. "Now there's a possibility for you. Dan's good-looking and much more, um, cerebral than Tony. Of course, I think he's on his third divorce," she added, frowning.

"Linda," Sarah said patiently. "What does Tony have to do with Trish Cowens?"

"He and Dan are in charge of her case," Linda said, surprised. "Didn't I mention that already?"

"No," Sarah said absently. "No, you didn't."

"And that's not all." She moved closer, glancing around to make sure they were alone. "They think vampires are doing it."

Sarah blinked in confusion. "Doing what?"

"Stealing those girls!" Linda exclaimed, as if it was Sarah who wasn't paying attention.

"Girls? Plural? As in more than one?" she asked, already knowing the answer.

"Well, yes. I think it's three or four, I'm not sure. But, Sarah, vampires!"

"Yeah, I got that. Why?" she asked suddenly.

"Why?" Linda parroted, her expression confused.

"Why do they think a vampire's involved? I mean why would a vampire do that?"

"For blood, of course!"

Sarah frowned, thinking about Raphael and his gang, about Raj. She tried to imagine any of them kidnapping women off the streets, especially when there were beautiful women like those in that club Saturday night, women who offered themselves eagerly. "I don't think they need to do that, Linda. Not anymore anyway."

Linda scowled at her, dissatisfied with the reaction to her big news. "Well, I don't know," she said irritably. "Tony said the missing women had all been to those horrible blood houses or something. He didn't want to talk about it really, but his mother squeezed it out of him." Linda shrugged loosely as if shaking off the entire subject. "Anyway, I'm sure they'll find her. You know freshmen. First time away from home, they go a little nuts. Okay, sweetie, I've got to run." She gave Sarah a quick peck on the cheek. "See you at the party, and wear a dress, for God's sake!"

Sarah ignored the comment about a dress, putting it in the same category as her sensible boots. "I'll be there," she said, instead. "And give Sam my love."

She watched her friend dash off between the buildings, thinking about vampires and the dark, windowless room Regina had woken up in. The kind of room in which a vampire might choose to hide his victims.

* * * *

Later that afternoon, Sarah sat in her home office, hunched in front of her computer, staring intently at the monitor, waiting for the secrets of the universe to be revealed. Or at least the next chapter of the book that was supposed to get her tenure. Unfortunately, there was nothing but a blank screen staring back at her. When the monitor reverted to her screen saver, she jerked back in surprise. How long had she been sitting here lost in thought? She pushed away from her desk with a sigh, not even bothering to save her work. She hadn't typed more than a hundred words and none of it was worth keeping. Her stomach growled, reminding her it had been hours since lunch.

She thumped noisily down the weirdly narrow stairway, heading for the kitchen. The duplex she lived in had once been a single home.

When someone had divided it in two, they'd made her half slightly smaller, with the cut right down the middle of the existing staircase, leaving each unit with a squished set of stairs, like something you'd see leading to an attic that no one ever used. Fortunately, Sarah was petite, five-foot-four in her stocking feet, if the socks were thick —although her much taller brothers had simply called her Shrimp. She wasn't skinny, but she was fit and toned, so who cared about a number on the scale?

Rounding the newel post at the bottom, she scuffed her way in stockinged feet to the kitchen and pulled open her freezer door. A dazzling array of Tupperware containers greeted her, all carefully labeled, courtesy of her landlady Mrs. Maglietto. Mrs. M. had sort of adopted Sarah, when she'd discovered there was no family nearby. An inveterate gossip, she always seemed to know when Sarah was coming and going, and frequently met her on the porch with whatever casserole she or one of her many daughters had prepared that day. Sarah didn't mind. She'd been close to her family before everything fell apart. Sometimes she missed that sense of belonging, of knowing someone cared about her, that they'd miss her if she died . . . or if she was taken by one of the human monsters who haunted her dreams.

Sarah shivered, and realized she was still standing in front of her open freezer lost in thought. First her computer and now the freezer. Next she'd be drifting off while driving her car. She had to figure out a way to deal with the dreams before she suffered something more drastic than freezer burn. She slammed the freezer door and took a yogurt from the refrigerator instead, staring out the window as she spooned it into her mouth, barely aware she was eating. There had to be some way she could find out what the police knew. She could call Linda's cousin, of course, but what would she say? Even if he remembered her, she couldn't imagine he'd be eager to spill all the secrets of his investigation. After all, who was she? An Assistant Professor of History at the university, hardly an expert on . . .

Her spoon clattered into the sink. Why hadn't she thought of that sooner? Hadn't she just spent the weekend with two of the most powerful vampires in the country? And wasn't her best friend practically married to one of them? She'd call Linda's cousin. She didn't know his last name, but that'd be easy enough to find out. She'd call him and offer her services as a vampire expert. Well, maybe not an expert, but a resource. There was probably nothing to the rumors anyway, but that wasn't the point. It would give her a chance to find out what the police knew without giving herself away. And anyway, who else could the police turn to if they had questions about vampires? The real vampires were all in Manhattan. She'd seen them in Raj's club. What self-respecting vampire would live in Buffalo when he had Manhattan to play in?

Chapter Ten

The sun went down and the vampires rose. Raj opened his eyes to the instant knowledge of where he was and how he'd gotten there. And hunger. He'd left the city in such a hurry last night that there'd been no time to eat a full meal. Normally, he kept a supply of bagged blood in the bar refrigerator here for emergencies, but his last visit to Buffalo had been weeks ago and the refrigerator was empty of everything but ice. Which meant, Krystof be damned, Raj's first order of business was finding a willing donor. Demented or not, Krystof was a powerful vampire, and Raj had no intention of meeting him at anything but his best.

Besides, finding a woman shouldn't be difficult in this part of town, even on a Wednesday night. It was one of the reasons he'd built his lair here.

He stood and headed for the bathroom, groaning at the stiffness in his neck. He'd fallen facedown into bed this morning, which always left him feeling a little mean when he woke up. He twisted his neck with a loud crack of vertebrae and stared at his reflection in the mirror as he began to shave. He'd had a mustache, when he was human, and hair down to his shoulders. Now his face was bare and his thick, blond hair barely touched his collar. He turned on the shower and let steam fill the bathroom before stepping under the steady spray—one of the greatest inventions of modern man.

As the hot water pummeled away his uncomfortable day's sleep, he thought about Krystof and what this latest crisis might be. The old man had very little contact with the world outside his own small circle these days. He'd lived in Buffalo for hundreds of years, the last ninety of them in a big, turn-of-the-century house in the Delaware Park section of town. A fear of fire had forced him to rewire the entire building some years ago, but there was no television, no sound system and just one computer, which was used by his minions to monitor security.

Remarkably, Krystof also owned an entire penthouse floor in a downtown high rise, with both offices and bedroom suites. But he never used it, unless there were visitors to impress—which meant once every eight years when it was his turn to host the annual meeting of the North American Vampire Council.

As for the city itself, Buffalo had once been fat and satisfied, its steel mills and ports thriving and new people arriving all the time. Raj had come here four decades before the American civil war, looking for a different future than that offered by his own country, which was being slowly torn apart by competing foreign interests. Pure chance had brought him into contact with Krystof, who had already been a vampire for centuries by then. Krystof was the first master vampire to travel to the new world. With no competition, he had established his own territory and made himself a vampire lord. And he had been constantly on the lookout for potential recruits from his native Poland, men who were accustomed to the hierarchy of nobility and would not chafe under his rule. That the men he recruited didn't always volunteer to serve him didn't matter. Once they were turned, like Raj, they had little choice.

Unfortunately, Lord Krystof's fortunes were, of necessity, tied to the city's, and Buffalo's heyday was far in the past. Krystof's refusal to see the truth of the decline, to move his seat of power to Manhattan or one of the other profitable Northeastern cities, was an indication of how out of touch he was; but his failure to maintain order in the territory was far more serious. Raj wasn't the only vampire who'd begun siring an army of loyal followers. If nothing was done, the Northeast would soon be a honeycomb of fiefdoms, weakening the whole until it shattered into pieces—or attracted the attention of some strong outsider who would come in and do a little permanent dusting.

When the shower's water began to lose its heat, Raj turned it off and stepped out, wrapping himself in a big towel and drying off as he strolled over to his closet. His choice of clothing usually ran to black denims and leather jackets, especially in cold weather. But tonight, he pulled out a charcoal worsted wool suit instead. Krystof would be pleased. And for right now, that was Raj's goal. He wanted the vampire lord smug and complacent in his own power, totally unprepared for the not-too-distant day when Raj made his move. He tossed the towel away and began to dress. His hunger was growing by the minute. It was time to hunt.

* * * *

The woman moaned softly as Raj drank, the chemicals in his saliva turning the experience into one of orgasmic pleasure for her, instead of the brutal act it really was. Raj slowly withdrew his fangs from her neck and ran his tongue sensuously over the two small puncture wounds, speeding coagulation and healing. He licked his mouth and teeth, savoring the bouquet of her blood before retracting his fangs into his gums. Her blood was sweet with youth and warmed by the rum she'd drunk earlier.

He heard voices and moved quickly, hiding her small body behind his bulk as two waiters came down the dark hallway toward them, keeping his back turned until they were gone. He then walked the groggy woman back into the crowded main room, skirting the edge of the dance floor to an empty booth. She'd awaken soon, probably a little embarrassed at the obvious evidence of her orgasm. But there would be no memory of Raj and no lasting or negative effects. He'd taken only what he needed, less than if she'd donated at the local Red Cross. He strode out to his car, feeling strong and alive once again. It was still early, although no doubt later than Krystof would have preferred. But the old vampire lord's house was only a short drive and whatever waited for him there, he would now face it at full strength.

Chapter Eleven

The BMW responded readily when he turned onto Delaware Avenue, and he had to force himself to back off the accelerator. That was the danger of drinking too well. It left him feeling high and invincible, never a good combination when facing one's Sire.

He went in through the back door, nodding to the two guards stationed just inside the house—their faces were familiar, and they clearly recognized *him*, although he didn't know their names. He swung through the empty kitchen and into the hallway, where he took the basement stairs downward, resisting the urge to take them two at a time.

The room below was crowded with vampires, but they were little more than a wall of meat between Krystof and whoever came down the stairs. Krystof preferred to surround himself with weaklings, vampires who presented no challenge to the vampire lord's authority. If the old man had known ahead of time how powerful Raj would turn out to be, he probably would have drunk him dry and left him for the undertaker all those years ago.

But the truth was no one knew the full extent of Raj's power, not even Emelie. He kept it carefully shuttered for the most part, using only what he needed to get the job done. It was dangerous enough that Krystof considered him a threat. There was no reason to advertise just how much of a threat he really was. Of course, it was Raj's strength that brought him to the vampire lord's lair this evening. He'd had a chance to think about Krystof's abrupt summons, and that scenario was the only one that made sense. Whatever was going down in Buffalo, it was serious enough that Krystof wanted Raj's power at his back. Raj only hoped he'd survive whatever it was.

One of the newer vamps—a bulky Latino male Raj had never seen before—emerged from the crowd and thrust out his considerable chest in challenge. He was physically imposing, but registered not even a trickle on the power scale, which was all that mattered. Raj studied the younger vampire through half-lidded eyes and gave him a lazy smile. "Jozef," he drawled as he looked over the idiot's shoulder. "If you value this pup, you better call him to heel right now."

Across the room, Krystof's head of security looked up and swore as the pup in question shoved himself into Raj's face with a snarl.

"Morales, you fucking idiot, stand down," Jozef snapped. He crossed the basement and shoved at the vampire's thick chest. Morales stiffened against the push and only stared harder.

Raj chuckled. "This one might be too stupid to live. You sure you want to save him?"

"I said stand the fuck *down*." Jozef shoved harder, sending the other vampire crashing through the crowd to smash into the hard wall on the other side. At Jozef's nod, two of the others held the idiot back when he would have rushed right back into the fray. The security chief shook his head in disgust. "Sorry about that, Raj. He's so new we have to lock him up at sunrise or he'll stand out there and watch the pretty lights in the sky."

"Maybe you should put him down then, do us all a favor. What's he doing here?"

"Krystof likes him."

Across the room, Morales grinned at him in triumph, but Raj only laughed. The puppy obviously didn't know it, but Krystof's favor meant a vampire was too stupid or too weak to pose even the tiniest threat.

"Our master's waiting for you," Jozef said. Which meant Raj was late and Krystof was pissed.

Raj shrugged, unconcerned. "It was late when he called last night. I barely made it into town before dawn, and I needed to eat. What's this about?"

"Rajmund."

Every vampire in the room—except for Raj—went down on one knee as Krystof appeared in the doorway to his office. The kneeling was an affectation he insisted upon, and one Raj hadn't granted him in years.

"Sire," Raj said with a bend of his neck, nothing more. He lifted his head and met Krystof's gaze directly, daring him to force the issue.

The vampire lord's thin mouth tightened briefly before curving into an insincere smile. "It's good to see you again, Rajmund." His voice was strong and even, which meant he'd probably just fed. Over the last few years, it had become apparent that Krystof was feeding more and more often. It was another sign of his growing weakness, that he was reverting to a schedule closer to that of a newborn than a vamp of his considerable age and power. When he was hungry, his speech would become hesitant and uncertain like an aging human's, although he never *looked* old. It wasn't his body that was aging. It was his mind.

"Do come in," he said now, sweeping his hand across his body in a graceful gesture of invitation. He started back into his office, but stopped, frowning as he gave Jozef a pointed look. "Clear this room, Jozef. Rajmund and I will require privacy."

The security chief rose from his kneeling position and stared moodily at their master's departing back. A long minute later, he turned his head and gave Raj an unreadable look before giving the vampire closest to them a quick push. "Everyone upstairs," he barked.

Raj shrugged, gave the fuming Morales a wink and strolled through the doorway to Krystof's inner sanctum.

Krystof was alone but for a young woman lolling on an elaborate, velvet settee against one wall. She was half-naked, her blouse hanging open on small, pale breasts, her skirt scrunched up nearly to her waist and her underwear gone, if there had ever been any. Fresh blood, red and wet, seeped lazily from the big vein on her neck and she was humming softly, a dreamy expression on her face as she twirled a lock of purple-streaked hair with one finger.

"Lovely, isn't she?"

Raj swung his attention immediately over to the vampire lord, irritated that he'd permitted himself to be distracted by the human female. Distraction could be deadly in Krystof's presence, no matter that the old man was half senile. "Young," he commented. But then Krystof had always liked them young.

Krystof bared his teeth in a grin that showed far more than a hint of fang. "Over eighteen and plucked from one of the blood houses, so you know she's legal." He turned his back and walked silently across the deep pile carpeting to sit behind a fussy antique writing table with inlays so beautiful that even Raj could appreciate them. Velvet curtains in a full, rich red hung behind the vampire lord's desk—purely for effect since there no windows in any of the basement rooms. The remaining walls were bordered by a deep mahogany wainscoting against subdued satin wall paper.

Krystof seated himself on a delicate chair and folded his soft-looking hands on the leather-trimmed blotter. His long, dark hair was bound with a black, velvet ribbon, framing an unlined face and brown eyes which were remarkably clear, showing no signs of stress as he gazed up at Raj expectantly. Raj was reminded of an old, Russian saying about a person whose face was untouched by the wind. It referred to someone unmarked by the hardships of life, and it wasn't a compliment. Here was a vampire lord who had lived for centuries, who had enslaved hundreds, if not thousands, of both humans and vampires, who killed brutally for no reason but his own convenience. And yet, there he sat, the picture of a pampered young aristocrat whose hands had never been soiled by anything so crude as blood.

Raj stared at this creature who had so changed his own life and was nearly overcome by the urge to leap across the desk and choke the unnatural life from him.

"Why am I here?" he growled.

Across the desk, Krystof's lips tightened and he cocked his head in rebuke. "Do not presume too far, Rajmund. I am still master here." His eyes went abruptly flat, and Raj realized they could do it right now, decide this thing between them once and for all. But not with all of his own supporters hundreds of miles away in Manhattan, while Krystof sat beneath a house full of minions whose very lives depended on his continued existence. They would defend him to the death out of a raw instinct to survive, no matter their feelings about him personally.

Raj lowered his eyes and bent his head briefly. "My apologies, my lord."

Krystof smiled graciously, the benevolent lord with his servant. Raj ground his teeth so hard he thought the old vampire could surely hear it.

"So," Krystof began in the bored, dulcet tones of a born aristocrat. "Tell me what Raphael wanted."

Raj looked up and shrugged carelessly. "A holiday in Manhattan for his mate."

Krystof frowned. "Why New York?"

"Shopping, I suppose. That's what she and her friend did all day. "

"Is there no shopping in Los Angeles?"

"The friend works in New York, here in Buffalo, as a matter of fact. She teaches at the University. As for Raphael's mate . . ." Raj hooked an uncomfortable-looking chair over with one foot and slouched down onto it. "She's a rich American and clearly used to having her own way. Raphael indulges her."

"Does he?"

Krystof's note of interest sharpened Raj's attention, although he was careful not to show it. "To a point," he clarified. "She's quite beautiful."

The old vampire lord laughed. "So even Raphael has a weakness. I never thought I'd see the day."

Raj didn't say anything. If Krystof wanted to believe Raphael's mate, Cynthia, made him weaker somehow, that was his choice. Raj had seen enough this weekend to know that while the Western Vampire Lord clearly loved the human woman, he hadn't let down his guard at all. If anything, he might be more secure now than ever. Having finally met her, Raj was inclined to believe many of the rumors he'd heard about Cyn's determination and her willingness to kill if necessary. And he had no doubt she'd defend Raphael to her death, if that's what it took. As for Raphael, only a fool would think to bring harm to Cynthia and survive.

"Well, this is all very interesting, but that's not the main reason I wanted you here, Rajmund. We have something of a situation involving the humans and you know I've never been comfortable dealing with them. One doesn't *talk* to the livestock, after all." He chuckled at his own jest. "Still, this is America and one must adapt."

Raj ignored him. Krystof had been in this country for nearly three hundred years and he still spoke as though he'd only arrived a month ago.

"I'm afraid the human police are concerned, Rajmund."

That got Raj's attention. "The police? About what?"

"Apparently some women have disappeared. As if that's a rare occurrence in a human city. They butcher each other so casually, we're far less of a threat to them than they are to themselves. Unfortunately, an influential man has become involved—his daughter is among those missing, and he's convinced the police we've something to do with it. Ridiculous, of course. The girl is no doubt fucking her minimal brains out with someone unsuitable and will come home pregnant and diseased when she realizes her mistake. But in the meantime, we are all forced to play this silly game."

His voice was no longer that of a bored aristocrat, but had grown almost coarse with some emotion. Could it be fear? Did Krystof know more about these missing women than he was saying and was *that* the real reason Raj had been called to deal with it?

"In any event," the vampire lord continued, "you will be meeting the police this evening—"

"Tonight?" Raj demanded.

Krystof raised one eyebrow in disapproval at the interruption. "This evening," he repeated. "At nine p.m. I told them—"

"Why talk to them at all?"

Krystof's patience snapped. His chair crashed behind him as he stood, his eyes twin coals of fire in the suddenly dark room, his power sweeping out to encompass not just the house on Delaware Park, but the entire city of Buffalo and beyond to Manhattan where Raj's own vampires would be feeling the swell of his power and wondering if they were about to die.

Raj sprang to his feet as, around them, the ancient mansion shuddered with the force of Krystof's will. Plaster dust filled the air as old wood groaned beneath the sudden pressure. Krystof's young donor had begun to whimper in fear, while in the outer room, crystal sang its death throes as something crashed to the ground and shattered into a million pieces. On the floors above them, all movement ceased as Krystof withdrew the very life force which kept his minions alive, demonstrating his power in the most cruel fashion.

Raj sensed their terror all around him as they fell to their knees, as their hearts grew still in their chests and their breath was sucked away. Not even he was completely immune to the pull of Krystof's will. But unlike the others, he fought back, releasing enough of his power to keep his heart pumping, his lungs drawing in air against the demands of his Sire.

In the silence that was the vampire lord's will, Raj's single heartbeat was a loud drumbeat of sound. Across the room, Krystof heard it. Their eyes met.

"So," Krystof said finally. He blinked and the light returned. All over the city, Raj knew, vampires would be collapsing in relief, overwhelmed by the touch of their master, sucking new air into their lungs, feeling the stolen blood in their veins begin to pump sluggishly once again. The young woman on the settee coughed spasmodically, her face blanched white with fear, her lips tinged blue from oxygen loss. Krystof gave her an idle glance, then sighed impatiently and walked over, dropping to one knee at her side. He rolled up his sleeve and casually ripped open a vein with his fangs, holding his wrist out and allowing several drops to fall between the girl's gasping lips. She nearly choked as the viscous fluid dribbled down her throat, but her distress was quickly followed by ecstasy as the full richness of the vampire lord's blood hit her system. She moaned and rolled to her side, curling up on herself to lie there trembling.

Krystof licked his own vein shut and smoothed his cuff down, buttoning it with crisp, efficient movements, as he sat on the edge of the settee. A single drop of blood stained the pristine white cloth and he frowned at it. "I should have let you die, Rajmund," he said without looking up. "To this day, I'm not certain why I didn't."

Raj remained silent.

Krystof gave him a dismissive glance. "I could kill you now, of course," he continued conversationally. "They'd all die willingly if I called upon them." He waved his hand over his head to indicate the vampires in the house above. "I could drain the city dry, if necessary, to defeat you, and what could you do?" His eyes burned again, but the fire was the cold of death. "Nothing," he snapped, glaring at Raj. "I am master here. Do not forget that, Rajmund. You and I may come to a challenge some day, but that day is not today and we both know it." He pursed his lips in annoyance as he contemplated the mess around him, bending slightly to straighten a fallen chair before returning his attention to Raj.

"You will meet with a Detective Scavetti and some others this evening at nine p.m.," he said. He slipped his fingers beneath his jacket and extracted an ordinary-looking business card with the police department's logo. He held it out to Raj. "You will answer all of their questions within reason. I hardly need tell *you* to be discreet. Regardless of our personal animosities, I know I can trust you to handle this to the best of your considerable abilities." He paused, his gaze never wavering. "Do you have any further questions?"

Raj studied his Sire for the space of a heartbeat, reminding the vampire lord that his heart no longer beat of anyone's will but his own. He took the proffered card and asked, "Is this wise, my lord? We have survived for so long by remaining beneath their notice."

For a brief moment, Raj thought he saw something like cunning in the old vampire's eyes and then it was gone. "The latest girl disappeared after attending one of those ridiculous vampire costume events," Krystof said, his mouth twisting with distaste. "My lawyers have explained to the humans that we have nothing to do with those, but . . ." He shrugged gracefully.

Raj nodded. "I will keep you advised."

Krystof nodded and turned his attention to the shivering young woman, one smooth white hand stroking her bare thigh. "Close the

door on your way out, won't you, Rajmund?"
* * * *

"Everything okay, Raj?"

Raj spun away from the closed door to Krystof's office and found Jozef standing a few feet away, a sharpened stake in one hand. Raj gave the stake a pointed glance. "You planning to use that?" he asked, almost hoping the other vampire would say, "Yes." He could use a good fight about now.

Jozef looked down as if surprised to find himself holding the deadly weapon. He swore and tossed it aside. "Some of the younger ones didn't make it," he explained, and then he grinned. "Including Morales."

Raj's only reaction was a slight arching of one eyebrow. He checked his watch. "I'd like to catch up with you, Jozef, but it will have to be later. Krystof has asked me to look into—"

"I know about the cops," Jozef snapped, his mood suddenly changing. "I'm his chief of security, Raj. I know why you're here."

Raj regarded the other vampire silently. *Definitely some resentment there*, he thought. And who could blame him. "Look," Raj said, leaning in conspiratorially. "If I'm going to deal with this quickly, I'm going to need your help. These aren't my streets anymore."

Jozef studied him for a minute before nodding in agreement. "I'll tell you what I can," he said. "Call me later. Now that I think on it, you should come by the house. Celia'd love to see you. She gets tired of the same old faces."

Celia was Jozef's human wife. They'd wed in the old way long ago, for the benefit of Celia's now dead family, who had never known the true nature of the man she married. They'd been together for more than a century, long enough that although Celia was still human, her life was completely tied to that of her vampire husband. If Jozef ever decided to put her aside, to stop giving her blood, she would die within days. But that would never happen. Celia was a diminutive ball-buster of a woman and completely dominated the bulky vampire. Raj would rather meet the sun than be saddled with someone like Celia for even a day, much less forever.

"I'd enjoy that," he lied. "We'll set something up."
* * * *

Raj went out through the front, glad to leave Krystof's nest of neurotic vampires far behind. The air outside was fresh, and for once he didn't mind its cold bite. It was a relief after the lingering miasma of the house, with its half-mad lord and pandering sycophants. He clicked the remote to open the BMW's locks and slipped inside, enjoying the smell of good leather, the smooth rumble of the engine when he turned the key, and the sad, gravelly voice of Leonard Cohen murmuring from his stereo. He picked up his cell phone and speed dialed Manhattan.

"Raj!" Em answered before the phone had finished its first ring.

"Is that how you answer the phone now?"

"I'm sorry, my lord," she said. "Are you . . ."

"I'm fine, Em," he relented. "But Krystof confronted some unhappy realities tonight. Everyone there come through all right?"

"No problems. A few headaches and some panic among the younglings, but mostly . . ." She paused as if unsure whether to continue. "I was worried, Raj," she said in a low voice.

"So little faith in me, Em?"

"No," she said quickly. "Not really," she amended. "It's just . . . you're there alone and Krystof has his whole gang behind him—"

"In front of him, you mean. Krystof leads from the rear."

Em laughed and he could hear the relief in her voice when she continued, "So, are you coming back soon?"

"I wish. There's trouble here. Women have gone missing, including the daughter of a man rich enough to make the cops pay attention. The girl was at a vamp party before she disappeared, so the police are following up on what they regard as a vampire connection."

Em snorted. "*What* vampire connection? No pun intended, but none of us would be caught dead at those silly parties."

"That's what Krystof told them, but you know how it goes. And frankly I'm not sure the old man's as innocent as he claims. He's a little too worried about this whole situation."

"Well, fuck. Just what we need. More bad press. Why not let Krystof clean up his own mess?"

"Because something like this could hurt us all. Besides, if there's any truth to it, and it's *not* Krystof, I'll have to get rid of whatever vampire is behind it. God knows Krystof won't get *his* hands dirty."

He heard Em's long sigh over the phone. "Let me send some people, Raj. Now that Krystof knows—"

"Not yet. It's too soon. I need to get the lay of the land and find out what's really going on. All I have so far is what Krystof has told me, and his main concern is always his own ass. I'm on my way to meet the cops, if you can believe that—Krystof set it up before I got here. I'll call you after that."

"If it's not too late, I could still get some troops—"

"Let it go, Em. I'll call you." He hung up before she could protest any further. He loved Em like a sister, and she was a first-rate lieutenant, but she could be a bit of a mother hen sometimes.

He turned up the music and pulled away from the curb, heading for the police station—the one place he'd never expected to visit.

Chapter Twelve

Sarah hadn't been inside a police station since California, hadn't had so much as a parking ticket in those twelve years. She stood at the bottom of the short, concrete stairway, staring up at the glass doors, and wondered why it felt as if she was giving up her freedom by walking into that building. Intellectually, she knew it was just a building. Moreover, a building filled with men and women who put their lives on the line every single day for people like her. And it wasn't as if they were going to arrest her or anything. She was going to have a nice conversation with Tony Scavetti about vampires, then go back home to her little duplex with its weird staircase and Tupperware-filled freezer. So why was her body in full fight or flight mode?

"Vampires, Sarah," she muttered to herself in a low voice. "You're just going to talk about vampires." And if Tony happened to let fall some tidbit of information and she happened to suggest something in return, what harm could there be in that? Right. She hitched her purse higher on her shoulder and went up the stairs.

The door opened as she reached for it, two men in suits—and guns, she noted—coming out as she went in. One of them held the door for her, his gaze moving up and down her body, finally lighting upon her face with an appreciative smile. She'd worn pants today—no matter what Linda said, it was too cold for anything else. But they hugged the curve of her hips and she knew she had a figure that looked good in sweaters, even with most of her body hidden beneath her long wool coat. She smiled back, murmured, "Thanks," and stepped into the station.

The first thing that hit her was the smell—sweat, dirt and under it all the lingering scent of pine cleaner. Unfortunately too many unwashed bodies had passed through too recently for even the most rigorous cleaning to have made a difference—and she had a feeling the cleaning hadn't been that rigorous. Next was the number of people crowding the barren lobby. She'd scheduled her appointment with Tony for later in the evening, thinking it would be a quieter time. So much for that idea.

To her right was a reception counter—and Mayberry this wasn't. The bottom half was wall, the top half a double layer of presumably bulletproof plastic. She could see various people in uniform moving around behind it, with one well-fed, middle-aged officer sitting at a counter behind the plastic and more or less facing the waiting room. She walked up to the small perforated oval near his head and stopped, waiting for a reaction. It took a while, but eventually he looked up. "Can I help you?" he asked.

Reminding herself that she had a reason for being here that didn't include antagonizing the first cop she came into contact with, Sarah smiled and said pleasantly, "I'm Professor Stratton. Sarah Stratton. I believe Detective Scavetti is expecting me."

The cop regarded her silently for a few moments, but then punched some buttons on his console and spoke into his headset. "Scavetti. You got a visitor." He paused, listening. "Nah, it's a lady. Says her name is—" He looked at Sarah for guidance.

"Stratton," she reminded him. "Sarah Stratton."

"Sarah Stratton," the cop repeated. "Yeah, okay." He punched another button and said, "He'll be right out. Have a seat."

Sarah surveyed the seating options and decided to stand. A few minutes later, the single, windowless door across the lobby opened and Tony Scavetti appeared. She'd all but forgotten what he looked like; he hadn't made much of an impression the one time she'd met him. But she recognized him immediately. He was one of those Italian-American males she passed every day on the streets of this city, with dark hair greased back, olive skin and deep brown eyes. He was good-looking, if you liked the type, and he clearly spent a lot of time in the gym, with a trim waist and broad shoulders beneath an ill-fitting sports coat. She walked over and held out her hand. "Detective Scavetti."

His eyes never made it to her face as he shook her hand briefly, seeming in a hurry to get her inside and close the door on the lobby. "Sarah," he said. "Come on back."

She followed him down a short hallway, through a bullpen crowded with desks and people. Phones rang almost constantly and there was a steady murmur of voices, broken by the occasional loud exchange. More than a few heads turned, most of them simply curious, as she followed Tony to a glassed-in office with four desks, none of which were occupied.

"Have a seat," he said, moving to the desk furthest from the door. There were two padded, straight chairs in front of the desk, and she took the one that didn't have a torn seat cushion. "So, Sarah," he said, smiling. "What can I do for you?"

Sarah put her purse down on the floor and leaned forward. "I hope it's what I can do for you," she said, laughing slightly. "As I said on the phone, I was talking to Linda yesterday, and she mentioned you were the lead detective on the Trish Cowens case."

Tony didn't look happy about that, but he nodded.

"She also said you thought vampires might be involved, and since I—"

"Fu—" He looked at her quickly. "How the hell did Linda—"

"I think your mother told her."

"Fu—" He sucked in a breath and smiled, leaning way back in his chair until it hit the wall behind him. "Sorry. Bad habit. I guess I'll have to arrest my mom for talking out of turn. I'm sorry, Sarah, but you may have wasted your time in coming here. I'm not free to discuss any ongoing investigation. I'm sure you understand."

"I do," she assured him. "And I'm not here to ask questions. I'm actually hoping I can answer some for you. I'm very good friends with some people high up in the vampire hierarchy. If you needed—"

He smiled patronizingly and dropped his chair forward. "I believe we have the vampire angle covered. I don't think—" His phone rang and he picked it up quickly. "Scavetti." He listened for a minute and swore, "What the fuck—" His eyes flashed to her once again and he turned away slightly. "What's he doing here? Nobody told me— Yeah. Great. Fan-fucking-tastic. What about— All right, you bring him back and I'll meet you in the conference room."

He slammed the phone down and she could see the tendons in his neck straining as he fought for control over his anger. He stood abruptly, and Sarah knew her few minutes were over. "Come on," he said tersely. "I'll walk you out." He came around the desk and took her arm, propelling her quickly back through the bullpen, not letting go until they crossed into the hallway.

Sarah felt her chance, slim as it was, slipping away. What did he mean when he said they had the vampire angle covered? Was there someone in town who knew about vamps? No one at the University, that was for sure. Who could he . . . Her eyes widened as she suddenly remembered someone just a short flight away who knew a hell of a lot more than she did about vampires.

* * * *

Raj pulled into the parking lot behind the police station, backing into a spot in the second row with a good line of the sight on the entrance. He wasn't comfortable being here, although he dealt with cops all the time in Manhattan. There was always some idiot with a death wish who decided to take on one of his vampires, or who got drunk and started a fight in the waiting line as it wound its way down the block. But Manhattan was Raj's city and he knew its cops. He knew who worked what beat around his clubs and he always donated to the various police charities when called upon, which was often. This, on the other hand, definitely *wasn't* his city, and he wasn't dealing with some asshole on a drunk and disorderly. The Cowens girl had been gone a few days; the odds were she was already dead, which made this a potential murder investigation. And Raj had a feeling the Buffalo Police Department wasn't going to be impressed with his donations to the NYPD Policemen's Ball.

A taxi cab pulled up to the station house, its left front tire dropping visibly into a water-filled pothole before the driver edged forward to sit spewing exhaust in front of the stairs. A woman climbed out of the back seat, her hair uncombed, her clothes obviously pulled on in a hurry. She shoved some money at the driver and he took off, swerving at the last minute to avoid hitting the pothole a second time, driving right by Raj on his way to the exit, windows open despite the frigid air.

As the taxi whipped onto the street, it cut right in front of a limo which had slowed down for its own ponderous turn into the lot. Raj chuckled softly. Who knew sitting in a police parking lot would be so entertaining? The long, black vehicle made its stately way across the width of the building, the driver deftly avoiding the water-filled pothole while taking up almost the exact position the taxi had occupied earlier. The right passenger door opened almost immediately and a man jumped out, his ready demeanor and discreet weapon proclaiming him a bodyguard even before he scanned the area carefully. The driver had disembarked and circled the car by then and, after getting an affirming nod from the bodyguard, opened the back door and said something to whoever was inside before stepping out of the way.

A large man emerged first, his longish blond hair uncovered, his camel-colored cashmere coat buttoned tightly. He turned just enough to offer a good look at his face and Raj swore softly. Edward Blackwood—a traveling snake-oil salesman if there ever was one.

A second man stood from within the limo, almost as tall as Blackwood, but not nearly as bulky. In his late fifties, with carefully styled dark hair, he wore a black winter coat and had a scarf wrapped around his neck against the cold. Unlike Blackwood, he didn't wait, but went immediately up the stairs and into the building, his bodyguard in tow. Blackwood seemed taken aback by the rapid departure and hurried to keep up, hustling along behind. Raj frowned. Given Blackwood's habit of hanging around rich men who had nothing better to do with their money than waste it on Humanity Realized, Raj had to figure the dark-haired man was William Cowens, the missing girl's billionaire father. Which didn't make him happy. He had come prepared to deal with the cops, not a distraught father.

The limo driver pulled the vehicle deeper into the parking lot to wait for his boss's return. Raj sat there a few minutes longer, then switched off the ignition and climbed out of the warm car. Time to find out how much the police knew. And how much they didn't.

Time to get the job done and get out of this town before it sucked him dry.

Raj crossed the parking lot swiftly, taking the stairs two at a time. The scent of a woman's perfume drifted on the air, something light and flowery, something oddly familiar. It persisted as he crossed to the reception desk to confront a human policeman sitting behind a bulletproof barrier and studiously ignoring everyone on the other side.

Raj tapped on the plastic and the cop looked up.

"My name's Gregor, Raymond Gregor," he said, using the American version of his name. "Detective Scavetti is expecting me."

"Mr. Gregor?" The man's voice came from behind him and Raj

spun, tensing slightly.

"Detective Dan Felder," the man said, stepping forward. "Scavetti and I are partners." Felder was tall and slender, probably considered good-looking in a subdued sort of way. He smiled as he extended his hand. "Didn't mean to startle you. I was passing through and heard the name."

"Detective," Raj said, accepting the handshake.

"So, no problem entering the building, huh?"

"Pardon me?"

Felder looked away, uncomfortable. "I kind of thought you might, you know, need an invitation or something."

Raj's first instinct was to scoff, but he thought better of it. It was a generous gesture, and besides, it might come in handy later to have a friendly contact inside the department. "No," he said. "But thanks for thinking of it, Felder. Public places like this, I can do just fine."

"Oh, right. Makes sense." Felder gestured toward a closed door. "We're down this way." He jerked his head at the desk cop who pushed a button somewhere. A loud buzz sounded and Felder pulled the door open, indicating Raj should go ahead of him. He would have preferred the cop go first, but that would have looked a little too paranoid, so he went on through.

They had taken only a few steps when that same perfume hit his senses. He lifted his head and grinned. Sarah Stratton was coming down the hall, along with another detective. She was obviously uncomfortable and embarrassed by whatever the detective was saying, and not yet aware that Raj was standing there.

"Look, I appreciate your effort in coming down here, Sarah," the cop said, as they came closer. "But like I said, we have our own experts on these things."

"Of course. I just thought, well, since I do have contacts with the local vampire lord—"

She did? That was news to Raj. And it didn't make him happy. He didn't want Sarah Stratton within a hundred yards of Krystof or any other vampire. Except, of course, himself.

"Tony," Detective Felder said.

The other detective looked up impatiently. "Yeah, just a minute, Dan. Look," he said quietly, taking Sarah's arm. "Why don't you leave me your number and I'll—"

"No," she said instantly. She glanced up nervously and froze, her eyes growing wider when she saw Raj watching her.

His lips curled into a pleased smile, although what he wanted to do was knock *Tony's* fucking hand off her arm.

"Tony," Felder insisted. "This is Raymond Gregor."

Tony, presumably the Tony Scavetti Raj was supposed to meet, paid attention at last. He forgot the woman at his side to focus on Raj.

"You're the vampire?"

Raj nodded. "And you must be the detective," he responded. He took a cynical pleasure in Scavetti's automatic bristle of reaction as the human drew himself up to his full height—which was no more than five, eight—and flexed gym-built muscles beneath a too-tight jacket. Raj regarded him evenly. He'd met too many Scavettis in his long life, the ones who picked fights for no better reason than to prove no one was tougher than they were.

"Good to get those details out of the way," Felder said, playing peacemaker. Something he probably had to do often if Scavetti was his partner. "Uh, Professor Stratton?" he reminded Scavetti.

Scavetti frowned, but switched his attention back to Sarah. "Yeah. Sarah, I'm sure Gregor here can answer any questions. In fact, you two probably know each other, right?"

A bright pink blush spread along her cheek bones as she looked up at Raj, staining her otherwise porcelain-pale skin. Her hazel eyes darkened almost gray with emotion and lingered a heartbeat too long before dropping to hide behind thick eyelashes.

"Mr. Gregor," she said softly.

"Professor Stratton," Raj purred. He took her hand and tugged, smoothly extricating her from Tony's grasp and drawing her close enough that he could breathe in her scent, shutting out the smells of sweaty cops and burned coffee. His action startled her into looking up and meeting his eyes again.

"I hate to interrupt," Scavetti said snidely. Raj just barely held back a furious snarl at the interruption, and he felt Sarah's jolt of surprise, as if she'd forgotten Scavetti was even standing there. "Could we get on with this please?" the detective asked.

Raj glanced at Scavetti and permitted a cloud of disdain to cross his expression before he shut it down completely. "Of course, Detective," he said. "I'll just walk Professor Stratton out to her car first."

Sarah flashed him a startled look, but Raj only bowed slightly and gestured down the hallway. She gave him a weak smile and shivered slightly when she walked past him. Raj swallowed his grin and followed, watching the muted sway of her hips beneath that bulky winter coat and wishing she was wearing something light and silky like before. Maybe a soft skirt, something to play around her slender legs above those sexy high heels she seemed to favor. He glanced back to find the two cops staring at him and shrugged gracefully. "This will only take a moment," he assured them.

"What the fuck?" he heard Scavetti swear before he'd gone ten steps. "What's he going to do to her?"

"Looks like they know each other, Tony," Felder responded in a bored tone. "What do you think he's gonna do? Drain her in the parking lot? Besides what do you care?"

"Fuck you, Dan. I might not want her on this case, but that doesn't mean I want some fucking vampire sucking on her neck either."

Raj chuckled and stopped listening. He caught up with Sarah just as she pushed open the outside door, letting in a rush of much fresher air.

Chapter Thirteen

Sarah put her shoulder into the heavy door, sucking in a cold breath and telling herself she'd done everything she could to help Trish. Scavetti had been—well, not polite, but probably as polite as he ever got. Every other word out of the man's mouth was an expletive, although he had tried to censor himself for her benefit. And she was sure he'd only agreed to give her the five minutes he had because, according to Linda, he was hoping to hook up with her.

And then, of course, there was Raj. She'd looked pretty stupid once *he'd* shown up. If she'd known he would be here, she'd never have come down in the first place. And not just because he made her look foolish with the cops, either. That man, that *vampire*, was nothing but trouble. Every time she got within two feet of his gorgeous self, her IQ seemed to drop about forty points. And he knew it, too. The arrogance just oozed out of him, he was so damned sure of . . . The weight of the thick glass door suddenly disappeared as a long arm reached over her shoulder. The light from the lobby disappeared, casting her into shadow, and she looked up, not surprised to see Raj right behind her, his easy grin not fooling her for a second.

She murmured her thanks and stepped out onto the landing, pulling her coat closed and hunching deeper into its warmth. "I'm fine, Raj," she said quickly. "You don't have to—" She jerked her gaze sideways as the solid thunk of a car door punctuated the night. Across the parking lot, a chauffeur had just stepped out of a long, black limo to grab some fresh air. She couldn't be positive, but she didn't think the vehicle had been there when she'd arrived at the station. It could be anyone, of course. Limos weren't common—except on prom nights—but they weren't completely rare in the city either. But for some reason—maybe it was the phone call Tony had received while she sat in his office— she was convinced this one belonged to William Cowens, and that meant Edward Blackwood was nearby. She immediately turned her back on the lobby and stepped away from the lights, just in case. Raj caught her reaction, naturally, and slipped an arm over her shoulders, his great bulk effectively hiding her from both the limo and the lobby. She could feel him studying the limo and its driver over her head.

"Come on, Sarah," he said. "I'll walk you to your car." He started down the stairs with her firmly in the curve of his arm. "And you can tell me why you don't want Williams Cowens to know you're here." Sarah nearly missed the next step, but his solid strength kept her upright. He tucked her against his body with a low chuckle. "I love the boots, sweetheart," he murmured. But they're not the best choice for the icy streets around here."

Sarah felt a rush of pleasure that he'd noticed her admittedly sexy high-heeled boots, but cursed her own clumsiness. "I didn't expect to be walking much," she muttered. "And I'm not worried about William Cowens."

"No? Then maybe it's the limo driver. A former lover, perhaps?" He said it lightly, but there was a definite growl on his last words.

Sarah laughed. "Right, it's the limo driver. I was just startled, that's all. I'm not used to hanging around police stations."

They had reached her car by then. Sarah beeped the locks open and Raj reached around her to open the door. "Is it Blackwood?" he persisted.

She threw her bag across the seat and gave him an exasperated look. "I told you. I don't even know—"

Raj placed one hand on the door and braced himself against the roof of her car with the other, effectively trapping her. He was so damn *big*. She stifled a brief, irrational urge to run, looking up to meet his amused gaze instead. "Do you know how lie detectors work, Sarah?"

She frowned in confusion at the seeming non sequitur. "Of course. When a person lies about something, there are physiological changes that give him away. Pulse rate, respiration . . . and probably some other things too. It's not exactly my field, but what—"

He leaned down until his mouth was at her ear. "Your pulse and respiratory rates just rocketed, little one. And your luscious heart is going pitty-pat. Either you're madly in love with me, or you're not being totally honest. Although it might be both." She felt the soft touch of his tongue along the curve of her ear. "Delicious," he whispered.

She shivered and forced herself to meet his icy blue eyes. Except they weren't quite so icy anymore. She licked her lips, and those eyes followed the movement of her tongue before returning to meet her gaze with a slow, sensuous blink. *Ice can be hot, too*, she reminded herself.

"Why do you care?" she managed to say.

"You didn't come down here to offer advice on vampires," he chided her gently. "Of course, there's your close relationship with Lord Krystof . . ." He let the words trail off suggestively.

"I *don't* really know him," she admitted. "Although, I did, er, *see* him at a University reception once. And I could probably get Cyn to set up a meeting or—"

"I don't think so," he interrupted harshly.

Sarah looked up at him in surprise and caught the dying flash of some emotion in his eyes. "If you have any questions about vampires, you can ask me," he said. "No one else."

"Excuse me?" she said, his high-handed attitude restoring some of her usual backbone.

Raj gave her a charming smile, one that almost made her forget her newfound determination. "Lord Krystof doesn't deal with humans much. Whereas I—" He nuzzled her cheek softly, placing his lips once again at her ear. "I am at your *complete* disposal."

Sarah didn't need a vampire to tell her that her heartbeat had just gone into overdrive. She turned her face into his, struck by the smoothness of his cheek, by the warm, masculine scent of his skin. "Raj," she murmured.

"Yes?"

"What are we doing?"

He laughed. "I must be out of practice if you need to ask me that."

Sarah smiled up at him, feeling relaxed and warm, just like she had in the club. It was strange how he could make her feel that way—strange and a little troubling. She started to turn, intending to slip into her car, but Raj had other ideas. He wrapped an arm around her waist, lifted her up to her toes and kissed her—a long, soft, sensuous seduction of mouth and tongue. When he finally ended the kiss, tracing her jaw with his lips as he set her carefully back on her own two feet, she held onto him, not entirely certain she could remain standing on her own.

"I have to go back inside," he murmured, even as he continued to taste her, his mouth moving slowly from cheek to cheek and down to her neck, where he lingered. "Why don't I come by your place later." He bit gently into her neck and then kissed away the small pain. "And we can talk all about what's really going on here."

Sarah forced herself to breathe, to take a half step back. She stumbled into the doorframe of her car with a jolt and Raj steadied her with a hand on her arm. She stared up at him, a bit stunned to realize she was actually considering it. He was a vampire. She'd known him only a few days, really only a few hours, and she was seriously considering inviting him over to her house. To talk. *Right.*

"Are you messing with my mind, Raj?" she asked softly.

"I sure as hell hope so."

She laughed and shook her head at her own foolishness. "Not all of us can stay up all night. I've got to teach tomorrow and it's already late."

"Tomorrow night then," he persisted.

She smiled, thinking of Linda's birthday celebration for Sam—what would her friend do if she showed up with a vampire as her date? "I'm already committed to a friend tomorrow night."

"What kind of friend?" he demanded, scowling.

She gave him an exasperated look. "Not that it's any of your business," she said pointedly. "But she's a friend from the University. It's her husband's birthday party."

"Fine. I'll meet you after."

"Maybe. I don't know—" Her next words were cut off as he lifted her effortlessly and covered her mouth with another lingering kiss. She heard herself moaning softly against his lips and knew if he'd asked at that moment, she would have gone with him anywhere he wanted. He let her go gently, her body sliding down his in a slow, suggestive glide that left little doubt as to the state of his own arousal. She leaned against his chest, feeling safe in the circle of his arms as she caught her breath. "Do you know where I live?" she asked softly.

She could hear his grin when he said, "I can find out." She had no doubt that was true. In fact, she had no doubt Raj could do pretty much anything he set his mind to. "All right," she said. She forced herself to pull away from him, to put a few inches distance between them, so she could think. She turned and threw her purse across the seat. "I guess I'll see you tomorrow."

"Yes, you will."

Sarah trembled at the heat in those three words and wondered if she'd finally lost her mind for real, just as her parents and her therapists had thought she had way back when.

* * * *

Raj stood back and watched Sarah drive out of the parking lot. He found himself eager for their next meeting, and not just because he was attracted to her, although, there was no question about that. In fact, his feelings for her went a little deeper than he was comfortable with. He'd wanted her in New York. If not for her rather unique position at the time, as a member of Raphael's entourage, he'd have taken her. But she wasn't with Raphael anymore. The scent of her perfume lingered and he grinned. Oh, yes, he was definitely going to taste his sweet Sarah, and very soon, too.

But he was also curious about what she was hiding. And she was definitely hiding something. He could have taken it from her mind easily. The lightest exploratory touch had already told him she was amazingly susceptible to his will, maybe more so than most humans. But it also told him she was both physically and emotionally exhausted from whatever secret she was keeping. A secret Raj would uncover before too long.

Of course, it didn't hurt that the secret came wrapped in a package he intended to unwrap slowly and with great relish. He wouldn't take her quickly, as he did the women he drank from usually, not like that woman in the bar earlier. Raj didn't pretend to be anything but what he was. He was a predator and humans were his prey. And he was very good at what he did. But for some reason he didn't want to trick Sarah Stratton into doing his bidding. He wanted her to go with him knowingly, to invite him into her home because she wanted him there, not because her mind was clouded with lust. Although, she did desire him already. She hadn't completely surrendered to it yet, but the subtle notes of her body told him she would soon. He smiled to himself. Oh, yes, he was going to enjoy unwrapping Sarah Stratton very much indeed.

Chapter Fourteen

"Fucking Commissioner's throwing a wild card at us, Dan." Raj heard Scavetti's blustering from down the hall. "Captain says he didn't know about it until a few minutes ago, but he could be lying through his teeth, covering his own ass. They want in on the meeting."

"What meeting and who wants in on it?" Raj asked, strolling into the conference room.

Scavetti gave him a scathing look. "Just a quick bite, huh, Gregor?"

"You're a crude man, Scavetti," Raj said, not even glancing at the detective as he dropped into a chair at the end of the table, leaving a wall at his back and his face to the open door. "But Felder here seems like a decent sort, so I'll assume that you're a good cop." He leaned back into the chair, perfectly at ease. "Shall we continue?"

"You got somewhere else to be, vampire?"

Raj gave him a smug glance. "I do now."

"Son of a bitch," Scavetti muttered. "What is it about vampires and women?" He shook his head in disgust, but his voice held an undercurrent of admiration that he couldn't disguise.

Raj permitted himself a slight smile, knowing it would irritate Scavetti. The burly detective responded on cue, giving him a final glare before turning his delightful personality on his partner. "Cowens and Blackwood are in on the meeting."

"Do they know—" Felder began.

"That we have one of the bloodsuckers here? Yeah, they know. No offense," he added, giving Raj a look that made it clear offense was very much intended.

"Mr. Gregor—" Dan Felder started.

"Call me Raj."

"Raj?" Tony drawled, stretching out the single syllable.

"A nickname, Detective. We bloodsuckers are quite big on them."

Scavetti's eyes went flat as he tried to decide if he was being played, but Felder intervened once again. "Come on, Tony. Mr. Gregor . . . er, Raj is here to help us. We *asked* him to come down here, remember?"

Raj pitied Felder, having to work every day with such a noisome partner. But the truth was he *did* have an interest in getting this case solved quickly, so he tried to be more diplomatic. "Lord Krystof is very interested in resolving this matter, gentlemen. He's asked me to assist in any way I can."

"*Lord* Krystof, huh?" Scavetti sneered predictably. "Well, isn't that fucking sweet. I thought we were in America, Dan."

"Jesus Christ, Tony, what the hell is wrong with you?" Evidently even Dan Felder could only take so much.

Scavetti snapped his mouth shut, sucking back whatever he'd been about to say. He scowled at Raj, as if daring him to say anything. When Raj remained silent, Scavetti gave his partner an apologetic look. "I'm all right," he muttered. He turned his back in an obvious attempt to keep his next words private. It didn't work. Raj could have heard him easily, even he'd been standing outside the room and down the hall. But Scavetti didn't know that.

"It just threw me off, that's all," Scavetti said softly to Dan. "The Commissioner showing up at the last minute like this. This case is important to me; you know that."

"Which is why you should welcome help from the vamps," Felder replied. "What do we know about their community? Nothing, that's what. So play nice for a change, you idiot."

"Yeah." Tony gave a nervous laugh and steeled himself visibly before turning back to face Raj. "You okay with William Cowens and his fucking spiritual adviser being in the room?"

Raj shrugged easily. "I have no problem with that. The more information we have, the sooner we can solve this case and get back to our own lives. Believe me, Detective, I am no happier to be here than you are."

Disbelief flashed quickly in Tony's brown eyes, but he nodded in agreement. "Cowens and the Commissioner had a private meeting first." He crooked his fingers in the air, giving the last two words air quotes for emphasis. "Blackwood's with them. They should be here any minute."

Raj sighed, thinking every extra minute spent in Scavetti's company had to be taking at least an hour off his immortal life. But he waited, letting thoughts of the lovely Sarah Stratton, and what he had planned for her, make those minutes pass more pleasantly.

He jerked his thoughts away from Sarah and fixed his sight on the door moments before a big man in a dark suit walked into the room. He recognized Police Commissioner Thornton from his picture in the lobby behind the bulletproof glass. With him were William Cowens, his bodyguard, and Edward Blackwood. Commissioner Thornton took a look around, his gaze lighting briefly on Raj before moving on to Scavetti. "Have you begun the briefing yet?"

"No, sir," Scavetti said. "Captain said to wait for you and Mr. Cowens."

"Then let's get this started. William," he said, addressing Cowens, "these are Detectives Scavetti and Felder." He indicated each man in turn. "They're heading up Patricia's case and I have every confidence in their abilities. He pulled out two chairs, offered one to Cowens and sat in the other. "Edward Blackwood," he continued, with a nod toward the HR founder, "is Mr. Cowens's advisor in this matter and will be serving as his press spokesman unless we decide a more personal statement is warranted." He didn't bother to introduce the bodyguard, of course. It wasn't appropriate and no one took offense. The man eyed the room carefully, his gaze lingering on Raj before he moved to take up a position between his client and the door, while still having a clear view of everyone in the room.

"And you, sir," Thornton said, addressing Raj directly, "must be the representative from our local vampire community." He all but choked on the words, which Raj found amusing. That most humans preferred to believe vampires didn't exist was understandable, even preferable, to the vampire community. As he'd told Krystof, vampires survived largely by living below the radar, so to speak. If the humans thought too much about what walked among them, they might be prodded into doing something about it. And as powerful as vampires were, they were few in number, especially compared to the billions of humans now walking the Earth.

But it always surprised him when the human authorities permitted themselves to remain equally ignorant. Thornton was the Police Commissioner of a major American city—a city which was controlled by a vampire lord, no less; a city that hosted the most powerful vampires on the continent at the Vampire Council meeting every eighth year—and the man couldn't even say the word *vampire* without choking on it. But Raj kept these thoughts private. He rose slightly, just enough to extend his hand halfway across the table, establishing the pecking order by forcing the Commissioner to do likewise.

"Raymond Gregor," he said. He noticed the Commissioner avoided looking at him directly and once again had to stifle the urge to laugh out loud. Television and movies had spread many myths about vampires, most of them utter foolishness, although some played into the vampires' hands quite nicely. The need for eye contact was one of them. It helped sometimes to focus the target's attention, but if Raj wanted to seize control of a human's mind, he certainly didn't need to waste time staring into his eyes to do so.

"Always an honor to meet some of our fine men in blue, Detectives." Blackwood's voice broke the sudden tension. "Even if you wear a suit," he added, with his patented charming smile. He shook hands with the two detectives. "And Mr. Gregor," he enthused, shaking Raj's hand in turn. "This is indeed a pleasure. My institute would love to open a dialogue with your people. I believe we have much in common."

Raj accepted the handshake without comment. Humanity Realized had been after the vampire community for years, trying to "open a dialogue." Vampires were all but immortal, and HR wanted to know why so they could sell the secret to wealthy humans and thus fulfill their mission of realizing what they considered to be the full human potential. Since the last thing the people of Earth—or vampires either, for that matter—needed was a competing bunch of rich, immortal assholes running around, every vampire council on the planet had issued a firm edict. There was to be no cooperation of any sort with humans when it came to researching vampire physiology. It was the one thing, possibly the only thing, every council member agreed upon wholeheartedly, and they enforced that edict absolutely. The penalty was death—permanent and instant death—for any vampire caught breaking the edict. No trial, no appeal. Vampire justice had its own code, and it was uncompromising.

"I'd like to make something clear right now," Cowens said, his tone suggesting he was accustomed to having strict attention paid to everything he said. And indeed, silence fell as everyone in the room turned to look at him. "My daughter is missing." He breathed deeply in and out through his nose, his jaw clenched, visibly struggling to bring his emotions under control. "I know how this works," he said bluntly. "I know you all think she's dead already." His eyes grew hard and he stared at Felder and Scavetti. "I don't believe that. I won't believe that until I have a body to take home. I want a full investigation, do you understand me? I don't care if you resent me talking to you this way. You can complain to your Union, to the Commissioner, to God himself. I don't care. I want my daughter found. Dead . . ." He closed his eyes against the pain. "Dead or alive," he continued hoarsely. "Or heads will roll. Do you understand me?"

Felder and Scavetti returned his stare and Raj gave them credit for not being cowed by the explicit threat. Cowens had more than enough influence to get a couple of city detectives broken down to street cops if they failed him, and they had to know that.

"And you," Cowens said, turning his angry gaze on Raj, who regarded him impassively. "I don't give a fuck who you are or who your so-called master is. If one of you monsters has my daughter, if you've harmed a single hair on her head." Cowens rose and leaned forward across the table. "I have resources you cannot imagine, vampire. No hole will be deep enough to hide you." He kicked his chair out of the way suddenly, raked all of them with an angry glare and strode from the room, his bodyguard racing to hit the doorway before he did. Blackwood scrambled to his feet only steps behind, but the Commissioner merely stood and watched them leave.

When he turned back, his expression was somber. "This is a difficult case, gentlemen. Not just for you, but for the Department. I'm trusting you to take care of it." And he, too, departed, leaving just the three of them once again.

"Well. That was useful," Raj commented dryly. He straightened from his casual slouch to put both elbows on the table. "So tell me, gentlemen, why exactly was Sarah Stratton here tonight?"

Scavetti swung around and stared at him for a few silent minutes, and then shook his head, chuckling in disbelief. "She called, said she had an in with the local honcho." He gave Raj a skeptical look. "Your boss, I assume."

"One would think. What's Blackwood's involvement?"

"Fuck if I know. He seems to like *you* well enough. Maybe you should ask him yourself, *Raj*."

Raj studied Scavetti lazily, thinking how easy it would be to grab the foulmouthed detective some night and make him disappear. Would anyone miss him, he wondered. Could even a Neanderthal like Scavetti have people who loved him?

"Are you married, Detective?" he asked. "You have a wife? A family?"

Scavetti regarded him suspiciously. "What the hell do you care?"

Raj shrugged. "Just curious."

"Well, leave me the fuck out of your curiosity. And if you want to know more about Stratton, you can ask her yourself. Asshole."

Felder rolled his eyes. "How about we get on with the briefing, Tony? Raj here isn't the only one with a social life. I've got a late date with my next ex-wife."

Scavetti brooded a few minutes longer, staring blankly at the wall. And then with no outward warning, both hands slapped the table, rattling Felder's already chipped coffee cup and knocking over a couple of unopened water bottles. "Fuck, yeah!" he announced. "Let's do this."

He stood and stomped over to a whiteboard which ran along the entire far wall. There was a roughly five by six foot piece of thick poster stock leaning against the board, and Scavetti moved it aside to reveal a series of photographs and notes taped to the whiteboard itself. "We've got three women over the last month who match the profile," he said, suddenly all business. "All three missing, no bodies found yet."

"What *is* the profile," Raj asked curiously.

Scavetti gave him a dirty look, but said, "We're going on the assumption that there's a vampire link for now, so that's fucking number one. The rest is the usual—age, appearance, access. William Cowens's daughter, Patricia, eighteen and single, was last seen at a vamp party. It was an open affair, advertised in the dorms and various places on campus, on bulletin boards and so on. We spoke to her airhead roommate who says she persuaded Cowens to go to the party at the last minute, that she'd never been to one before. At this point, we don't think she was specifically targeted. There've been no calls to her father, no ransom demand, not even with all the publicity—which doesn't say much for her fucking chances. Unless one of you guys has her?" he asked with faked curiosity. "I understand you keep 'em alive for a few days."

Raj didn't bother to respond, and Scavetti continued with a grunt. "Anyway, for now, it looks like a random snatch—she left the party early and, as far as we can tell, alone, and no one has seen her since.

We do know she never made it back to the dorm.

"Going back to the most recent incident before Cowens . . ." He moved down the board to the picture of another young woman who looked older than Patricia Cowens, but not by much. "Regina Aiello, twenty-one years old, living with her mother who filed the missing report. Mother says she went out with friends, kind of a girl's night out before someone's wedding that weekend. We talked to the friends who say they all went to a fucking blood house—"

"That's apparently the in thing for bachelorette parties these days," Dan interrupted to add. "No more Chippendale dancers, I guess. Now it's vampires."

"The others didn't realize she was missing," Tony raised his voice slightly over his partner and kept talking. "Until the mother started calling around the next day. Apparently several of her group peeled away during the festivities to do God knows what, and they just assumed Aiello had done the same. The mother says she didn't know they were going to a blood house and seemed pretty shocked by the idea. Talking to the girl's friends, I get the impression Aiello wasn't exactly a player."

Raj listened with half an ear to the facts—interviews with Aiello's friends and so on—but pushed away from the table and stood, walking over to the board where he studied the pictures of the missing women. Trisha Cowens's disappearance might be questionable—those ridiculous vamp parties had nothing to do with anything truly Vampire—but Aiello disappearing from a blood house was troubling.

Raj frowned and kept reading as Scavetti's expletive-laced recitation moved on to the next woman, the first one taken, as far as they knew. Martha Polk, nineteen, engaged to be married, but living with her parents. She was employed by an upscale catering company and had worked a private party downtown, after which several people, including some of the wait staff, went to another of the blood houses.

Raj saw a definite pattern developing, but whether it was vampires or someone who wanted it to look like vampires was the big question. Not that everyone went right home from the blood houses. Scavetti wasn't far off on that point. When a vampire found a tasty and amenable partner, it wasn't unusual for the two of them to spend a few days together, especially on a weekend. The very young woman who'd been lounging around Krystof's office earlier was a good example. But Polk had been gone nearly a month and that was far too long.

"Polk's group have all developed fucking amnesia about the night in question," Scavetti was saying. "Not one of them will say for sure that Polk was with them at the blood house, but they won't say she wasn't either. Apparently her fiancé's the jealous type and no one wants to pony up and get her in trouble. Like she's not in fucking trouble already."

Raj studied the young woman's picture, which was from her work photo ID. She seemed too young to be getting married. Her face was open and expressive, with a big smile and brown hair that was swept into a bouncy looking ponytail.

"And then there's Dr. Estelle Edwards," Scavetti continued. "She fits the time frame, disappearing about a week before Polk, and there's a vamp connection, but she's older than the others and travels in radically different circles. She's a research MD at the university."

Raj moved down to Edward's profile, which was set apart from the rest. He leaned closer, straining to read someone's uneven handwriting. He frowned. Her husband said she'd gone out to meet a local vampire connection? What the hell was that about?

He shifted his gaze once again to scan the pictures pinned across the top of the board. Scavetti was right. Estelle Edwards stood out. She was only in her late thirties, but with her carefully coiffed and highlighted blond hair, and her well-fleshed face, she appeared much older, almost matronly. Each of the three others was petite and dark-haired, with a youthful ripeness to them that Raj recognized as the kind of women who many vamps—including him—enjoyed feeding from. That ripeness gave them a special glow, softening their cheeks and plumping their lips into a pouty fullness that invited a vampire to crush them with his mouth and sip at the juice of life.

He turned back to the image of Estelle Edwards. Everything about her said settled, married, matron. She was attractive enough, but she'd never have turned heads the way the other three did.

"What kind of research?" Raj asked, interrupting Scavetti's flow.

The detective looked over with a predictable scowl which transformed to quick interest when he saw the picture Raj was looking at. "I'm not sure. You remember, Dan?"

"Yeah." Felder was flipping through his notes. "Uh . . . hematology?"

"Blood," Raj said unhappily.

"Her husband said she's been trying to get funding for a study of vampires," Felder added. "Wants to figure out whatever it is that makes them—" He jerked a look at Raj, as if he'd forgotten for a moment there was a real vampire in the room with him. "That is, why you all live so long and everything."

"A dangerous subject," Raj said thoughtfully. "How did she plan to do it without a test subject?"

"What do you mean?"

He turned all the way around and looked between the two detectives, trying to decide how much to say. "I mean it's hard to study blood without a sample, and no vampire would have cooperated, not willingly anyway. Or unless he had a death wish."

"Why not?"

"We don't share," Raj said flatly. "How do you know she's part of this case? Maybe she pressured a vampire who didn't want to cooperate and got killed for her efforts."

"We're not sure she is, actually. Like Tony says, the timing fits, and there's a definite vamp connection, but for the rest of it . . ." Felder shrugged. "You might be right about some vamp getting pissed and taking her out, but her husband was pretty insistent that she'd made contact with someone in the vampire community. Someone who was willing to cooperate in her research. And he told us she'd already met whoever it was at least once before."

"Did this supposed contact have a name?"

Scavetti snorted a dismissive laugh. "I asked him the same thing. He says she's very secretive about her work. We took a hard fucking look at the husband, I'll tell you, but I don't think there's anything there. As in *nothing's* there. I got the impression they don't spend that much time together. No heat, if you know what I mean."

"He's a doc at the University too," Felder added. "Heads up a big psychiatric clinic or something. He seemed awfully certain his wife was going to get her samples, though. Says she had drug companies lining up to sponsor her. A lot of money, too."

"How much money?" Raj asked curiously.

"The good doctor almost choked on his own tongue trying to avoid answering that question, but I got him to admit we're talking well into the tens of millions."

"Interesting," Raj said, concealing his rising concern. "I'll check into that angle for you," he said. "Someone may have been playing her along, either human or vampire, and if that's true, I'll find him. Or her. I'd like to talk to Edwards's husband," he said. "And maybe visit her lab."

"I'll set something—" Felder started to say, but Scavetti interrupted, ignoring his partner's look of surprise.

"That's not gonna happen, Gregor. We appreciate the cooperation and all, but I can't have you contaminating my case, going around talking to people, muddying up the investigation."

Raj didn't bother arguing. It no longer mattered what the detective did or didn't want. Krystof had sent him here to cooperate with the police in their investigation and he'd done so. But Raj had assumed going in that there was no vampire involved in these crimes, that all of this cooperation was just for show. He'd learned enough tonight to make him doubt that assumption, and that meant any real cooperation with the authorities was now over. If vampires were involved, it was an internal matter and it would be handled accordingly. If Edwards's husband was right and a vampire was providing blood for this research— well, there was only one possible outcome for that vampire and any humans involved with him. And that outcome probably wouldn't be acceptable to the human authorities.

Raj glanced once again at the board, memorizing the salient facts of all four missing women, before turning away to stroll around the table.

"I guess we're done here, then?" He glanced at Scavetti, who seemed surprised by his quick capitulation even though he'd been the one insisting Raj get off the case and out of his life. "Excellent," Raj said, when no one objected. He started for the door, but a sudden thought made him stop and turn. "If there is a vampire mixed up in any of this, I will find him and he will be dealt with. For your own safety, gentlemen, leave that part of the investigation to me. If I learn anything that might help your own efforts, I'll let you know. In the meantime . . ." He pulled a slim, gold case out of his inner jacket pocket. "My numbers," he said, opening the case and dropping a few thick, white business cards on the table. "Call anytime, although night is always better," he said with a quick grin.

Scavetti was still growling when Raj walked through the lobby and out into the dark night to begin searching for answers.

Chapter Fifteen

The temperature had dropped a few more degrees while Raj had been inside. Damn Buffalo and its weather. It reminded him of his hometown on the Baltic coast of Poland. The cold and wet had seemed to last forever there too, days passing one after the other without even a glimmer of honest sunshine. His father had been a dock worker and every once in a while, especially in winter, a crate of oranges from Italy or Spain would just happen to break open, spilling its cargo all over the dock. On those days, his father always brought home a few of the ripe, succulent globes wrapped in thin tissue paper like priceless treasures. The thick perfume of the citrus oil as his mother peeled away the skin, the sweetness of the juice as they savored each portion—a much younger Raj had dreamt of sun-drenched hillsides filled with beautiful women in skimpy dresses plucking the golden rounds into their aprons.

A bus drove past on the street, spewing exhaust and crashing into his reverie. Raj sighed. It had been centuries since he'd seen the sun. On the other hand, there had been no shortage of beautiful women in skimpy dresses. He thought of Sarah Stratton and her red dress. Unfortunately, Sarah would have to wait until tomorrow. He had a vampire to talk to tonight.

The drive to Krystof's was a short one, the streets mostly empty of traffic. It was late for mortals, but the middle of the workday for vampires. Raj pulled out his cell phone and scrolled through the stored numbers, finding the one he wanted.

"Yeah," Jozef answered.

"We should meet," Raj said.

There was a moment of silence. "Give me a couple of hours."

"I'll be outside." Raj hung up. Two hours to kill. The luscious Sarah Stratton came to mind once more, but she was probably tucked safely into her bed by now, all toasty and warm. Ah, well. Two hours. He might as well check out the house where Patricia Cowens was last seen.

He made a quick U-turn and drove back to his lair, staying there just long enough to get rid of the suit and pull on his usual cold weather ensemble of sweater, jeans and leather jacket, all in black.

Back in the BMW, he called up the address of the missing girl's last known location from memory and entered it into his dash GPS for directions. There was a time when these streets had been as familiar to him as the docks of Poland, and this part of the city hadn't changed much in the intervening years. But unlike the streets of his childhood, Buffalo had no nostalgic hold on his memories. He'd let them go as soon as he'd left. This was no longer his town, if it had ever been.

Cruising down the silent streets, he parked a couple of blocks away from the house where Patricia Cowens had attended the vamp-wannabe party. No one knew exactly where or when she'd disappeared. She'd left the house a little after eleven, telling her roommate she intended to catch the bus back to campus. But she'd never made it back to the dorm and the driver on the only bus running that night didn't remember picking her up. Of course, after awhile every passenger probably looked the same to those guys, but the police were going on the assumption she'd been taken between the house and the bus stop, probably before she ever reached the busy main street.

The area was quiet when he climbed from his car and looked around. Nearby, a dog barked briefly but quickly gave up the effort as Raj moved down the street. The neighborhood was older, rows of modest houses on lots just big enough to give the illusion of privacy. They were well-kept for the most part, the driveways filled with minivans and mid-size cars. It was a work night, so all the good citizens were sound asleep, their houses locked up tight, with only the occasional gleam of a nightlight through a window or the rare porch light to chase away the dark.

Raj walked right up to the house where the party had been held, climbing the stairs and turning around to stand on the porch and stare outward. There were street lights here, but plenty of trees, too. In the summer, the trees would block much of the light from the overhead lamps, but with winter only a couple of weeks gone, most of the trees were still bare, their branches casting twisted skeletons of shadow on the sidewalk and empty front yards.

There'd been no sign of a struggle, he remembered from the report on Scavetti's board. No blood—not that the human police could find anyway—no torn bits of clothing or discarded possessions. More significantly, no one had heard anything at all. The dog down the street hadn't barked enough for the owner to notice and there'd been no screams, no shouts. But if William Cowens was right and his daughter's abductor was a vampire, she would have gone willingly. And if that vampire had hung around long enough, the dog would have grown used to him and stopped barking, just as he had for Raj tonight.

He studied the silent street. Whoever had taken the girl had been waiting. Not for her specifically perhaps, but for someone from the party. And if Scavetti's working theory was correct, the abductor had done it at least twice before. So he'd have found someplace dark where no one would notice him, but with a clear view of the house so he could see people coming and going, waiting for a woman who left alone, a young woman like Patricia Cowens.

Raj concentrated on the pattern of shadows and light, places where one of his own could have hidden. Three houses down and across the street, in between two older brick homes, was a space of roughly ten feet. The far house had a porch light burning, but none of that light made it to the dark canyon between the two houses.

He scanned the neighborhood slowly and stepped off the porch, striding down the cracked walk and across the street. As he drew closer to the hide, his head came up and his already enhanced vampire senses snapped to attention. He drew a breath deep into his lungs, tasting the air as he moved closer, his boots nearly soundless on the dry grass.

If a vampire was powerful enough, he could wrap himself in darkness and all but disappear, especially at night and with no direct light. In shadows as deep as these . . . There. Some sort of cologne. It was faint, but Raj's sense of smell was far stronger than a human's and, though it had been cold, there'd been no rain or snow since Trish had been kidnapped only a few days earlier. He inhaled again and wrinkled his nose in distaste. Too sweet. But mingled with the cologne was the old blood scent of Vampire. *Damnit.* He'd come here hoping to prove himself wrong, to find evidence that it was a human preying on his own, not some rogue who'd decided to break every rule of vampire society in the new age.

He drew another breath, fixing the scent in his memory. It took power to hide in the shadows, to come upon the victim without her seeing anything. Other than Raj himself, Krystof didn't generally keep people around who were strong enough to do something like that. If anything, the vampire lord's newest minions were weaker than ever, probably because Krystof knew his control was weakening as well.

Had an outsider sensed this vulnerability and moved in without Krystof's knowledge? Someone who was scouting the area in preparation for a takeover? If so, the intruder would have no choice but to hunt in order to feed. The human donors at the blood houses would be unavailable to an outsider, someone who wasn't supposed to be here and had to hide his presence. But why *abduct* the women? Why not simply find a willing companion and wipe her mind as Raj had done earlier?

He took a step out of the shadows between the two houses but retreated quickly when he heard a car approaching from down the block, moving slowly, as if searching for an address. He watched as the driver almost stopped in front of the party house, but then kept going to park in front of the neighbor's instead. The engine was turned off and the interior light came on as the driver got out and closed the door, her eyes glued to the house where Trish Cowens had been seen last.

Raj grinned, not at all surprised that the driver was Sarah Stratton. If anything, it gave him a moment of personal satisfaction. He'd been right about her. She was involved in this case somehow, and in a way she didn't want anyone to know.

Wrapping the darkness around himself, just as the abductor must have done, Raj crossed the street, no more than the shadow of a cloud passing over the waning moon as it slid through the night. He approached her in perfect silence, until he was standing only a few feet away, beneath the bare branches of an elm. She was close enough that he could hear her every breath, hear her heart beating rapidly with nervousness or perhaps fear.

Not so bold as Raj, she walked only halfway up the uneven walk toward the house, muttering softly under her breath the whole way. What little he could make out of her words made no sense to him. She stopped and stared at the dark porch and then turned and headed quickly back toward her car, seeming suddenly eager to leave. Still unaware of him standing there, she hurried down the sidewalk, her stiletto heels clicking sharply on the cement. She passed right by him, arms crossed tightly, holding herself in a way that suggested the chill was coming from something other than the weather.

Raj stepped out behind her and pulled her back against his chest, holding her there with one hand over her mouth to catch her scream.

"I thought you'd be safe in your bed by now, little one," he murmured close to her ear. He gentled his hold without letting her go, exquisitely aware of her body against his, the thud of her heart against his arm where he held her tightly, and the fading shivers of fear as she realized who it was holding her. She was tiny compared to him. He could have lifted her bodily and carried her away easily, even as Trish Cowens had been carried away only days before. But he wasn't some rogue vampire, and this wasn't Trish Cowens.

"If I take my hand away, will you promise not to scream?"

She jerked her head downward in what he took for assent. He dropped his hand from her mouth, resting it on the swell of her hip instead, still holding her in place. She drew in a long breath, but didn't try to break free. She relaxed in his arms briefly, letting her head fall back against his chest.

"You're trembling," he said quietly.

She stiffened in outrage. "You scared me half to death!"

Raj chuckled, shifting his grip and turning it into a caress, enjoying the feel of her soft curves beneath his hands, the warm weight of her breasts against his arms. "What are you doing here, Sarah?"

She made a move then, but he only held her more securely. "I was just curious," she insisted. "And, I'm worried about Trish—"

"Sarah, Sarah," he chided. "You're lying again."

He let go of her as she spun around to glare at him. "What are *you* doing here?"

He raised an eyebrow at her. "*I'm* cooperating in an active police investigation. You, on the other hand, were told your services were not required. And yet, here you are."

He felt more than saw the heat of her blush. "At least I wasn't sneaking around in the shadows, spying on people," she muttered, refusing to meet his gaze.

Raj gestured at the wide open space. "I was hardly sneaking. You simply didn't notice me, for which I am deeply wounded."

He expected a smile, but instead she looked up at him with eyes filled with fear. "She didn't see him either," she whispered. "He was just . . . there."

"Who?" Raj asked suddenly intent. He stifled a sudden irritating urge to reach out to her, to pull her close and reassure her that nothing could harm her as long as he was with her. He wanted answers. "What do you know, Sarah?"

She stared at him with haunted eyes, searching his face, looking for . . . *What? Raj* wondered.

"Nothing," she whispered. "Nightmares. They don't mean anything." Her voice caught on the final words.

He did reach out for her then, but she beat him to it, taking hold of the front of his jacket with both hands and gripping the leather like a lifeline. She was trembling again and he wrapped his arms around her in confusion.

"Tell me their names, Raj," she demanded unexpectedly, raising her head enough to give him a searching look. "The other women. Tony wouldn't tell me—"

Raj frowned. "Why do you need their names, Sarah?"

She choked out a harsh laugh and lowered her forehead to his chest. "Because I need to know whether or not I'm going crazy." Her voice was muffled against his sweater, but he could hear the desperation in her voice. It troubled him more than it should have, but it made his decision easy.

"You know about Trish; she's been in the papers."

Sarah looked up at him in surprise, as if she hadn't expected him to answer her plea. She nodded.

"There are three other women, Estelle Edwards, Martha Polk and Regina Aiello."

Her face seemed to crumple, a sob escaping her lips, as she hid her face once more against his chest. "Regina," she said softly. "I'm so sorry."

"Sorry for what, Sarah? Tell me what's going on."

"Nothing," she said, stepping back from him to stand on her own, even as one hand stroked the front of his sweater, wiping away the wetness of her tears. "Regina's mother is someone I know. She's been worried, and when I heard about this case . . . I don't know what I'll tell her now."

She was lying again, damnit. "We need talk about this. Your place, now," he said impatiently. "I'll follow you—"

"No." She met his angry gaze, the gold flecks in her hazel eyes glinting in the street lights. "It's late," she offered as an excuse. "I shouldn't have come at all. I don't know what I thought I'd find here."

Raj studied her silently, debating. She knew something, or thought she did. On the other hand, she hadn't even known the names of the missing women, beyond Trish Cowens, so whatever she thought she knew didn't get to the heart of whoever was doing this. Probably. And he still had to meet with Jozef tonight.

"All right," he said, unsmiling. "Tomorrow night then."

She stared back at him, as if not quite trusting his easy surrender. "So we're good, right?"

Raj smiled then, a slow curving of his lips. "Oh, yes, Sarah. We're very good."

She backed several steps away from him, retreating as she would have from a dangerous animal, as if she was worried he would suddenly leap upon her and ravage her right here on this cold, Buffalo street. The thought kept him amused as she turned finally and hurried to her car.

She passed him when she drove away, giving a little wave through her open window. Raj smiled. And when she was gone, he punched a speed dial number.

"My lord," Emelie answered instantly. "How may I serve you?"

Raj winced. He hated that formal vampire shit and Em knew it. She only fell back on the formalities if she was pissed at him, or if someone else was listening. And he couldn't think of anything he'd done to piss her off lately. "Get rid of whoever it is, Em. We need to talk."

"Yes, my lord."

Raj waited, listening as Em moved herself, rather than asking the others to leave. He could hear her steady breathing as she walked, a door opening and closing and then another. "Okay," she said in a far more casual tone. "I'm in the office. What's up, boss?"

"Congratulations," he said dryly. "You win. Get some of my people up here. Not an army, not yet anyway. Just some back up. And no one but my own children, people I can trust absolutely."

"Yes," she breathed in obvious relief. "We're ready to go, my lord. I put out a heads-up right after you left, just in case. If we leave immediately, we can be there before dawn."

"Tomorrow night's soon enough. There's nothing specific yet, but there's a possibility someone from out–of–town is moving in on Krystof and I'm not going to let that happen."

"Only give the word, my lord."

"What would I do without you, Em?"

"You'd manage. Not as well, of course," she added. "But you'd manage."

"Thanks. One more thing, Em. I want to know everything we've got on the woman who visited Manhattan with Raphael and his mate last week . . . Sarah Stratton. Put Simon on it and tell him to go deep. I already know she teaches at the university here in Buffalo, so that's a place to start, but I want everything Simon can find. If he needs a picture, she should be on the security video from the club."

"Okay," Em said slowly. "You picking up stray kittens again, boss?"

Raj laughed. Her curiosity was fairly burning through the ether, but Raj didn't feel like saying anything more. Not yet.

"I'll talk to you later, Em," he said, ignoring her question. He disconnected the call, pocketed his phone and opened the car door, sliding into the comfortable interior. As he drove away in the opposite direction Sarah had taken, he thought about stray kittens and about Emelie. She was always telling him he had a weakness for damsels in distress. And she should know, since the damsel he'd rescued once upon a time had been Emelie herself.

* * * *

Albany, New York 1918

Raj strolled down the darkened street, drinking in the excitement, the fear. The United States was at war. Men were lining up to go fight in Europe, seeking a glory in battle that would never be found on the streets of their hometowns. Raj could have warned them. Could have told them there was nothing exciting about the stink of a battlefield, the blood and excrement, the screams of your friends dying all around you while you could do nothing but fight to save your own miserable life. But he said nothing. They wouldn't have listened anyway.

Eager young men roamed the streets of Albany, drunk for the most part, enjoying a final fling before Uncle Sam sent them out to become soldiers. By tomorrow, they'd be regretting this last night of indulgence— when their heads were throbbing, their stomachs rebelling, and they were stuck on a hot, crowded bus for the journey to some dismal boot camp.

But for some of them, most of them probably, tonight was their first real taste of freedom, their first time away from the family farm, the small town scrutiny. Fights were common, but the police paid little attention, recognizing the futility of trying to bring order to a chaos that would dissipate itself in a day or two anyway. And as long as the new recruits limited themselves to pounding on each other, no one cared.

He turned away from the main boulevard, seeking the side streets, the dark alleys where fledgling soldiers could be found sleeping or passed out. Either way they were a quick, easy meal for a hungry vampire.

The noise of a crowd drew his attention to what should have been a quiet side street. A rowdy group of men had gathered, shouting encouragements and threats. Yet another fist fight, no doubt. Raj almost turned away. There was nothing for him in these squabbles. But something made him turn back and take a second look. It wasn't the words the men were shouting; he could barely make those out. But the taunts carried a raw brutality, a gutter meanness that burned against his senses. Raj frowned, pushing his way through the crowd until he drew close enough to see what was going on over the shoulders of others.

He swore viciously and shoved the rest of the way forward with a purpose, tossing bodies aside in his fury. A young woman lay at the heart of the circle, half-naked, bloody and beaten, her latest rapist grunting between her legs. Raj kicked out, his thick boot breaking ribs with a resounding crunch. The man screamed as he flew through the air, the noise cut off with a choked gurgle when he hit a nearby wall.

Raj crouched and spun, ready to fight, mouth open, fangs fully displayed, seeing the faint gleam of blue as his Vampire-enhanced eyes burned ice-cold with rage.

Young men who moments earlier had been full of bravado at the prospect of raping a helpless woman fled before the wrath of Vampire. Screams faded down the alley as they ran, trampling each other in their hurry to escape. To one side, the injured rapist was struggling to crawl away, whimpering wordlessly. Raj took a step forward, intending to drain him dry, to ensure he never again brutalized a helpless woman, but from behind him came a small, lost sound.

He turned back toward the woman. She'd curled in on herself, thin fingers struggling to pull the tatters of her clothing around her battered body, to cover her nakedness. He whipped off his jacket and covered her, careful not to touch her, letting her grasp the ends of the fabric to her chest as she shook silently.

"Let me help you, child," he said softly. His voice was deep and melodic, the same voice he used to seduce the unwary, to persuade the unsuspecting to open their veins for him. She stilled, trembling like a small animal beneath the gaze of a predator, refusing to look at him, as if that would somehow save her.

"Do you have family?" he asked.

She started crying then, quiet sobs that racked her entire body. Raj wanted to reassure her, to tell her he could make it all go away. His blood might not be as strong as that of his master, Lord Krystof, and she was very badly injured, but he was Vampire nonetheless. And his blood was stronger than most, strong enough to heal her injuries, strong enough that he could wipe this night from her mind, make it as if it had never happened. But in her present state, she wouldn't have heard him, much less believed something so fantastic.

"Let me help you," he repeated instead. He laid a single, gentle hand on her back, wincing as she jerked away from his touch, her cries finally finding voice as she grew more frantic.

He sighed. The last thing she needed was a man's hands on her, but the sun was rising and he had to get inside. "I'm sorry, sweetheart," he said. He scooped her up easily, silencing her cries with a quick, mental jab that stole her consciousness and left her limp in his arms. It was crude but effective, and time was running out.

As he sped down the side streets toward his hideaway, racing the sun, he thought to wonder what he was going to do with her now that he'd saved her.

Chapter Sixteen

Buffalo, New York, present day

Raj pulled into the curb near Krystof's and turned off the engine, climbing out of the car to lean against its warmth in the chilly, early morning, waiting for Jozef to appear. He sometimes thought about the men who'd attacked Emelie all those years ago. They'd been ordinary men—sons, fathers and brothers. Some of them had no doubt died in the war. Others would have come home, raised families and grown old. One way or another, they were almost certainly dead by now. Had they ever remembered that night in the alley? Had they ever watched their own daughters grow and been ashamed of what they'd done? There were people who called him a monster, people who would have wiped out every vampire on Earth. But did they ever look at their own neighbors and wonder?

He looked up as the front door opened on silent hinges. A deeper shadow resolved into Jozef's bulk, reminding Raj that Jozef too possessed the power to manipulate shadow if he chose. But Jozef wasn't the assailant. Raj dismissed that idea almost as soon as it occurred. Jozef was powerful enough, but it took intelligence and discipline to climb high in the vampire hierarchy. And that's where Jozef fell short. He was the perfect tool—reliable but completely without imagination. It was both an asset and a weakness in a security chief. He would never stage a rebellion, but he might not see someone else's rebellion coming either. In Raj's estimation, no one knew this better than Jozef himself. He had a good position here with Krystof and a vested interest in keeping it that way. The security chief passed between the twinkling lights along the front walk, cutting across the yard, making directly for him.

"Raj," Jozef said when he got close enough. "It's been awhile since you visited Buffalo."

Raj smiled to himself. Like Krystof, Jozef preferred it when Raj was far away from the city. He shrugged carelessly. "The old man doesn't like me around, and I'm content with Manhattan."

Jozef raised his eyes to meet Raj's. "So how can I help you?"

Help me get back to Manhattan, Raj thought, smiling. "I see a lot of new faces," he said.

The other vampire didn't respond immediately, turning to gaze up the street instead. Raj didn't hurry him. If Jozef wanted Raj gone, this was the best way to make that happen. Eventually, his mind would work around to that conclusion. In the meantime, Raj waited.

"Too many new faces," Jozef said abruptly. "Krystof's turning five, sometimes ten a month, and every one of them's as stupid as that idiot Morales," Jozef continued.

"An army?" Raj asked sharply.

"Cannon fodder more likely, but against what threat? None that I know of."

Raj considered this in light of his suspicions. "Any new vamps move into the area? Anyone who's strong enough to challenge Krystof?"

Jozef barked a laugh. "Other than you, you mean?"

"It can't be me he's worried about. I've given him no reason." *Yet*, he added to himself. "I'm talking about someone else, an outsider. Maybe someone in town unofficially."

Jozef's gaze sharpened. "You know something I don't?"

Raj shrugged and said, "I went by the house where Cowens's daughter was taken last weekend. The sign was old, but there had been someone there. Someone strong enough to stalk his prey undetected on an empty street."

Jozef stiffened. "If Krystof thought someone was poaching, someone who could do what you say, I'd have heard about it. You know how he is. If there was any real danger, he'd be shoving everyone he could find between him and the threat." He paused, making the connection. "You think that might be what this is? Why he's got all this new meat hanging around? But why not tell *me* about it?"

Now *that* was a good question. Krystof understood Jozef's limitations every bit as well as Raj did, which was why he kept Jozef close and Raj far away. But if the vampire lord truly was falling into senility, he might not be thinking as logically as he once did. Raj scraped his fingers back through his hair in frustration. Damn that old man.

"Okay, look, I'm going to talk to some people about these missing women. Witnesses, family members, the usual. I *will* find whoever's doing this, and if it's one of us, I'll make him go away." He paused thoughtfully, remembering that too sweet cologne. "Or her."

Jozef's head came up. "Her? You think it's a woman?"

"No, I don't. But I can't rule it out either," he added, thinking of Emelie—not as a suspect, but as an example. Like humans, female vampires were generally weaker than their male counterparts, but if the vampire had enough power, physical strength became less important, especially if the victim was a little girl like Patricia Cowens.

Jozef frowned, as if trying to wrap his mind around the idea. "Are the cops really letting you in on their investigation?"

"No, they're not. They pretty much just wanted to go through the motions so they could say they'd tried. But I don't need their permission to ask questions." He started to say something about Sarah, but changed his mind. He might not trust her right now—she was definitely keeping something from him—but he still wanted to keep her as far away as possible from Krystof and his clowns.

Frowning, he tossed his keys up and caught them. "I've got to go.

You stay in touch, Jozef."

He spun around without waiting for Jozef's reply, walked around the car and opened the driver's door. By the time he was pulling away from the curb, the other vampire was already gone and Raj was wondering why the very idea of another vampire coming anywhere near Sarah made his hackles rise.

Chapter Seventeen

Sarah struggled to keep her eyes open the next day, listening with only half an ear as the faculty meeting droned on. She'd gotten little sleep last night, partly because she was afraid the dreams would come back. The other part was because she'd tossed and turned like a silly teenager, thinking about Raj and slow, soft kisses. She told herself it was just because she hadn't had a serious relationship with a man in a very long time. Not since college, and even then it hadn't been really serious. She'd learned early on to avoid close friendships, because questions always got asked about the past, about where she grew up, where her family lived. The kind of questions Sarah didn't have good answers for. Cyn had been an exception to the rule, because simply put, Cyn didn't pry. And now, of course, there was her new friend, the incredibly sexy Raj.

She remembered a professor she'd had in graduate school. He'd been born in Poland before the war, had survived the destruction of his small Jewish village, the obliteration of everyone and everything he knew, not only his entire family—although that was horrific enough—but of an entire way of life. She'd been his teaching assistant for a year and had spent a lot of time with him, drinking tea and listening to his stories of a world that was gone forever. He'd told her all sorts of things, but what she recalled now was a bit of wisdom from the old country. She'd never mastered the Polish words; it was a difficult language and one you could study for years and still not get the nuances right. But a rough translation had been something like, "For every monster, there's a monster to love him."

Maybe that's what she saw in Raj. They were both monsters of a sort, freaks in a world of people who went about their lives, never having to worry about dreams of tortured women or . . . well, whatever it was vampires worried about. Blood, she supposed, and where to get it.

She became aware of movement around her and realized the meeting was breaking up at last. Across the table, the Department Chairman was giving her an odd look, and she tried to look thoughtful and scholarly, instead of bored, as she gathered up her papers and shoved them into her oversized purse. She must have succeeded because he gave her a short, approving nod before joining a group of the more senior, i.e., male, department members who would now troop over to the nearest bar and drink themselves into a stupor. One thing she'd noticed right away about academics. They drank a lot. At least the older ones did. And who knew? A few more years of these meetings and she might be drinking a lot too.

She started for the elevator with everyone else, but a glance at her watch sent her racing for the stairs instead. She wanted to shower and change before tonight. She might *be* a monster, but that didn't mean she had to look or smell like one.

* * * *

Raj woke in a much better mood on his second night in the city. He'd had plenty of time this morning to get back to his lair, strip off his clothes and even enjoy a nice, cold shot of vodka before settling down to sleep the day away, safe in his personal vault below the streets of downtown Buffalo. And it didn't hurt that he'd be paying Sarah a personal visit very soon. The taste of her skin had been sweet. Her blood would be even sweeter. He frowned. There was, however, a lot more to Sarah Stratton than a sweet taste. She was hiding something and he intended to know what it was before this night was over.

He checked his watch. It was just after eight. There was one stop he needed to make first—some preparations for Em and the troops. And then sweet Sarah would have his undivided attention and he would have his answers.

His phone rang as he pulled up to a big industrial building not far from Buffalo's international airport. "Where are you, Em?" he answered.

"My lord," Em said, speaking loudly to be heard over the considerable background noise of a small airport. "We're loading supplies, now. We'll be there before midnight."

"I'm at the safe house," he said, staring out the windshield at the darkened building. "I'll turn on the lights and warm it up, but I won't be here when you arrive. I'm meeting someone in a few minutes."

"Dinner, boss?"

"You could say that. Speaking of which, you've all fed tonight, right?"

"You have to ask?"

"Right. Have everyone stay close when you get into town. I'll come by later and fill you in, but something is majorly fucked up in this city, and I don't want any of my people going out there blind."

"Will do, boss."

"Later."

Raj slipped the phone into his jacket pocket and got out of the car. The old warehouse loomed two stories above him, lit only by the big security lights all along its substantial length, and above the door. Its brick walls were old and blackened from years of airport pollution and hard weather, and it appeared deserted. An astute observer would have noticed, however, that the light fixtures were new and enclosed in sturdy cages to deter vandalism. That although the windows were dirty and flecked with bird droppings, not a single one of them was cracked or broken, the panes filled with safety glass and firmly sealed. And the single pedestrian entrance was a solid steel door with a heavy duty lock.

Raj had always known that someday he'd be making a move against Krystof. He'd bought this property years ago, snapping it up at a bargain price when its former owner had needed a discreet sale and Raj had had the cash on hand. Of course, the title had changed several times since then—on paper, anyway. As he stared up at the building, it hit him for the first time that before the month was out he would be the Northeastern Vampire Lord. It never occurred to him that he would fail. He would defeat Krystof and take his place as one of the rarified few who controlled all of Vampire society. It was not something he particularly lusted after. If Krystof had been a different sort of master, Raj would have been content to stay in Manhattan with his clubs and his children, insulated against vampire politics.

But Krystof had always been a petty tyrant, forever the spoiled, younger son of an aging royal house to which he'd been born to as a human. The recent deterioration of his mind had only exacerbated inborn weaknesses. And, as for Raj, he'd had enough of one master; he had no intention of serving another.

He unlocked the sturdy metal door. A soft security light came on to reveal a small vestibule, with a second door a few feet beyond. The interior door opened readily, once the exterior door was fully closed, and Raj stepped into the main building, immediately flipping switches to bring up the overhead lights.

While the building's exterior only hinted that it was more than it looked, the inside left no doubt. The only windows were high above the floor and sealed with thick steel shutters. Long banks of industrial lights illuminated every corner of the vast, empty space. And when Raj's people arrived later, they'd drive their vehicles right into the warehouse through the roll-up bay doors, which were currently secured by thick rods drilled into the concrete floor.

There was a mezzanine over the loading bay, with several rooms for his human guards—a few trusted men and women whom Em would bring in from Manhattan along with the vampire contingent. As with Raj's much smaller, private warehouse downtown, the main sleeping quarters for the vampires were below ground, safe behind a bank-like vault door.

His booted footsteps echoed loudly as he crossed the warehouse floor. Down two short flights of stairs, he keyed in a digital combination and opened the vault. The accommodations inside were Spartan, but then this had never been intended as a permanent headquarters. It was a staging area, nothing more. He turned on the lights there as well, checked the temperature on the thermostat and headed back upstairs, leaving the door open behind him. Upstairs, there was a microwave to serve the dual function of heating food for the humans and blood for the vampires. A refrigerator sat next to the counter, which doubled as a bar, and against the far wall, near the stairs, a large blood storage unit hummed happily. It was empty now, but not for long. He verified that it was working and glanced again at his watch. Time to go.

Leaving the main lights on, he closed and secured the vault and exited the building, locking it behind him. Em knew this place; she'd been the one who'd helped him set it up. She certainly didn't need him to tell her how to get their people settled. And besides, Sarah was waiting.

Chapter Eighteen

Sarah linked arms with Linda as they walked out of the restaurant. The cold night air bit hard after the warm restaurant which, in this case, was a good thing. She'd probably had too much wine to drink, but it had tasted so good and for just a little while, she'd been able to forget everything else and just enjoy the party. Unfortunately, she could never forget for too long or too well. Which was why Linda would soon be back inside with Sam and his friends, getting even tipsier, while sober Sarah went home like the good girl she'd never planned to become.

"Are you sure you won't stay, sweetie?" Linda's breath was fragrant with the lovely Chateau Margaux they'd been drinking all evening.

"Yes, I'm sure. I've got to get some sleep or I'll be useless tomorrow, and I need to get back to my research." She hadn't told Linda that Raj was coming over later and didn't intend to. Her friend would probably begin planning the wedding if she found out Sarah had an actual date.

"I do research, too," Linda said happily. "Just not very often." She laughed, as if that was the funniest thing she'd ever heard. In the restaurant, she'd insisted on walking Sarah safely out to her car, but now Sarah was wondering who was going to walk *Linda* safely back inside.

"Maybe you should go back inside," she said now, trying to turn them back toward the restaurant. "I can find my—"

"Good evening, Sarah."

She jumped at the sound of Raj's voice, turning to find him leaning casually against her car, looking like a cross between the bad boy every mother warned her daughter about and a model in a Calvin Klein aftershave ad. His broad shoulders were encased in leather, his narrow hips and long legs covered in snug fitting denims that made her stomach— and lower parts of her anatomy, too—ache. He gave her a wicked smile, as if he knew exactly what she was feeling.

"Raj," she all but squeaked.

"Raj?" Linda stopped dead in her tracks, suddenly completely sober as she took in this new development. "And who might this be, Sarah, my darling?" she asked silkily, scanning the vampire head to toe with unabashed curiosity. "That research you had to get back to, perhaps?"

"Um." Sarah felt herself blushing and hurried to say, "Linda, this is Raymond Gregor. Raj, my friend Linda Hoffman."

Raj gave Linda a cool glance and held out his hand to Sarah. She took it without thinking and found herself pulled away from Linda's embrace and into the curve of his arm. He secured her there before saying, "A pleasure, Linda. I'll see to it that Sarah gets home safely."

"Will you?" Linda said archly, with a speculative glance at Sarah.

"Well, well."

"Linda, Raj and I—"

"Are old friends," Raj interrupted. "I was in town and looked Sarah up. It's been a while, hasn't it, sweetheart?" He kissed her temple, his breath warm on her skin, and she shivered with something other than the cold.

"Hmmm." Linda clearly wasn't buying it, but she was just as clearly willing to wait for the *entire* story. "I'll just leave you two to *catch up*, then." She laughed a little and said, "We'll talk, Sarah darling," before strolling back across the parking lot with a little wave over her shoulder.

Sarah turned to demand an explanation from Raj but found herself swept literally off her feet as he lifted her directly into a searing kiss that made her anger disappear, along with about half of her brain cells. He crushed her against him, kissing her as hungrily as if they truly had been separated for too long, even though it had been only hours. She felt her own response rising to meet his with an intensity she couldn't recall ever experiencing before. She didn't want to think about anything except the taste of his mouth, the sweep of his tongue against hers, the feel of his big body enclosing her, sheltering her from the unfriendly night. She moaned softly and wrapped her arms around his neck, whispering his name against his lips.

"I think—" Raj began, but whatever he thought was delayed by her renewed demand for his mouth. "Sarah," he tried again, succeeding in getting his lips close enough to her ear for her to hear what he was saying. "Your friend is still watching."

She stiffened at the reminder they were right outside Buffalo's most popular restaurant. She buried her face against his shoulder and he chuckled softly. "I'll drive you home."

"No," she protested. "I can—"

He tightened his hold. "Well, I can't," he growled. "I don't want you out of my sight."

Fresh desire rolled through her body on a wave of warmth. "Okay," she whispered.

Raj's car was parked right next to hers. He beeped the locks open and all but lifted her into the passenger seat, closing the door with a solid thunk. Sarah jumped a little at the sound, a jolt of adrenaline clearing her head long enough to wonder what she was doing in Raj's car, getting ready to drive back to her house and—

Raj leaned over from the driver's seat to give her a quick, hard kiss. "Don't think so hard, sweetheart. I'm not dangerous." He spun the wheel in a tight circle, taking them past the startled valets and out of the parking lot. "Not to you anyway," he muttered.

Sarah gave him a worried glance, but quickly realized she *liked* the idea that he might be dangerous. She liked this big, lethal vampire lusting after her, wanting her so badly that he'd been ready to take her right there in the parking lot. And he *had* been ready. She might not be experienced, but she knew when a man wanted her. Of course, she hadn't exactly been fighting him off either. She smiled, feeling just a little satisfied with herself.

Raj reached out at that moment to take her hand, raising it to his mouth for a soft kiss before settling it on his hard-muscled thigh. "Your place or mine, sweetheart?"

Sarah gave him a surprised look. "You have a place?"

He laughed. "Of course, I have a place. Where do you think I sleep, the local graveyard?"

Sarah blushed. "No," she protested. "Of course not. I just thought . . . I don't know. Maybe a hotel?"

He snorted in dismissal. "Have you *seen* the local hotels? I'm from Manhattan, darling. I'm accustomed to a higher standard. So, what's it to be? I've got a turn coming up."

"My place, I guess," Sarah said, beginning to worry again about what she'd gotten herself into. "I live—"

"I know where you live. I was supposed to meet you there."

"Then why—" She frowned at a sudden thought. "How'd you know which restaurant?"

He shrugged easily. "You said it was a celebration. There aren't that many places worth celebrating in around here. I got lucky and saw your car."

Sarah wasn't sure she believed him, but couldn't figure out any other way he'd have known where to find her. "Look, Raj—" He kissed her hand again, one finger at a time, with a lingering caress of his lips and just a touch of tongue.

"You're thinking again," he said. "And besides . . ." He pulled to a stop in front of her house. "We're here, and I've earned at least a good-night kiss for seeing you home safely."

Sarah opened her mouth to reply, but he was already out of the car and at her open door, holding out his hand to help her. She knew better, but she took his hand anyway, letting him pull her into his embrace, knowing she'd feel that same tug of desire the minute . . . *Oh, God, yes.*

* * * *

Raj followed Sarah up the front stairs to a turn of the century duplex with a pair of old and slightly warped doors. The unit on the left was dark, but the twitch of a curtain told him someone was watching. Beneath the porch light, Sarah inserted her key and unlocked the crummy piece of shit masquerading as a deadbolt. The door opened and Raj breathed in the scent of her home, feeling a deep satisfaction flowing in, along with the unique fragrance that was Sarah. She looked up at him, her long hair a golden spill over soft shoulders, and his brain was suddenly filled with a single word. *Mine.* The thought hit him before he could stop it, and he frowned even as his body kicked hard into an instinctive response. His fangs were pushing eagerly through his gums, hungry for a taste of her blood, and his cock was stiffening with an entirely different sort of hunger. He'd never felt this instant attraction to a woman. He wasn't sure he liked it, but he definitely wanted it.

"Are you going to invite me in?" he asked lazily.

She looked up at him with wide, uncertain eyes. "Do you think I should?"

He gave her a shark's grin, tugging her close enough that she could feel his body's reaction. "Unless you'd rather do this on the porch so your neighbor can enjoy it too."

Sarah blushed hotly and stepped inside the house. "Come on in."

Raj paused long enough to wink at whoever was watching next door, and then followed Sarah, immediately closing the door behind him. She threw her coat over the stairway banister, kicked off her heels and started toward the back of the duplex. Without her coat, he could see she was wearing a skirt and sweater. It wasn't the silky, sheer dress of summer he'd wished for the other night, but it was very nice indeed, the skirt tight and clinging to her hips, accenting a very nicely rounded ass. He watched that ass as he followed her into the kitchen. She was muttering some nonsense about a cup of tea, lifting the kettle and shaking it before putting it back on the burner and twisting the knob to bring up the flame. When she turned to find him standing right behind her, she gave a little squeak of surprise.

"Are you afraid of me, Sarah?" he asked quietly, pushing her hair behind one ear with a gentle finger.

"Terrified," she said with a nervous little laugh. "But not the way you think."

Raj's lips quirked up in a smile as he let his finger travel down her neck and over the fragile arc of her clavicle, coming to rest just above the full swell of her breasts, where he could feel the gentle beat of her heart. "I think you look good enough to eat."

"Oh," she breathed. Her eyes, when they met his, were still wide, but no longer uncertain.

He closed the distance between them, pulling her against his body with a possessive arm around her waist, his hand on her hip as he bent down to breathe deeply of her warm scent. Her heart was racing, her breathing fast and shallow. Her breasts were soft against his chest, her nipples hard. He slid his hand beneath her sweater to touch the soft, warm silk of her skin and she melted into his embrace, reaching up to wrap her arms around his neck, her slender fingers playing with the ends of his hair, as she raised her face to his for a kiss. Wanting far more than playful kisses, Raj growled and fisted his fingers into her silky tresses, lowering his mouth to her bare neck. He could smell the blood flowing hot and sweet, could feel the rush of her jugular against his lips as he bent to taste. His fangs emerged slowly to graze the velvet of her skin, as hard and ready as his cock against her belly. She moaned softly, and he felt it as a gentle vibration against his heart. His woman. Her blood, his to drink; her body, his to take.

Raj froze. He raised his head and his hands stilled. He blinked against the nearly overwhelming need to sink his teeth into her, to lift her up onto the counter and take her right there in the kitchen. Sarah whimpered his name softly, hungrily.

What the hell? He placed his hands on her shoulders and straightened his arms, forcing her away from him, putting enough space between them that he could draw a breath without inhaling the intoxicating aroma of her arousal. "Sarah," he said, shaking her slightly. "Sarah!"

She protested softly, looking up at him in confusion with eyes that were blurred with desire. "Raj?" she said in a small, hurt voice.

"Fuck!" He pulled her against his chest once more, wrapping his arms around her tightly and trapping her arms between them. She struggled fitfully to touch him, stroking him with aborted little jerks of her hands. His own arousal tormented him, screaming at him to go ahead and take her. He buried his face in her hair and groaned. It would be so easy to lift her up, to slide that tight skirt up to her waist, spread her legs and pound his aching cock into her until they both came screaming. She wanted it. And God knew he did; his entire body was throbbing, aching with the need of it. But the very strength of his desire made him stop, because Raj didn't do this sort of thing, didn't lose control with any woman, much less one he barely knew. He was in control, always in control.

"Sarah," he commanded. He took her delicate jaw in one hand and forced her to look at him.

"Raj," she responded impatiently.

He sighed, regretting what he was about to do, wishing he was a bit more of a selfish bastard. But he wasn't. With a gentle nudge of her mind, he sent her to sleep, erasing her memories of the evening since her return home. She collapsed, but he caught her easily, lifting her in his arms, holding her against his chest, her head resting on his shoulder.

He carried her upstairs, twisting nearly sideways on the ridiculously narrow stairway, knowing the nosy neighbor was probably listening to every step. There were two rooms up there, one obviously an office of some sort. He ignored that one for the time being and opened the door to her bedroom with a gentle kick. A queen-sized bed filled most of the space, a single bedside table in the corner. A jewel-toned Tiffany style lamp sat on a dresser near the door, providing minimal light, but more than enough for his vampire sight.

He laid Sarah's limp form on the bed, shoving a huge pile of lace-trimmed pillows to the floor. He left her clothes on, although with slight misgivings. Not that he didn't want to see her sweet little body naked—he definitely wanted *that*—but he didn't want her to wake up wondering what he'd been doing with her while she was unconscious. Especially since he'd denied himself the pleasure of doing exactly those things she would have wondered about. It was one thing to pay the price for one's sins, but another entirely to pay the price without the pleasure of sinning first.

He tucked Sarah under the comforter, sliding her between the fresh-smelling sheets. She murmured softly, curling onto her side and snugging the remaining pillow beneath her cheek. Raj watched her breathe, in and out, indulging himself with a lingering touch on her pale cheek. He didn't understand what was going on. He had beautiful women lining up to bed him every night of the week. So, what was it about sweet Sarah that had him contemplating mayhem against any male who dared touch her? Had him acting like a raw child panting after the first fresh blood he'd ever tasted? Raj didn't like things he didn't understand, especially not when those things had the power to make him vulnerable.

He stood and crossed the hall to her office, which was even smaller than her bedroom. There was the usual computer paraphernalia, but mostly, the room was filled with books. Books on shelves, books in boxes, books stacked on the floor. Curious, Raj glanced at the titles. A lot of academic volumes with those convoluted titles the eggheads were so fond of. He moved to the next bookcase and grimaced. Romance fiction, a lot of it vampires. Em read these books by the dozen. She got a real kick out of passing them around to the guys and suggesting they could learn a few things.

He retrieved one of his business cards from its golden case and tucked it under her phone where she'd be sure to see it, then flicked off the desk lamp. Across the hall, Sarah was sleeping peacefully, her hair a tousle of gold, her long lashes dark against a barely visible pale cheek. Cursing himself for every kind of fool, Raj spun and took the narrow staircase quickly, walking back to the kitchen, where the damn tea kettle was screaming hysterically. He turned it off and stormed to the front door, his mood darkening with every step.

"Fuck!" he swore and just managed to stop himself from putting a fist through her wall. He had the whole damn night ahead of him, hard as a rock and walking away from the one woman he was aching to fuck. Someone was going to pay the price for his bad mood. Maybe it was time to question a few of the local vampires. He wanted to see some blood flowing and it sure as hell was not going to be his own.

Chapter Nineteen

The blood house where Regina Aiello had disappeared was in the small village of Corfu, well beyond the main city, on a few acres bordered by the colorfully named Murder Creek. Raj had always wondered if that creek had been Krystof's motivation to purchase the property—a house on Murder Creek for the vampires to play in was just too great a temptation to pass up.

Outwardly, the place looked much the same as when Krystof bought it just after World War II—a nicely maintained, two-story clapboard with a covered porch. The front yard was covered by a manicured lawn, but the remaining acreage had been permitted to grow wild, with tall grass stretching out to either side, providing a buffer of privacy for what was really going on inside that simple white farm house.

Raj pulled the BMW over to the side of the road. There were no curbs this far out of the city. The house was filled to the brim and more, with people spilling out onto the porch and even into the yard where tables and chairs had been set up to accommodate the overflow. As far as he could see there was no control over who came and went, and sure as hell no one was checking IDs. What the fuck?

He strode across the uneven grass, his tread heavy on the soft ground. Couples were all but having sex in the front yard, vampires sinking fang in full view of the public road not twenty-five yards away. He grabbed a handful of long hair and pulled one of the offending vampires off his donor *de la nuit*. The vampire whipped around with a furious roar, fangs fully distended and dripping blood, hands curled into claws.

Raj gave him a bored look. "Who's in charge here?" he asked.

"Who the fuck are you?" the vampire snarled.

Raj didn't say a word. Using a small thread of power, he drove the vampire to his knees and then bent him backwards until the sound of vertebrae popping was so loud it could be heard over the pounding music coming from the house. The vampire could do little more than grunt in pain, but his eyes were wide with fear, gleaming golden yellow as they begged silently for mercy.

"I believe I asked you a question," Raj said calmly. He released the vamp without warning, causing him to snap forward with such force that he did a full face plant in the grass before slowly, painfully, raising himself just enough to answer Raj's query.

"Mick is in charge, my lord," the vampire rasped. "He'll be in the first room on your right."

"Thank you," Raj said cheerfully and walked away. Behind him he could hear the vampire's companion making concerned noises until she was driven away by a vicious snarl of profanity. Raj smiled. His evening was looking up already.

He crossed to the front porch without incident. Every vampire outside the house had witnessed his display of power and backed off quickly, jerking their humans with them. As he suspected, there was no bouncer at the door—which meant there was not even a record of consent, much less signed waivers. This house was a disaster waiting to happen—and tonight that disaster's name was Raj.

Once inside, he found Mick easily enough. The fool was lying in the middle of a big four-poster bed, surrounded by women. He was a big man, tall and thick, with a headful of unruly red hair and a broad chest that was as naked as the women who were draped all over him. He had power, too. Enough to control this house and its vampires. But not enough to face down a true master.

Fortunately for Raj, he was too arrogant to realize it.

Raj strolled into the room casually, looking like a prospective home buyer checking out the furnishings. Mick's gaze followed him warily, but he didn't move from the bed.

"There are vampires sinking fang in the front yard," Raj commented, running his hand along the silver frame of a particularly fine antique mirror.

"Shocking," Mick said dryly. His women tittered.

Raj glanced at him. "And there appears to be no one checking the IDs of your lovely guests," he continued, giving a little nod of inclusion to the half-naked women who preened under his gaze.

Mick growled out a command, drawing the attention of his adoring fans back to him alone. "What's it to you?" he demanded. "And for that matter, who the fuck *are* you?"

"I didn't introduce myself? How rude. Raymond Gregor," he said, continuing his perusal of the mostly gaudy furnishings. He paused and shifted his gaze to the big vampire. "Raj to my friends, but I'm afraid that doesn't include you, Mick."

The redheaded vampire snorted in disdain and began shoving away his unhappy playmates to climb from the bed. Raj was grateful to see the vampire *was* wearing pants which he zipped with a quick jerk before turning to face him.

"So you're Raj. I've heard about you."

"Have you? I, on the other hand, have never heard of *you*."

Mick squinted angrily and drew himself up to his full height, thrusting out his chest in challenge, much the same way the human Scavetti had the night before.

"Mick," Raj said gently. "You might want to clear the humans from the room first."

The other vampire looked puzzled for a moment and then laughed. "Frankie," he said to a short, scared looking vampire standing near the door. "The house is closed, get everybody out. Five minutes ago," he added with a snap, when Frankie just stood there staring at him.

Raj waited patiently while the house was closed down and emptied of human witnesses. There was a lot of complaining from the humans, but none from the vampires. They moved through the house in taut silence, hustling their visitors out the door, hurrying them to their cars and shoving them inside. Raj only hoped there wasn't a rash of accidents on the way home. That wouldn't be good for business.

"So, *Raj*," Mick said finally. "Where do you wanna do this?"

Raj smiled and slowly released a measure of his true power. It was an exquisite rush, as delicious as blood from the most succulent woman he'd ever taken, as sweet as that first slow glide of blood down his throat after a long drought. He skewered Mick with derisive look. "We can do it right here. It won't take long," he said with an arrogance born of certain knowledge.

Mick's eyes widened, and Raj saw the first flash of fear, as he recognized the true depths of Raj's power. But he didn't back down. He had to know he couldn't win this battle, but he stood his ground, and Raj decided in that moment not to kill good ol' Mick. He would need vampires with this kind of courage when he took over Krystof's territory. And he was definitely going to take over the territory.

Mick attacked first, understanding that it was his only, slim, chance. He aimed a spear of concentrated power at Raj's chest and attacked physically in the same moment, throwing himself across the room. His considerable bulk hit like a pile driver, and Raj grunted with the impact, but repelled it easily, using power alone to toss the other vampire into an elegant armoire that rose almost to the ceiling. Or it had before Mick crashed into it and reduced it to a pile of shattered wood. *A shame, really*, Raj thought idly.

Mick stood with a roar and would have attacked again, but Raj— wanting, *needing,* a more physical violence—crossed the room in two hard strides and caught the big vampire with a roundhouse punch, breaking his jaw and spinning him away to crash into the bed, toppling the canopy and tangling him in a dusty shroud of blue velvet. Mick shook his head—a grotesque sight with his jaw hanging loose—and stood once again, fists bunched at his sides. Muscles strained and veins bulged as he concentrated his remaining strength, throwing everything he had into a last desperate burst of power, his mouth open in a furious howl, as if the sheer volume of his voice could add weight to the attack.

Raj raised a hand and deflected every ounce of that power and more back on its owner, driving Mick to the floor and pressing down on him until his joints groaned and he screamed in agony beneath the crushing weight.

"Yield," Raj demanded softly. "Yield and serve me willingly, or you die right here, right now."

Mick twisted beneath Raj's greater strength, his face contorted with rage and pain as he fought to the last shred of his power. He pounded the floor with one fist, driving it through the old wooden planks and shattering the bones in his hand before finally forcing his gaze up to meet Raj's implacable blue stare. He ground one word from his ruined mouth. "Master," he said.

Raj nodded and released him, and then immediately drew off his jacket and rolled up his sleeve, slicing his own wrist with a slash of his fangs. "Do you come to me of your own free will and desire, Mick?" he asked formally.

Mick's eyes met his briefly in surprise, but then he nodded, his hungry gaze lowering to the bounty of rich blood so tantalizingly close. "I do, my lord."

"And is this what you truly desire?"

"My lord, it is my truest desire."

Raj lowered his bloody arm to the vampire's ruined mouth. "Then drink, Mick, and be mine."

Mick closed his mouth over Raj's wrist, drawing the powerful blood into his body with great gulps. Raj could feel the tug not only on his wrist, but on his very soul as yet another vampire became his—his to command, his to live or die. One more stone added to a burden of responsibility that was already too heavy.

When he felt the bond seal into permanence, he withdrew his arm from his new minion's eager mouth. He didn't bother to wipe it clean. The wound would heal on its own in a few minutes, and there was nothing in this room he cared to clean it with. He rolled down his sleeve, drew his jacket back on, and stood to survey the assembled vampires. Some stared in open-mouthed shock, others seemed almost relieved. It was a testament to the failure of Krystof's authority that not a single one of them protested his takeover, or even made a dash for the exits to report in.

"This house will reopen in two nights under new management," Raj announced. He glanced down at Mick who was already beginning to heal with the surge of Raj's blood through his veins. "Mick will see to its proper administration. Won't you, Mick?"

"Yes, Master," Mick said fervently. When he looked up this time, his gaze held nothing but respect. "We've been waiting for you a long time, my lord."

"I know," Raj said somberly. "But I'm here now." He spun around and left the house the way he'd come in, ignoring the vampires who knelt in obeisance as he passed. In taking Mick's oath, effectively stealing him from Krystof, he'd openly declared his intention to overthrow the Vampire Lord. It was possible Krystof's mind was so weakened that he wouldn't even notice the loss, or that he'd just write it off to rivalry among his minions. After all, he'd brought Raj to Buffalo to clean up his mess. But whether Krystof appreciated the true significance or not, Raj knew what he'd done. And he knew it could only lead to the ultimate confrontation with his Sire. He also knew he should be reeling in triumph at the ease of his first victory, and a part of him recognized the importance of this night. But all he could feel was a keen awareness of the terrible burden that was about to be his. The burden every vampire lord carried, the weight of thousands of vampires who would draw their next breath by his will alone. He climbed into the comfort of his BMW and turned for the city, trying to remember when he'd ever felt this alone.

It was nearly dawn when he pulled into the garage of his private lair. He'd meant to drive by the warehouse near the airport and check on Em and the others, but he'd found himself sitting on the docks of Lake Erie instead. He watched as the longshoremen unloaded a single, huge cargo ship, the giant cranes lifting big, metal containers so different from the crates and barrels, and even occasional livestock, that had been the norm when he'd worked these docks log ago. Until a chance meeting had brought Krystof into his life. He'd often thought about that night—if he'd gone straight home after work to the mean, little room he'd rented for far more than it was worth, or if he'd stopped at the bar a block further on instead of the first one he'd come to, feeling flush with money in his pocket on payday. A whim, not even a real decision— such an insignificant thing to have changed his life forever.

* * * *

Buffalo, New York, 1830

Rajmund made his way back to the table, dodging flying fists and stumbling drunks, balancing three mugs of foamy beer which sloshed liberally over his fingers to join the layer of old spills lacquering the filthy floor. It was a seedy place, this tavern, set on the edge of a dark pier and stinking of wet grain from the docks only yards away. But it was one of the few bars that would serve him and his friends, immigrants the lot of them, with accents as thick as a slice of his mother's bread, when they could come up with the American words at all, which wasn't often and not nearly fast enough.

He sidestepped an Irish headed for the bar and slid into the chair Maciek had saved for him, dropping the mugs onto the table with a thud and a final splash of golden liquid.

"Easy there, Rajmund," Maciek said in Polish. "There'll be nothing left for drinking."

"Raj," Rajmund corrected. "I've told you, Maciek. The Americans don't have the tongue for Polish names. Call me Raj."

"Raj," Zosia said, her voice a low, sultry purr that made him think of dark corners and lifted skirts. Preferably hers. "It makes no sense, Rajmund."

He shrugged and leaned over to steal a kiss from her luscious lips.

"Perhaps not, my sweetness, but the Americans like it, no? And we're all Americans now."

"Maybe you are," she said, lifting a shoulder to brush him away. "I'm still Polish." Rajmund slung an arm around her and grinned, ignoring Maciek's frown of disapproval. His friend's brain was stuck back home in Poland where a proper girl would be spending the evening with her mother, not drinking in a filthy tavern with the likes of Rajmund Gregorczyk. But they weren't on the docks of Gdansk anymore. This was Buffalo, New York. America. And this was their future.

Maciek drew a long draft off his beer and put it down on the table. He wiped his face with the back of one dirty hand, spreading nearly as much of the thick foam around his scruffy beard and moustache as he wiped off. "I'll tell you what I think," he began.

But they never had a chance to hear what Maciek thought. The door flew open with a shudder, as though a storm was blowing off the lake fit to tear the building down around them. The thick wood slammed against the wall with a sound like a ton of bricks hitting the dock.

Silence. Every head in the place turned toward the empty doorway and stared. More than a few crossed themselves and muttered a prayer to the Virgin. A man stepped into the silence. A rich man. Raj could tell by his clean clothes, his white hands and buffed fingernails, his neatly combed hair. And the disdainful look he was passing over the assembled drunks.

There were others with him. Strange, Rajmund thought, that he'd not noticed them before, though they'd certainly entered the bar first. There were four of them, two in front and two flanking the rich man to either side, their bulky physiques and meaty fists describing them, just as the rich man's fine clothes had him. They were bodyguards, hired muscle to ensure the rich man's white hands stayed clean.

The dandy sniffed once, immediately raising a delicate white handkerchief to his nose. "Well," he said in strongly accented American. "They will have to do."

What followed next was a blur of blood and violence, as the four bodyguards tore into the crowd, their mouths gaping wide with impossible fangs, their fingers curled into claws like some sort of vicious beast. The hardened men in the tavern, men who tossed two hundred kilo crates like children's toys, screamed in terror, crawling on the filthy floor now slick with red as throats were torn and blood spilled everywhere. Rajmund grabbed Zosia and threw her behind him, backing against the wall and trying to remember if there was a rear door and if it was barred. He saw Maciek pick up a heavy chair and swing it, breaking it across the back of the one of the beasts, but the creature turned and laughed—*laughed*—as it sank fangs into Maciek's throat and he began to scream.

Behind him, Zosia was screaming as well, her voice rising above the others, a shrill female cry in the room full of men. Rajmund saw the rich man notice, although he no longer looked so fine as he had—his expensive clothes were stained with dark blood and gore, his white hands buried in the flesh of a dead Irish whore. He raised his head, his eyes glowing like an animal's in the dim light until Rajmund thought surely he could feel the heat of them against his skin.

"Quiet, Zosia," Rajmund hissed. He could feel her trembling behind him, her hands clinging to the thin fabric of his shirt.

The rich man smiled and began walking toward them, gliding through the chaos as if God himself was clearing the way, men and monsters brushed aside as if they were no more than silk curtains. "What are you doing here, boy?"

Raj stared in shock. The monster was speaking to him in Polish. "I . . . I work the docks," he stuttered, not knowing what else to say.

The rich man grinned and it was a horrible sight. "Not anymore."

A single swipe of one delicate, white hand tore out Rajmund's throat. He fell to his knees, feeling the warmth of his own blood as it drained through his fingers to join the growing pool on the floor. Zosia screamed his name, and he watched helplessly as she was dragged over his useless body, her heels kicking weakly as the rich man buried his teeth in her neck and drank.

The last thing Raj saw before a curtain of black fell over his eyes was Zosia's lovely face slack with death, her once bright, blue eyes pale and lifeless.

Rajmund opened his eyes to darkness. He could see men, no not men, monsters moving in the shadows, could heard their growls of pleasure as they sucked the juices from bits of meat he didn't want to think about. Was this death? Was this the hell the priests had warned him of, the corruption of his soul they predicted if he left the lands of his birth and traveled so far away?

"He's awake," someone growled.

"Ah, at last." Rajmund recognized that voice. The rich man. The one who carried evil with him like an elegant cloak.

"Bring him the girl."

The girl? Did he mean Zosia? Was she alive then?

A young girl was pushed out of the darkness—not Zosia. He didn't recognize this pathetic child. She stumbled and fell hard against him, crying pitifully. Her body stank of sex and sweat and she shook with fear. He reached out to comfort her as she turned toward him, her eyes full of a silent plea. He touched the bare skin of her arm . . . and an unreasoning hunger roared through him. He could hear the rush of her blood and the terrified pounding of her heart, could smell a sweet, fresh scent so close beneath her paper-thin skin. It was intoxicating. He leaned closer, wallowing in the scent, his tongue lapping out to feel it pulsing, like a small animal begging for release.

His felt his gums split, felt something hard and sharp tearing his lips and knew they were fangs as he pressed them against the soft flesh of her neck. One pointed tip punctured her skin to release a single drop of blood. He closed his eyes at the exhilarating flavor, his head thrown back as if it was a flood pouring down his throat instead of a meager drop.

His gaze fell to the small, red puncture wound. To the thick, ripe vein. He buried his face in her neck and for the first time, he fed.

Rajmund pushed the girl's body aside, his jaw cracking wide as he sought to release the tension of his feeding. He sat for a moment in silence, rolling his head from side to side, hearing the pop of vertebrae as he stared around the room. He froze when he took in the carnage, when he realized what he'd become, what he'd done. Horrified, he scrambled across the littered floor until he felt a wall at his back.

Someone laughed and he looked up to the find the rich man staring down at him, once again clothed in fine fabrics, his hands and face pristine and white.

"Zosia?" Rajmund croaked. "Maciek?"

The rich man gestured around the room with an elegant hand. "I'm afraid they're all dead. To a worthy cause, if it's any consolation to you." His gaze bored into Rajmund. "But not you, Rajmund. You're very much alive."

"Why?" Rajmund asked, more the cry of a tormented soul than a man's question.

The rich man smiled. "Because I can. Come along, boy. You're one of us now."

Rajmund threw his head back and howled.

* * * *

The ringing of his cell phone brought Raj back to the present. He pulled his phone from a pocket as he climbed out of the car, not bothering to check the ID.

"Yeah."

"Raj?" Em's voice was troubled.

"Yeah, Em. Anything wrong?" He punched in the security code on the private warehouse door, making certain it closed and locked behind him before he crossed the empty space and descended the stairs to his private apartment.

"No," Em said cautiously. "Not on this end. We're all here in the warehouse, the guys are settling in downstairs. I expected you—"

"Something came up."

"Right, okay. Will we see you tonight?"

"Yeah." The vault door swung shut behind him. He entered the code to engage the full security of his building and heard the vault's heavy locks slide home for the day.

"Let me think a minute, Em." He rubbed his forehead, trying to put the next twenty-four hours into place. He'd have to see Sarah again. He still had to find out what she was hiding, the real reason she'd been so eager to be a part of the police investigation. And Krystof was probably waiting for a progress report, but he could fucking wait until Raj had time for him. His own people were far more important. "I'll come by right after sunset. It's a real mess here, Em. Worse than I thought."

"Then I'm glad we're here for you, boss."

"Yeah. See you tonight."

He hit disconnect and stared at the phone, thinking about Sarah Stratton. She was a complication he didn't need right now, and if the thought brought a twinge of unexpected pain, he ignored it. This wouldn't be the first time he'd been forced to leave behind a human he cared about.

He immediately dialed her number, relieved when it gave him the option of going straight to voice mail.

"Sarah. We need to talk. I'll be over around ten tonight." He left it at that and hung up. She'd get the message when she woke this morning. And if she wasn't home when he got there, he'd track her down and get what he needed, one way or another.

Chapter Twenty

Regina forced herself to sit up, open her eyes and stay awake. Vampires had her; she was sure of that now. But not just vampires. There were regular humans, too. The thing was, she couldn't figure out what they wanted. The one she sort of knew—the one she'd danced with at the house and who must have knocked her out somehow and kidnapped her—came to see her almost every night. But everything that happened after his visits was kind of a blur. And she was grateful for that because what little she remembered about the other vampires and what they did to her . . . She didn't want to think about those things. She ran her hands up and down bare arms, pimply with cold; she'd lost even her thin jacket somewhere. Her fingers ran over a sore spot on her left arm and she looked down, touching it gingerly. Dark bruises marred her skin, visible even in the low light. There had been another room. One with bright lights and the cold sting of an alcohol rub, her blood filling the little glass tube. A woman had talked to someone as she bent over Regina's arm. But what had the woman said? And who else had been there?

Regina tried to recall, but a wave of dizziness hit her, making her empty stomach roll with nausea. She lay back down and closed her eyes, wishing it away. It was so ironic. She'd always been one of the good girls—no drugs, no drinking and hardly ever a date. She'd finally decided to break out of the mold, her first tiny rebellion, and what happens? Some wacko nut job kidnaps her.

She sighed wearily and shifted on the uncomfortable bed. It was so hard to think. Maybe that's what they wanted, to keep her confused so she couldn't think straight, couldn't remember their faces when they let her go. Because she had to believe they were going to let her go. Or that someone would find her and the others. It was the only thing that kept her going. She shivered and reached for the blankets he'd finally brought her last night. That was a good sign, wasn't it? It was just . . . the blankets had smelled of perfume. It was a scent she recognized, a musky scent she'd never worn. And she couldn't help wondering who'd been using these blankets before they'd given them to her?

Her eyelids drooped closed and the tears came unbidden. She wanted to go home; she wanted her mom. She drifted off to sleep. Maybe when she woke up, the police would be there, maybe they'd find her. Maybe it would be in time. Before they did to her whatever they'd done to the girl who wore the musky perfume, the girl who didn't need her blankets anymore.

Chapter Twenty-one

Sarah woke to the sting of tears running down her face, the pillow damp beneath her cheek. The tears weren't only Regina's this time. They were Sarah's, too. Tears of anger, of frustration, of despair at the girl's fragile courage and the hope that rescue was near. But how could they find Regina before it was too late, before she ended up like all the others Sarah hadn't been able to save? She sat up in bed, drawing a deep breath. She'd only been a teenager then, she reminded herself sternly. A child. She was an adult now, a woman with resources and contacts of her own. Surely she could figure out some way . . . Her phone rang and she knew it wasn't the first time. It was the ringing that had woken her.

She twisted automatically, reaching for her bedside table where she always left her cordless phone overnight. But it wasn't there. It rang again . . . in the other room. She frowned. She never went to sleep without her phone nearby. Never.

She started to climb out of bed and had a second surprise. She was wearing the clothes she'd worn last night—her sweater and skirt, of all things, and her bra. That was just wrong. No sane woman slept in a bra. It was one of the first things she took off when she walked through the door, along with her shoes. She must have been drunker than she thought when she left the restaurant last night. It was just luck that she'd managed to get home without hurting herself or someone else. *Stupid, Sarah.* She should have called a taxi. Her phone rang a final, futile time, the ring chopped off as the call was routed automatically to voice mail.

She stood, shivering slightly, as she shuffled on bare feet over to her closet for a pair of slippers and then a quick stop in the bathroom. Crossing into her office, she found her cordless sitting on the desk in its charger. She picked it up and noticed a business card sitting there, a thick, white card with crisp edges and a familiar name . . . And it all came back to her in a rush.

She *had* gone to the restaurant, but Raj had been waiting in the parking lot. He'd driven her back here and they'd . . . They'd what? She remembered opening the door, remembered letting him into the house. Mrs. M. had been listening at her window like always; Raj had told her that. But then what happened? And how had she ended up in bed fully dressed?

The light on her phone flashed, reminding her she had messages. She called voice mail and discovered there were two. She hit the play button absently, still trying to remember—

"Sarah."

Raj. She collapsed into the chair, suddenly overwhelmed by a wave of lust so strong it took her breath away. She leaned forward, hugging herself, her nipples stiff and painfully erotic against the lace of her bra, her thighs clenched tightly against a need so powerful that she groaned out loud. She wanted to strip away her clothes and—

"We need to talk. I'll be over around ten tonight."

And that was it. He hung up without identifying himself, without saying good-bye, just assuming she'd be waiting for him tonight like a good little pet. "Arrogant bastard," she muttered, albeit somewhat breathlessly. She pressed one hand over her heart, waiting for her body to recover, only half-listening as her voice mail went on to the next message, which would be the call that had woken her. It was Linda, demanding Sarah call her immediately and tell her all about this gorgeous Raj person and why hadn't Sarah ever mentioned him before. Sarah smiled at Linda's description of Raj. He was pretty gorgeous with those beautiful blue eyes and hunky body. She shivered as another wave of longing hit her.

"Son of a bitch," she swore suddenly.

She ran to the bathroom and began ripping off her clothes, her sweater first, her bra. Half-naked, she leaned closer to the mirror, holding up her hair and searching her neck for any telltale marks. She was perversely disappointed when she found none, but immediately stripped off her skirt, shimmying it over her hips and down to the floor. She'd read all those books about vampires; there was a big vein in the thigh that some of them were very fond of. She stared at her bare thighs in the mirror and then sat down to look with her own eyes. Nothing. No bite marks of any kind.

Perched on her closed toilet seat in the chilly bathroom, mostly naked, she suddenly felt pretty stupid. If he'd ravished her, why would he have bothered to put her clothes back on? "Stupid," she muttered. She stood and stared at her reflection. "He did something, though. I know he did."

She shivered viciously and began picking up her scattered clothes. Walking back into the bedroom, she folded the sweater and threw the rest into her clothes hamper, then stripped off her underwear and went to take a hot shower, standing under the pulsing jets for awhile and letting them warm her up. The first thing she'd done after moving into the duplex was replace the "water saver" abomination Mrs. M. had frugally provided with a decent showerhead. She believed in conservation, but enough was enough. Sometimes a woman needed a good, hot pummeling—of the watery variety, that is.

Once out of the shower and dried off, she pulled on her warmest sweats and sheepskin-lined slippers and headed downstairs for coffee. As the first shot of caffeine flowed deliciously through her system, she again considered her murky memories of the night before. She definitely remembered arriving back here at the house with Raj, because she remembered specifically inviting him in. He'd closed the door and then . . . A jolt of desire swept her from head to toe, just like before. Something had happened to her. Something to do with that damn vampire. And she intended to find out what it was.

She stomped back up to her office and found the white business card he'd left on her desk. She dialed his number, knowing he'd be down for the day and hoping the ringing phone would make his rest a hell of a lot less restful.

* * * *

Raj was uncharacteristically edgy and dissatisfied as he dressed for the night. And it wasn't the usual hunger making him feel this way. He was old enough, and powerful enough, that he didn't need to feed nightly. The woman at the bar two nights ago should have been more than sufficient to keep him strong for another day at least—not that he *had* to go that long, but he could. He considered stopping in for a drink somewhere on the way to meet Em and the others, but if he needed blood that badly, he could always tap into the bagged supply at the warehouse. And besides, for some reason the idea of feeding from an anonymous stranger was unappealing.

No, it wasn't for *some* reason. It was for a very specific reason, one with blond hair and a tidy little body he was eager to taste in every way possible. Too eager. Raj didn't believe in self-indulgence. Yes, he drove nice cars and wore nice clothes, and his penthouse in Manhattan was well beyond comfortable in its amenities, but those were things, meaningless possessions he could walk away from without a thought. When it came to his personal life, he was all about discipline and control. He had the occasional vodka, but never drank to excess. He preferred blood from the vein of a beautiful woman, but he never overindulged and always left his women happy and sated. He had his vampire children, but he was their master and their sire. He was not their friend or their drinking buddy. Emelie he trusted utterly, but she was the only one.

Which was why this sudden irrational attraction to Sarah Stratton was so irritating. His need to protect her, to taste her, to steal her away and make her his and his alone, was powerful and instinctive. He didn't have to think about whether he wanted her; he *did* want her—totally and in every way possible. It took an effort to stop himself from ripping her clothes off and to hell with the consequences. He shook his head in disgust. If he had a choice, he'd fly back to Manhattan tonight and never see Sarah Stratton again. Since that wasn't an option, he'd simply have to act like a civilized man instead of a ravening beast, even if the latter was closer to the truth.

He pulled on his leather jacket and picked up his cell phone, noticing there was an incoming message from the lovely Sarah herself. He frowned, thinking she was canceling their appointment tonight, which was unacceptable. When he heard her message, his frown deepened.

"I know you did something last night, vampire, and I want to know what it was. No one screws around with my head, you got that? Not even you. And to hell with ten o'clock, Mr. High and Mighty. I want you here ten minutes after sundown or I'm going to the cops."

There was a pause during which he could hear her give a frustrated sigh.

"Okay, so I won't really go to the cops, but I'm not waiting around either. If you're not here by nine, I'm leaving and you can just use your stupid vampire tricks to try and find me."

Part of him wanted to chuckle at the exasperation in her voice. And part of him, completely irrational, wanted to applaud her determination in standing up to him. The more rational part demanded to know why she remembered anything at all about what had happened last night. Had he unconsciously *wanted* her to remember him and left a weakness in the memories he'd planted? That would be both stupid and dangerous. Only one way to find out. He punched in Em's speed dial. His vampires were awake and ready to go. He could hear their voices in the background when she answered.

"My lord."

"I've got an errand to run on the way over, Em. It won't take long."

"I hope not," she said dryly. "Being stuck in this warehouse is like being trapped in a monkey cage. These guys need to be let out."

He laughed. "Not much longer. I'm on my way." *But first,* he thought to himself, *there's the matter of a stubborn little human to deal with.*

Chapter Twenty-two

Sarah pulled her sweater over her head, smoothing it over her hips and checking to make sure the lace on her bra didn't look lumpy beneath the fine weave. Her freshly shampooed hair shone in the overhead light of her bedroom, and she'd put on just enough makeup to give her eyes a slightly smoky quality, the gold flecks like bits of fire in the smoke. *Oh, get a grip, Sarah. Flecks of fire in the smoke, for God's sake.* She laughed at herself. Clearly she'd been reading too many of those romance novels she was so fond of.

Of course, she was nothing like the kick-ass heroines in those books. She had never fired a gun, never used a knife—unless the ones in her kitchen drawer counted. And although she kept herself fit, there was no way she was going to high-kick anyone into submission. She was too short for one thing, and a little too curvy and five pounds too heavy, no matter how many mornings she ran her five-mile circuit. Some men liked her curves, though. Not usually the *right* men, but at least it proved she wasn't a total toad.

And why was she spending so much time getting ready anyway? This wasn't a date. Quite the opposite. She intended to read Raj the riot act and send him on his way. That was it.

"This definitely isn't a date," she scolded her reflection for the umpteenth time. Of course, *that* begged the question of why she was wearing her best lace push-up bra and had taken the time to put on eye shadow in the first place. Oh well, gotta create the smoke for those flecks of fire, right?

She laughed out loud, like a crazy person, and sat on the edge of the bed to pull on her shoes. They weren't designed by anyone famous—like most women, she didn't have the budget to spend five hundred dollars on a pair of shoes. But they were nice and, more importantly, they had a four inch heel so she wouldn't feel like such a shrimp standing next to Raj. Not that this was a date or anything. She stood and turned off the overhead light as she walked out of the bedroom, ready to beard the lion in his den. Or her den. Or whatever. Because this definitely wasn't a date.

* * * *

Raj took the stairs up to Sarah's porch in a graceful leap. He was in a hurry to get over to the warehouse and didn't have time to waste pretending to be human. He put his hand on the doorknob and, finding it unlocked, twisted it open and walked in, knocking as he did so.

He caught Sarah halfway down the stairs. She was wearing a different bra, one that made her obvious curves even more obvious beneath a soft wool sweater. And what the hell was he noticing that for? She was looking at him in shock, which quickly changed to outrage.

"Just come on in, why don't you?"

"I did, thanks," he said, ignoring her sarcasm. "You ever think of locking your door?"

"What would be the point? It wouldn't stop *you*, would it?"

"Nice. You about ready to leave?"

"Leave? Are we going somewhere?"

"Yes. I have a stop to make and then I'm taking you to dinner."

"Are you?" she asked, in a tone that implied quite the opposite. She came down another couple of steps but stayed on the staircase which put her at eye level with him. "What happened last night? And I want the truth, not more of your vampire bullshit."

"I wasn't aware I'd given you any vampire bullshit," he said mildly.

"Ha, ha. What happened, Raj? And don't say *nothing*, because I know damn well you did something to my memories, and it sure as hell wasn't consensual."

Raj pulled back in surprise. First of all, she shouldn't have remembered anything, but secondly, her choice of words made him distinctly uncomfortable. He didn't take women against their will. Not ever. Not since that first night in the tavern when he'd been too out of his mind to realize what was happening. Sarah was waiting for an answer, glaring at him accusingly. She'd done something with her eyes that brought out the gray but didn't hide the gold flecks that were always there.

"We talked about the missing women," he said slowly. "It was . . . you were upset. More than upset. I didn't understand why, but it bothered me to see you like that, so I put you out and took away the memories so you wouldn't have nightmares."

It was a version of the truth, anyway. She hadn't been upset precisely, although she'd definitely been out of control. And he *didn't* want to add to her nightmares by inflicting himself on her life.

Sarah was watching him, searching his face, looking for the truth, he figured. He stared back at her calmly and knew the moment she decided to believe him. "Don't ever do that again, Raj," she said softly. "Not for any reason. My memories are mine, good and bad, and I'll deal with them. I can't stand the idea of anyone messing around in my head."

There was more to that than what she was saying, and it made him wonder what had happened in her past. Did it have anything to do with whatever she was hiding? "I'm sorry," he said.

She smiled all at once, as if he'd surprised her. "Well, that's something you don't hear every day." Her expression abruptly became serious again and she gave him a funny look. "Er, Raj, we didn't, that is, um . . . we didn't—"

"Sarah," he said softly, catching her eyes. "If I'd made love to you, you'd remember it."

Her face flushed a delightful pink. "Arrogant bastard," she muttered, but she smiled at him again, and he felt a weight lift from his soul. "Okay. Let me get my coat."

He watched her walk past him down the rest of the stairs, watched her tight ass swing by beneath a pair of dark blue slacks, with those damn sexy heels she was always wearing. "Better make it a heavy coat," he said. "It's cold out. Maybe the one you had on the other night." *The one that hides the temptation of your sweet little body,* he added to himself.

"Okay," she said agreeably and pulled out the long, brown coat. He took it from her, holding it while she slipped it on, sliding it up over her shoulders. He let himself run his hands down her arms ending with a light brush of fingertips, but resisted the urge to bury his face in the warm gold of her hair.

Jesus, Raj, you're in trouble.

She looked up at him over her shoulder. "So you're taking me to dinner? Are you hungry?" she asked innocently.

"Are you offering?" he couldn't help retorting.

She snorted delicately. "In your dreams, bud."

He leaned down to murmur directly in her ear, "Or maybe in yours, sweetheart."

She shivered and he smiled in satisfaction. He might not have any intention of taking her, but he didn't want her completely immune to him either.

Sarah pulled the door open, but he stepped in front of her, his attention directed next door where someone was watching once again. "Your neighbor pays a lot of attention to who comes and goes here."

"That's just Mrs. M.," she said blithely, walking around him and out onto the porch. She gave him a warning look. "She keeps on eye on me."

"You get a lot of male visitors?"

"Not at all," she said, patting his arm, as if he needed reassurance. "Mrs. M.'s just a bit overprotective."

Good, he thought. But he kept it to himself. "Lock your door," he instructed her.

"Yessir, Mr. Raj, sir."

He walked ahead of her down the stairs. It was going to be a long night.

* * * *

Sarah watched Raj out of the corner of her eye as he maneuvered through the Friday night traffic. He seemed different tonight, still friendly and overprotective, but cooler somehow, except for that one slip about being hungry, which had been a pretty stupid thing for her to say. She *hadn't* meant it as a come-on. Had she? She had to admit she was attracted to him. Who wouldn't be? He had that whole tall, dark and handsome vibe going, except he was blond and blue-eyed, of course. His hair was thick, brushed straight back to his collar, just long enough that she wondered what it would look like if he let it grow even longer, maybe past his shoulders. And with those gorgeous blue eyes, kind of an icy blue, except for when they burned with an undeniable heat. She shivered inside her warm coat. Yeah. She was definitely attracted to him. And sometimes she was sure he was attracted to her too, but then it was like he threw a switch and disappeared behind that all-business exterior.

"You're different from the others," she said suddenly.

In spite of the busy traffic, he turned to stare at her, his eyes practically glowing in the dim light. "Others?" he asked, his voice so low and deep it was nearly a growl.

Sarah licked her lips nervously. "The other vampires here in Buffalo."

"You've met other vampires here in Buffalo?"

There was something about the way he said it, the way he was looking at her, that suddenly made her aware she was trapped in a car with a vampire. A very big, dangerous vampire. She was sorry she'd brought the whole thing up now, but he was waiting for an explanation, so she said, "Sort of. I mean, I didn't actually *meet* anyone, but there was a University reception last year. It was supposed to be a showcase of local Buffalo talent. Manhattan's gotten so expensive that some people are actually moving back to Buffalo to live. Not many, of course, but someone decided it couldn't hurt to remind people that there is a major university here, with a medical center and lots of eggheads and artists. It's not Manhattan, but it's not Outer Mongolia either."

Raj gave her a skeptical look. "The vampires?" he reminded her.

"Right. Well, I'm just a historian, and a junior one at that, but my friend Linda—you met her the other night—her husband's kind of a star in the art department."

He nodded, and Sarah thought it was possible she'd told him about it last night and didn't remember. "Well," she continued, "they invited me to go with them to the reception. All the local bigwigs were there including your boss, Krystof Sapieha."

"He's not my boss," Raj snapped.

Sarah frowned in confusion. "But I thought he was the local vampire lord, and that—"

"It's complicated. Go on with your story," he commanded.

She gave him a dirty look—he really *was* going to have to stop giving her orders. "Anyway, Sapieha was only there for maybe an hour or so with a couple of other vamps—bodyguards, I guess—although I wasn't too impressed."

"No?" Raj gave her a quick, amused glance before switching his gaze back to the road to stop at a red light. "What did you expect?"

"Giant eunuchs. You know, gold earrings and stuff."

He laughed. "I'm sure they were quite capable, despite their absence of gold and gelding, and there were probably others in the crowd you didn't know about. Krystof is very aware of his own safety."

"Maybe. But I thought it would be interesting to meet him. You know, because of Cyn and Raphael. I figured they're probably friends."

"You spoke to *Krystof?*"

She was suddenly aware that the light had turned green but they were still sitting there. Raj was regarding her intently, overwhelming her, not just with his size, but with a sense of menace, as if everything rested on whatever she said next.

"No," she said carefully. "I tried to, but he was talking to this woman, like really involved, you know? I went over anyway, but when I got too close, one of the other vamps stopped me." She shrugged. "Maybe Krystof was lining up his next meal or something. He left right after that."

Raj seemed satisfied with her answer. At least he relaxed so that she no longer felt as if her life hung on her next words. He glanced up at the light and accelerated across the intersection. "Just as well," he said at last. "Krystof is very old," he said, as if that explained everything.

He turned into an industrial area not far from the airport, taking several turns until they were driving along a dark side road, fronted by what looked like a bunch of abandoned warehouses. He pulled into the parking lot of one of those warehouses and stopped right by the door. Sarah looked around, leaning forward to see through the windshield. There were no other cars anywhere and no lights coming from inside. "You're living up to your stereotype, you know," she said.

"Stereotype?"

"Big, bad vampire, innocent, helpless female, abandoned warehouse, middle of the night. You know. Stereotype."

"I've done nothing lately that was bad, and *you* are hardly helpless and probably not that innocent either," he added with a sidelong smirk. "Also, this warehouse is not abandoned. I *will* give you middle of the night, however. Think of it as vampire noon."

"A sense of humor? Be careful, Raj, your stereotype is slipping."

When he didn't so much as crack a smile, Sarah thought maybe he didn't have a sense of humor after all. Leaving the keys in the ignition and the car running, he turned and met her eyes directly.

"Wait in the car. I'll only be a few minutes."

"Yes, Master," she intoned.

He shook his head and climbed out. Before he'd taken two steps, the warehouse door opened and a woman emerged—a tall, beautiful woman who Raj looked awfully happy to see. Curious, Sarah opened her car door, intending to join the party.

The woman looked over at the sound and grinned. "Who's for

dinner?" she asked, jerking her chin in Sarah's direction.

Raj glanced quickly over his shoulder and turned to face Sarah, blocking her view of the other woman. "Get back in the car," he ordered grimly.

"Don't be a party pooper, boss," the woman said clearly. "Let your little friend join us."

Raj spun back around, and Sarah saw his fangs flash for the first time. "Shut the fuck up, Em!"

The woman's playful expression froze at his words, but what replaced it was not outrage, which Sarah would have expected from a girlfriend. Instead the woman dropped to her knees, head bowed. "My lord," she murmured. "Forgive me."

Sarah stared from the kneeling woman to Raj and wondered if she should be afraid too.

"Get back in the car, Sarah," he repeated, walking toward her, his fangs once more out of sight.

Wait. *My lord?* This woman was a vampire?

Sarah heard Raj swear softly as she stepped around him, walked over to the woman and stuck out her hand. "Sarah Stratton," she said.

The woman gave Raj a startled look, her eyes questioning. He made a disgusted noise and gestured his okay. The female vampire stood and took Sarah's hand, shaking it firmly. Not one of those fingers-only girly shakes, but a real handshake. "Emelie," she said. "No last name, like Prince," she added with a quirked smile.

Raj snorted and Emelie scowled at him over Sarah's shoulder. "Everyone's waiting for you, my lord," she said pointedly.

"Give us a minute," Raj said.

"As you wish," Emelie replied. "Nice meeting you, Sarah. Maybe next time we can actually have a conversation."

"Over my dead body," Raj muttered.

"Too late," Emelie said sweetly, and strolled back into the warehouse, closing the door behind her.

Sarah spun around as soon as she was gone. "My lord?" she repeated.

Raj closed his eyes briefly and then opened them, giving her a patient look. "Vampires live a long time. We've developed a highly structured society in order to survive, for protection from each other as well as from humans with torches and stakes. When that structure was first conceived, there was no such thing as a democracy. And it wouldn't work anyway. Vampires are more than just humans who stay awake at night." He stepped closer suddenly and locked his gaze with hers. "Remember that, Sarah. Vampires are dangerous and unpredictable, no matter how human they might appear."

"Okay," she said in a small voice. "I'm properly terrified."

He moved back a bit. "No need to be afraid of Em."

"Are you two . . ." She let the words fall away, embarrassed that she'd even asked the question.

Raj smiled a little too smugly. "Would it bother you if we were?"

"No, of course not. I just—"

"Well, we're not. Em's my best friend and my lieutenant. But there's never been anything else between us."

"Oh. Well. Okay." Sarah cleared her throat nervously. "So what now?"

"Now, you get back in the car and stay there. This won't take long." He took her arm and bundled her back into the BMW, shutting the door firmly. "Stay there," he said through the window as she hit the button to lower it. "And put the window back up. Emelie's not the only vampire in there."

As he walked away from the car, Sarah thought she heard him mutter, "And I've no intention of sharing." But she might have been wrong.

Chapter Twenty-three

Raj did a final scan of the area, checked that Sarah was sitting in the hopefully locked car as promised and pulled open the warehouse door, ready to apologize to Em. The lights were on inside, too low for human eyes but just right for a vampire. And the large space was no longer empty. Four big SUVs, all black with black-tinted windows, were parked near the loading bay doors. Over near the big refrigerator, the eight members of the team Emelie had brought from Manhattan were engaged in various activities. Some lounged, watching the big screen TV, wearing cordless headphones to preserve the façade of silence from outside the warehouse. Others were checking gear, mostly guns and knives. Vampires didn't need much in the way of hardware. With their strength, speed and fangs, they were their own deadliest weapon. But a gun came in handy sometimes, and knives were always fun.

Em was in conversation with Abel, one of Raj's oldest and most reliable children. Abel caught Raj's eye and nodded to him, the big diamond in his ear winking happily against his nearly black skin. Emelie finished whatever she'd been saying and walked over, detouring around a table loaded down with computer gear and electronics. The team's tech wizard, a human named Simon, was set up there, fingers flying over a keyboard while ear pods blasted music so loudly that Raj could hear it from where he stood.

Emelie's eyes were downcast as she drew closer. To his horror, she went down on one knee and said, "My apologies, my lord. I did not realize—"

"Jesus Christ, Em, get up!" Raj pulled her to her feet. "I'm the one who has to apologize. I shouldn't have snapped at you like that. I don't know what's wrong with me."

Em studied him, her dark, brown eyes solemn, the lovely planes of her face showed off to advantage by a tight ponytail pulled up high on her head. "Raj, my friend," she said softly. "That's not true. I only spent a few minutes with the two of you, but I know what's happening. And so do you."

Raj matched her serious gaze for a few breaths. When he looked away, he swore viciously. "Fuck! Why now? Why *her?* Jesus Christ, Em, this city's a total mess. Krystof's making new vampires like they're nothing but toys, someone's kidnapping women from blood houses, and now her! I don't fucking need this!"

His voice had gotten louder and louder until it drew the attention of the vampires on the other side of the room. They'd all stopped what they were doing. Even the TV watchers had pulled their headphones off. They might not mean to eavesdrop, but they couldn't help it if he was going to shout like an idiot. He drew a deep breath and let it out slowly. "I can't deal with this right now. There's too much at stake. I can't afford to be distracted by some little bit of a girl who thinks vampires are something she reads about in books with half-naked men on the covers."

Em's mouth tightened in an obvious effort to keep from laughing, but her eyes gave her away. "Why not just take the girl, boss?" she asked practically. "Maybe that's all you need—a quick sip, a roll in the hay and you're a free vamp."

"And if not? Then she's bound to a fucking vampire for the rest of her life. Not to mention, things are about to get hairy around here, and there are plenty of vampires who'd love to get their hands on her if she's linked to me. She doesn't deserve to get tangled up in all this."

Em shrugged. "Maybe you should let Sarah make that decision for herself. She's a grown woman, you know, not a child. Besides, there are worse things in life than being bound to a vampire, especially one as powerful as you are."

Raj just scowled at her. "Why don't we drop the subject of my love life?"

Em shrugged and said, "You're the boss. You want to tell me what's going on, or you want to brief everyone at once?"

"Let's do it all at once. I don't like leaving Sarah out there alone."

"So bring her inside."

"No," he said instantly.

Em raised her brows significantly, shaking her head as she led Raj over to where the team waited.

"All right, people," Raj started. "Here's what we've got. Several human women have disappeared in the last month, all connected somehow to vampire activities. The last one is the daughter of William Cowens." He looked around and saw every member of his team nodding knowledgeably.

"It was Cowens who insisted the police follow up on the vampire angle. Krystof agreed to cooperate, mostly, I think, because he was sure there was nothing to it and it was an easy way to get some good citizen credit. He called me in to take the heat, and if there was fallout, to make sure it didn't fall on him. No surprises so far.

"But." He paused, meeting the eyes of every one of his people. "Recent information leads me to believe there might actually be a vampire involved. I'm not certain if Krystof knows about it or not, but he clearly feels threatened by someone or something, and I don't think it's just me. He's making new vampires left and right, so many that Jozef doesn't even know about all of them.

"The key is the blood houses. With all these new vamps running around, the houses are bound to be crowded and someone might be dipping on the sly. I want you to split into teams of two, civilian dress. There are four blood houses in the greater Buffalo region. I already stopped at the Corfu house and there's been . . . a change of management." Emelie gave him a sharp look. "I didn't get a chance to ask too many questions first, so I'll still want a team out there, and at each of the other houses on a rotating basis. With all the new vamps, it shouldn't be a problem for you to blend in, but let's not push.

"Em and I will be at large; you have our cell phone numbers. You find anything weird, you call us. Unless your lives are threatened, and then you do whatever it takes. Questions?"

"You want us on the bag, or can we feed?" Abel asked.

Raj thought about it for a minute and said, "Go ahead and feed at the blood houses; you'll stand out otherwise. But don't overdo it. I need you alert and ready to move."

Abel nodded his understanding and Raj looked around. "Anyone else?"

There were no other questions, so Raj turned to his lieutenant. "Em," he said, indicating she should walk with him to the door.

Once outside, he verified that Sarah was where he'd left her. He was surprised when she gave him a cheery little wave, but then glanced over his shoulder and scowled to find Em waving back.

"Christ," he swore again. "Stop that." He positioned himself between Em and the car, effectively blocking any view of Sarah. "Look, Em," he said quietly. "This might be really bad. Some of what I'm hearing makes me think . . . Ah shit, I don't even like to bring this up." He looked away, shaking his head, then looked back at her. "I think someone's selling vamp blood for research."

Em's eyes widened in a shock that mirrored his own feelings. "Not one of ours!"

"Hell, no. Someone local. One of the missing women was a researcher at the university. Her husband claims she was meeting someone who said he could guarantee access to vampire blood samples."

"Krystof?" Em asked in disbelief.

Raj shook his head. "It seems out of character. I've never seen him risk so much as a paper cut. And for something like this? The Council would crucify him at midnight and leave him for the sun, and he knows it."

"A lot of money in something like that, though."

"Yeah, but he doesn't need money. I thought maybe it was about finding a fix for whatever's wrong with him, but then why bring me here to dig into it?" He shook his head. "I don't think this is Krystof. I'm not ruling it out yet, but it doesn't feel right." He glanced quickly over his shoulder and saw Sarah watching them closely, even though she couldn't possibly hear what they were saying.

He turned back to Em, lowering his voice even further. "I'm going to talk to the husband of the missing researcher tomorrow. The cops don't want to let me in, but I don't need their permission, and if this involves vamps, it's none of their business anyway. I'll be in touch with you afterward. In the meantime, take care of what's mine. Make sure no one goes out alone and that includes you, Em. You go out with one of the teams or with me. I don't want to lose anyone over this."

"I love you too, boss. I'd kiss you, but your new girlfriend over there wouldn't like it."

"Em." He shook his head in disgust. "I'm leaving now, but I'll be in touch."

* * * *

Sarah watched Raj as he turned away from Emelie and strode back to the car, moving with that lethal grace of his, every muscle coiled and ready. He glanced up at her and she could see his eyes had gone that strange icy-blue again. She smiled and caught his look of surprise, followed quickly by a scowl. It made her wonder why he was trying so hard not to like her.

He yanked the driver's door open and settled into the car, barely waiting until his door was closed before spinning them out of the dingy parking lot with a tire-squealing turn. He didn't say anything as they headed back toward the city, but Sarah didn't mind. She'd learned a lot about Raj tonight, probably a lot more than he'd intended her to know. You could learn things from watching people relate to one another, even without hearing what they were saying. In fact, sometimes it was better *not* to hear the words because words didn't always tell the truth, but the body usually did. For example, she knew for certain that Raj had told her the truth about Emelie. There was nothing sexual between them and never had been. They were friends, very old, close friends who were totally at ease with one another. But that was it. Not a hint of sexual tension between them. No flirting, no posing for effect, even unconsciously.

On the other hand, there was Emelie's reaction to Sarah, and *Raj's* reaction to *Emelie's* reaction. Sarah smiled very privately. Yes, she'd learned some things about Raj tonight and it was all beginning to make sense to her.

"You still hungry?"

She interrupted her private thoughts to look over at him. "Pardon?"

"Dinner," he said patiently. "Are you still hungry?"

"Oh, sure. Yes. Um, do you go to restaurants?"

He laughed. "Not usually. Well, not to eat food anyway."

She blushed at this unsubtle reminder. "I'm not starving. I mean it's okay if—"

"I know a place," he said. "And we still need to talk."

"About what?" she asked nervously.

He glanced over at her. "About those lies you keep telling me."

* * * *

Boy, did he know a place, Sarah thought to herself. She forked up a final bite of the most succulent salmon she'd ever tasted. They were in a small restaurant, one she'd passed almost every day on her way to campus without ever realizing what a treasure it was. In one of those frustratingly rapid-fire mood changes she was beginning to associate with Raj, he'd become almost cheerful once they sat down. He seemed to be old friends with the Polish proprietor—at least that was the incomprehensible language the two of them were speaking. Only Polish had that many variations of the letter S.

Raj was even drinking vodka, much to her surprise and his obvious amusement. "It's not that we *can't* eat regular food, sweetheart," he'd said, leaning across the table to whisper conspiratorially. "It's just that the flavor pales compared to our usual diet." He'd winked at her then, those cool blue eyes flashing icy hot, and she'd begun to wonder just what it would be like to have all of that vampire sensuality focused on her for a single night . . . or maybe two.

Raj had given her a confident smile, as if he knew what she was thinking, and she'd glared back at him. Which had only made him laugh yet again before the proprietor stopped by and the two of them downed yet another vodka. Not that it seemed to have any effect on Raj. She, on the other hand, was carefully nursing her single glass of white wine. It was hard enough to resist his charms while sober.

"Mr. Gregor," a hearty voice boomed out across the room and Sarah looked up in shock to find Edward Blackwood bearing down on them. The proprietor gave Raj a questioning look, but Raj shook his head slightly and slid out of the booth, standing next to the table and not looking much happier to see the HR founder than Sarah was, although perhaps not for the same reason.

"Mr. Blackwood," he said smoothly. "This is unexpected."

"An unexpected pleasure, surely," Blackwood oozed. "I was sorry we didn't have the opportunity to chat more the other night. Perhaps we could take a moment now, if your companion wouldn't—" He swept a glance over Sarah, and she stiffened, convinced he had paused for a brief second with something close to recognition. Raj seemed to sense her discomfort. He stepped in front of her again, blocking Blackwood's inquisitive eyes.

"Sorry, Blackwood," Raj said, not sounding sorry at all. "We have plans."

"Of course, you do. Rude of me to think otherwise. How is the investigation going, if I might presume for just a moment of your time?"

"Investigation?"

"Well, yes, with the police. Have you made any headway?"

"You'd have to ask them about that. I'm afraid I've been politely requested to stay out of it."

Blackwood frowned. "But I thought, that is, it was our understanding you would be involved."

"No," Raj said, shaking his head. "I'm looking into it on my end, and I wouldn't mind talking to some of the witnesses, but I can't get access. Not officially anyway."

"Really. Well. Maybe I can make a few calls." He retrieved a slim wallet from the inside pocket of his suit jacket and extracted his business card. Handing it to Raj, he said, "In return, perhaps you'll agree to meet with me when this is all over." Raj took the card and slipped it into his pocket while Blackwood waited in obvious expectation of a reciprocal offer of some sort. When none was forthcoming, he smoothed his tie nervously, coughed and said, "Well, I'll make those calls then. You have a pleasant evening."

Raj didn't move until Blackwood had crossed the main dining room and turned out of sight into one of the smaller, private rooms. Without sitting down, he made some sort of gesture to his proprietor friend and slipped a hand under Sarah's arm. "We're leaving," he said, all but lifting her from her chair.

Sarah didn't protest since she wanted nothing more than to get as far away from Blackwood as possible. She let Raj propel her out of the restaurant, but finally dug her feet in when he would have dragged her like some sort of stuffed toy down the street to where his car was parked. "Stop," she said, shaking her arm loose from his firm grip.

He gave her a cool look. "I was under the impression you wanted to avoid Blackwood."

Sarah blushed, but raised her chin defiantly. "That doesn't mean I want to be dragged down the street like a recalcitrant child. I *can* walk, you know."

"Yes, I know," he said in a way that made her blush even harder.

"How do you do that?"

"What?"

"Make everything seem like some sort of foreplay. It's just *walking*," she complained.

He laughed and wrapped an arm around her waist, getting her moving again toward his car. "Not when you do it, sweetheart. And not with those heels you're wearing."

Sarah smiled despite herself as he opened the car door and she slid inside. But her smile faded when she saw Blackwood standing outside the restaurant looking their way.

"He's watching us," she murmured as Raj settled into the driver's seat.

"I know." He spun away from the curb, executing an illegal U-turn that took them in the opposite direction they wanted to go but avoided driving past the restaurant and Blackwood's prying eyes.

Sarah expected him to turn somewhere, but he caught the main road out of town instead.

"Where are we going?" The words were no sooner out of her mouth than he was crossing several lanes of traffic and pulling to a stop on a dark street of quiet homes and very little traffic. He left the engine running, but put the car in park and turned to face her, one long arm along the back of her seat.

"I think it's time for our little talk, Sarah."

"Here?" she asked.

"Here. We can begin with why you're afraid of Edward Blackwood. The guy makes used car salesmen look like boy scouts, but he's fairly harmless. Unless you happen to have a few million stashed away in a trust fund somewhere?" He gave her a questioning look.

"No." She drew a deep breath and stole a quick glance at Raj. He sat watching her with that cool blue gaze of his, looking as if he had all the time in the world and was ready to spend it waiting for her to spill her guts. She restlessly played her fingers on her thigh until he reached out and placed his hand over hers, stilling them.

"Look at me, Sarah." She did. "Whatever it is, whatever's going on . . . it can't be that bad. I'm a vampire, sweetheart. I drink human blood on a regular basis. What can you possibly have to tell me that would top that?"

She laughed and, to her horror, felt tears pressing against the back of her eyes. "It's just . . . I've spent years getting away from it all, and now—"

"The other night you asked me about the other women. You wanted to know their names. Why?"

The tears were threatening to overflow and roll down her cheeks. She wanted to tell him the truth, and something told her he'd understand if she did. Maybe he was right, maybe it was because he was a vampire and nothing she could tell him would be worse than that. But—

"Tell me, Sarah."

"I left home when I was sixteen," she whispered miserably, hating herself. "I couldn't live there anymore. I changed my name and cut off all contact so they couldn't find me." It was close to the truth, close enough, she hoped, that he wouldn't know the difference.

He frowned at her in the dark car. "Why? Did something happen?"

She nodded, refusing to meet his gaze. "It just wasn't a good place for me."

"So where does Blackwood come in?" he asked, clearly puzzled.

"What?"

"Blackwood," he repeated. "I saw your reaction at the police station and again tonight. You're really spooked by him."

"Blackwood . . ." Sarah said, thinking quickly, ". . . knew my parents. He'd recognize me and then . . . It's been twelve years since I've seen any member of my family. I'd like to keep it that way."

Raj was quiet, tapping on the steering wheel lightly, his gaze on the nighttime traffic, but his thoughts seemed far away. Abruptly, he looked back at her and asked, "So why this case? Why your interest in the missing women?"

"I just . . . I read about Trish in the paper. I felt sorry for her and I thought . . . Since I knew Tony sort of, and Cyn's my friend. I thought maybe I could *do* something instead of just waiting for Trish to die." That part, at least, was true.

She waited for Raj's reaction, waited for him to blow up at her, accuse her of lying yet again, but he just tapped his fingers on the steering wheel some more, then checked his watch and said, "I've got to get you home."

* * * *

When they reached the house, Sarah threw the car door open without waiting for Raj to turn off the engine. She started up the walk to her stairs, digging her keys out of her purse as she went. Behind her, she heard the beep of the BMW's remote and then he was next to her, beating her to the door and waiting while she unlocked it. She opened the door, stepped inside, and threw her purse on the stairs, shrugging out of her coat. Aware of him towering over her, she kept her heels on, but could still feel his cool stare following her every move. How much did he see? she wondered. Could vampires read human thoughts? Some said it was just a myth, but vampires weren't exactly lining up to be studied, so who really knew the truth?

"I'm going to put some water on for tea," she said, not quite knowing what else to do. Raj followed her into the kitchen. As she reached for the kettle, his shadow fell over her and she had a moment of déjà vu so strong, she had to grab onto the stove or fall over. She could feel him right behind her, blocking the doorway, his gaze icy hot against her back. Her heart began to race and a cold sweat covered her skin as she fought for her next breath.

"Sarah?"

She spun around at the sound of his voice, overwhelmed by the desire to close the distance between them, to reach up and touch his face, to run her fingers through his thick hair and see if it felt as silky as it looked. To feel his arms holding her effortlessly while he picked her up and plunged his cock deep inside her again and again, until she was screaming his name.

Shocked by her own thoughts, she forced herself to look away. Avoiding his touch, she slid sideways down the counter, until she came to the refrigerator. She turned her back to him and opened the door, pulling out of a bottle of cold water and holding it to her overheated face. "Sorry," she said. "I'm a little tired. I haven't been sleeping well."

"I should go, then. Let you sleep."

"No," she said quickly, and then rolled her eyes at her own stupidity, grateful she was facing away from him and he couldn't see. She drew a deep breath and turned around, her gaze riveted to the water bottle as she twisted off the cap. "I was thinking I might be able to help with your investigation. You probably want to talk to some people on campus, and I could go with you, maybe, you know, since I work there. I thought we could be like partners," she said reasonably. Unfortunately, when she raised her eyes, he wasn't looking at her like a partner. It was more like she was steak and he was a starving man.

* * * *

Raj leaned in the doorframe, denying himself another step, afraid to get any closer to Sarah. His gums ached and his lips were closed tight over fangs that wanted nothing more than to sink into her soft flesh and drink the sweet nectar of her blood. He'd noted her reaction, known the moment her body remembered what had happened in the kitchen the night before, even though her mind had been wiped. He'd heard her heart speed up, had seen the sudden gleam of sweat above her lip, and known that the delicate valley between her breasts would be warm and damp.

He straightened away from the door, as much to relieve the pressure in his groin as anything else. "All right," he said, thinking this was a very bad idea. He should be avoiding any contact with her, not setting up a fucking partnership. But for some reason, his mouth just kept talking. "I do need to talk to people," he said. "Witnesses, families, that sort of thing. And some people find me intimidating."

"Really?" she said in a thin voice.

"You, on the other hand . . ." He couldn't help himself. He closed the distance between them and reached out to twirl a lock of her blond hair around his finger. "You're apple pie and Sunday school. People probably come up to you on the street and tell you their secrets. Small children seek you out in a crowd when they've lost their mothers."

Sarah scowled at him, clearly not knowing if she should be flattered or insulted by his description.

Raj laughed, feeling the sexual tension drain away.

She gave him a little half smile. "What the hell," she said. "When do we start?"

"Tomorrow night, if you're available."

"Sure, why not? Who needs sleep?"

"I want to begin with Dr. Edwards's husband. He's a man *and* an academic so your presence should be particularly useful."

"Gosh, thanks. I love being *useful*. Who's Dr. Edwards?"

"Estelle Edwards. A medical researcher and the first woman to disappear. She doesn't fit the profile and I'd like to know why."

She shrugged. "Okay."

Raj smiled. "I'll let you get some sleep then," he said. He strode down the hall, pleased to have made a clean get away, already thinking of ways to get out of meeting her tomorrow night. God knew he wanted to spend time with her. But he wanted it too much and that wasn't healthy for either of them. He reached the front door and turned around to call a good-bye, but Sarah was right behind him.

She stood there looking up at him, her hands behind her back like a well-behaved child. She drew a deep breath that did nothing for his newfound restraint, and said, "Don't you want to kiss me good night?"

He froze. "What?"

"A good night kiss," she persisted.

He frowned. "Sarah . . ."

She gave him an impatient look. "What's the problem, Raj? You kissed me last night, didn't you? And the night before that. Have I suddenly grown a second head or something?" She patted her shoulders, as if searching for the new growth.

"Fine." He bent down, intending to give her a chaste kiss on the cheek, but Sarah had other plans. She turned her head at the last minute so that their lips met. And he was lost.

Her lips were soft and warm, melting beneath his as her mouth opened with a breathy little moan. He picked her up with an arm around her waist and spun around, trapping her against the wall, pressing his body to hers as he explored her sweet mouth. Their tongues tangled, her slender arms coming around his neck and pulling him closer until he thought they'd fuse into a single entity, trapped forever in a searing embrace. And surely there were worse ways to end one's life?

She cried out as his fangs nicked her lip and he pulled back, lost in his first taste of her blood, the dizzying spell of it as it raced through his system. He held her a moment longer, relishing the feel of her warm, willing body, the image of her arousal, her cheeks flushed and her eyes foggy with desire, and then he let her slide down until her feet touched the floor.

"Be careful, little one," he whispered roughly. "Don't tease unless you're prepared to deal with the consequences." He held her until she could stand on her own, permitting himself one tender kiss against her hungry little mouth before he pulled away. "I'll call you tomorrow," he said, and then he left, her frustrated protest echoing down an empty sidewalk behind him.

Chapter Twenty-four

Raj secured his private vault door and went directly to the bar, pouring a shot of vodka and tossing it down his throat. But nothing could wash away the lingering taste of Sarah's blood. Maybe if he'd never tasted her beyond the sweetness of her skin, he could have stayed away from her. But now . . . That tiny sip of her blood had sealed his fate. He could still leave her behind, could run back to Manhattan on the fastest jet he owned, but he would never erase the memory, the need. She was his, and he'd be damned if he'd let anyone else, human or vampire, have her. But would Sarah be damned instead if he took her?

He slammed the empty glass back onto the bar and tore off his clothes, aware of the sun rising, draining away his energy. When he fell at last into his bed, he welcomed the sweet oblivion of daytime sleep. For a few hours at least, he would be free.

When he awoke that night, there was a message from Tony Scavetti waiting for him on his voice mail asking him to call. It was hardly expected, but it was nice to know his business cards hadn't gone to waste.

Raj showered and dressed before punching in the detective's direct number.

"Scavetti."

"Raymond Gregor, Detective. You called."

"Yeah," Scavetti said, sounding as if he'd rather have pulled every one of his own teeth than to have made that call. "I understand you'd like to talk to some of the witnesses."

Since this was about the last thing Raj expected the man to say, it took him a minute to respond. "I would," he said finally.

"Yeah, well. I've made some calls. Dr. Edwards will be home tonight if you want to see him."

"I'll be there close to nine," Raj said. "Why the change of heart, Detective?"

"I don't know what—"

"Let's not play games, Tony. Not between us," Raj added dryly. "Why the sudden courtesy?"

He heard Scavetti's harsh breathing and then something that sounded like a chair hitting a wall. "You've got friends, Gregor. I'll give you that. Friends with a lot of fucking money. And money talks, even when it should keep its fucking mouth shut."

And the real Scavetti returns, Raj thought. It was almost reassuring.

"William Cowens called the Commissioner and *requested* our cooperation," Scavetti added. "Requested, my fucking ass. Captain came down on us hard. So you got your fucking interviews. That good enough?"

"It is, and thank you."

"Yeah, whatever. Hey, Gregor, since we're being all buddies and everything, why are you here?"

"Excuse me?"

"I mean your usual territory's Manhattan, right?"

Raj hadn't told him that, and it shouldn't have been easy for anyone to dig out information about him and his businesses. Maybe the cops had someone inside Krystof's circle.

"There must be more than a few local guys who could handle something like this," Scavetti was saying. "So why bring a ringer like you all the way from the big city? What're you guys trying to hide?"

Raj wished he had the answer to that question, but all he said was, "You'd have to ask Lord Krystof that question. Like you, I only do what I'm told."

"Right," Scavetti said, clearly not believing a word. "Just like I'm sure you'll let me know if you find out anything about those missing girls."

"You and I have the same goal, Detective. I'm sorry you don't believe that."

"Yeah. Whatever."

The phone went dead against Raj's ear. He disconnected and punched Sarah's number by heart.

"Hello?"

He didn't announce himself. "We've got an appointment with Dr. Edwards at nine tonight. Can you make it?"

"Well, good evening to you too, Raj."

He was silent for a moment, and then he said, "Sarah."

"Yes."

"Can you make it or not?"

"Yes, my lord."

He frowned. *Damn Emelie.* "Don't call me that."

"But Emelie—"

"Emelie likes to play games."

He could hear the slight tap of computer keys and realized she was continuing to work on something else while talking to him. "Am I interrupting something?" he growled.

"Well, someone certainly got up on the wrong side of the coffin tonight. So are you picking me up, or what?"

Raj had a fleeting thought about the "or what" portion of that sentence, but he said, "I'll be there before nine."

"See you then."

"Yes, you will," he said and hung up, determined to get the last word.

His phone rang almost immediately. It was Sarah. He mashed the button with his thumb, and before he could say anything, she said, "Good-bye, Raj," and hung up.

Chapter Twenty-five

"We'll go by the University after we meet with Edwards," Raj said, when Sarah answered his impatient knock on her front door. She'd made a point of locking it, and he'd made his irritation plain when she finally let him in. "I want to talk to Trish's roommate, too," he continued. "You can call ahead and make sure she's there."

Sarah gave him a dark look. "Who put you in charge of this partnership? Maybe I had something else in mind."

"Did you?" he asked curiously.

She pursed her lips in annoyance and stomped over to pick up her coat from the back of the couch where she'd thrown it earlier. "No," she snapped and began yanking the coat up her arms. She was surprised when Raj took it from her, sliding it over her arms gracefully, his hands remaining on her shoulders a few seconds too long.

She shivered and he lifted his hands immediately.

"We'll take my car," he said, holding the door open. He cocked one eyebrow. "That is, unless you have another plan?"

She stuck out her tongue as she walked past him, startling a short bark of real laughter from him. Apparently even Raj could be surprised. Good to know.

* * * *

It was a half hour drive to the Edwards's house, which was a sprawling ranch-style on a big double lot out in one of Buffalo's many suburbs. This particular suburb had a faux-country theme, with white rail fences and wide stretches of lawn that would hold six houses in other parts of the county.

"Do the Edwards have children?" Sarah asked as they pulled into the U-shaped driveway.

"No. They have careers." He glanced over to find her eying the house doubtfully. "You don't approve?"

"I don't really care either way, as long as they're happy. It's just, I look at this huge house and try to imagine the two of them roaming around inside. They could probably go days without seeing each other."

"Maybe that's what's happened. Maybe Estelle's actually working somewhere inside the house and Dr. Edwards doesn't even know it." He turned off the engine. "Let's go."

The house was all lit up, both inside and out. It was a single story, probably with a basement, but the ceilings were high and the windows took advantage of that, reaching from close to the ground to nearly the roof line. Tall double doors were flanked by clouded cut glass panes, and they could see someone moving around inside when they rang the doorbell.

"I'll take the lead," Sarah said. "He's probably upset, and a woman—"

Raj snorted. "For all you know this guy killed his wife. The husband's always the prime suspect in cases like this."

She eyed him thoughtfully. "You're either a big fan of cop shows . . ." Raj rolled his eyes. "Or you haven't told me all of your secrets."

He gave her a dry look.

"Okay, so you haven't told me *any* of your secrets. But you will," she said confidently. "People always—"

The front door opened, interrupting whatever it was that people always did in Sarah's world. Donald Edwards was only a bit shorter than Raj, but looked half his weight. Brown corduroy slacks, a white shirt and a gray wool cardigan hung loosely on a heavy-boned frame, as if he'd either been ill or lost weight recently. His hair was black and cut close to his head, liberally sprinkled with strands of silver.

"Doctor Edwards?" Sarah said. "I'm Sarah Stratton. I believe you're expecting us?" She held out a hand, which Edwards stared at blankly, as if he didn't know quite what to do with it. When he finally responded, it was slow and methodical, a loose grip that he released almost immediately.

Sarah gave Raj a troubled glance.

"Raymond Gregor," Raj said, holding out his hand in turn. Edwards's handshake came faster this time, as if having done it already with Sarah, he was reminded of the proper response. Long thin fingers wrapped around Raj's and he could feel the heat and pulse beneath the man's skin.

They waited for Edwards to say something, to invite them in or maybe send them away. "Detective Scavetti told us he'd called you?" Raj reminded him.

The man's brown eyes shifted to him and he nodded. "Yes, of course. Come in," he said. He walked away from the door, giving them room to enter. His voice was dry with disuse. This was either a man in deep mourning for his missing wife, or one who was hitting the pharmaceuticals a little too hard.

They followed him into a sitting area just beyond the foyer. It was an odd room, big and high-ceilinged, with a sunken center that featured an L-shaped couch and several chairs, as well as a fireplace. A wide screen television sat to one side, positioned so that it was inconvenient to almost every seat in the room. Edwards sat in a chair far too small for his height and gestured toward the adjacent couch.

Sarah sat on the edge of the cushion, radiating concern, her knees together, hands clasped, body leaning slightly forward. Raj sat on the arm of the couch close to her. He wasn't getting a clear vibe from Edwards and it made him nervous.

"Is she dead?" Edwards's face held no expression. He didn't even glance at Raj, but stared at Sarah, as if knowing she was the one who would deliver the bad news.

"No! Oh, no, Dr. Edwards." Sarah reached out one hand to touch his knobby, corduroy-clothed knee. Raj had to restrain himself from snatching her hand back when it lingered long enough for her to say, "I'm so sorry. We're not here for that."

Edwards's whole body seemed to collapse. Raj smelled the tears before he saw them leaking from beneath the man's closed eyelids. Scavetti had been wrong about this half of the Edwards marriage. This man loved his wife.

"I'm so sorry. Detective Scavetti should have told you," Sarah added grimly. "We don't—"

"We're part of a new investigation," Raj interrupted. "Certain information has come to our attention that leads us to believe your wife's case may be part of a larger pattern. Our purpose in being here is to collect whatever new details we can in the hope of drawing a clearer picture of the crime."

Sarah frowned up at him, but Edwards responded to the businesslike tone. He straightened visibly, sitting up in the chair and drawing in a stabilizing breath. He looked at Raj directly. "Of course," he said, seeming alert for the first time since they'd arrived. "Although the police have been here several times already. I don't—"

"Fresh eyes, Dr. Edwards," Raj said briskly. "And a new perspective. Just a few questions."

"Of course. I'm sorry. Would you like something to drink? I just made coffee."

The coffee sat cold and untouched, and Edwards still hadn't told them much more than they already knew. He claimed to know almost nothing about the vampire contact his wife was planning to meet, which Raj found unbelievable. If a woman he cared about had been off on a late night rendezvous with an unknown vampire, he sure as hell would have known whom she was meeting. Hell, he'd have been going with her.

"You didn't worry about your wife meeting someone, maybe even a vampire, so late at night?" Raj asked bluntly, which earned him a shocked look from Sarah.

Dr. Edwards seemed taken aback by the question as well. He didn't respond immediately, staring at Raj and then away, as if debating whether to answer. When he looked back, his eyes were full of loss, and something else—guilt.

"We were supposed to have dinner that night," he said quietly. "It seems meaningless now, but at the time . . ." He drew a breath before continuing. "I'd scored something of a professional coup and we were going to celebrate. Estelle cancelled at the last minute. I was angry. She'd done this sort of thing so many times before, always putting her work before everything else. She left a phone message, canceling our plans and telling me about her meeting. I didn't even call her back."

"Does your wife keep a calendar? Anything that would list her appointments?"

Tears sparkled in Edwards's eyes and he swallowed hard before nodding. "On her computer, but the police already took that. I don't think they found anything."

"Does she have a secretary?" Sarah asked. "Someone who might have called her contact?"

Edwards shook his head. "Estelle was very careful about her work. Medical research is a highly competitive field, cutthroat some would say, and she'd been burned before by a colleague. She rarely shared any of the details beyond her lab, and even then her assistants know only what they're actively working on, very little of the larger project."

Raj stood to leave. *This was useless.* "Thank you, Dr. Edwards, for—"

Edwards stood also, interrupting him. "You must understand. We live well here, but it was not always so. It's difficult to see beneath her professional persona, but Estelle is very street smart. She told me she was meeting someone in the vampire community, someone high enough to ensure access to the blood samples she needed. I believed her, Mr. Gregor. And I believe whoever she met . . ." He drew a breath before continuing, ". . . whoever she met knows where she is."

Raj frowned and nodded sharply. "For what it's worth, I think you're right, Dr. Edwards." He gestured at Sarah, indicating it was time to leave.

Sarah set her untasted coffee back on its delicate saucer and stood. She'd slipped out of her coat when she sat down and now gathered it up, getting ready to leave. Something caught her eye, and Raj saw her cross to a large sideboard against the entryway wall.

"Is this your wife?" she asked Edwards, touching a silver-framed photograph.

"Yes," the doctor replied, seeming puzzled. "But I already gave the police a photograph."

"You did, sir," Raj said quickly. "Dr. Stratton is new to the case. Thank you for agreeing to see us on such short notice. We'll be in touch," he added and hustled Sarah out the door.

Chapter Twenty-six

Sarah waited until they were in Raj's car and back on the main road, before saying, "Remember when I told you Krystof was talking to some woman at that university reception?"

"Mmm," Raj said absently.

"It was Estelle Edwards."

He glanced at her in disbelief. "Why didn't you say something before?" he demanded.

"I never saw her photograph before," she replied calmly.

"But you met with Scavetti—"

"For five minutes, so he could tell me all the reasons I didn't belong on his precious case. I only know what Trish looks like because she was in the paper."

"Goddamn it."

"I don't get it, Raj."

"What don't you get?" he asked. He seemed angry suddenly, although not necessarily at her.

"What's the connection? Why Estelle Edwards, and why those women?"

"Blood," he said succinctly. "That son of a bitch."

"Explain please."

He scowled. "Vampires stay young forever. Humans would like to also. It's all in the blood."

Sarah's eyes opened wide in understanding. "Oh, my God," she said. "And Estelle Edwards is a hematologist! She could make a fortune."

"Exactly."

"But why hasn't someone done it before now? Hell, why haven't you all set up a corporation and raked it in?"

He stopped at a red light and twisted around to look at her. "How long do you think vampires would remain free if humans figured out a way for our blood to make them live forever?" he asked grimly.

She stared at him as realization struck. "Right," she said. "Got it." The light changed and the BMW took off like it was on a raceway. "So is Krystof in trouble?" she asked.

Mr. Inscrutable just shrugged, ignoring her question, and Sarah had a sudden, strong urge to throw something at him. Unfortunately, there was nothing handy, and besides, at the speed he was going, the car would probably crash spectacularly and she'd die. He'd be fine, of course. Stupid vampire.

Staring straight ahead, he whipped the powerful sedan down the empty streets, his anger fairly radiating off of him. She expected him to take her straight home and dump her at the curb, so she was surprised when he turned toward the university.

"The roommate's name is Jennifer Stewart," he said abruptly and rattled off her phone number. "Give her a try."

"Yes, my lord," she responded, which earned her a sideways glare. She punched in the number.

"If she's not there, I'll drop you off—"

"Hi, is this Jennifer?" Sarah made a face at Raj. "Jennifer, my name's Sarah Stratton."

* * * *

Jennifer Stewart could have been Patricia Cowens's twin sister, Raj thought. They had the same heart-shaped face surrounded by long, curly black hair, the same newly ripe body, fairly begging to be plucked.

"I told the police," she was saying. "Trish never went to one of those parties before. She was really sweet, but she hardly went anywhere. It was a big deal for her that her dad let her move into the dorm, and she didn't want to do anything to make him change his mind. He's pretty protective, like totally obsessed almost. Did you know he bought a house here just so he could visit on weekends? It's out in the country and it's like huge."

"He bought a house because Trish was going to school here?" Sarah asked.

"Yeah. Trish didn't mind, though. She said it was because of her mom being dead. He's actually a really nice guy for being so massively rich."

Raj was getting impatient with the conversation. They'd already gone through a needlessly long set of introductions, during which Jennifer wisely asked to see their identification. Raj could understand that. After all, her roommate was missing. But the ID check had been followed by a lengthy explanation of why they should called her "Jen" and not "Jennifer" and never "Jenny." Raj would have called her anything she wanted if it meant he'd get some answers before the next millennium.

"I don't think she had a good time at the party, though, *Jen* was saying. "It's kind of a weird vibe there sometimes, you know?"

Raj didn't know. He didn't want to know. What he *wanted* to know was whatever Jen had to say that could possibly help him discover if Krystof was trading in vamp blood. Christ, if that was true, the old man really had lost it. He wandered over to the small student desk next to the window, leaning over to peer at a photograph of the two roommates which was stuck to a cork bulletin board. Without even glancing over his shoulder, he ripped the photograph off the board and tucked it into his pocket before turning around to lean against the desk.

"Did you or Trish ever go to anything more serious than these parties?" he asked impatiently. "Anything involving vampires?"

Jen looked at him with those wide, little girl eyes and shook her head. "Oh. You mean like a blood house or something?"

That was exactly what Raj meant and he found it curious that the innocent-eyed Jennifer had homed in so quickly. "Among other things," he said. "Anything like that?"

"No, sir," she said, shaking her head vigorously and tossing her shiny curls. "Never."

Raj straightened from his slouch against the desk. "Jennifer," he said in a low, seductive voice. Her gaze swung to him as quickly as a compass to due north.

He went to one knee in front of her and took her hand, like a courtier before a princess. *Jennifer, you know what I am don't you?*

Yes. Even her mind voice was young and breathless. It made him smile.

I'm trying to find Trish, Jennifer, and I know you want to help, don't you?

She nodded eagerly.

I'm going to help you remember some things, is that okay?

Is this kind of like hypnosis or something?

That's exactly what it's like.

She frowned. *You won't make me cluck like a chicken or anything, will you?*

Raj wanted to laugh, but he replied seriously. *No. That would be a betrayal of your trust, and I would never do that, sweetheart.*

Okay, then.

Raj heard Sarah moving restlessly behind him. The entire conversation with Jennifer would have taken only minutes, but he had a sudden image of what Sarah must be seeing. Him kneeling in front of the young woman, her gaze locked on his, her face suffused with happiness, as if he was the most wonderful person she'd ever met. He cleared his throat and spoke out loud. "Jennifer, did you lie earlier when I asked about the blood houses?"

The girl's eyes filled with tears that spilled down her cheeks. "I'm sorry," she whispered.

"Why did you lie, sweetheart?"

"I'm not allowed," she said in a childlike voice. "My parents would get really, really mad at me."

"Did you tell the police about it?"

"No! They'd tell!"

"I won't tell."

She smiled happily. "I know."

"So you can tell me the truth, can't you? You can tell me about the blood house."

"Yes," she nodded vigorously. "My friend Kara and I went twice. It was scary at first, but the vampires were really nice. And some of them were good-looking too, just like the romance books say."

Raj turned his head to share his amusement with Sarah and was startled to find her glaring at him. He frowned, but switched his attention back to Jennifer, not wanting to lose her or the perfectly clear image he was getting of a blood house he recognized from his own tenure in this city. "Did you meet anyone at the blood house, Jennifer? Anyone special?"

The young girl blushed. "There was one guy. He really seemed to like me. We danced all night, and he said I should come there again, that maybe we could go out or something."

Raj frowned at the image he was getting from her, which was no image at all. Whoever it was had spent enough time with her to seduce her mind and alter her memories.

"He really liked my jacket."

Raj blinked. "Your jacket?"

"It wasn't really mine," Jen confided, leaning closer to him. "I borrowed it from Trish. She has such nice clothes." Jen looked sad. "She was wearing our jacket when she went away."

Raj stared at her intently. "Do you remember the vampire's name, Jennifer? The one who danced with you?"

She frowned. "I can't remember."

"What did he look like?"

She frowned again, looking down at their joined hands and concentrating. "I can't remember that either. I'm sorry." She looked up at him and he could tell she was growing increasingly distraught as she tried to break through the other vampire's conditioning in order to please him. He didn't want that.

"That's all right," he said quickly, soothing her. "You've been very helpful tonight."

"I have?"

"Absolutely." He took her arm and led her over to one of the twin beds. "You should sleep now."

"I *am* tired," she said, yawning widely and curling up on the bed.

He leaned down, pulled the covers over her and touched her shoulder. "Good night, Jennifer."

He stood upright and found Sarah standing right next to him, almost vibrating with anger. "What—" he began.

"Outside," she said furiously.

He gave her a narrow look, not used to anyone giving him orders. "What is your problem?"

"Out fucking side."

"Look, Sarah, if you want to leave, go ahead. I need to make sure that—"

"I'm not leaving you alone with her."

Raj felt his own anger rising to meet hers. He grabbed her arm, holding on when she tried to yank away, pulling her from the room and down the battered stairway, not letting go until they stood next to his

BMW.

"What the hell is wrong with you?" he demanded.

"Me? What's wrong with *you?*" she demanded. "You practically raped that girl!"

"Are you out of your fucking mind?" he said, every word enunciated clearly. He was holding onto his rage by the thinnest of threads. That she would accuse him of—

"Why? Because you didn't touch her? You think rape only happens to the body? Guess again. I *know* what it's like to—"

"You don't know shit because I would never hurt a woman," he growled, stepping so close he could feel her body trembling. "Don't you *ever* accuse me of something like that. Never. You got it?"

Sarah stared at him. "Fuck you, Raj," she whispered. She spun around and stomped away through the parking lot, pulling her cell phone out of her purse.

Raj used his vampire speed to place himself in her path. "Get back in the car. I'm not leaving you here."

She laughed. "Well, I'm not getting in the car with a rapist, so tough luck for you."

Raj stared at her, not quite believing what she was saying. How could she think that of him? How could any woman think he was that kind of a monster, much less *this* woman?

She was talking on the phone to someone and he realized she was calling a cab. He considered picking her up bodily and throwing her back in his car. Hell, he could erase this whole fucking nightmare from her mind and she'd never remember a thing. But he wouldn't do that. Not again. And not to Sarah.

He watched her storm across the parking lot, heading for the street where, presumably, the cab would meet her. Maybe it was better this way. He'd wanted an excuse to walk away from her. To make her walk away from him. To get her as far away as possible from vampires in general and him in particular. This wasn't what he'd had in mind, but it would do. It would do nicely. And they'd both be better off in the long run.

He strode back to his car without another word, sitting there until he saw the cab arrive, until Sarah was inside and safe. And then he drove into the night alone.

Chapter Twenty-seven

Raj pulled up to the warehouse and twisted off the ignition key. He sat there for a while listening to the ping of the cooling engine, the occasional whine of a big truck on the nearby Genesee Road. The airport was silent. The last passenger flight came in from Chicago around midnight. After that, the terminals pretty much shut down until morning and the first cargo flights at six.

He had the connection he'd been looking for. Jennifer, sweet Jennifer, had given it to him. It was the blood houses. Trish Cowens had never made sense to him. Why would any vampire stalk a victim on the streets, when he could find plenty of women at the blood houses who were willing to spend an hour or a weekend if that's what he wanted? But it wasn't Trish Cowens the vampire had been after. It was Jennifer Stewart, who looked so much like her roommate and who'd worn a leather jacket the night she'd gone to visit a blood house. The same jacket Trish was wearing the night she was taken.

But what was the connection between the kidnapped women and Estelle Edwards's vampire research project? Would she need human subjects to test her research? And what about Krystof? Even if he was behind this scheme, he certainly hadn't been the one who'd danced with Jennifer Stewart at the blood house or, for that matter, the one who'd taken Trish Cowens off the street. And he kept coming back to the fact that it was Krystof who'd brought him to Buffalo to figure out what was happening.

Raj swore and shoved open the door. Too many damn questions and not enough answers. He strode over to the warehouse, expecting it to be empty. But when he stepped inside, he found Em heading for one of the big SUVs, the only one left in the warehouse bay.

"Raj," she said, veering toward him. "I didn't expect you here."

"Do we have any human assets in town, beyond these guards?"

She blinked, obviously taken aback by his cold demeanor, but he wasn't in a friendly mood.

"None I would trust, my lord, but I can have someone here by daybreak."

"Do it. I need more daylight guards for this place and a twenty-four hour watch on Sarah."

Emelie paused in the act of punching buttons on her cell phone. "You think she's—"

"I don't have time to baby-sit her, but I need to know what her involvement is. She's been lying to me all along and I need to know why. Did Simon find anything more on her?"

"Nothing relevant, my lord, but he's still digging. There is one oddity—"

Raj looked at her sharply. "What's that?"

"She doesn't seem to exist before maybe ten years ago. A little less."

"What does that mean?"

She shrugged. "There's no birth certificate, no high school graduation, no driver's license that we can find before then. Of course, it's possible she was home schooled and really didn't drive a car until she broke away from her parental units, but it makes Simon's Spidey sense tingle. He's looking deeper."

Raj frowned. "Let me know as soon as you find something. Where is everyone?"

"Throughout the city, as you ordered, my lord. We've been rotating the blood houses between us, and I can tell you this much. There's no one in charge here. None of the local vamps raised an eyebrow when I showed up, and I don't exactly blend."

Raj nodded. Most vampires were men, although it was more by happenstance than planning. Contrary to what popular fiction would have one believe, there weren't that many vampires in the world. Only master vampires had the power to make and hold a child, and the most common reason for a master to make children was to defend his territory. There was a strong cultural bias among all but the youngest vampires that put women in the to-be-protected category, while males were seen as defenders. And then there was the need for blood—if a vampire had a female lover, even for a short time, he wanted her to remain human so he could continue to feed from her. All of which resulted in more male vampires than female, which in turn meant that Emelie definitely should have been noticed.

"Jozef told me my first night in the city that Krystof was making children left and right," Raj said. "The local blood house managers are probably so used to new faces they don't bother to question anyone."

"Or maybe they're overwhelmed," Emelie said. "The houses I've been to are far too crowded. The ventilation systems aren't working properly, and the humans are drunk on vampire pheromones."

Raj nodded, not surprised by this. "The blood houses are the key, Em. I think Trish Cowens was a mistake. Someone meant to grab her roommate and got Trish instead." He frowned. "And Sarah says she saw Krystof talking to Estelle Edwards at a university reception."

Em's face reflected her shock. "That's pretty damning, boss."

He nodded. "It looks like it, but damnit, Em, it just doesn't fit. Krystof wouldn't have brought me here if he was the one. He *knows* I'll figure this out. I'm missing something. I just don't know what it is." He drew a troubled breath. "It doesn't matter," he said finally. "If it's Krystof, I'll deal with him sooner than planned, that's all. And he can't be the one taking the women from the houses, because the house managers would damn well remember if Krystof had visited. I was out in Corfu the other night and no one said a word to me about Krystof. So even if he's in on it, he's not acting alone."

"Whoever they are," Em said. "They've got to be getting a little frantic by now with all the press this is getting. We need to find those women before the bad guys start getting rid of the evidence, assuming they haven't already."

Raj shook his head in disgust. "Make your calls, Em. Get some more of our human assets here. And then you and I are going to visit the East Amherst blood house. Jennifer Stewart, Trish's roommate, went there twice. I want to see what it looks like."

Chapter Twenty-eight

The house was pretty much as he remembered it. Built in the early seventies, it was a wood and glass tract house—two stories, with an incongruous A-frame that would have looked ridiculous except for the identical homes all around. A sort of mini-Swiss chalet bedroom community in upstate New York.

The inside was just as firmly stuck in the seventies as the exterior. A short entryway led to a sunken living room with walls that alternated wood paneling and gold-veined mirror. No doubt the carpet had originally been some sort of shag, but that was long gone, replaced by something sturdier, something that wouldn't show blood stains. The interior was dark and smoky, music pulsing with a heavy backbeat that caused the cheap floor to vibrate beneath his feet. And Em was right. The air was foggy with pheromones and human sweat.

Raj stood in the doorway and waited for someone to challenge him, or to at least acknowledge he belonged there. But no one did. He glanced at Em and started toward the back of the house, ending up in a kitchen which had been gutted to make room for two big subzero refrigerators standing side by side. Raj strode over to the units and pulled one open.

Rows of bagged blood were stacked inside. Either the house manager had a deal with the local blood bank or he was draining more from the human donors than anyone knew. He closed the heavy door. He still had not been challenged by anyone. "Upstairs," he told Emelie.

She nodded and led the way back down the hall, taking a U-turn upward around a flimsy iron banister. The stairway was crowded, but once they got upstairs, the hall was more or less clear as activities were taken behind closed doors. The usual sounds were emanating through those doors—women, men and vampires, in the throes of sexual passion and release. Not a few of the outbursts were punctuated with cries of pain; some vampires didn't even try to be gentle.

Raj felt his own fangs pushing for release. He hadn't fed from the vein since the woman in the bar his first night in the city, and while bagged blood contained all the nutrients he needed, it held none of the visceral satisfaction he craved almost as much. Between the bad ventilation system and the crowds of willing humans, it was like asking a starving man to walk through a McDonald's without tasting so much as a French fry. The door to the master suite opened behind him and he spun around, fangs fully distended. A vampire stood there, his arm around the waist of a young man who would surely have collapsed if not for the vampire's assistance.

"Raj!" the vampire said. "I heard you were in town. What's up, big guy?"

"Lose the human, Kent," Raj growled.

"Sure thing," Kent said agreeably. "You go on back inside, darling," he said to his companion. "You're looking a bit peaked." He turned the human around in his grasp and gave him a gentle shove toward the big bed in the background. The young man barely made it, falling face down when his knees hit the mattress.

Kent watched, shaking his head fondly. "A sweet boy, but a cheap date." He pulled the door closed and turned back to Raj with nothing but business on his face.

"Let's talk," he said. He tugged a set of keys from the pocket of skintight jeans and opened a door right next to the master suite. It was a small office of sorts, with an industrial-looking metal desk and two chairs. There was no window, and from the configuration, Raj figured this space had been chopped off the master next door.

Kent propped himself on the desk, his back against the outside wall, and indicated the two chairs, eying Em curiously before he said, "I'm surprised to see you, Raj. Pleasantly, but surprised, nonetheless. So what's up?"

Raj didn't sit. He stood just inside the door, aware of Emelie at his back and the houseful of vampires all around him. Kent was a friend, or had been once, but Raj wouldn't go so far as to say he trusted him. Raj didn't trust anyone who had remained within Krystof's grasp. He studied Kent and saw a fine sheen of sweat betraying the nerves behind his relaxed façade, saw his hand gripping the keys so tightly blood had begun to leak between his fingers. Raj met his eyes and held them until Kent dropped his gaze with a low groan. He slid to the floor and onto his knees.

"Master," he forced out from between lips pressed tight with pain.

Raj left him there a few minutes longer, while Emelie stood stock-still next to him, probably fighting her own urge to drop to her knees.

"Get up, Kent," he said finally, and swung into the larger of the two chairs, pushing it back against one wall.

Kent breathed a sigh of relief and, after glancing at Raj, climbed shakily to his feet to slump weakly against the wall over the desk.

"How can I serve you, my lord?" Kent asked in a much subdued voice.

"I'm not your lord, Kent."

The other vampire dared a quick look at Raj's face and away. He shrugged. "Krystof doesn't bother with anything outside the boundaries of Delaware Park anymore. You're the only master I've seen in two years."

Raj concealed his dismay. "No one checks on the houses?"

"Jozef, sometimes. He comes around every few months, but he was here last month, so I don't expect him for awhile yet."

Raj was quiet, thinking. "Has anyone asked you about missing women?"

"Women?"

"Three women, Kent. Three separate disappearances, but each had visited one of the blood houses, including this one. A fourth—" He considered how much he wanted to say. "A fourth woman has a different connection to the vampire community, but she's also disappeared. No one told you?"

"No. This is the first I've heard of it."

Raj shook his head. Kent was telling the truth, which meant Krystof hadn't even taken the basic precaution of warning his house managers. He pulled out the picture of Jennifer Stewart and Trish Cowens he'd snagged from the bulletin board in their dorm room and ripped it in half so that only Jennifer remained. "You recognize this girl?"

Kent studied the picture carefully, but shook his head. "I'm sorry, my lord, she could be one of a hundred, a thousand, women around here. They come and go and, you know me, I don't pay that much attention to the ladies."

"What's with all the bagged blood downstairs, Kent? Where's it coming from?"

The other vampire seemed to freeze for a moment and Raj growled softly, "Kent."

"Orders," he gasped, and Raj could tell he was fighting the compulsion of some other master. He would have fallen to the floor again, but Raj was already on his feet and caught him before he could hit the ground.

"Whose orders, Kent?" he asked intently.

Kent shook his head, as if trying to clear it, then threw back his head and screamed. Raj reacted instantly, grasping the other vampire with both hands and surrounding the two of them in a sphere of pure power. Kent collapsed against him and Raj sorted through his mind, undoing the tangle of commands and counter-commands some clumsy master before him had left behind.

Whoever had done this had the strength to take over another vampire's will, but not the finesse or experience to do it without damage. He cursed the ignorance that could easily have left Kent permanently damaged and tasted the essence of the other. It was familiar, but . . . who? Someone he knew? Or just someone whose power he had crossed paths with before? Raj withdrew gently and lifted Kent in his arms. Emelie was standing ready, and she responded to a jerk of Raj's head by opening the door and stepping into the hall to look both ways.

"It's clear, my lord."

Raj carried him into the master suite. He considered leaving him on the bed with his lover, but there were too many windows in this room and he couldn't be sure Kent would wake soon enough. He settled for the walk-in closet, tucking the unconscious vampire into the back corner and covering him with a pile of blankets that had obviously been used before. Stepping out of the closet, he closed the door, checked on the sleeping human and led Emelie back out to the hallway. She looked at him, her eyes full of questions, but he shook his head. "Later."

They were out the door and back into the SUV before anyone in the house was aware of their passage. Raj didn't say anything for a long while, trying to remember where he'd run across that power before, the taste of the vampire who'd messed up Kent's head so badly. It wasn't until Em took a turn onto a side road, which wound behind the airport to the warehouse, that he snapped his fingers in sudden recollection. "Trish Cowens," he said.

"My lord?" Em took her eyes off the road to give him a worried glance.

"The bastard who messed with Kent's mind. It's the same asshole who took Trish Cowens. He's strong enough to conceal his identity, but not strong enough to keep from making a mess doing it. And that sure as hell is not Krystof, even as fucked up as he is lately." He tapped his fingers on the door panel, thinking. "You and I are going to visit every blood house in the city in the next couple of days. Kent was too screwed up for me to make an identification, but maybe the others won't be. Maybe our man has improved his technique with practice." He left unsaid the possibility that Kent *was* the improvement and the others would be worse—dangerously worse. He glanced at his watch. Less than two hours 'til dawn. The houses would already be shutting down, and if he didn't want to sleep at the warehouse, he had to do the same. "We'll start tomorrow night. I'll be at the warehouse after sunset. The others can go ahead, but you're with me."

Emelie's cell rang and he waited while she answered the call, said a few words and hung up. "The additional human staff will be here by morning, my lord. Whom do you want on Sarah?"

"Any women in the bunch?"

"Yossi's here already, so Angel's coming in," she said.

Yossi was one of Raj's vampires. Angel was his human lover of several decades. "Put Angel and one of the guys on her during the day. I want someone who can stay close if she goes out. I want to know everyone she sees and what they say."

Em gave him a puzzled look as she pulled into the warehouse lot and parked near the door, leaving the engine running. "You think she's up to something?"

Raj frowned. "I don't know. But someone with a grudge against me might think she's important and an easy target."

"So, you think there are more humans involved than just Estelle Edwards?"

"Maybe. I ran into Edward Blackwood last night at a restaurant. He'd love to get his hands on some vamp blood for research, and his institute sure as hell has the money to fund something like that."

"Maybe this other vamp, the one trying to move in, is offering his own blood as the sample," Em suggested.

"Would that be enough? Dr. Edwards's husband seemed to think she'd need more than one donor."

"Hell if I know, boss. We need someone who knows blood."

"Not just blood, but vampire blood," Raj said thoughtfully. "Okay, Em, I'm out of here. I'll see you tomorrow."

He didn't waste any time, spinning tires out of the parking lot, heading straight for his lair downtown. There was only one person he knew of who might have answers to his questions and be willing to talk to him. That was Peter Saephan, Raphael's very private human physician. Raj wouldn't even have considered such a thing before his recent meeting with Raphael. But if the Western Vampire Lord was serious about cooperation, this was the perfect opportunity to prove it. Besides, if someone was selling vampire blood, the vampire community worldwide would be affected. Peasants with torches would be nothing compared to the hunt that would ensue if humans found out what vampire blood could do for them.

He checked his watch again. It was still early on the west coast and he might have just enough time for a call before the sun took him.

Chapter Twenty-nine

Sarah stayed in bed late the next morning. She kept her eyes closed, hoping to go back to sleep, but it wasn't happening. Not that she wasn't tired. She hadn't slept well again last night, but it wasn't dreams that kept her awake this time, it was a guilty conscience. And she was beginning to think she preferred the dreams.

The problem was she didn't know exactly what she was feeling guilty about. Was it because she'd stood by while Raj had his vampire way with Jennifer Stewart's head? Or was it because she'd accused Raj of something horrible without any real evidence?

She'd replayed the scene in Jennifer's dorm room over and over in her head, lying there in bed staring at the ceiling all night. And she couldn't help thinking she'd missed something. Something vital.

She sighed. The sun was beaming into her room. Her windows faced east, and only the lower part was shuttered. Normally, she liked that her bedroom was sunny and warm in the morning, especially in winter. Today, it just highlighted the dust on her dresser and reminded her that Raj was beyond her reach. Of course, even if it had been nighttime, he probably wouldn't talk to her. He'd been pretty pissed last night.

On the other hand, Jennifer was eighteen years old and probably slept with her cell phone glued to her ear. Sarah got out of bed and dug her own cell phone out of her purse. A quick check of her call log gave her Jen's number from last night, when she'd called from the Raj's car.

The girl answered immediately with, "Jen." She certainly sounded chipper enough, Sarah thought.

"Hi, Jen. This is Sarah Stratton. I came to see you last night at the dorm, remember? About Trish?"

"Yeah, sure. Hi, Professor Stratton."

"I had a couple more questions for you. Could I meet you later today?"

"I guess. I'm kind of working, though. I have a kiddy lit paper that's like thirty percent of my grade due the day we come back from break. What kind of a moron makes a paper due on the day after spring break?" she groused, and then seemed to remember whom she was talking to. "Anyway," she mumbled. "I have a couple hours. My brother's picking me up later to go up to my parents' house. I guess I could meet you."

Sarah ignored the lack of enthusiasm and said, "Great. Are you in your room?"

"Right," Jen said, laughing in a way that told Sarah she'd asked a stupid question. "Like anyone could study in that place today! It's like a tomb. No. I'm over at the Union. I guess I could do a food break or something, in like maybe an hour?"

"Okay," Sarah agreed, suddenly feeling ancient and out of touch. "I'll meet you by the front doors."

"Will Raj be with you?" Jen asked with a sudden burst of enthusiasm.

"Um, no, Jen, he's—"

"Oh, duh! Vampire." She laughed. "Okay, look I gotta go."

"Wait, how do you know—" But Jen was already long gone.

* * * *

"Of course I knew he was a vampire!" Jen was looking at Sarah like she'd lost her mind. "Gorgeous guy, spooky eyes, talks in my head. What else would he be?"

Sarah glanced around the crowded dining room, but no one was paying attention, or at least no one who thought it was odd to talk about vampires. "I don't know," she said. "I just thought—"

"You need to expand your horizons, Professor Stratton. That's what my lit teacher said last week. 'Expand your horizons.' Of course I don't think he meant vampire lit, but, hey, to each his own, right? Isn't that like Shakespeare or something?"

"Um, no, that was Cicero. So you don't think he, I don't know, took advantage of you last night?"

Jen gaped at her, seemed to realize what she was doing and shut her mouth, checking around quickly, before saying, "Raj was like the sweetest guy I've ever met. And come on, Professor Stratton, even *you* must have noticed he's a total babe. I wish my last boyfriend had been half as nice. All he wanted was—"

"Okay." Sarah held up her hand. She wasn't really interested in hearing what Jen's last boyfriend had wanted. "That's great. I'm going to go now. I just wanted to make sure you were all right."

"Sure," Jen said, seeming puzzled. "Why wouldn't I be?" Her face brightened. "Listen, if you see Raj tell him 'hi' for me, okay? And tell him—"

"I'll tell him," Sarah said quickly, standing up. "Thanks, Jen. If we need anything else, I'll call."

"Or Raj could call," Jen called after her as Sarah hurried from the dining room. "I'm up really late every night."

* * * *

Sarah was not only exhausted, but depressed by the time she got home from meeting Jen. Her first reaction had been relief that the girl was all right, but as she drove home, all she could think about were the things she'd said to Raj the previous night before storming off. She remembered the look on his face, his disbelief that she would accuse him of rape, and then his look of betrayal as the meaning of her words sank in. What an idiot she'd been. What a total moron. And still he'd waited until the stupid cab arrived and she was on her way before leaving the parking lot himself. She closed her eyes against a wave of regret. What had she done?

She parked in front of her house and dragged herself up the front stairs, wondering if she should call Raj and apologize. It was still daylight, which meant she wouldn't have to risk having him hang up on her. She could just leave a message on his voice mail and slink back into her corner of guilt. But, maybe he wouldn't even listen to it, maybe he'd hear her voice and hit delete, which was no more than she deserved. *Damnit.*

She unlocked her front door, grateful that Mrs. M. was over at her son's house today and not waiting to pounce with another Tupperware container. Her cell rang as she was pushing the door open and she dropped her purse on the floor, fumbling her keys as she patted her pockets looking for the phone. She grabbed it on the fourth ring, just before it would have gone to voice mail.

"Hello," she said, somewhat breathlessly.

"Sarah Stratton?"

She grew still, listening hard. The voice was familiar, but . . . "Yes," she said cautiously.

"This is Edward Blackwood. I believe we met, in a manner of speaking, the other night. You were having dinner with the vampire, Raymond Gregor."

"Oh." Her lungs strained to produce enough air for that one syllable, to keep breathing in and out. She sank down on the stairs, heedless of her purse sitting on the floor by the still open front door.

"Of course, we weren't properly introduced," Blackwood was saying. "But I was speaking to that police detective, Mr. Scavetti, and he mentioned your name."

"I see."

"I thought perhaps we could have lunch, Ms. Stratton."

She could feel her heart laboring in her chest, but there didn't seem to be any blood going to her brain. Had there been something snide about the way he said her name? Or was she hearing things that weren't there because she was so terrified?

"That's very kind," she managed to say, "but I'm afraid I'm rather busy right now, what with exams and my own research. I couldn't possibly—"

"I was under the impression you were working with the vampire on the Cowens case."

Sarah put her head between her legs, forcing the blood to rush back to her brain so she could think. It made breathing more difficult, but she would have fainted otherwise.

"Are you all right?" Blackwood's oily voice was full of concern.

"Yes," she all but gasped. "Yes, I'm sorry. You caught me in the middle of my exercise routine; I'm a bit out of breath is all."

"Ah. I am sorry to interrupt. We at the Institute believe firmly in a healthful exercise regimen. I myself work out with a trainer regularly, although I do have a weakness for fine food." He gave a self-deprecating laugh that was as phony as every other word he'd uttered since she had stupidly answered the phone without checking her caller ID. Not that it would have mattered. Blackwood was a persistent man. She remembered that much.

"Shall we have lunch tomorrow?" he said, proving the accuracy of her impression.

"Forgive my bluntness, but why, exactly, do you want to have lunch with me?" Sarah asked, reminding herself yet again that she was no longer a scared teenager. She was a grown woman and if she didn't want to have lunch with someone she didn't have to.

"Well, as you may know, I'm helping my friend William—that is Patricia's father—get through this terrible experience. And as you seemed to have information—"

"Mr. Gregor is a friend, Mr. Blackwood. We were having dinner, nothing more. I don't know why you would think—"

"Come now, Susan, there's no need for that with me."

Sarah's heart jumped so hard, it jolted her into the sharp ridge of stair behind her back. "Pardon me?" she whispered.

"You hair is somewhat darker and, of course, it's been over ten years, but, if I may say so, you've grown into a lovely woman, Susan." He repeated her name with emphasis.

"Don't call me that," she managed to say with some conviction.

"Of course," he said smoothly. "I certainly understand your desire for privacy. The tabloid press has always been intrusive, but now with the Internet scattering images around the world in only moments, they've gotten quite out of hand."

Sarah found her anger. "Is that a threat, Mr. Blackwood?"

"I'm offended you would think so," he protested, but he didn't put any real effort into it. "My only purpose in contacting you is to help a dear friend save his daughter before it's too late." He paused for calculated effect. "It isn't too late, is it, dear? I mean why else—"

Sarah closed her eyes, feeling the weight of inevitable destiny bearing down on her. "What is it you want?" she asked dully.

"A simple meeting. A pleasant lunch perhaps between old friends."

We're not friends, she thought viciously, but only to herself. Blackwood would be a formidable enemy, and she had little or no defense against the kind of campaign he could wage against her. "When?" she asked.

"Tomorrow at Chloe's. Say, two o'clock? Noon is so common."

And Edward Blackwood would never want to be *common*. "Fine."

"Marvelous. I'll look forward to it, then. Good afternoon . . . Sarah."

She sat and listened to the dead air, feeling panic welling up in her chest until it became a physical pain. She wanted to scream in frustration, anger, desperation. Tears filled her eyes. She wanted to talk to someone; she *needed* to talk to someone. She wanted Raj. But she couldn't have him, because she'd been too stupid, too blind, to see the man behind the vampire before letting her own fears run away with her emotions and taking it all out on him.

She pulled her knees up and dropped her face into her hands, letting the tears come as the setting sun dropped below the horizon, its fading light shining through her half-open front door.

It was the sound of voices that woke her. Sarah raised her head. The room was dark and it took her a minute to figure out where she was. She shivered with more than the cold, realizing she'd fallen asleep sitting on the stairs, her door standing half open. Her back ached as she straightened from the uncomfortable position, and she held tightly to the banister when she stood, supporting legs that were cramped from sitting too long. The slamming of a car door made her jump and she hurried to the door, closing and locking it before peering cautiously out the window. But no one was there. She turned on the porch light anyway and wearily climbed the stairs, hoping she would sleep . . . and not dream.

Chapter Thirty

Raj drove up to the warehouse, parking in the shadows between the security lights. Inside, it was dim and quiet. A few of the human guards were lounging in the living area, playing what looked like a video game, headphones on. Em was leaning against one of the SUV's, talking to Yossi's Angel, or rather listening intently to what the much smaller woman was saying. Raj didn't know what Angel's real name was, but given her true age and Japanese ancestry, it was unlikely that it was Angel. To everyone in the vampire community, however, she was Yossi's Angel. She was also one of Raj's best human assets, with a quick mind and an even temper, and training in several martial arts. Perhaps more importantly, she could change her appearance and attitude in remarkable ways. Tonight, she looked like herself, an eighteen year old with black, waist-length hair. When Em saw Raj, she motioned him over. He sighed impatiently and checked his watch, but there was still some time before he could call the West Coast. He walked over, giving Em a questioning glance.

"Tell our master what you told me," she said to Angel.

Angel dropped to one knee. "My lord," she murmured and waited for permission to speak further. Raj gave Emelie a pained look and gazed down at the perfectly straight line of pale scalp down the middle of Angel's dark head. He hated this vampire shit.

"Get up, Angel," he said gently. "And tell me what's going on."

"Yes, my lord." She stood with her usual economy of motion. "As instructed, I followed Sarah Stratton throughout the day. She remained home until late morning at which time she traveled to the local university and met with a student, Jennifer Stewart. Jennifer is the room—"

"I know who she is. Go ahead."

"Jennifer and Sarah met for lunch. I was unable to hear most of their conversation, as the dining room was extremely noisy. However, as Sarah was leaving, Jennifer called out to her, telling her that you, my lord, could call her at any time." Angel kept her eyes lowered in embarrassment, clearly thinking Raj was targeting the young human. It reminded him uncomfortably of Sarah's still-fresh accusations. "What else?" he asked too sharply.

Angel ducked her head briefly and continued. "Sarah was visibly distraught after the meeting. She went directly home, but as she was opening her front door her cell phone rang. In her urgency to answer the phone, she dropped several items and left her door standing open while she talked, so I was able to hear her side of the conversation. It was Edward Blackwood calling her, my lord."

Raj stiffened to attention. "Blackwood? What did he want?"

"From what I could deduce, he wanted to meet her. Sarah was

clearly reluctant to do so, but did finally agree to a meeting."

"Details?"

"Chloe's restaurant at two o'clock tomorrow afternoon. I have already coordinated with Simon. He will provide a small transmitter which I will contrive to place on Sarah's person. Simon is quite confident that he will be able to record the entire encounter."

Raj wanted to pound something. Why was Sarah meeting Blackwood? She'd told him he was a family friend, someone she wanted to avoid. Had she lied about that, too? "All right," he said finally. "You stick close to her tomorrow, Angel. Whatever happens, I don't want her going off with him alone. Em, let's put Simon in close. He can monitor the bug and back up Angel at the same time."

"Yes, my lord. I've spoken to him, and he'll set up right across the street. Chloe's has windows all along the front, so there's a good chance we'll have a visual, as well."

"Forgive me, my lord. But there's more."

Raj looked at Angel. "More?"

"My lord . . . it would seem, that is, I assume . . ."

"Just say it, Angel," he said impatiently, thinking maybe he *was* a monster if even Angel was afraid to speak openly to him.

"I don't want to presume, but I thought you'd want to know . . ." She drew a breath through her nose and forged ahead. "After the phone call, she was even more upset. Her front door was still open and I could hear her crying," Angel said softly, no longer looking at him directly.

Raj stared at her, his thoughts blanked by a rage that threatened to swamp every ounce of self-control he possessed.

"Go get some sleep, Angel," Em said quietly.

"Yes, ma'am. My lord," Angel whispered.

Raj barely registered her departure. His hands were clenched against a nearly overwhelming desire to shove a fist through the gleaming black fender of the SUV next to him, his jaw tightened against a howl of frustration. He looked up and even Em took a backward step at the fury on his face.

"Who's on Sarah tonight?" he ground out.

"Cervantes."

"Get him on the phone." As Em dialed, Raj turned and stormed toward the exit. Em followed, handing him the phone as they stepped outside. He put it to his ear. "Where is she?"

"I believe she's retired for the night, my lord. Her door was still open when I arrived, but she closed and locked it soon after. The porch light came on and then the lights upstairs."

Raj swore softly. She'd left her door hanging open? That wasn't like her, was it? But how the hell would he know? He barely knew her. *Damn it.* What he wanted to do was rush over to the house and make certain she was safe, but since she clearly counted him among her nightmares, he didn't think a visit from him would make her feel any better.

"Thanks, Cervantes. Let me know the minute anything changes." He handed the phone back to Em. "We're going to Corfu and I've a call to make on the way."

"My lord," Emelie ventured, "perhaps we should stop by—"

Raj spun and speared her with a steely gaze. "That wasn't a suggestion, Emelie."

She caught her breath. "Yes, my lord."

He strode outside and over to the BMW, yanking open the passenger door and throwing his keys over the roof toward Emelie. "You're driving," he growled.

Em caught the keys one-handed and slid into the driver's seat. As she pulled smoothly out of the warehouse parking lot and onto the street, he punched in Duncan's number.

"What's going on, boss?" she asked.

He ignored her, staring out the window and thinking about Sarah crying on the stairs of her damn rickety duplex. From his cell phone's speaker, Duncan's voice said, "Good evening, Raj."

* * * *

Raj thanked Peter Saephan and disconnected. He'd promised to keep Raphael informed, assuming this matter turned out to be something other than a local dustup.

"What was that all about, boss?" Em's voice interrupted his thoughts.

"That was Raphael's pet doctor," he said casually. Em turned to stare at him. "Watch the road, Em." She jerked her attention back just in time to avoid running a red light. "I called Duncan last thing this morning. There was a message waiting for me when I woke up tonight."

"Raphael let you talk to Saephan?"

The light changed and Raj winced as she floored the accelerator. "He did," he said, answering her question. And then he shrugged. "If someone really is selling vamp blood, it could come down on all of us. And all I wanted was to ask a few questions."

"Wow. Maybe he really meant all that alliance bullshit you told me about."

Raj nodded staring out the window. "Maybe he did."

"So, what did Dr. Saephan say about our missing researcher?"

He looked at her. "He says if Edwards is doing this, she'd normally need as many donors as possible, but since it's vamp blood we're dealing with, he thought two or three would do it."

"Vamps or humans?"

"Both. He said the choice of women is probably just the vamps' preference. She can't just use bagged blood for the humans, because the physical bite changes the chemistry."

Em was staring at the road, listening to every word. "So the women are probably still alive then. That's something."

"For a while anyway, yeah."

They turned down Lake Road and the blood house came into view. Raj studied the white clapboard farm house and said softly, "Well, that's an improvement."

Em's head swiveled his way. "I meant to talk to you about that," she snapped. "I can't believe you came out here with no backup. What if—"

Raj gave her a cool glance. "Are you suggesting I'm incapable of defending myself, Emelie?"

Em blinked and swallowed hard, but held her ground. "Not at all, my lord," she said formally, but then added with a snarl, "And you know it. But that doesn't mean you're invincible. A simple phone call, that's all I'm asking."

Raj permitted himself a bare smile. "Done. Can we go inside now, Mommy?"

"Fuck you," Em said cheerfully and threw open her door.

They crossed the uneven lawn together, bypassing an orderly line of club goers waiting for admittance. Two vamp bouncers stood at the door, checking IDs and producing waivers, which were then signed and delivered to a third vamp sitting at a small table just inside. The bouncers gave Em the once over, which she ignored, and nodded respectfully to Raj, holding the crowd back so he could go ahead. The music was just as loud as before, but then everyone seemed to prefer it that way. Why have a blood house in the boonies if you couldn't crank up the sound? There was a steady stream of vamps and humans heading for the private rooms upstairs, and more than a few cries of pleasure emanating from dark corners downstairs. But as long as it stayed inside the house, Raj didn't much care what they did.

"My lord."

Raj turned to find Mick waiting for him. When their eyes met, Mick dropped his gaze immediately and bowed from the waist, holding the bow for several seconds before straightening with a grin. "I'm honored at your return, my lord, and with such a lovely companion." He admired Emelie's shapely form, his appraisal resting somewhere south of her face.

Em gave Raj a *"Can I smack this fucker"* look, but, to her obvious disgust, Raj only shook his head in amusement. "My lieutenant, Emelie," he told Mick. The other vamp's eyes widened slightly at Em's title, and Raj felt the jump in power as the big vampire instinctively challenged Em for her position. He stifled a smirk of satisfaction as Emelie flicked Mick off with a surge of power and a vicious grin. She might *look* like a runway model, but Em was tough. Certainly tougher than any of Raj's other vampires, and that was saying something.

Mick stumbled back a step, his expression grim, but he gave Em a grudging nod of acknowledgment and turned back to Raj. "I trust everything is as you wanted, my lord?"

"Yeah, it looks great. Listen, is there somewhere we can talk?"

The other vampire's eyes widened in surprise a second time. "This way." He led them back through the house to what had probably been a closed-in porch at one time, but when Mick closed the door to the house, the loud music shut off as if a switch had been thrown. "A vampire can't think with that racket sometimes," he joked. "Please, my lord." He waved at a cluster of chairs, then sat down himself, leaning back and looking completely relaxed, despite his confrontation with Raj only a few nights ago. Raj had noticed this about vampires. They were most comfortable when there was a clear chain of dominance. Mick sat easily under Raj's power as long as Raj demonstrated his superior strength. Problems arose only when there was no obvious hierarchy, or when, as with Krystof, the would-be dominant held the reins so loosely as to be ineffective.

"So, Mick," Raj started, "You know why I'm in town, right?

Mick shrugged. "I know what I've heard. Krystof brought you in to deal with these missing girls because the cops have him worried." He eyed Raj speculatively. "Jozef thinks it's bullshit. He's not entirely thrilled to have you back."

"Yeah, I noticed that," Raj said dryly. "I'm not all that thrilled to be here either." He had a sudden thought and leaned forward, head cocked curiously. "Jozef doesn't think there's a vamp connection to these crimes?"

"He didn't come right out and say it, but I got that vibe from him. Why, do you think there is?"

"I notice a lot of new faces in town," Raj said, changing the subject. "And not just in the blood houses. Half of the meat in Krystof's basement the other night was new to me."

Mick snorted. "Why do you think everything was so out of control here? The old man's making new bodies so fast I'm surprised the cops aren't investigating *that* instead of a few missing pieces of—" His gaze swung to Emelie. "—er, young women. At least some of those guys have to be from out of town, or maybe right off the boat, so there's no one to miss 'em."

"Any theories on why Krystof's so eager for converts? Any threats you know of?"

Mick snorted. "Other than you, you mean?" he said in an unconscious imitation of Jozef. He shook his head. "Nah. A couple of the old ones have disappeared, though. Maybe Krystof's worried—"

"Old ones?" Raj interrupted. "Like who?"

"I can only tell you what I've heard. But you know Byron?"

Raj nodded.

"Yeah, well, his partner Serge disappeared a few weeks back. At first I thought he'd just moved on, what with Krystof the way he is. But Serge wouldn't have gone without Nina—that's his longtime squeeze. She's a fucking ghost since he's been gone, and Byron's not saying nothin'. That's who you should be talking to."

Raj frowned. "They still have that video store in the city?"

"Yeah, but you're just as likely to catch them at home. I hear Byron's not really paying attention to business these days."

Raj and Emelie stood up, followed by Mick. "All right," Raj said. "Thanks, Mick. Good job here, by the way."

Mick put a hand over his heart and bowed again. "Thank you, my lord."

"Yeah," Raj said. "Okay. We're out of here, Em."

* * * *

Em followed Raj's quick steps across the grass and back to the BMW. "Keys," he snapped. She handed them over with a sigh.

"I knew it couldn't last," she muttered.

Raj barely heard her. "You or any of the guys hear anything like that in the other blood houses?"

"No, my lord. Not a whisper. Just that the houses are overcrowded, and like I told you before, no one so much as blinked at our unknown faces, although I did tell the guys to tamp down the power levels, make it seem like they were fresher than any of them really are."

Raj frowned. *Old vamps.* He had to find out *who* was missing besides Serge. If the missing vamps were strong enough to pose a challenge, it could be someone eliminating the competition before making a play, but if not . . . He didn't know Byron and Serge that well, but Serge had never struck him as the type to strike out on his own and Byron was weak.

He dropped into the driver's seat and started the car. "Byron and Serge live in the city close by the store, maybe even the same lot. See if—" But Em already had the address and was entering it into his dashboard GPS, her Blackberry in hand. "Nice," he said.

"I live to serve, my lord."

"Right," Raj snorted.

The video store was dark when they arrived, which was consistent with what Mick had told him, but still surprised Raj. Byron and Serge had always stayed open late, since their fellow vampires were some of their best customers, especially the old ones who were slow to accept the newer technologies. He circled around the block to the modest house which sat right behind the store. This was an older part of town, from when a lot of merchants lived in the same building as their businesses. With the rise in inner city crime, most of the stores had relocated long ago, but two vampires had no need to worry about crime. A single demonstration of the consequences, and the local hoods pretty much left the store alone.

He and Em crossed to the small, neat house. "Think anyone's home?"

"Everything's closed up pretty tight, but there's at least one human inside," Em said, concentrating. "And a vamp too."

"Byron and Nina, if Mick's right. Okay, let's ring the doorbell like the unwanted guests we are."

They made no effort to be quiet, letting their boots thud on the wooden porch and hitting the pretty, little doorbell hard and long. Raj waited one minute and rang again. If Byron had the brains God gave a hamster, he'd know that not only were there two vamps on his doorstep, but that either one of them could rip the door open without the courtesy of ringing the fucking doorbell.

A slice of dim light split the doorframe as the door cracked open and Byron's pale face came into view. He stared at Raj for a long time, glanced at Emelie and back at Raj, then pulled the door wider and pushed open the screen door. "Come on in," he said listlessly.

Emelie pushed past Raj to go in first—she was becoming a regular pain in the ass when it came to his security. He caught a brief flash of movement in the back hallway—Nina, he assumed. Byron made a soft sound of distress, and Raj turned to find the other vampire watching him fearfully.

"I won't hurt her, By. You should know that."

Byron's shoulders slumped. "I don't know anything anymore, Raj. Not a fucking thing." He looked around as if not knowing where to sit, as if it wasn't his own house they were standing in. Finally, he gestured toward what was obviously the living room and led them in that direction, flipping a switch as he walked into the room. A standing lamp came on in the corner, highlighting a big comfortable chair and an old table filled with books. Flanking it was a long overstuffed couch, with one of those handmade blanket things thrown over the back. The light was bright enough to read by, but soft enough for a vampire's eyes.

"Have a seat," Byron said. He headed for the big chair, but paused, and with a glance at Raj, settled on the couch instead, scooting down to make room for Em, careful to leave enough space between them that they wouldn't have to touch.

"Thanks," Raj said. He sat on the big chair, but didn't settle back into it. He felt like an intruder in this house, in this room. "Sorry to bother you, By."

"It's no bother. I guess I knew you'd get here eventually."

"Why was that?"

Byron studied Raj's face carefully before answering. "Because something's going on." His voice trembled with an anger that grew with every word. "And someone told you about Serge, or you wouldn't be here. So don't play fucking games with me, okay?"

Emelie bristled, but Raj held out a hand, easing her back. "What do you think's going on?" he asked softly.

"How the fuck do I know? Krystof sends word he wants Serge, so Serge goes. That was something like six weeks ago and we haven't heard a single word from him since. Nina says he's still alive, that she'd know if he was dead. But where the fuck is he then?" His voice broke on the last sentence and Raj looked away, giving him the privacy of his grief.

"Mick said there might be others missing too," he said quietly.

"Yeah," Byron mumbled. "Maybe. There's a couple of 'em used to come around the store a lot, but I haven't seen 'em lately. One of 'em's Barney. He's an old timer who likes movies, especially the classics that are hard to find. Charles is younger . . . I mean, you know, relatively speaking. He likes the video games and porn—our big sellers, you know?"

Raj nodded.

"Yeah, well. I haven't seen either one of them for a while. 'Course it could just be they're like me and too fucking scared to leave their own houses."

Raj stood and jerked his head toward the door, telling Emelie they were leaving. Byron looked up in surprise and stood quickly. He wobbled awkwardly and Raj frowned. "You taking care of yourself, By? You won't do Nina or Serge any good if you starve yourself."

"Nina doesn't want me to leave the house. She's afraid I'll disappear, too . . ." His voice trailed off. "She's not eating right, not sleeping. I can't risk her—"

"I'll have some blood sent over—" Raj glanced at his watch and frowned. "Tomorrow night. In the meantime, you need anything, you call me or Em here." He handed Byron one of his cards before walking back to the front door. He started to pull it open, but Byron's voice stopped him.

"You'll let me know?" he called.

Raj turned around.

"Whatever you find out," Byron pleaded. "Whatever it is, Raj. Let me know. Nothing could be worse than not knowing."

He nodded. "I'll let you know. In the meantime, take care of yourself and Nina." He couldn't get out of the house fast enough, striding down the walk and through the gate to where his car was parked. He beeped the locks open, but instead of getting in, he paced down the alley with hard strides and back again. "Goddamn it, Emelie. What the hell is Krystof thinking?"

"Maybe he's not," she said. Raj stopped and looked at her as she added, "You've been telling me for months, hell, years, that the old man's not right in the head. Maybe he's finally lost it for good and he's not thinking at all anymore."

"Fuck. All right, it's come to Jesus time. I'm going to pay a visit to the old man tomorrow night. See what he knows about all of this." He closed his eyes, feeling the sun threatening on the horizon. "I can't do anything more tonight. Let's get going. I don't want to end up bunking with the monkeys in the cage," he said echoing Em's earlier comment about the rest of his vampires.

"But it's okay if I do?" Em observed as she slid into the BMW's passenger seat.

"Yeah, because you live to serve, right?" Her only answer was a raised middle digit. Raj smiled, and it occurred to him that it might be the last thing he had to smile about for a while.

Chapter Thirty-one

Sarah was running a little late as she hurried down the street toward Chloe's elaborate red and gold awning. She'd been reluctant to use the restaurant's valet parking, preferring to park her own car for a quick getaway. But that had meant using the public lot two blocks over. She rushed past the long bank of windows which sat several feet above street level and overlooked the main square. Blackwood was already there, sitting at a window table in full view of anyone who happened to pass by—no doubt quite intentionally. The maitre d' was hovering as his famous guest sipped a glass of red wine and chatted amiably.

The light was perfect, highlighting the gold in Blackwood's fake blond hair. Granted it was probably very expensive fake blond hair, but a bleach job by any other name . . . She smirked, and for the first time since getting up that morning, felt a little better about things.

Not that it lasted very long. She went up the stairs, stepping aside to avoid being knocked over by a herd of suited businessmen who pushed through the door just as she reached for it. She'd taken no more than two steps inside the restaurant when Blackwood caught sight of her. He waved and said something to the maitre d', sending the twitchy little man scurrying across the restaurant in her direction.

"Ms. Stratton," he said breathlessly. "Permit me to—"

"The ladies' room?" she inquired, interrupting.

"Oh," he said, clearly stunned that she wasn't rushing over to the great man's table. "Yes, of course. Just that way. I'll tell Mister—"

"Thank you." Sarah escaped down the ornate hallway, calling herself every kind of a coward. It wasn't as if she could get out of the meeting altogether, so what was the point in delaying it the five minutes it would take to wash her hands? She sighed and pushed open the door, nearly gagging on the scent of perfumed air freshener. She washed her hands quickly, drying them with a paper towel from a tidy wicker basket sitting on the sink. Tossing the damp towel, she dug into her purse for her lip gloss. Not that she cared how she looked, but it delayed the inevitable for a few more seconds.

A young Asian woman came in behind her and stuttered to a halt, waving a hand in front of her face. "Yech! It reeks in here."

Sarah smiled over her shoulder. "I know."

The woman walked over to the sink next to Sarah and washed her hands quickly, leaning forward as she did so to study her perfect, golden complexion. Obviously content with what she saw there—*and who wouldn't be*, Sarah thought enviously—she reached for a paper towel, inadvertently knocking Sarah's purse to the floor. She made a quick grab for it, but so did Sarah. They caught it together and the woman relinquished it with a touch on Sarah's shoulder and an apologetic smile.

"Sorry."

"That's okay," Sarah said. "There's nothing in there but junk anyway."

"Tell me about it. Not yours, I mean. But I swear my purse gets heavier every day and I can't figure out why." They shared a knowing grin as Sarah slung the purse strap over her shoulder, gathered her courage and walked out to face the music.

* * * *

Blackwood raised his big ass off the chair in a semblance of courtesy and said, "Thank you for meeting me, my dear."

Sarah barely acknowledged him, concentrating on sitting down, hanging her purse from the chair and opening the buttons on her coat. She didn't take it off; she didn't plan to be here that long. Blackwood stared at her intently. She took a nervous sip of water as he started talking.

"So, tell me, Susan," he began. She flashed him an angry glance and he backpedaled immediately, pretending to be flustered. "How silly of me. Of course, it's Sarah now, isn't it?" He smiled ingratiatingly. "I do understand your desire for secrecy, you know. The glare of the camera can be exhausting." He waited for Sarah to respond, to comment on their shared misery perhaps, but she remained silent, sipping her water and counting the threads on the table cloth. "Well, then," Blackwood said, filling the silence. "I wonder how you came to be working with the vampire on this matter? I wasn't even aware you were in town and believe me, I have excellent sources."

"I told you, Mr. Blackwood—"

"Edward, please."

"Mr. Blackwood," she repeated firmly. "Mr. Gregor is a friend. Nothing more." *And probably not even that anymore*, she thought to herself, feeling an unfamiliar ache in her chest at the thought. "We were simply having dinner together when you saw us."

Blackwood's cheeks flushed and his mouth tightened in obvious irritation, but he shifted tactics, saying, "William is quite convinced the vampires are behind it, you know. But I'm not so certain."

Sarah looked up at him. "You don't think there are any vampires involved?"

"No, I—" Blackwood began, but then gave her a curious look and leaned forward conspiratorially. "Unless you have something to tell us? I've always felt the police would do well to listen to what you have to—"

"I don't have any knowledge—"

"Don't play games with me," Blackwood snapped, any semblance of friendship disappearing in an instant, replaced by hard intent. "I understand why you haven't gone to the police," he said. "The idiots wouldn't know a true talent if it bit them in the ass. What I don't understand is why you've chosen to throw your lot in with those disgusting blood drinkers. If you're having dreams—"

"Those dreams were years ago," Sarah insisted. "I don't do that any—"

"This is bullshit!" Blackwood nearly shouted. The room around them was suddenly quiet. Blackwood drew a deep breath and sat back with a broad smile, smoothing his ruby-colored tie over the bulk of his gut and waving off the maitre d' who was looking their way anxiously. He took a long drink of his wine and patted his mouth prissily with the neatly pressed napkin.

"We both know what you're capable of," he said in a low voice, that phony smile once again firmly planted on his broad face. "So, *don't* insult me by pretending otherwise."

"What is it you want from me?" Sarah asked tightly.

"What I want is whatever you know about Patricia Cowens and this entire affair."

"I told you. I don't know *anything* and I don't *want* to know anything. Do you have any idea what they put me through back then? The police treated me like a murderer and my parents thought I was crazy. They institutionalized me, *Edward.* I've spent the last ten years doing whatever it takes to forget this so-called gift and nothing you say will change that."

Blackwood regarded her with a smug smile. "Nothing? Well, *Susan,* I'm quite certain the tabloid press would be thrilled to discover that their favorite teenage psychic is alive and well and living right here in Buffalo. Why, I imagine it would make the front pages for weeks if you turned up. You'll be right alongside the two-headed cows and Elvis. And, of course, the tabloids are all over the Internet now too, aren't they? What do you suppose your University colleagues would make of that?"

Sarah sat rooted to her chair, her heart in her throat, watching the last ten years of her life go a little further down the drain with every word from Blackwood's mouth. She'd been so wrong about Raj. He wasn't a monster. He wasn't even close. The real monster was sitting across the table from her in this elegant restaurant, a smug smile on his fat face that said he didn't give a damn about her or anyone else.

"Your refusal to face the truth of your talent is a loss for the entire human race," he was saying. "A true loss. And, may I say, selfish on your part. Surely you owe it to—"

"I don't owe anyone anything," she managed to whisper. "Least of all you." She grabbed her napkin blindly, laid it on the table and shrugged the strap of her purse over her shoulder. She scooted her chair backward to stand, but Blackwood placed a firm hand over her arm on the table, holding her in place. "Now, Sarah, I don't think either of us—"

"Director Blackwood?" She looked up to see a woman bearing

down on them, middle-aged and wearing enough jewelry to feed a small village for a year. "It is you! I'd heard you were in town—"

Blackwood was on his feet in an instant. "Of course, my dear, and what a delight to see you." The woman took his arm, turning him away from the table as she called to someone across the room. Sarah saw her chance and made a break for it, all but running from the restaurant. She passed the wide-eyed maitre d' and shoved her way past a trio of matrons who gasped at her rudeness. Like she cared.

She almost fell down the stairs in her urgency to get away. There was a big, black van parked right in front of the restaurant, and some part of her registered the valet arguing with the driver as she ran past. But she left it behind, along with the curious looks of the suited executives and iPodded teenagers she shoved out of her way. She took a shortcut through a reeking passage between two buildings, dashing around trash cans, nearly tripping over a homeless person who muttered angrily as she disrupted his afternoon nap. She reached her car, keys in hand, thankful for the remote to beep open the doors, because she didn't think she could have gotten a key in the lock with her hands shaking the way they were.

Once inside her car, she locked all the doors and leaned her forehead against the steering wheel, trying to think. She'd have to run. Get out of Buffalo, out of New York. Everything she'd built over these last years would be gone—her career, her education—none of it would matter now. She'd start all over again. She'd saved some money, enough to last her a year if she was careful. A scrape of sound had her sitting up quickly and looking around. No one there, but she shouldn't be sitting here in the open like this. She drew a deep breath and started the car. The car at least was hers, free and clear. She'd paid cash for it, one less thing for her to worry about, one less trail to lead them to her.

She drove out of the parking lot and headed for home, knowing as she did so that by tomorrow, she wouldn't have a home any longer.

Sarah turned onto her street, driving past the duplex and around the block to park in the alley. A worn fence with a rickety gate opened from the alley to the scruffy back yard she shared with Mrs. M. There was a padlock on the gate, but it was on the inside and it hung open most of the time. Neither one of them spent much time back here, except to take out the trash. Sarah fumbled with her key ring as she crossed to the house, trying to remember which one opened the back door. She'd never used it before, but she was sure Mrs. M. had given her a key when she first moved in.

She found the right key and shoved it into the lock, slipping inside and closing the door behind her. Her first thought was to check every shutter and curtain downstairs, closing them all before hurrying upstairs to drape towels over the uncovered halves of her bedroom windows. It was dark with the windows covered, so she turned on a few lights and walked from room to room taking inventory. There was really nothing in the way of furniture that she couldn't leave behind. Maybe she'd done that unconsciously over the years, never buying anything that meant something to her. Maybe a part of her had known this day would come when she'd have to abandon everything once again.

In her study, she opened a small safe tucked into her lower desk drawer. Her passport and a spare driver's license were there, although she'd need a new ID before long. Credit cards would be the easiest way of tracking her, so those would have to go right away. She swiveled her chair around and logged onto the computer, going to her bank's web site. With a few key strokes, she'd transferred all of the funds from her checking account into a separate account under her maternal grandmother's name. Gramma Maude was long dead and wouldn't mind. Sarah had been her only granddaughter and they'd been close. She'd died before everything fell apart, which was probably a good thing. In any event, the account wouldn't remain open long. Eventually, someone—the press or the police—would trace the transfer. But by then the money would be gone, withdrawn in cash from banks or ATMs on her way to wherever she ended up.

That done, she took a look around her study. None of the furniture mattered, but her books would definitely come with her. So would the desktop computer and, of course, her laptop. The boxes from when she'd moved in were downstairs in the closet beneath the stairs. She could start packing tonight and be gone by tomorrow. Her rent was paid through the end of the month, but she'd give Mrs. M. enough to cover an additional month to make up for her sudden departure.

She crossed the hall to her bedroom. There were no memories here. No lost loves, no hot nights of passion. She thought again of Raj. He'd be a passionate lover, there was no doubt of that. Memories of their few encounters still sent shivers through her bones and tightened her gut with longing. What would it have been like if they'd made love?

She closed her eyes and deliberately put the thought away. That was never going to happen. Unless she ran into him at a stop sign on her way out of town, she'd never see him again. Pain swelled in her chest at the thought and she rubbed it absently, surprised to find herself crying. "Don't be stupid, Sarah," she scolded herself. "He's not even speaking to you."

She drew a deep, stabilizing breath. *Clothes,* she thought purposefully, marching over to the closet. All of her clothes would go. She didn't have that many, and couldn't afford to leave them behind, in any event. Not if she was going to be living on her savings for awhile.

She was standing there, staring around and wondering where to start, when the doorbell rang downstairs. She froze, listening, and jumped when her phone rang loudly in counterpoint to the persistent doorbell. She ignored the phone; whoever it was would go to voice mail. Instead, she moved quietly over to the window, wincing when the old hardwood floor creaked noisily beneath her feet. Lifting the corner of one of the towels she'd slung over the curtain rod, she saw a black van parked out front. It was a cargo-type van, with no windows, and there was something about it—a disheveled man emerged from the back, looking as if he'd been sleeping inside, or maybe living there. He slammed the double doors noisily and shuffled around to the side where he opened the big sliding door as well. The interior was surprisingly well lit and filled with equipment, some sort of . . . Sarah drew back in dismay. It was a press van and she knew now where she'd seen it before. It had been in front of the restaurant where'd she met Blackwood; she remembered it from her mad dash down the street.

Her heart sank as Blackwood's phony smile filled her thoughts. The press had been there the whole time. No wonder he'd planted himself so prominently in the front window, he'd *wanted* them to see her, to get pictures of the two of them together. He'd lied to her. Whether she agreed to work with him or not, he already had plans in motion to publicize the whole thing.

She cursed the sleazy con man, fighting off the panic that was trying to rear its ugly head. No sense in panicking. It was only one guy—her doorbell rang again and she heard someone shout down below. Okay, two guys. The man in the van looked up and shouted something back. It was most likely one of the tabloid newspapers, or maybe one of those entertainment magazines. They followed Blackwood's adventures closely, although she'd never been able to figure out why.

Okay. She could deal with this. She'd pack quickly, taking only what she needed for the next month or so. Most of her clothes, even her books would be safe here as long as she paid the rent. She could use the time to set up her new identity, find a new place to live and then when everything had calmed down, come back and get the rest of her stuff. That was a plan. Yes. She could definitely do that. She grabbed a suitcase from her closet and started packing.

* * * *

Two hours later, the local press had arrived in force, not to be outdone by the tabloids when it came to a story about one of their own. They'd knocked repeatedly on her door until she thought their knuckles must be bleeding. They'd even questioned Mrs. M. next door, cameras rolling. Sarah had called and warned her, and her landlady had taken it all in stride, even seeming to enjoy the notoriety a bit.

Sarah thanked her landlady again and hung up, and then just for the hell of it, she checked her voice mail, deleting one message after the other, pretty much on the first syllable uttered. That ass Blackwood had called several times, offering the dubious safety of William Cowens's home as a refuge. How kind of him, Sarah thought viciously, considering he'd sicced the press jackals on her in the first place.

She went upstairs to continue packing, telling herself this whole thing would blow over quickly. Some other story would capture the tabloid's attention and they'd move on from Sarah and what was really not much of a story at all. She peeked out the window again. The anchor woman from the local news was down there, doing some sort of live feed. But the tabloid guys seemed to be packing their gear. It was supposed to be cold tonight, and besides, there was only so much coverage they could milk out of a locked and shuttered house. Once they were gone, she'd load a few things into her car and be gone before sunrise with no one the wiser.

* * * *

This was not good. Sarah peeked out the upstairs window for the umpteenth time. This was definitely not good. Rather than giving up and going home once the sun went down, the crowd of reporters crowding her front lawn had only grown. Tears filled her eyes and threatened to spill over, but she brushed them away, just as she had ten minutes ago, and ten minutes before that. Crying wouldn't do a damn thing. She'd considered going out there and making a statement, but dismissed that idea almost immediately. She knew from past experience that the media's hunger only grew with feeding. And it was never sated, especially not in this day and age when there was no secret too personal, no detail too intimate, to be blared across the pages of papers, magazines and web sites, where they were sucked up in turn by a public who had wholeheartedly embraced the peoples' right to know every damn thing.

A siren burst had her rushing back to the window. Red lights flashed as a police sedan arrived. About time, she thought furiously. All of those reporters and cameras had to be violating some regulation or other. Let the cops clear them out and she'd be right behind them, running as far and as fast as she could. A pounding started on her door downstairs, but she ignored it as she had all the others.

"Sarah Stratton," a deep voice shouted. "Police. Open up."

Okay, well *that* was new. She hurried downstairs, taking the time to open one shutter enough to verify it was the cops. Okay, so it wasn't the cops; it was just one cop. Tony Scavetti. And what the hell was *he* doing here? "Open the door, Sarah!" He pounded again, shaking the cheap door in its frame, and she began disengaging the various locks while she still had a door to open.

* * * *

Sarah stood in her front room facing down Scavetti who was angrier than he had any right to be. She hadn't asked for any of this. "Look," he was saying. "This is bullshit. I want this media circus over now. I'm taking you into—"

"I'm not going anywhere," she insisted, refusing to be bullied. She knew her rights. "If you want this to end, I suggest you start by getting rid of those clowns outside." She stabbed a hard finger in the direction her overrun front yard. "I've done nothing wrong."

Scavetti took a step closer, intruding on her personal space, trying to threaten her with his greater height and bulk. "If I have to arrest you—"

"On what grounds?" Sarah demanded, getting right in his face. She'd spent her entire life being smaller than most everyone else. He'd have to come up with something a lot better than size if he wanted to intimidate her.

"Interfering with an ongoing investigation, withholding evidence, and—"

Sarah barked a laugh. "What evidence would that be, Tony?" she scoffed. "You want to tell the D.A. I've been keeping my dreams from you? What are you now, my shrink?"

Scavetti flushed angrily and opened his mouth to reply, but someone else had started pounding on her door. "Sarah," a woman was shouting.

Sarah frowned. Her first instinct was to ignore it, just as she'd ignored all the ones before, but there was something familiar about the voice. She started toward the window closest to the door, but Scavetti got there first.

"Who the fuck is that?" Scavetti snarled.

Peering around him through the half open shutter, Sarah did a double take. It was the woman from the restaurant bathroom. The one who'd knocked her purse over. What the hell was she doing here?

As if she'd heard Sarah's unspoken question, the woman called urgently through the door, "Sarah, my name's Angel. I work for Raj. I want to help you. Let me in."

Sarah's heart did a little flip. Raj? But that meant he'd known about her meeting with Blackwood. Had he been spying on her all this time? Why would he do that unless . . .

"Sarah, please. Let me help you."

Sarah hurried over to the front door. If there was one person in this whole mess she trusted, she realized suddenly, it was Raj.

"What the hell are you doing?" Scavetti demanded. He reached for her, but Sarah snapped the locks open first, pulling the door open just enough to peek out cautiously. "How do I know Raj sent you?"

"I don't know," the woman Angel said, seeming flustered by the question. She started to say something, but cut herself off with a curse, placing her fingers to one ear as though listening. Looking closely, Sarah saw she was wearing some sort of radio earpiece, like Raphael's security wore. She nodded at whatever the other person was saying. "Go ahead and call Raj," Angel said to Sarah. "No, wait. Call Emelie. She says to tell you—"

If the woman knew both Raj's and Emelie's names, then she had to have been sent by Raj. Sarah opened the door and stepped back.

Angel pushed her way inside and closed the door quickly, shutting out the rush of noise and bodies that tried to follow her. "Thanks," she said breathlessly. "And I really do work for Raj."

"You were at the restaurant today."

"I was. We knew about the Blackwood meeting and didn't want you going there alone. For good reason, as it turns out."

"I don't understand," Sarah said. "Why would Raj—" Scavetti cleared his throat noisily behind her. "Ah," she said turning slightly to indicate the pissed off detective. "This is Detective Scavetti, Buffalo PD. He wants—"

"You don't have to go with him," Angel said immediately, giving Scavetti an unfriendly look. "Raj will be here—"

"What the fuck does that damn vampire have to do with any of this?"

Angel cut him off with a cold stare. "We will wait until he gets here before anything is decided."

"Who the hell appointed him God?" Scavetti snarled. "I don't have to wait for any fucking vampire—"

"Stop," Sarah shouted at Scavetti. "We'll wait," she said told him firmly. "Unless you're prepared to take me out of here kicking and screaming in front of all of that." She gestured at the crowd of overheated press people.

Scavetti frowned, clearly thinking about doing just that.

"Come on, Tony," she cajoled. "What can it hurt to wait until Raj gets here? If you drag me out there it'll be all over the papers. And what good will that do? You don't want me involved in your case, and that's pretty much the last thing in this world that I want either. Maybe together we can figure something out."

Scavetti stared at her, and she could tell he wasn't happy. But she also knew she'd touched a nerve about the press being all over the story. He finally gave her a short, unhappy nod.

"Fine. We'll wait." He checked his watch. "Ten minutes. After that, I don't give a fuck what you say. I'm taking your ass out of here."

Sarah knew when to quit. "Thank you, Tony. I'm going upstairs to pack a few things, just in case," she said.

"Good idea," Angel said. She gave Scavetti a smug look as she followed Sarah up the stairs. "I'll help you with that."

Chapter Thirty-two

Raj opened his eyes to the familiarity of his Buffalo lair. The lights were already up, set on a timer so when he woke there would be the little bit of light he needed to see by. As he swung out of bed, the light increased until it reached a steady, soft level of illumination. His first thought was hunger, but he didn't have time to stop for a live donor. Or so he told himself. He was unwilling to face his growing reluctance to tap anonymous women for blood and sex. Unwilling to deal with the significance of that reluctance in light of his feelings for Sarah Stratton—who was history, he reminded himself firmly.

He went over to the bar refrigerator and pulled out a unit of bagged blood. Loosening the release valve enough to prevent the contents from exploding all over his microwave, he set it for a quick warm up. Less than a minute later, he rolled the bag between his hands to even out the temp and downed it quickly, trying not to think about the woman he'd rather be drinking from instead.

The memory of Sarah's sweet blood hit him anyway—the sudden burst of it when he'd nicked her full lip with his fangs, the warmth as it caressed his tongue and slid down his throat with exquisite slowness. His brain moved on, thinking how delicious it would be to tap her vein, to pierce the velvet softness of her neck as his cock slammed into her tight little body. He could feel her soft curves beneath his hands, could hear her hungry little cries as he'd pressed her against the wall— *Enough!*

He threw the empty bag aside in disgust and forced his thoughts elsewhere. Sarah wanted nothing to do with him, and he had far better things to do than to chase after a woman who thought he raped little girls for fun. He felt the heated rush of righteous anger and welcomed it, letting it fill his gut with determination as he started the shower. He leaned against the tile wall, eyes closed, arms stretched straight ahead of him as the hot water pummeled his neck and back, reviewing what he knew so far. He pictured again the faces of the young women, imagined the scenes at the blood houses where they'd disappeared. When he came to Estelle Edwards, his thoughts skiddedto a halt. It all came down to her. She was the orange in the bowl of apples, the lone rose in a bouquet of daisies. She was the key. A researcher who specialized in blood, who'd been seen talking to Krystof and then told her husband she had a contact in the vampire community who could provide—

He swore viciously when the thought hit him. He slammed his fist against the tile so hard it cracked beneath the strain.

Young women were missing, but *so were old vampires*! Old, but not powerful. That was the crucial element. They were old enough to have fully manifested the one aspect of most interest to human researchers—resistance to disease and aging—but not powerful enough to master children of their own or to bend other vampires to their will. What if the missing vampires were prisoners, just like the young women? What if all of them—vampires and humans—were nothing more than Estelle Edwards's lab rats?

But then why bring Raj in to unravel it? Krystof had to know he'd never stand for something like this. Unless that was the old man's plan all along? Maybe he'd lost control of the project and didn't know how to shut it down himself. Christ! That didn't make sense, either.

He turned off the shower, disgusted with the whole business. Drying off quickly, he was halfway dressed when his phone went off. He picked it up, not surprised to see it was Emelie.

"Em," he said, by way of greeting. "How'd it go today with Sarah and Blackwood?"

Emelie sucked in a breath on whatever she'd been about to say and said, "Right, let's start at the restaurant, then." Raj frowned, but Emelie had launched into her report, so he listened carefully. "Angel managed to get a bug on Sarah ahead of time, so we got the whole thing. Blackwood tried to blackmail her, threatening to go to the press with her true identity—"

"Blackmail her? Wait, what identity?" Raj interrupted.

"Okay, this is where it gets tricky. Blackwood seems to know Sarah from back in California."

"Yeah, she told me. A friend of the family or something."

"Not exactly. Sweet little Sarah hasn't been quite forthcoming with us. Her real name is Susan Siemanski. That name familiar to you at all?"

Raj frowned. Sarah wasn't really *Sarah?* What the fuck? "No," he said. "Should it be?"

"Not unless you spend way too much time on the Internet."

"I pay people to do that for me," he said impatiently. "What the fuck's going on, Em?"

"Susan Siemanski pops up on several web sites, every one of them dedicated to the weird and unknown. Paranormal shit. Our guys cruise those sites looking for supposed vampire activity. It's sometimes a cover for the real thing and we—"

"I know this, Em. Get to the point."

"Sorry. Susan, aka Sarah Stratton, was fifteen when she claimed to be—I guess the word is *channeling* kidnapped women in her dreams. There were two cases made public, a few months apart. In each case a woman was found dead after the police ignored Siemanski's warnings. She drops off the radar after that, which explains why Sarah didn't exist until ten years ago. She must have changed her—"

"Right," Raj cut her off, feeling his own anger grow. She'd been lying to him the whole time, had let him think she'd run away to escape a bad home situation, had let him conjure all sorts of possibilities. And none of it was true. She was a fucking psychic. Was that her connection to this case? Was she getting hints of the missing women in her dreams or whatever the fuck she did? Goddamn it, she'd played him for a complete fool.

"Raj, you there?"

"Yeah. So what's Blackwood want?"

"Tell me your dreams kind of bullshit, but it was obvious he wanted her working exclusively for him, no one else, and especially not us *disgusting blood drinkers*. I believe that's how he put it."

"Imagine that," Raj said absently, pulling a shirt out of the closet and working his way into it without putting the phone down. "And he seemed like such a nice man, too."

"Yeah, well, fortunately one of his fans stopped by and Sarah made a clean getaway. She went back to her house and stayed there. *Unfortunately*, the slick asshole had a camera crew waiting out front to film his triumphant rediscovery of the long lost teenage psychic, or barring that, to follow through on his threat of exposing her. Which, apparently, he's decided to do."

He stopped what he was doing. "What's happening?"

"We have a situation."

Raj heard Emelie talking to someone else, a one-sided conversation, like she was on a second cell phone. He heard her swear and then shout orders to someone in the warehouse. "That was Yossi," she said, coming back to him. Sarah's house is swarming with reporters wanting to know why a psychic has been called in to help find William Cowens's daughter. The police are there too, with that Scavetti guy. He wants to take her into custody—"

"No!" Raj all but roared. He heard Em talking on the other cell again.

"Angel thinks she can persuade Sarah to let her inside. Do you want her to—"

"Yes. I want someone inside that house. I don't want Sarah disappearing into police custody. I need to know whatever she knows about this case. Tell Angel now, Em. I'll wait."

Em spoke briefly and came back. "Okay, Yossi and Cervantes are staying outside, but Angel's hitting the door now. What next?"

Raj was already pulling on his jacket, the phone snugged between his shoulder and his ear. He could hear a lot of noise from Em's end, SUV engines revving to go.

"Em!" he shouted, wanting to be certain she heard. "We need a getaway car, something anonymous."

"Will do, boss," her words were jumping as she ran to join the guys in the SUVs.

Raj punched the exit code for his vault and waited impatiently as the door swung open. "I'll meet you at Sarah's," he said and hung up, racing for the garage.

* * * *

"What the fuck?" Raj took one look at the street in front of Sarah's duplex and circled around the block, remembering an alley of some sort and assuming she had a back door. He'd been a bit distracted the two times he'd been in her kitchen. The east end of the alley was blocked by a chain link fence. He swore viciously and circled around again, turning down the west end of the alley and speed dialing Em as he drove up to and parked behind Sarah's car.

"Where are you?" he asked, before she could say anything.

"We're in three vehicles, two SUVs and the rental sedan. The two SUVs are holding at either end of the block. It's a mess out there, boss."

"Yeah, I saw that. I'm in the alley behind Sarah's. There're a few reporters hanging around back here, but nothing I can't handle. Too dark for the rest of them, I guess. I want both SUVs to come in the front. Tell them to make an impression. You bring the sedan around back; you and I will go in this way. Is Angel in the house?"

"Yes, my lord, along with Detective Scavetti who is not a happy camper, according to Angel. Sarah has dug in her heels and refuses to do anything until you get there. Scavetti's about to blow, but Angel doesn't sound too worried about it."

"I've met Scavetti. I'll put my money on Angel any day. Give her a call, tell her what's about to happen and tell her to brief Scavetti. I don't want a gun in my face when I come through the back door."

"I don't think you're Scavetti's favorite person right now."

"I'm crushed." Raj looked up as a white Taurus appeared in his review mirror, with Em at the wheel. He executed a quick U-turn so the BMW was facing the open end of the alley. Em did the same, pulling up behind him. She got out of the car and gave him an excited grin.

"Fun times tonight, huh, boss?"

Raj shook his head. He had to remind himself sometimes that behind Emelie's cover model exterior was a total adrenaline junkie. She lived for this kind of thing. "Everyone set?"

She nodded. "At your word, they'll hit the gas. Two minutes to the front of the house, two minutes inside."

Raj surveyed the situation in back. The grubby yard was surrounded by a battered wooden fence, and if there was a light, it wasn't lit. A lopsided gate was standing wide open, its padlock hanging uselessly on the fence's U-ring, probably put there by the ten or so diehard press types huddled around their Blackberries in the darkness. Occasionally, one of them would glance up at the house, but nothing was stirring up there, either. Sarah's windows were all covered, blinds drawn and curtains closed, but he caught the flash of the landlady's curious face from an upstairs window next door. The woman would have made a great spy. There was no light leaking into the yard from inside Sarah's duplex, and behind him, the alley was just as poorly lit, with no street lights. A motion activated flood lamp, which had lit up when he drove past, had gone dark again. Three cars were parked along the side, all of them heading into the dead-end, and presumably belonging to the reporters, because the residents would know better. "All right," he said to Em. "I'll give these people a nice nap and then you and I go in the back at the same time Yossi and the others hit the front. They make a big noise, take Angel out as a decoy and storm away. She's about the same size as Sarah, we'll just cover her hair. You exit back here with Sarah and take her to the warehouse. I'll handle Scavetti and whatever else comes up and meet you there later."

"I can handle the cop if you'd rather—"

"He knows me. You take Sarah."

Em studied him briefly. "You're the boss."

Raj nodded. "Give Yossi the go ahead."

* * * *

Sarah sat huddled halfway up the stairs, hugging her knees to her chest, utterly miserable. Poor Mrs. M. was next door, as trapped as Sarah herself. Scavetti couldn't decide if he was more pissed about Raj, or the fact that everyone would now think the Buffalo Police Department, i.e. Tony Scavetti, was using a psychic to solve their very high profile case. Once he'd agreed to give Raj ten minutes, the detective had thrown his hands up in disgust and disappeared into Sarah's living room where she could hear him swearing at someone on his cell phone. Angel was doing pretty much the same, albeit with a lot less swearing, whispering into her headset like some sort of special ops agent in an action flick.

For her part, Sarah didn't know if Raj's imminent arrival was good news or bad, but she did know he could make her disappear faster than she could have on her own and without involving the police. So she sat on her stairs where no one could see her from the outside, listening to the competing mutterings of Scavetti and Angel, and waiting for Raj who probably hated her.

She sat up abruptly, as two things happened all at once. Angel shouted, "They're coming in," and a sudden roar of truck engines and squealing tires sent Scavetti racing for the front door. He cursed violently when Angel whipped the door open ahead of him, but then both stood back as four men in black combat gear stormed through the crowd of shouting, angry reporters, stomped up onto the porch and into the house. Angel slammed the door behind them and Sarah's small hallway was suddenly crowded with big, hulking vampires, while Scavetti was all but thumping his chest in anger. The testosterone was so thick in the air she looked up at the ceiling, expecting to see clouds of it hovering visibly over their heads.

"What the fuck?" Scavetti yelled. "Who the hell authorized—"

"I did," Raj said from the kitchen. With all the fuss and noise at the front door, Sarah hadn't even heard the back door open. She realized that had been the plan, that the team entering through the front had one purpose—to cover their master's entrance from the backyard.

At the sound of his voice, all four vampires turned as one, muscles quivering like horses at a starting gate as they dropped to one knee, along with Angel. Scavetti stared, mouth agog, his gaze traveling from the kneeling vampires to Raj and back again in disbelief.

Sarah heard heavy footsteps, and then Raj's head and shoulders came into view through the banister to her right. Wearing black leather and denim, radiating a dangerous sort of authority, he looked larger than life and twice as lethal as the vampire minions kneeling before him. And while he had to be aware of her sitting there, he didn't so much as glance her way. Her heart clenched painfully. Em strolled in behind him, dressed in black combat gear and looking far better in it than Lara Croft ever did. Raj gestured to the kneeling vamps and they jumped to their feet.

"Detective Scavetti," Raj said calmly. "Is Ms. Stratton under arrest?"

Sarah jerked at the sound of her name, while the police detective glared daggers all around. "I don't fucking need this crap, Gregor," he snarled.

Raj's heavily armed vampires bristled with outrage at this disrespectful treatment of their master, and Sarah shrank back against the wall, expecting violence. But Raj only smiled. "Let me take this off your hands, Detective. I assure you it is none of Ms. Stratton's making. If you're looking for the person who leaked her identity, you should call Edward Blackwood."

So she'd been right about Blackwood. Not that there'd ever been any doubt. The bastard had been phoning almost nonstop all afternoon, clearly figuring Sarah would have no one to turn to but him. He didn't know that she'd rather let Scavetti arrest her than put herself into his greasy hands.

"For all the fucking good it will do," Scavetti muttered in response to Raj's comment about Blackwood. He looked around. "Obviously, you have a plan."

"Angel here will serve as a decoy." He gestured at the diminutive woman. "My people will exit through the front door, as though spiriting away Ms. Stratton, taking off into the night with great fanfare and drawing as much attention as possible."

Sarah looked at Angel who caught her gaze and grinned

conspiratorially. She was leaning into the heavily muscled vampire standing behind her and Sarah wondered if they were a couple, if that was why Angel, who obviously wasn't a vampire, was a part of Raj's company.

"Meanwhile, my lieutenant," Raj was saying, indicating Emelie who snapped off a quick salute in response. He gave her a quelling look, but there was a small smile playing around his mouth as he did so. "My lieutenant," he continued, "will take Ms. Stratton out through the back and transport her to a location known only to my people."

Scavetti had looked satisfied up to that point, but now he scowled. "We'll want to know where you're taking her. And where the fuck will you be during all of this?"

Raj gave the detective a patient look. "I thought you and I could take this opportunity to update one another on our progress, Detective, including, of course, Ms. Stratton's location. Our goal in this matter has consistently been to assist in your investigation, not impede it. Once we have concluded to your satisfaction, I will rejoin my team."

Scavetti looked like he had swallowed something rotten, but he nodded.

For her part, Sarah had some pretty real doubts that Raj had any intention of informing anyone about her whereabouts once they left this house. She also couldn't help noting that it was Emelie who'd be taking her away, not Raj. So much for the knight-on-a-white-horse scenario. She was pretty sure none of those scenes involved having the knight's sidekick ride away with the rescued maiden. She also wondered if anyone was going to ask her opinion about any of this, or if she was going to be treated like just so much baggage—

"Is that acceptable to you, Sarah?"

Jerked out of her thoughts, she raised her head and found Raj looking at her for the first time since he'd shown up out of nowhere. She studied his ice-blue eyes and found not a trace of warmth for her anywhere in their cold depths. She swallowed around the tightness in her throat and nodded. "Yes. Thank you."

Raj held her gaze a moment longer. "You should call your neighbor and see if she wants to be rescued as well," he said in a cool voice.

"Okay," Sarah whispered. She rose quickly, grateful for the excuse to go upstairs and away from the speculative looks of Emelie and the other vampires. She had taken only one step when a thought occurred to her. She stopped and turned around to ask, "What about my car?" Raj just looked at her. "I'll need my car wherever we're going," she insisted. She didn't know exactly what she'd do or where she'd go, but she definitely knew she didn't want to endure this frigidly polite Raj any longer than necessary.

He held her gaze a moment longer and then glanced at Emelie. "Give me your keys," she said, addressing Sarah. "I'll have one of the guys bring it to the safe house later."

"Okay," Sarah agreed. She went upstairs to call Mrs. M. and to grab the duffle bag she'd packed earlier, before the press had descended and thrown all of her plans into the dumper. She'd go along with Raj's escape plan for now. But at the first opportunity, she would be gone. If he didn't want anything to do with her, that was fine. She didn't need him to get away from this town. She'd orchestrated her first disappearance when was she eighteen years old and broke. She could sure as hell do it now. Raj wouldn't have to worry about her much longer.

Chapter Thirty-three

The maneuver went off like clockwork. Not that Sarah expected anything else. Emelie seemed to know what Raj wanted before he could ask for it, and there was no arguing once something was decided. His vampire guards paid almost fanatic attention to every word he said, but then, what he said seemed to make sense, so why not?

Mrs. M. had agreed to be evacuated and plans were quickly made to drop her at her son's. Raj said he would take care of her after everyone else was gone, and he and Scavetti had finished their discussion. And he hadn't said a single word to Sarah since asking her to call Mrs. M.

When the time came, every light in the house was doused, and Raj's team of black-clad vampires, with Angel tucked amongst them, stormed through the front door and into the yard as if the Dogs of Hell were on their heels. Before they were off the porch, Emelie was hustling Sarah out the back door and through the yard, where she almost tripped over someone's body. She stifled a shriek and grabbed Em, who laughed quietly.

"Don't worry. They're still alive."

"What happened to them?" Sarah whispered, maneuvering around what she now saw were several people, looking particularly ghostly in the bluish light of their Blackberries and cell phones.

"Raj happened to them," Em said, with some satisfaction.

"What does that mean?" Sarah snapped irritably.

Em tsked, holding up a hand for quiet as they went through the gate and into the alley, where a boring white Taurus was parked behind Raj's sedan. There were tens of thousands of white American sedans just like this one all around Buffalo. They were as common as the wind, and Buffalo was a very windy city.

In minutes, they were out of the alley and onto the street. Emelie made one disparaging comment about the car's gutless engine, but she stayed within the speed limit as they headed toward the airport. She glanced at Sarah and said, "I'm taking you to the warehouse for now."

"Why didn't Raj leave with us?"

"Because anyone can drive this tedious little car, but only Raj can do what Raj does."

"What does that mean?" Sarah demanded again.

"Make all the reporters go away," Emelie said in a spooky movie voice and laughed.

"Great," Sarah muttered, not seeing the humor.

"Don't worry. He'll mess with their memories a bit, but they'll all be fine, even that nasty police detective—or at least as fine as he ever gets. Raj just doesn't want anyone to remember a bunch of vampires arriving en masse to save your cute little ass."

Sarah blushed. "I don't care what he does to them. I hate those people."

Emelie gave her a longer look. "Is there somewhere you'd rather go? Family maybe?"

Sarah stared out the window and shook her head. "No. No family."

"What about your parents, or your brothers?"

Sarah turned and gave Emelie a flat stare. "You checked me out."

Emelie nodded easily, no embarrassment, no apology. "It wasn't easy, if that's any consolation," she offered.

Sarah took a deep breath and let it out. "It doesn't matter anymore, does it?" She jerked a thumb over her shoulder. "They all know who I am now. I'll have to start all over again."

"Raj could help you with that. The vampire community has resources."

Sarah laughed bitterly. "I don't think Raj would give me the time of day unless he had to."

Emelie gave her a puzzled look. "He rode to your rescue today, didn't he?"

"Yeah," Sarah admitted. "But only because he wants this case solved and I'm the best lead he's got. So far, anyway. I probably won't even be that for much longer."

Emelie startled her by reaching out to snap her fingers in front of Sarah's face. When she recoiled, Emelie said, "Huh. Well, you're not blind, so the only alternative is stupid."

"Excuse me?"

"Raj is crazy about you, little human."

"Raj hates my guts, skinny vampire."

Emelie laughed. "*Skinny vampire*," she repeated. "Awkward, but accurate. So tell me, Sarah," she said deliberately. "What exactly did you do to my master to turn him around the way you have? He's been a bitch to get along with the last few days and I think it's your fault."

Sarah met Emelie's certain gaze and turned away, unwilling to admit what she'd done.

"Oh, come on, Sarah. We're going to be spending a lot of time together for a couple of days. It'll be more fun if we can talk girl talk— you know, guys, makeup, hair, shit like that."

It was Sarah's turn to laugh at the idea of Emelie being interested in *girl talk*. "What did Raj tell you?" she asked.

"You may not have noticed, Sarah, but Raj can do a fair imitation of the Sphinx when he wants to. He hasn't told me shit. And that's saying something, because Raj tells me pretty much everything. He's my Sire and that makes him pretty damn important, but he's also my best friend. He was the first person ever to see me as something other than what he needed me to be. I would die at his command without hesitation and I *will* kill anyone who harms him."

"Oh."

Emelie grinned. "Don't worry, that wasn't a threat. Raj'd kill *me* if I harmed a hair on your pretty head. But I'm thinking whatever you did had to be something bad because that vamp *is* crazy about you."

Sarah sighed. "Did Raj tell you we went over to the university the other night and talked to Jennifer Stewart? Trish's roommate?"

"Yes. We've been doing the three dollar tour of Buffalo blood houses the last couple of nights because of it."

Sarah blinked in surprise. Raj had been continuing the investigation without her? It was stupid, but she was sort of hurt to discover that.

"And?" Emelie said impatiently.

Sarah cringed. She had a pretty good idea of what Emelie's reaction would be to what she was about to say.

"I don't know anything about how you all do stuff. I mean, I know you can make the act of drinking blood feel really good—not that I've ever *done* that."

Emelie hooted loudly, obviously amused by Sarah's inexperience.

Sarah scowled at her and continued. "Apparently Raj was talking to Jennifer, um, in her head, I guess you'd say. You know, telepathically or however you do it. I think he only had her talk out loud eventually so I could hear, but I didn't figure that out until later. I didn't know *then* what was going on."

Emelie's face grew solemn. "What did you say to him?" she asked, her eyes suddenly dark with accusation.

"I told him what he'd done was the same as rape," Sarah said in a small voice. "That he'd raped Jen's mind instead of her body."

Emelie closed her eyes briefly, as if in pain, shaking her head slightly. "You and I have to talk," she said somberly. But then she lapsed into silence, making a left turn down a long, dark street, eventually pulling up in front of the same abandoned-looking warehouse where Sarah and Raj had stopped what seemed like a lifetime ago. Back when he'd still liked her.

Sarah sighed as Emelie drove past the office door, stopping instead in front of one of the three big loading bay doors. Jamming the car into park, she reached over to the back seat and dug into a black canvas duffle bag, emerging with what looked like a heavy-duty garage door opener. Point and click, and the left-most door rolled up on nearly silent tracks. Emelie dropped the remote into her lap and drove the car inside, clicking it again to close the door behind them as soon as they were clear.

"Home sweet home," Emelie announced and turned off the engine.

"What is this place?" Sarah asked, staring through the window.

"This, my dear, is why Raj is going to be the next Vampire Lord of the Northeast. Raw power is good and he's got lots of that, but it's brains that makes the difference, and Raj is a fucking genius when it comes to strategic planning. He bought this place years ago in anticipation of this day."

Sarah gave her a skeptical glance. "This day?" Either Emelie was talking about something other than her own predicament, or Raj was more than a strategic genius, he was a damn fortune teller.

Emelie laughed as she swung the car door open and climbed out. She grabbed the duffle from the back and said, "There's a lot more to this day than you realize, little human. One hell of a lot more."

"Tell me something I *don't* know," Sarah snapped back.

"How much time do you have?"

Sarah swung around. "What?"

"You said tell you something you don't know. Well, how much time do you have?"

"Har, har." Sarah watched enviously as Emelie strode away from her. She looked like a model on a runway despite the heavy bag thrown over one shoulder and the functional black combat gear she wore. Or maybe because of it. The contrast only accentuated her very feminine appeal. As if aware Sarah was watching her, she turned around and walked backward for a few steps, grinning. "Come on, Sarah. I've got a story to tell you and I'm going to need a drink first."

"A drink? But—"

"Don't be such a wuss." Emelie dropped her bag near a pile of similar gear and sauntered back to hook Sarah's arm, leading her across the large, empty space toward some sort of living room in the corner. Since Emelie was as strong as any other vampire, Sarah had a choice between going along or being dragged like a rag doll. She went along.

They crossed into the faux living area which was about the size of Sarah's entire first floor. It was defined by a thick-pile carpet, or maybe just a really big throw rug. Several couches and chairs were scattered at odd angles, although every one of them was turned toward a wide-screen display worthy of a private theater and complete with a dizzying variety of electronic devices. Emelie dropped Sarah's arm and walked over to a bar which stood along one wall, with several rows of bottles lined up on a counter behind it. Emelie grabbed one of the bottles and poured herself a shot of some clear liquid. She offered the bottle to Sarah who shook her head.

"Raj got me hooked on vodka decades ago," Emelie said. "When it was still only commies who drank it." She laughed at her own joke and threw the shot of liquor down her throat. Sarah almost coughed in sympathy, but Emelie didn't seem at all bothered by the alcohol. "Tastes better with blood in it, but I don't want to sully your innocent sensibilities." She winked at Sarah and poured herself another shot, downing it the same way.

"Okay," she said, drawing a deep breath and letting it out, as if reaching some momentous decision. Hands resting on narrow hips, she gave Sarah a speculative look. "Have a seat, Sarah. I'm going to tell you a story. It's one that very few people know—in fact, only two people in the world know it, and that includes me."

"Uh, I'm not sure—"

"Oh, pooh. You're a scholar, right? Where's your curiosity? You're about to hear how I became a vampire."

Chapter Thirty-four

Em poured another shot, swallowing it quickly. "I was gang raped." She glared at Sarah, as if daring her to comment. When Sarah said nothing, she continued. "The circumstances don't matter. Let's just say I was more attracted to the cook's daughter than the young men who called at my parents' house to play suitor, and I did something stupid trying to make up for it.

"Raj found me while . . . Anyway, he pulled some of them off me, scared the rest away. I don't remember much about that part. I don't really try very hard. But I remember afterward. He took me back to his lair. It wasn't fancy, but it was safe."

She leaned back against the bar, a half smile on her face. "I know what you're thinking. He's a vampire, right? A sensible girl would have run from him screaming. But I knew who the real monsters were and it wasn't the nice vampire offering me some hot soup."

Rubbing her hands up and down her arms, as if suddenly cold, she walked over to one of the couches, picked up someone's discarded jacket and slipped it on. "The true monsters were altogether human. Those men could have been my cousins or uncles. Hell, for all I know, some of them were. I was beaten and raped nearly to death. She stared down at the floor, her face blank of any emotion. "Stupid," she said at last, then drew a deep breath and met Sarah's gaze.

"Raj offered me a choice that night. He would heal me, wipe my memories of the rape and send me back to my parents. Or freedom. A chance to be myself. The choice was easy."

"Have you ever regretted—"

"Never," Emelie said immediately. "Never. Raj might say differently. As good a leader as he is, as powerful a vampire, he never asked to be turned. But I love my life, and I love Raj. Not as a lover. We were never that. I have no interest in men, and Raj would never, ever force himself on anyone. You were way off base on that. But I love him as my master and my friend, my true creator. He's the best man I've ever met, Sarah, vampire or not, and I've lived a long time." She leaned forward intently, forcing Sarah to look at her. "And I will not tolerate *anyone* causing him pain."

Sarah sighed. "I really fucked up, didn't I?"

Emelie barked out a laugh. "Yeah, you really did. And he's not happy you lied to him about who you are, either."

"I lie to everyone about that," Sarah said dismissively. "No one knew before today."

"What about your friends?"

"No one," Sarah repeated.

Emelie cocked her head as if listening, then took two steps and crouched in front of Sarah. "Listen to me. Raj is almost here. I've never seen him care about a human the way he does you. This whole thing tonight? He wouldn't have done this for anyone else. But if you want him—and you're a fool if you don't—you've got to make him believe he's not a monster."

"He's not!" Sarah said, outraged at the very suggestion.

"No, but he sometimes thinks he is, and you pretty much told him you think so too."

"I—" Sarah remembered the things she'd said to Raj and blew out a long sigh. "Damn."

"That about sums it up," Emelie agreed. She stood and began walking toward the exit. By the time she reached the door, it was opening and Raj was striding through.

"My lord," Emelie said, her voice full of affectionate respect.

"Em," he said, not even glancing at Sarah. "When you send someone back for the car, tell him to check inside and around the house. I want to make sure we didn't miss anyone."

Sarah sank deeper into the cushions and stared at him, brooding. Granted, she'd been way out of line the other night, and if he ever gave her a chance, she'd be happy to apologize profusely, but he didn't have to be such a dick about it. She'd never told anyone her real name, never trusted anyone that much, not even Cyn, so why would he think she'd spill her guts to him? She tried to build up some anger toward him, but it wasn't working. Of course, it didn't help that he looked so damn delicious standing there in his tight jeans, his t-shirt straining over his broad chest beneath the leather jacket. She remembered the smell of that jacket, the soft leather against her cheek, the zipper rubbing . . . *Ah gods.* She twisted around on the chair, turning her back on him and slouching down so she didn't have to look at him. He was probably relieved not to have to look at her anymore, too. Not that he'd been looking anyway. Son of a bitch.

* * * *

Raj knew Sarah was watching him, knew she was waiting for some acknowledgment from him. He saw her flinch when he told Em to have one of the guys check the house and felt just a bit guilty. She'd been through a lot today and the worse was yet to come. She'd probably lose her job over this, and it would be difficult, if not impossible, to get a new one with all the publicity. That asshole Blackwood would no doubt be happy to give her a job at his phony institute, but Raj knew she wouldn't even consider that. He wondered if she had enough money to get by for a while, and then wondered why he cared. It wasn't like she'd been honest with him about anything at all.

Besides, he knew if he gave an inch, if he let himself care even a little, that inch would become a mile and she'd be right back in his gut, her presence gnawing away at him until he was forced to touch her, and then . . . Well, there was no doubt where that would end. He shook his head, disgusted with himself. Jesus, he was nearly two hundred years old. Maybe he should grow a pair and stop acting like a Goddamned love-struck teenager. He heard a little hitch in Sarah's breath from behind the sofa and wondered if she was crying. *Damn.* He had to get out of this fucking warehouse.

He switched his gaze to Em and found her fighting a smile. Great. Just fucking great. "I think it's time we paid Blackwood a call," he said gruffly. "He's got the resources to back something like this, and I'm curious why he was so set on keeping Sarah to himself."

"Plus he's kind of an asshole."

"That too." One of the bay doors rolled open suddenly to admit the two SUVs carrying Angel and the decoy team who'd whisked her away. The doors closed behind them and they piled out of the trucks, their excited post-op chatter falling quiet when they saw Raj standing there. "Problems, Yos?"

"None, my lord."

"Good. Simon, I need to know where Blackwood is right now, then you, Danny and Cervantes are with me. Everyone else, check your gear and take the rest of the night off. We'll meet first thing tomorrow night and see where we stand."

Emelie leaned in close, speaking low enough that only he could hear. "I'm not well-suited to the role of babysitter, boss. Yossi and Angel are here. They can take care of—" She stopped at the look on Raj's face. "Yeah, yeah." She gave a long-suffering sigh. "You were a lot easier to work with *before*—"

"Don't say it, Em," he warned.

She shrugged. She didn't have to say the words. Sarah Stratton had gotten under his skin good, and if he didn't get away soon, he never would. It was probably too late already, but he wasn't ready to admit that, fool that he was.

* * * *

Sarah heard Raj leave. Not so much that he was noisy as that his vamps all became very quiet when he was around. The bay door slammed down and the noise level rose as his minions went about their usual activities. Several were heading in her direction and she wiped her eyes quickly, not wanting anyone to see she'd been weeping like a big baby. She dried her face on her t-shirt and glanced around, trying to remember where she'd dropped her duffle bag. Or if she'd even brought it in from the car.

"Your bag's back by the sleeping quarters." Sarah jumped at the sound of Em's voice right behind her. She sat up and looked around to find Raj's lieutenant regarding her with a carefully blank expression. "Why don't I show you where you'll be sleeping?" Em asked.

Sarah nodded her agreement. She had to think about what she was going to do next, but she was too tired right now. Tomorrow she would drive . . . Wait a minute. "My car?" she asked Em.

"We'll send one of the human guards over in the morning. He'll check out the house and pick up your car then. Why? You in a hurry to go somewhere?"

"No," Sarah said quickly. "I just feel better, you know, having my own transportation."

Em gave her a skeptical look. "Sure. Well, it'll probably be back here by the time you wake up. Come on, I'll show you around. You'll probably be with us a few days either way."

Don't count on it, Sarah thought privately. She'd be gone way before that.

Chapter Thirty-five

Raj and his team arrived well after midnight. It was a sprawling house on a quiet street full of sprawling houses. This one was a two-story redwood spread out over a lush two acres with a turquoise pool glimmering in the party lights. A big white tent had been set up and crowds of partygoers mingled inside and out, wearing full black tie regalia.

"This it, Simon?" Raj asked.

"Yep. He's still there. Several people are Tweeting from the party.

"Wait here. Danny, Cervantes . . . let's go."

Raj paused on the front steps, scanning the partygoers' minds, looking for Blackwood. He winced at the overload of anger, jealousy and greed he associated with a gathering of this sort, but eventually zeroed in on the HR founder and planted a suggestion that would take him into the house and away from the crowds. Telepathy was Raj's particular strength—but the fewer humans he had to deal with the better.

"No need to knock," he said, walking up to the door. "Mr. Blackwood is about to let us in."

True to his prediction, the door opened and Blackwood stood there, staring at them in confusion. "Gregor?" he asked. "What—" His eyes widened as he took in the two bulky vampires flanking Raj.

"Let's talk, Blackwood," Raj said pleasantly.

"Really, I don't think—"

"No," Raj commented. "You don't, do you? Well, maybe it's time you started. There must be someplace in this monstrosity we can speak undisturbed?" He looked around coolly.

"Yes," Blackwood said, suddenly becoming aware of the potential embarrassment. "Of course. This way."

He led them down a hall and into a split-level library. Danny and Cervantes shut the double doors and stood blocking the exit, while Raj crossed to stand in front of the big desk Blackwood had interposed between them, as if it would do him any good. The HR founder had rediscovered his testicles on the journey to the library and was now puffed full of righteous anger. "I'd like to know the meaning of this, Gregor. The mayor *and* the police commissioner are among the guests here tonight, so don't think you can—"

"Silence," Raj said quietly. Blackwood's voice stopped mid-sentence, his face reddening with effort as he struggled against Raj's command. The full import of what was happening seemed to hit him finally, and he sank into the leather desk chair, sweat popping out on his suddenly pale face.

"I was going to do this the nice way, Blackwood," Raj said. "But seeing you here at this big party in your fancy tuxedo while Sarah

Stratton is hiding out and wondering where she'll run to next . . . I find myself in the mood to inflict some pain. So . . . tag, Blackwood. You're it."

* * * *

Raj eyed the puddle of quivering humanity dispassionately and hoped the stains on the rug would come out. It was a very nice rug, Afghani, he thought and probably expensive. Blackwood twitched, moaning when Raj toed him experimentally with one boot. The trip out here hadn't been a total waste. He'd taken some personal pleasure in causing the HR founder pain, especially after what he'd found in the man's narcissistic mind. He wasn't the one behind the kidnappings and didn't know anymore about it than what the newspapers could tell him. The entire affair had meant nothing more to him than a chance to curry favor with William Cowens. Finding Sarah mixed up in it had been pure chance, like finding a diamond lying on the street. Mostly, he disliked her and was glad for her troubles after the way she'd treated him at their lunch meeting. This last had enraged Raj so much he'd almost killed the man. But he hadn't wanted anyone to see a connection between Sarah's uncovering and Blackwood's sudden death.

He kicked the human again, harder this time. Blackwood's eyes opened and he scuttled across the floor, coming to rest against the back of the desk where he jiggled into a sitting position, his eyes watching Raj fearfully.

"You're leaving town tomorrow, Blackwood. And you won't be back. Not Buffalo, not New York. I don't want you setting foot in this part of the country ever again, you understand?"

Blackwood nodded rapidly.

"You'll forget Susan Siemanski ever existed. Sarah Stratton is someone you've never heard of. You or any of your people contact her or come anywhere near her ever again and I'll know about it. You believe me, don't you, Edward?"

Another spasmodic nod.

"Good. Then we're done here. Just one more thing." He rested his gaze on Blackwood and blinked lazily. Blackwood's mouth opened and he tried to scream, but nothing came out.

Cervantes closed the doors behind them as they left the library, walking unhurriedly down the hall, their booted feet silent on the thick carpet. Raj snagged one of the waiters as they passed the kitchen, grabbing the man's arm and catching his gaze. "I think Mr. Blackwood might be having a heart attack," he said, and then wiped the man's memory of himself and his people and walked out the door.

Chapter Thirty-six

She was in a car, the rough fabric of the seat abrading her naked skin like steel wool. She groaned and tried to roll over, but she couldn't. She was weak, too weak. Something was wrong. There were voices, men talking, arguing briefly, and then the car swerved suddenly, crushing her against something metal. Her eyes cracked open to darkness and she realized she was not in a car, but in the trunk. Salty tears rolled down her cheeks, burning like acid.

The car stopped and the trunk lid opened, blinding her with the dim light. Someone was there, a big man reaching for her, picking her up like she weighed nothing. He walked a few steps, lifted his arms and . . . she was flying through the air, her scream of terror nothing more than a pitiful whine. Rocks bit into her flesh as she hit the ground and rolled down a hill, stiff weeds and brush tearing and scraping.

She lay still, unable to move, listening as the trunk lid slammed, as car doors closed and the engine faded into the distance. Shivering in the cold, nearly gagging with the stench of wherever they'd left her, she forced her eyes open and stared up at a moon that was little more than a curving slice of white in a clear sky. It was beautiful. Despite the overwhelming smell of rot, despite the freezing air biting into her bare skin, she smiled. And somewhere in her brain, a small voice told her what she already knew. She was dying. She quieted the voice, just turned it off. She gazed at the sickle moon, and at the brightly lit buildings much too far away to do her any good and then closed her eyes.

* * * *

Sarah sat up in with a cry, reaching automatically for the switch next to her bed. She fell to the floor with a hard thump, yelping at the feel of cold linoleum where there should have been a warm rug. Her heart hammered as it all came back to her in a rush. The crowds of reporters, the warehouse . . . Regina!

She crawled on all fours, finally locating the table next to the bed where she'd left her watch. She checked the time on its illuminated dial. Nine o'clock, but was it morning or night? She scrambled to her feet and opened the door. A wave of sound, truck engines and shouted voices, greeted her. She stumbled outside and down the stairs, almost falling against Danny, the lady killer who'd been Raj's bartender at the club that night in Manhattan a hundred years ago.

"Whoa, beautiful," Danny said playfully, standing her upright. "You okay?"

"She's alive," Sarah croaked. The voices died and she was aware for the first time that she'd interrupted a meeting of some sort. Raj was standing there, and so was Em and a bunch of other vampires and humans. And they were all staring at her. She found Raj's face in the crowd. "She's alive. Regina Aiello. We have to find her."

The expression on his handsome face remained dark and cold.

"Please," she begged him, tears of fear and frustration shielding her from the ice in his gaze. "You can hate me if you want, but please find her. Please, Raj. They never listened to me before, and they all died. But we can save Regina. Please. *Please.*" She sat down on the stairs, sobbing, her heart breaking. This couldn't be happening again. Not again. *Damnit!* She wouldn't let it happen again!

Angrily rubbing away her useless tears, she grabbed the railing and stood. Raj was still staring at her. She thought there was a glimmer of compassion in his gaze, but she couldn't trust it. Not when Regina's life was at stake.

"I know where she is," she told him, her voice growing stronger with every word. "And if you won't help me, I'll find her myself." A small sob escaped her lips with the last word, and she swallowed hard.

"Get dressed," he told her sharply. "Danny, you and Cervantes come with me," he ordered, his eyes never leaving Sarah. "Em, send the teams out, but stay in touch."

Sarah was still zipping her jacket when the industrial-sized door rolled up and they sped into the night. Danny was driving, so she told him what they were looking for. All she had to go on was what she'd seen through Regina's eyes, but she'd recognized those buildings in the distance.

"Which way, beautiful?" Danny asked, stopping at the first big intersection they came to.

Sarah sat on the front bench seat of a huge SUV, with Danny on one side and Raj on the other, his arm slung over the seat behind her. He shot Danny a scowl at the endearment and let his big hand drop to her shoulder, pulling her slightly away from the other vampire. She cleared her throat, determined not to be cowed. They couldn't do this without her. "We're going to the university campus. You know where that is?"

"Sure thing," Danny said, winking at her. "It's a big place, though. Anywhere special?"

"South of the medical center, but we're not stopping. I just need to position myself relative to the main buildings and we'll go outward from there."

"What?" Raj snapped.

"I know what Regina knows," Sarah said calmly. "She's on a hillside of some sort south of the campus. The distance is difficult to judge, but it smells like a dump or a landfill."

Raj swore beneath his breath, but nodded at Danny who grinned and turned right, gunning the truck well above the speed limit.

Sarah's heart lifted when they reached the campus. She'd been pretty sure she was right about the buildings, but seeing it brought tears of relief to her eyes. Buffalo was a very flat place, and she'd questioned the idea of anything like a hill in the vicinity. "That's it," she whispered. "That's exactly it." She gulped down her tears. "Okay, can you drive that way, Danny?" she pointed in a generally southward direction. "I'm not sure exactly . . ."

"I've got it, darlin'," he said with a charming grin. "I'll find your girl for you."

Raj growled softly over her head and Danny sobered immediately, becoming all business. She heard a snort of laughter from the backseat where Cervantes sat. He'd been silent until this point and she'd almost forgotten he was there.

Sarah fidgeted nervously as they drove further away from campus. She kept glancing back over her shoulder, trying to align their position with what she could see of the buildings. Cervantes was watching her every time she turned, his eyes gleaming a pale yellow in the low light. That would have startled her once upon a time, but the last couple of weeks had made her pretty much immune to the oddities of vampires.

Someday in the future, when all of this was over and her life was back to something close to normal, she'd do a little research. There were a lot of things her friend Cyn hadn't told her about vampires, like the fact that their eyes glowed in the dark or when they were angry, or about how perpetually aggressive they were, constantly testing dominance against one another. But maybe it was just the ones who hung around the really powerful vampires, like Raphael or Raj. There had to be hundreds, probably thousands of them, who lived quiet, uneventful lives.

"Sarah."

She jumped at the sound of Raj's voice. The truck had stopped. Danny's hands were clenched on the steering wheel, and she could feel the tension fairly zinging off Raj's body next to her. And there was something else. She drew a breath and nearly choked. The smell was disgusting. "Oh my God," she gasped. She began pushing at Raj, desperate to get out of the truck. "Get out," she demanded. "Let me out!"

"Sarah . . ." He started to say something else, but then he shrugged and opened the door, sliding out of the way, catching her when she would have fallen from the high seat. The ground underneath her feet was squishy with moisture, the dirt and debris broken down by the constant freeze and thaw cycle of this time of year. She spun around until she could see the buildings in the distance, and then took off.

"Wait!" Raj called after her, but she ignored him, trading glances between the uneven ground that she could barely see beneath her feet and the campus lights far away. "Sarah." His heavy hand grabbed her from behind, scooping her up and holding her when she tried to break way. "Stop it," he ordered. "We'll find her," he said in a softer voice, next to her ear. "Look."

Danny and Cervantes were standing nearby, eyes glowing in the pitch black night as their heads swiveled slowly from side to side, seeming oblivious to their surroundings and yet keenly aware of everything at the same time. Raj's arms around her loosened, but he didn't let go of her, preventing her from interfering in whatever it was his minions were doing. Almost as one, the two vampires stared at the same spot, down the hill from where they were standing.

"My lord," Danny said, but Cervantes was already moving faster than Sarah could follow. One moment he was five feet away from her and the next, he was so far downhill she wouldn't have been able to see him, if not for the pale glow of his eyes. Danny moved closer to Raj, as if whatever they'd found made him uneasy, bringing out the ingrained vampire need to protect his master that Cyn had talked about.

"Cervantes?" Raj called.

Cervantes was a big man, not huge like Raj or even Danny, but big nonetheless. He appeared out of the stinking darkness like a golem from a fairy tale, eyes glowing that pale yellow, his head a square block over broad shoulders, and carrying the limp form of a young woman in his arms.

Sarah cried out and would have gone to them, but Raj stopped her again. "Let go," she demanded, pushing at him.

"Take her to the truck," Raj ordered. "Danny, open the back and get that blanket from inside."

"She's alive?" Sarah asked, stunned. She hadn't really believed Regina could be saved. Not after everyone else had died.

"Barely," Raj said in a tight voice. He held onto her, almost dragging her around to the back of the SUV, waiting while Danny spread out a blanket and Cervantes laid the small form across the back of the cargo space.

Raj met Danny's eyes and then transferred his gaze to Sarah in a clear signal to the other vampire. Before Sarah could object the other vampire had taken hold of her, while Raj stepped up to the truck and the injured young woman's side.

"What's going on?" Sarah asked in confusion. She couldn't see what Raj was doing, with Cervantes standing next to him and Danny holding her in place. Then it suddenly occurred to her that they didn't *want* her to see what he was doing.

"Oh, sweetheart," she heard Raj murmur softly. "She's been drained nearly dry and not gently," he said more loudly. He whipped off his jacket and shoved his sweater sleeve up to his elbow. Sarah saw him raise his arm to his mouth and bend over the dying young woman.

"Wait. What're you doing?" she demanded.

Raj's sharp glance was a slash of brilliant, icy blue over his shoulder before he turned back to Regina. "He's saving her fucking life," Danny hissed next to her ear. "Now, shut up."

Sarah gasped in surprise that the genial Danny would talk to her that way, followed quickly by intense embarrassment that she probably deserved it. Once again, she'd assumed the worst of Raj, and this time it could have cost Regina her life. "I'm sorry," she muttered.

Raj ignored her, but Danny's grip eased slightly. Sarah shivered in the cold air, trying to imagine how much worse it must have been for Regina, lying naked and dying in a pile of garbage. Thrown away because she was of no more use to them.

"Put her in the car, Danny." Raj's voice drifted over to them, and it took Sarah a minute to realize he meant her, not Regina. She opened her mouth to protest, then closed it with a snap, letting Danny lead her around to the passenger compartment where he lifted her onto the seat and closed the door. Walking swiftly to the other side, he settled in the driver's seat and started the engine, turning the heater on. Sarah drew her knees up to her chest, hugging the warmth to herself, and waited.

She heard rather than saw Raj stand up. "Careful," he said.

Sarah twisted around and saw Cervantes wrapping Regina in the blanket before he picked her up, cradled against his chest, then came around to slide onto the back seat while still holding her in his arms.

"Let's go," Raj said in a tight, angry voice, as Sarah scooted over, making room for him in the front. He spat out an address and Danny took off.

She waited until they were back on the main highway before daring to ask quietly, "Are we taking her to a hospital?"

Raj glanced at her and away. "Home. We're taking her home."

Sarah blinked, swallowing her first instinct which was to demand to know why. Instead, she sat and thought for a moment, and then she understood. Raj had probably already done more for Regina by giving her his blood than a hospital full of doctors and medicine could do, and if they took her to a hospital, there would be questions. Questions neither she nor Raj wanted to answer.

"Does someone live with her?" she asked in a small voice.

"Her mother."

Sarah nodded, remaining silent until they pulled up in front of a two-story duplex very much like the one she shared with Mrs. M. The only difference was the neighborhood.

"Can I . . ." Her soft question faded away as Raj turned to study her. His face was blank, but his eyes still had that icy sheen to them. "Um," she swallowed nervously. "I don't mean . . . that is, your eyes."

Raj's expression changed in an instant, becoming more animated, more human. A quick blink and his eyes returned to their pale but perfectly normal color. "Cervantes," he said, opening the truck door. "You'll carry the girl. Danny, wait here. Come on, Sarah."

It was more of a command than a request, but since it was what she wanted anyway, Sarah didn't argue. As they walked up the narrow, concrete walkway to the dark house, Raj leaned close enough to say, "It's your turn, sweetheart. Use those all-American girl-next-door looks of yours and convince Mom we're the good guys. I don't want the cops coming down on our heads over this."

Sarah's heart began to pound. She glanced down at what she was wearing—jeans, Nikes and a t-shirt under a light-colored fleece jacket. She looked more like one of her students than a professor, but maybe she could make that work for her. She pulled the scrunchy out of her hair, finger combing it down and over her shoulders, knowing it softened the angles of her face and made her look younger. Raj stepped up to the door and stood to one side, looking at her for a go-ahead before ringing the doorbell.

It took a few minutes, and he had to ring the bell more than once. It was, after all, nearly midnight. But eventually Sarah heard the slap of mule slippers just like her landlady wore and then the porch light came on. The woman who answered the door could have been Mrs. M., give or take fifteen years, and just like that, Sarah knew how to convince her.

"Mrs. Aiello?"

The woman blinked, taking in the unlikely trio standing on her porch. "Yes?"

"Mrs. Aiello, my name is—" Sarah stumbled over the unfamiliar syllables. "Susan Siemanski. I've been working with the police." She saw the woman's eyes widen, saw her gaze fix on the bundle held so carefully in Cervantes's arms.

"Is that . . ." Mrs. Aiello's trembling fingers covered her lips, afraid to say it out loud.

"If we could come in, ma'am?" Raj said gently. "It's cold."

"Oh my God, oh my God." The woman's voice rose as she fumbled with the flimsy lock on the screen door. Sarah felt Raj tense next to her and knew he was worried about the noise attracting attention. She pulled the door open and pushed into the house, putting her arms around the distraught mother, hustling her back inside. "Quietly, Mrs. Aiello. Please. We don't want the press—"

"No, no. Of course not. I'm sorry. Do you want . . ." She seemed uncertain where to go, her face pale, hands shaking.

"It's all right, Mrs. Aiello. Regina's fine. Or she will be now that she's home with you." Out of the corner of her eye, she saw Cervantes laying the girl gently on a big overstuffed sofa. Mrs. Aiello snapped out of her shock, hurrying over to kneel before her daughter.

"My baby, oh, thank you, Jesus, Mary and Joseph." She bent her head over Regina, shoulders shaking with sobs.

Raj gave Sarah a long look. She flushed and stood aside, clearing the way for him to kneel next to the sofa. Cervantes moved away

almost reluctantly, as if unwilling to relinquish his claim on the injured
Regina, but a glance from Raj had him crossing back to the front door,
where he stood waiting.

"Mrs. Aiello." Her head came up and she turned to meet Raj's
gaze. She smiled when he took her hand, and Sarah was startled to see
Raj smile back. Not the half sneer she'd come to expect from him
lately, but a genuine smile, the smile you'd give a child. He leaned
closer and stroked her face with one of his big hands. It was a loving
touch, gentle and understanding, and Sarah was ashamed as the memory
of the awful things she said to him came back to haunt her.

"She's a happy person, my Regina," Mrs. Aiello whispered suddenly.
"Always laughing and smiling, even when we argue. She can never
hold a mean for long,"

Raj nodded silently, then placed the mother's hand in her daughter's
and stood up smoothly, meeting Sarah's gaze across the room. It was
everything she could do not to step back in fear. His eyes were gleaming,
seeming to bleed power as he stood there staring at her. She froze,
trapped in his spell. Then he moved, and suddenly, he was just Raj
again, handsome, arrogant, and impatient to get the hell out of here. He
strode across the room in two long strides. "Let's go," he said.

"Good bye, Mrs. Aiello," Sarah called softly, but Regina's mom
had already forgotten all about them.

Sarah stepped out onto the porch with a sigh of relief, breathing in
the fresh air, clearing her head of not just the warmth of the overheated
house, but the cobwebs that seemed to cling to her thoughts. Cervantes
was already climbing into the truck and Raj was not far behind. She
hurried to catch up with him.

"What did you do?" she asked breathlessly. When he ignored her,
she reached out and grabbed his arm, forcing him to stop or drag her
along. Raj spun around, his glare colder than the night. A little thrill of
terror raced through her, bumping her heart into a faster beat and
catching her breath in her lungs.

"What do you think I did, Sarah?" He gave her hand on his arm a
pointed look and she dropped it with a murmured apology.

He strode away once again and she raced to catch him again.
"You might as well slow down, damn it," she complained. "You're not
going to leave me here and you know it."

He ignored her, standing at the open truck door and waiting
impatiently as she clambered up and slid to the middle of the seat.
Apparently Raj was angry. What a novelty. If they'd been alone, she
might have demanded to know what the problem was *this* time, but
Danny and Cervantes were listening to every word, so she bit her
tongue and said nothing.

Raj yanked the door closed and snapped at Danny to "Get the fuck
out of here." Maybe Danny knew what the problem was, because he

spun the truck away from the curb and took off with a squeal of tires.

It was a silent ride back to the warehouse, but instead of going inside, Danny pulled the SUV into the parking lot and looked over at Raj, his eyebrows raised in question..

"You two check in with Em," Raj ordered, opening the door on his side. "Take one of the blood houses. Sarah's going with me."

Sarah jerked around to stare. She wasn't sure she wanted to go anywhere with him in this mood, or any other, for that matter. But neither Danny nor Cervantes seemed to care what Sarah wanted. The truck's taillights were already disappearing by the time she'd processed the fact that they were leaving.

"Get in the car," Raj said, beeping the locks open on his car.

"Maybe I should—"

"Get in the car, Sarah," he said, staring at her over the gleaming black roof of his BMW.

"Where are we—"

"Get. In. The. Car."

Sarah took a deep breath and looked around. She was in the middle of an empty parking lot, on a dark street, miles away from anyone or anything, with not even her emergency twenty dollars in her pocket. The warehouse was right behind her, of course, but somehow she doubted they'd let her inside, even if anyone was there. And she really *didn't* believe Raj would hurt her. She sighed, opened the car door and slumped into the seat, thankful that at least she didn't have to climb five feet straight up to get there. Small favors.

* * * *

Raj brooded as he sped down dark streets, not sure where he was going. Sarah sat next to him, silent for once, not demanding to know what he was doing or where they were going or any of the myriad explanations she was always insisting upon. She probably thought he was angry. Which he was, although not at her. What made him furious was what he'd discovered inside Regina Aiello's head.

Making a last minute decision, he took a hard right turn onto the thruway, the rear end fishtailing behind him on the slick surface. He caught the jerk of Sarah's hand as she grabbed for the armrest and smiled in satisfaction.

"What happened, Raj?" Sarah said suddenly, in a low, tense voice. "Please tell me."

So much for her silence. When he didn't say anything, she continued. "I know you got inside Regina's mind. I'd like to know what you found there."

"Why? So you can be certain I didn't rape her?"

She flinched away from him so hard her head bumped against the window. He could hear the tears in her voice when she said quietly, "I tried to call you. I left messages."

Raj ignored her and kept driving.

"I spoke to Jennifer," she added.

"I know. She told me."

"You talked to Jen? But—"

He glanced over and saw the hurt in her eyes that he'd called Jennifer but not her. But then Jennifer hadn't accused him of being a rapist, had she?

"I said I was sorry," she said softly. "I know you wouldn't . . ." She looked away from him and swallowed hard. "You have to understand what it's like for me. What it's like for *them*."

He gave her a sideways glance. "Them?"

"The women in my dreams, my nightmares. I'm inside their heads. I feel everything they feel—the pain, the terror, the awful, awful hope that someone will come in time." She shook her head and turned away from him, staring out the window. "Please drop me off somewhere," she murmured desperately. "I don't care where. Drop me at a phone. I can—"

"Running away again, Sarah?"

She swung on him. "How dare you—"

"Accuse you of something like that? Is that what you wanted to say, sweetheart?"

She sucked in a deep breath. "I said I was fucking sorry."

Raj laughed abruptly. "You know, I think that's the first time I've ever heard you swear," he said, just to irritate her.

"Yeah? Well, then, fuck you again. Let me out of this fucking car."

"No."

"*No?*" she all but screamed at him. "I am so sick of you—" Her words were chopped off as he cut across three lanes of traffic, slicing between two huge eighteen wheelers with only inches to spare, before zipping down an off-ramp and dumping into one of Buffalo's working class neighborhoods. Next to him, Sarah had released her death grip on the armrest and was looking around, scanning the streets. She probably had no idea where they were, probably never ventured too far away from the campus with its trendy restaurants and tidy bars.

Raj, on the other hand, knew exactly where he was going. He made a series of quick turns down narrow streets and pulled onto a smear of blacktop in front of a seedy-looking bar. He parked, got out of the car and started across the poorly lit lot without saying a word. He clicked the remote in warning and heard her swear softly. She opened her car door and he smiled, feeling the angry heat of her gaze on his back. He stopped at the bar's entrance, waited politely until she caught up and then opened the door and gestured for her to go in ahead of him. She paused to peer cautiously through the door, gave him a dubious look and crossed the threshold. Raj chuckled and followed her inside, letting the door swing slowly shut behind him.

* * * *

Sarah shuffled to a halt just inside, letting her eyes adjust. It was even darker inside than out, especially once Raj let the door close with a muffled thud. She was aware of him crowding impatiently behind her and she stepped aside, watching as he strode across the room. A trio of cheap, tin wall sconces hung on the opposite wall, the kind with a pattern punched into the metal to shed a dim, yellowed light on a row of banquettes. There was a long bar to the right, with tired-looking twinkle-lights around the mirror. Raj called out something to the bartender in Polish. The bartender grunted and headed for a small freezer unit sitting on the counter at the far end.

Sarah threaded through empty tables to the bar where she took one look at the dull, sticky surface and decided to stand. Raj had no such qualms, he was leaning forward with both elbows, one foot cocked on a railing which might have been brass in some long-ago former life. He glanced over his shoulder at her. "You want something to drink?"

"What are you having?" she asked.

"Vodka," he snorted, as if it was a stupid question.

"I'll have the same."

He barked out a surprised laugh and called to the bartender who reached beneath the bar and produced two shot glasses. Carrying the glasses in one hand and a frosty bottle of vodka in the other, he deposited both on the bar in front of Raj with no comment. The label on the bottle was in Polish, but it wasn't one of those trendy made-for-America Polish vodkas in a beautiful bottle, and Sarah had a feeling the alcohol content was quite a bit higher.

Raj picked up both glasses and bottle and headed for a booth in the darkest corner of the already dark room. Sarah saw little choice but to follow him.

"Have a seat," he said. He took his own advice and slid onto one of the benches, dropping the glasses onto the table and twisting off the bottle cap with a snap of metal seals. The vodka was so cold, it poured more like thin syrup than liquid, the alcohol preventing it from ever freezing solid.

"You guys drink a lot," she commented. She brushed off the bench seat across from him and sat.

He gave her a lazy look. "That's *all* we do, *sweetheart.*"

She hated it when he called her sweetheart like that. Like what he really wanted to say was *bitch*, but he was too polite. "That's not what I meant and you know it," she said.

He smiled and pushed one of the brimming shot glasses across the table to her. "Have a drink. You'll feel better."

She doubted that. She wasn't much of a drinker, but the few times she'd indulged it had made things far worse, not better. She looked down at the small glass, now frosted white from the cold liquid. His chuckle made her glance up quickly to meet blue eyes which were as icy as the vodka in front of her. His gaze moved slowly down to the glass and back up again in blatant challenge. *Damnit.* Sarah drew a breath, picked up the shot glass and brought it to her lips. Her eyes watered immediately from the alcohol fumes and she hesitated, but he was watching her with that patronizing smile of his.

She opened her mouth and threw the freezing liquid straight down her throat, feeling the muscles there contract in shock. She choked, fighting down a reflexive cough, refusing to give him the satisfaction, even as her stomach burst into flames. *Jesus Christ! How did anyone drink that stuff?*

Raj laughed appreciatively. "*Nazdrovia,*" he said and tossed back his own shot, slamming his glass to the table and immediately lifting the bottle again. He gestured at her glass, but she shook her head, still unable to speak, tears rolling unchecked down her cheeks. Raj slid out of the booth, strolled over to the bar and came back with a glass of water, no ice.

"This will help," he said, putting it on the table in front of her.

Sarah waited until she was sure she could open her mouth without gasping for air, then picked up the glass and sipped slowly. The water was just slightly cooler than room temperature, soothing her traumatized throat and washing away the residue of what was surely pure alcohol. She grabbed some cocktail napkins from the table and dabbed her eyes with them, their rough texture like sandpaper on her overheated skin.

"Not much of a drinker?" he asked.

"That," Sarah rasped, "is not drinking."

"It is where I come from."

Sarah took another sip of water and another, before she trusted herself to say anything more. "Will you tell me what you found out from Regina?"

He gave her a cool look.

"I'm the one who found her, not you," she insisted.

He still didn't say anything, just raised his eyebrows doubtfully.

She threw the wet napkins on the table. "You have got to be one of the most frustrating men I've ever met."

"That's because I'm not a man, sweetheart. I keep telling you that, but you're not listening."

"Fine. You're one of the most frustrating males I've ever met, how about that? You're still a male aren't you?"

"Oh, yes," he drawled suggestively. "Definitely that."

Sarah felt her face heat once again, and not from the vodka. "All right, I give. What are we doing here?"

He shrugged. "Having a drink."

She sighed and scooted further into the banquette, turning sideways to lean against the wall and bring her feet up in front of her. She wrapped her arms around her knees and let her head fall back and her eyes close. She was tired. She couldn't remember the last time she'd had a decent night's sleep, and didn't know how long it would be until the next one. She thought of all the things she had to do once this was over, once they found Trish and the others. The nightmare would be over for everyone else after that, but just beginning for Sarah.

She'd resign from the University, of course. She felt bad about leaving them in the lurch like this, but the term was almost over and they'd find someone to cover her classes. She was sure they'd prefer that to having her finish out the semester, in any event. It was bad enough that she was living under an assumed identity, although they probably could have gotten past that. She'd done nothing illegal. But a psychic? A woman who channeled captive women in her dreams? That was the stuff of those tawdry newspapers they sold at grocery checkout counters and not at all suitable for a faculty member at any decent university. She sighed again, more deeply this time, and was glad she'd already cried herself out from the vodka. The last thing she needed was to get all weepy with Raj the Perfect sitting across the table from her.

"Tired?" he asked.

Her eyes flashed open and she gave him a distrustful look. He'd sounded almost sympathetic for a minute there.

He gave a cynical laugh, more of a breath than anything else, as if he knew what she was thinking. "Regina doesn't know anything about where she was held," he said without preamble. "She was drugged at first and then . . ." He scowled across the table at her. "But you already know that, don't you, Sarah? What else haven't you told me?"

Sarah studied him for a minute and looked away. "Emelie said you wouldn't understand."

"Understand what?"

"Why I didn't tell you."

"You mean why you lied to me?"

She blew out a frustrated breath and gave him a disbelieving look. "Why should I have told you anything? What are we, best friends now, Raj? Hell, I don't even tell my best friends any of this."

"What about your buddy Cynthia. I bet she knows."

"Is that what's really bugging you? That Cyn might know something you don't?" His jaw tightened and she coughed a disbelieving laugh. "That's it, isn't it? No, wait. It's not Cyn, it's Raphael! You think Cyn told Raphael. This is just stupid vampire one-upmanship." She laughed bitterly. "Well, don't worry, Raj. Cyn doesn't know either. No one knows," she muttered. "Or at least they didn't until all of this happened."

She leaned her head back again, closing her eyes. She'd have to call Cyn when this was over, too, she thought tiredly. Have to explain it all over again. Although something told her Cyn would understand a lot better than Raj did.

Raj poured himself another shot and threw it down his throat, slamming the empty glass down with a crack of sound. "There's at least one vampire involved," he said suddenly, his voice heavy with disgust. "He's putting the women under his control so they only see what he wants them to see."

Sarah looked at him. "Can you tell who it is?"

"No. But I can tell who it *isn't*. He's got power, but he doesn't know what he's doing. His work is clumsy and potentially harmful."

"Regina?"

He shook his head. "She'll be all right."

"Wasn't she taken from one of the blood houses?"

Raj nodded. "Corfu, but that doesn't—"

"Were the others all taken the same way? I mean except for Trish."

"Pretty much, and I think whoever took Trish meant to get Jen. She was at one of the other houses the week before. Wait a minute," he said slowly. "Why?"

"Well, that's how we find him."

His gaze sharpened. "*We* don't do anything. I do. You're no longer a part of this investigation. It's gotten too dangerous." He slid out of the booth and stood next to it, waiting for her. "Come on, I'll take you back to the warehouse."

Sarah swung her legs down, scooted out of the booth and said calmly, "I'm not going back to the warehouse. I need to help with Trish and the others, and I can't—"

"No."

"Excuse me?" she demanded. She glared up at him towering over her and wished she was wearing heels instead of her Nikes.

"I told you," he explained with infuriating patience. "It's too dangerous for—"

"And I told you," she cut in, each word clearly enunciated. "I'll do what I want. I'm not one of your damn vampires, hanging onto every word—"

He grabbed her then, lifting her off her feet and swallowing her next words as he crushed her mouth against his. His kiss was hungry and demanding, his touch rough and familiar at the same time, full of anger and need all at once. She kissed him back, wrapping her arms around his neck with a little moan. God, she'd missed this. Missed him. Every frustrating, obnoxious, wonderful inch of him.

He deepened the kiss and she felt his fangs press against the soft flesh of her lip, felt the sting as her blood began to flow. He groaned and hitched her higher up his body, sliding one hand beneath her ass and pressing her against his erection which lay hard and long against the rough fabric of his denims. Sarah wrapped her legs around his waist with a sigh of pleasure against his mouth. "This isn't going to stop me from—"

He pulled back long enough to say, "You talk too much." And then she was lost in sensation. The feel of him was everywhere, his tongue caressing hers, his kiss moving from her mouth to her jaw and down to her neck where he lingered, sucking the skin just below her ear, stroking it with his tongue.

She was vaguely aware of the bartender yelling more indecipherable Polish, of Raj struggling to twist something out of his pocket. Money, she thought, as he threw it on the table and headed for the door. She didn't know how they got outside, but suddenly they were at the car, his heavy body crushing her against the cold metal, his hands beneath her sweater, shoving her bra aside until her breasts filled his hands and he was strumming her nipples to exquisite hardness. She could feel her heart beating wildly and knew he must be aware of it, knew he could sense the rush of her blood beneath her skin. She threaded her hands through his thick, wavy hair, urging him closer to her neck, feeling the press of his fangs against her skin, wanting to feel—

A trilling sound suddenly rang out, seeming unbearably loud in the quiet parking lot. "Ignore it," she gasped, tightening her legs around him. The ring came again and Raj froze, his breath shivering across her damp, hot skin. She felt him stiffen beneath her, and not in a good way.

"No," Sarah pleaded softly.

"Jesus," Raj said. "I shouldn't—"

The touch of his hands changed, no longer caressing, but an impersonal cage supporting her as her legs dropped to the ground. She slid down his body, feeling his obvious arousal as he set her on her feet, putting a few inches and a hundred miles between them. "I shouldn't have done that," he muttered. The damn phone rang a third time. "Fuck," he cursed and stepped away from her, digging into his pocket to retrieve his cell.

Sarah leaned against the car, too shocked to say anything, still reeling with the rush of feeling his mouth against her neck, his hands all over her body. She shook herself slightly. Raj glanced at her, his eyes no longer hot, but shuttered and blank, and Sarah ground her teeth, wondering if she could find a piece of sharp wood somewhere nearby. She straightened her clothes, refusing to look at him, refusing to see the look on his face. She heard the locks click open and slipped into the car, sitting sideways on the seat, running shaking hands through her long hair, trying to comb out the worst of it, remembering his thick fingers twisting it out of the way, his mouth . . . She closed her eyes against the sensory overload, shivering slightly.

Raj stood with his back to her, the phone at his ear. "Do not go in without me, Em. I'll see you in . . . Fuck, I'll get there as soon as I can." He jammed the disconnect with his thumb and shoved the phone back into his pocket, then spun around and headed for his side of the car. His door opened and he slid inside, filling the car with his presence, sucking all the air from her lungs. Sarah swung her legs into the car and closed the door.

"You okay?" he asked.

"Sure," she lied. She brushed nonexistent lint from her denims, avoiding his no doubt sincere gaze.

"I'll take you back to the warehouse," he said. "Some of the guards are there and Em should be back—"

"Don't worry about it," she interrupted. She could feel him staring at her across the endless gulf between their two seats.

"Sarah," he began.

"You don't have to say it. I understand." She turned and forced herself to smile at him, meeting his eyes briefly. "Sounds like you need to get going."

He frowned. "I've got people in the field, sweetheart, or I—"

"Don't call me that," she snapped.

He stared at her, clearly startled by the sharpness of her words. She shook her head. "I'm sorry. It doesn't matter."

He swore softly beneath his breath, but didn't say anything else, jamming the car into gear and gunning it out of the parking lot. Sarah sat there, staring out the window and telling herself it was all for the best. She'd be leaving soon anyway and the last thing she needed was one more complication, one more detail to clean up before she hit the road. Not that this particular detail needed cleaning up. Raj had made it pretty clear that he considered anything to do with her to be a mistake on his part. So, it was better this way. A clean break. She'd pick up her money and be free again, maybe take a few weeks off, drive around and see a few sights before she settled down somewhere and built a new life. She clenched her jaw and looked out the window, wondering why freedom tasted so bitter this time around.

Chapter Thirty-seven

Raj took surface streets back to the warehouse, breaking the speed limit all the way, skimming through stop signs and tearing around corners, not slowing until he was turning into the warehouse lot. Sarah's little sedan was sitting at one end of the parking lot and he frowned, not sure he was happy to see it there. She didn't need her car. What she needed was to stay put until he was sure it was safe for her to be out on the streets. *Right*, he scoffed privately. *Like she's any safer in here with you.*

He shook his head in disgust. He'd practically attacked her back at the bar. She'd been standing there giving him hell like she always did and something in him had just snapped. He tried to blame it on hunger. He hadn't fed properly in days; the bagged blood was good in a pinch, but he needed more. He wanted more. What he wanted was Sarah, and he wanted her in the worse way, hell, in *every* way.

He parked beside the front entrance and Sarah immediately opened her door, all but jumping from the car, clearly eager to get away from him. Smart girl. He followed, striding around to unlock the warehouse door, pulling it open and holding it while she stepped past him. He pushed open the interior door before she could get to it, holding that for her as well. Sarah gave him a silent nod of thanks and went directly for the stairs to the mezzanine.

"Sarah," he called softly, unable to bear the silence any longer. She stopped at the foot of the stairs, her back to him, head bowed. "I didn't mean," he began. "That is . . . Look, I'll probably be back too late tonight, but I'll be here tomorrow and we'll—"

She turned to face him, her hazel eyes dark and flat, the gold flecks all but invisible. "Don't worry about it," she said dismissively. "I'm fine." She turned away and began climbing the stairs. "I'm always fine," she said in words soft enough that if he'd been human he wouldn't have heard them. It troubled him and he took the first step to follow her, but his phone chose that moment to ring once again, echoing in the still warehouse.

"What?" he demanded.

"My lord," Em said in a tight voice. "I don't know how long—"

"I'm there in five minutes, Em. No one does anything—"

"I'm holding them, my lord, but I don't know how much longer—"

"No one goddamn moves before I get there," he snarled. He slammed his phone into his pocket and was already running out of the warehouse and into the car with the inhuman speed of his vampire blood.

* * * *

Some part of Sarah heard Raj leave, aware there was trouble

somewhere. That same part of her hoped no one got hurt, least of all Emelie, or even Raj. But most of her thoughts were on something completely different. She'd seen her car out front and wondered if they'd left her keys. Not that it mattered. She had a second set tucked into her purse, a backup she'd started carrying the first time she locked her keys in her car two years ago and decided the spare did her no good sitting at home in her desk when she was miles away. She walked down the mezzanine toward her temporary quarters, feeling the uneven tread of the metal surface beneath her feet, half-listening to the sounds of some sporting event drifting over from the living area where a couple of human guards were hanging in front of the big screen. His vamps, she supposed, were all out doing whatever it was they did in the middle of the night. She checked her watch. It was a few minutes before one a.m.

She pushed into the room, automatically checking to be sure everything was the way she'd left it. Control freak that she was, she knew the order of her rooms down to the placement of every pencil and pen. Linda had teased her mercilessly about it, but then Linda didn't understand. No one did. Once your life had been taken from you, your every moment given into the hands of strangers with clipboards and bureaucratic eyes . . . When you finally got it back, when your life was yours again, every moment, every detail, became important.

A quick survey of the small space told her that her laptop was where she'd left it, along with the few things she'd managed to stuff into her duffle before hurrying away from the duplex . . . not even two days ago? It felt like much longer than that. It didn't seem right that her entire world could be turned upside down in such a short time.

She pulled her duffle from under the bed and began repacking it, inventorying what she had, making a mental checklist of what she'd need to buy, matching it against her money. She'd have to stop at an ATM on her way out of town, and then first chance she got, she'd withdraw the entire amount through one of their brick and mortar locations. She'd pay an early fee for that, which seemed unfair, but at least she'd have all of it in cash, with no way for anyone to use the accounts to find her.

Shouldering her duffle and her laptop case, she checked the room one last time and slipped out to the mezzanine, closing the door behind her. The guards over by the TV looked up, and she thought at first they'd try to stop her, but she waved cheerfully, like it was no big deal and they relaxed. Holding her breath, she pulled open first one door and then the next, walked over to her car, beeped it open, threw her stuff inside and drove away. She didn't know where she'd go eventually, but she knew her first stop.

Raj might think this case had become too dangerous for her, but he didn't understand. The real danger was for Trish and whoever else was still being held by the vampires who'd thrown Regina away like yesterday's trash. And regardless of what Raj might think, Sarah wasn't running away this time.

As she drove through the sparse traffic, she flicked through her cell phone's call log until she found Jennifer Stewart's number again. It was way too late for Professor Stratton to be calling a student, but since Sarah wouldn't be a professor or a Stratton much longer, it didn't matter.

Jen's peppy voice answered. Sarah could hear music and laughter in the background and thought about how lovely it must be to be eighteen and carefree. Apparently, Trish's continued absence wasn't exactly weighing on her roommate's mind.

"Jennifer," Sarah said, "Hi, this is Sarah Stratton, Professor Stratton?"

"Oh yeah," Jen said, obviously confused and not terribly thrilled by the late-night call. "Hi, Professor Stratton."

"I just have a quick question, Jen. Raj asked me to call." Okay, so it was a lie—a small, very white lie.

"Sure!" Jen's enthusiasm ratcheted up about a thousand notches. "Anything I can do!"

"Thanks, Jen. Listen, you were telling Raj about that blood house you visited, but there're a couple of them in that area, and we want to be sure we have the right one."

"Sure, I understand. It's that one in East Amherst, kind of a funky pointed house with a way disco vibe going inside. Totally old school."

"Mmhmm," Sarah murmured. "Do you know the street?"

"Oh, let me think. I didn't drive and you know how it is."

"It's important, Jen," Sarah said absently, driving past her old duplex. "We're very close and it could help us find Trish." A little guilt never hurt.

"Oh, man. Trish. Yeah. Let's see, Evergreen or something Christmasy. Alpine! That was it. It was on Alpine, right off Stahley. I remember that 'cuz one of my friends has that last name and I asked her if it was like her grandfather or something, but she said no."

Sarah figured between that and an online map, she could find the place. If worse came to worst, she'd just drive up and down the street looking for a pointed house with lots of people going in and out.

"Thanks, Jen. That really helps. And sorry for calling so late."

"Hey, no problem, Professor Stratton. It's spring break, ya know?"

"Right. Party on, Jen."

"Uh. Okay. Bye."

By that time, Sarah had pulled around and parked in the unlit alley behind her duplex. The front had been completely dark, suggesting Mrs. M. was either already asleep or still at her son's house. Sarah hoped it was the latter because the woman had ears like a bat.

She hurried through the gate and across the dried grass of the back yard to her kitchen entrance, inserting the key and pulling open the door as quietly as possible. Setting her laptop on the table, she turned it on and then tiptoed up the stairs to her bedroom in search of something to wear. She didn't know what the dress code was at a blood house, but it probably wasn't jeans and a tee. And if she hoped to get any information, she was going to have to blend in.

Chapter Thirty-eight

Raj slid to a tire-squealing stop outside Krystof's. He left the engine running, threw open his door and stormed across the street to where Emelie and three others were gathered, his power thrumming around him like an electrical current, his eyes as bright as sun through glacial ice.

All of his vampires, even Emelie, fell to their knees at his approach.

"Get up and tell me what the fuck is going on."

Em stood gracefully, assuming a parade rest position, hands crossed behind her, shoulders back. She raised her eyes briefly to his, but quickly lowered them. "My lord," she started. "We were doing our usual rounds. Four teams, hitting each house for a while and moving on. I was with Abel when I got a call from someone using Simon's cell phone."

"Where was Simon supposed to be?"

"He was at the warehouse, my lord, but he'd called earlier to say he was going for electronic supplies of some sort."

"Who called you?"

"The caller didn't identify himself, my lord, just said if I wanted Simon back alive, I'd better find you and get you over here in the next half hour. That was . . ." She checked her watch. "Forty minutes ago, my lord."

He didn't hear any judgment in Emelie's voice. He didn't have to. He'd been humping Sarah in the parking lot while someone was kidnapping Simon out from under his nose.

"I called you first, of course," Emelie continued. "And then Abel and I came directly here, along with Danny and Cervantes." She nodded at the other vamps. I called the rest of the teams and sent them back to the warehouse in case this was some sort of a setup to pull everyone away."

"I just came from the warehouse. They weren't there yet."

"No, my lord. They were the farthest out, which is why I sent them to the warehouse while we came here. We arrived perhaps thirty minutes ago, but there's been no acknowledgment of our presence. Per your command, we made no attempt to approach the house directly."

"All right—"

Em's phone rang at that moment. She checked the ID, looked up at Raj and said, "Yossi." She listened for less than a minute and hung up. "He and the others are at the warehouse. Everything appears normal, but they're rousing the rest of the human guards as a precaution."

Sarah was at the warehouse. But he couldn't think about that now. "All right, let's see what the old man wants."

Raj led his vampires around the back and, not bothering to knock, threw open the kitchen door. He stared down the piece of meat Krystof had on guard there and strode past. He didn't run, he didn't fling things about, just walked through as though he had a right to be there and woe to anyone who dared tell him otherwise. He could feel Em and the others behind him, a wall of strength both physical and Vampire. He wasn't like Krystof. He didn't make vampires out of stupid humans and he never turned someone unwilling. His children were both smart and strong and served him out of personal loyalty and, according to Em, affection.

But Simon wasn't Vampire. He was human. He could outthink any of them, but he was not physically strong, which was probably why he'd been chosen as Krystof's sacrificial goat. He hadn't been harmed yet, however. Simon had been with Raj a long time, far longer than appearances would lead one to believe. He received regular feedings of Raj's blood to keep him alive and well, which meant Raj would have known if he'd been hurt.

The room at the bottom of the stairs was as crowded as it had been before, but he made no pretense of friendliness. He let his power swell, shoving everything and everyone out of his way like so much trash on the street—which was pretty much how he saw them. He didn't see Jozef, but perhaps the security chief was inside with his master . . . and Simon.

The door opened before he reached it, swinging wide in invitation. He sneered. If Krystof thought to impress him with a cheap parlor trick, he was mistaken. He gave Em a jerk of the head over his shoulder and knew she'd put the others on the door while following him inside herself. He would have liked it the other way around. Not because he didn't trust Em, but because he did. If it was going to come to a showdown between him and Krystof, he would have liked Em to be away from it so she'd have a chance of saving as many of his children as possible from the backlash. But he wouldn't do that to her. Wouldn't ask her to stay outside while he faced the greatest threat of their lives together.

"Rajmund," Krystof said smoothly. He was sitting on the same settee where the girl had lain the other night. He leaned back into a pillowed corner, legs crossed at the knee, one hand draped gracefully over the upholstered arm, while the other was on Simon's head, stroking his fine, brown hair as if he were some sort of dog kneeling next to his master. But Krystof wasn't Simon's master.

Raj felt his fury soar and tamped it down, knowing this was the reaction Krystof was hoping for. He watched the old man's face and saw the disappointment there. He smiled. "I believe you have something of mine," he said mildly.

Krystof laughed lightly, but the look he gave Raj was not amused. "But, Rajmund," he chided softly, his voice growing hard when he continued, "you're not supposed to have anything of your own."

Raj's smile only grew, and for a moment, he saw a glimmer of fear replace the smug look in his Sire's eyes. "Let's not play games, Krystof. What is it you want?"

The vampire lord shrugged gracefully and stood, leaving Simon behind. Raj didn't move other than to turn in place, keeping Krystof in sight. But he was aware of Emelie as she quickly stepped to his side, putting Simon behind them. Krystof settled at his desk and gestured at Emelie. "You've trained them well, I see. I couldn't even get that human—" He waved at Simon who'd risen to his feet. "—to tell me anything. Of course, I could have forced him."

"You could have tried," Raj corrected.

Krystof's mouth tightened in irritation. "What I *want*," he said, ignoring the truth of Raj's statement, "is a report on your investigation."

Raj gave him a look. "You couldn't phone?" he scoffed.

"I shouldn't *have* to," Krystof said petulantly, slapping one hand to the desk. "I brought you here to solve *my* problem, not to have your people running all over my city poking into my affairs."

Raj couldn't believe his ears. It was a struggle to keep the amazement off his face, and he could only hope Emelie was doing the same. Krystof, a fucking vampire lord, had effectively ceded his territory. He'd not only admitted to knowing about Raj's private army, but had complained, *complained*, like a child that they were infiltrating his home city.

"What would you like to know?" Raj asked.

"I would *like to know*," Krystof said, mimicking Raj, "what you've discovered. Is there a vampire connection to these crimes or not?"

Raj thought about what to say, about how much to admit of what he knew. He hadn't missed the fact that Jozef was nowhere to be found and wondered what that meant. Was the security chief getting ready to attack the warehouse while Raj stood here answering these ridiculous questions? Or had he absented himself as a passive show of support for Raj? *Too many unknowns*, he thought.

"There does appear to be some vampire involvement," he said carefully. "I am investigating further and expect to have a resolution within the next forty-eight hours. I'm sure you agree that whoever it is, he must be destroyed immediately."

Krystof looked up quickly at that, and Raj felt him pressing on his awareness, trying to force him to reveal more than he'd said. Raj stared back at him giving away nothing, but that alone spoke volumes. His Sire shrugged and looked away first. "Very well. You will inform me before taking any *final* action."

"Of course. Emelie," he said, and waited while she escorted Simon to the door and opened it. He watched in his peripheral vision as Cervantes and Abel grabbed the much smaller human and placed him between them, and he could feel the attention of his people, both vampire and human, focused solely on him, waiting for his command. He felt a surge of pride at their utter discipline and devotion. They would have stood with him at the Gates of Hell if he'd asked it. "We're leaving," he said.

He gave Krystof a short nod of acknowledgment and started from the room. "I wanted to grab your woman," Krystof taunted from behind him, "but I couldn't seem to find her."

Raj froze. He looked up and saw Emelie watching him, clearly worried at what he might do. He felt a moment's disappointment that she would doubt him and let it show in his eyes. Em flushed and lowered her gaze.

As for Krystof, Raj spun where he stood in the doorway and said in the coldest voice he could muster, "Don't ever touch anyone of mine again, Krystof. Not anyone."

He pushed through his vampires, hustling Simon ahead of him, feeling the others close in on his back. Emelie led the way up the stairs and through the kitchen, not stopping until they were out of the house and on the street.

"I'm sorry, my lord," Simon was saying miserably. "I was stupid and got distracted. I didn't see them coming until they were on top of me and—"

"Don't worry about it, Simon," Raj said. "If it hadn't been you, it would have been someone else." He checked his watch and saw he still had plenty of time to stop and tap a willing donor before the sun forced him back to his lair. He'd use one of the bars; they were always more crowded than the clubs midweek like this, and it was time he got over this fixation with Sarah. "Emelie," he said, "give Yossi a heads-up and take Simon back to the warehouse. I'm going to—"

Em's phone went off. He frowned but jerked his head, telling her to get it. Damnit, he needed to get going or it was going to get too late to—

He saw Em's face fall, saw her turn to him, her eyes wide with dread.

Chapter Thirty-nine

"Goddamn it," Raj snarled. "What the hell was she thinking?"

Em was on the phone talking rapidly, as Raj drove like a demon, skimming through red lights and screaming around corners. Sarah was at Kent's blood house. Sarah who was so susceptible to vampire suggestion that she'd almost had an orgasm after dancing with him for five fucking minutes at that Manhattan club. *Damn her.* He'd warned her about the dangers, but had that stopped her? No. Of course, the fault was at least partly his. He should have known better than to give her even the tiniest bit of information, should have known she'd go charging in and—

Em hung up and punched in another number. Raj looked over at her. "You're sure it's her," Em was saying. "If it looks like he's going to sink fang, you stop him. I don't care what it takes. We'll be there in fifteen minutes." She hung up and gave him a worried look. "That was Yossi. He and Gino are at the blood house already. Yossi's inside."

Fucking Kent. He'd kill that motherfucker dead if Sarah had so much as a scratch on her. He took a turn on two wheels and hit the gas pedal, feeling his anger growing hotter with every mile that passed. "What the fuck was she thinking?" he repeated.

"Probably that if you wouldn't tell her anything, she'd find out for herself."

Raj growled low in his chest, sparing her a cold glance. "Don't push your luck, Em."

She shrugged. "I don't know why you're playing this game with her or yourself. You want her, so take her."

"Fuck you." He pounded his fist on the steering wheel and would have snapped it in two had he not pulled back at the last second. "I'm a goddamn vampire. You think that's what she wants? To wake up every night to a dead man who drinks blood to stay alive? Besides, she accused me of mind-fucking Jennifer Stewart, for God's sake."

It galled him to admit that the woman he was obsessed with—the first woman since his turning who'd meant more to him than a quick meal—thought he was capable of the most heinous act a man could commit.

Em's gaze was burning a hole in the side of his face, but he ignored her. "Sarah made a mistake," Em said patiently. "She admitted it. But she didn't understand how we do stuff, not then anyway. And as for the rest . . . Raj, my friend, you're one of the best men I know. One of the best people I've ever met. So you're a vampire, so what? So am I. And Sarah's old enough to make her own decision. She's a damn university professor, for God's sake. You have no right to take that choice away from her."

"If she's been touched, I'll destroy everyone in that fucking house," he snarled.

"I know."

* * * *

Gino was waiting for them outside, standing in the shadows near the door. He came down off the shallow porch in a bound, meeting them halfway to the street, his gaze resting warily on Raj. Gino was a strong vampire, physically powerful and fearless. But he took one look at the fury on his master's face and dropped to his knees, speaking to the ground. "She's still in there, my lord. Yossi is with her."

Raj grabbed Gino by the front of his jacket and dragged him to his feet. "With her how?"

"Guarding her, my lord," Gino insisted. "Only watching. The others are—" His eyes widened in fear as Raj drew him closer, fangs fully distended, eyes gleaming an icy blue. "Master," he squeaked.

Em reached across and grabbed Gino's arm, pulling him out of Raj's reach and tossing him behind her. "This is a waste of time, my lord. We need to get inside." She gave Raj a shove that no one else would have dared and tried to step in front of him, but he snarled at her, pushing ahead onto the porch and into the house, ignoring Em's protest of, "It might be a trap!"

"Jesus, Em." Gino's complaint followed him through the door. "You think I'd let him walk into a trap?"

"Just cover our backs," Em snapped.

It was nearly as dark inside as out. The overhead track lighting had been dimmed until the small bulbs were barely glowing, even to a vampire's vision. The music was loud enough to give the humans a false sense of anonymity in the crowd, but not enough to disturb the neighbors. He heard Gino say from behind him, "Straight ahead, my lord, the back room."

Raj stormed forward, aware of both humans and vampires hurrying to get out of his way, letting the wave of his anger knock aside anyone who didn't move fast enough. Some of the vampires knew him personally; others only recognized the weight of his power. But all of them scattered. One or two of the more ignorant humans objected loudly, their words truncated by a vampire hand clamped over a foolish mouth.

Raj was aware of all of this and none of it, his mind completely occupied with the image of Sarah tucked away in some private room, drunk on the chemical overload of vampire pheromones he could scent clogging the air of the blood house.

He strode down the narrow hallway and into the large back room that had once been someone's family room. It was just as crowded back here, but the humans were more bold, more used to the vampire high. One woman, darkly beautiful and voluptuous, thought to offer herself to Raj. He stared at her, barely comprehending what he was seeing, and then she was gone, yanked away by Em or someone else. He didn't care which, because there was a flash of blond hair through the crowd and a familiar lilt of laughter. He saw thick fingers comb through that hair to grip the back of her neck. And everything else was lost in his roar of challenge.

Raj hit the crowded dance floor like a tornado, tossing bodies out of his way until he reached Sarah. Grabbing her around the waist, he swung her behind him, vaguely aware that Em was there to take her. With the same movement, he thrust his hand toward the vampire who had dared touch her and shoved him halfway across the room to slam into the wall with a loud crack. The vampire was as big as Raj, with long, dark hair that hung in curls around his shoulders and dark eyes burning red with anger, as his prey was stolen from him. He howled his fury and launched himself back to his feet, fangs fully distended, leading with a meaty fist at Raj's jaw. Raj didn't bother to duck, just stepped into the swing, letting the fist hit nothing but air and barely feeling the impact of the vampire's thick arm against his shoulder. Plowing his own fist into his opponent's gut, he seized the vamp's throat and let a hammer wave of power drive him to his knees.

The vampire's eyes bulged in pain and shock when Raj's power hit, when his brain finally registered who was attacking him. Some animal instinct of self-preservation kicked in and a confused whine strained to rise out of his throat, a plea for understanding, for mercy.

"Raj," Em said behind from him, her voice barely heard above the pounding rage in his head. "My lord," she shouted, louder this time, and he jerked an irritated growl over his shoulder without letting go of his victim.

"He could not have known, Raj," Em said intently, and then with greater urgency, "My lord, these are *your* people."

"Not yet they're not," he ground out.

"Lord Rajmund!" she demanded, her voice stiff with condemnation.

He stared at the terrified vampire on his knees before him, thinking, after days of playing politics with Krystof and with the cops, how very good it would feel to rip this vampire's throat out, to taste his blood and toss aside his lifeless body as it turned to dust before him. He became aware that the room had grown deadly silent, the humans all gone, hustled away by the few vampires left who could still think rationally in the face of Raj's thundering power. He raised his eyes and scanned the faces of the vampires who remained. Most refused to look at him, their eyes falling away from his stare, some going so far as to drop to one knee in submission. Others were eager, anticipating the feeding frenzy that would follow if Raj killed the dark-haired vampire. He held the gaze of those until every one of them had dropped to their knees, bowing before his greater power.

But there were a few, a very few, who knelt submissively, but who also watched. They knew who he was, knew he was likely to be their next lord, and they were judging him, waiting to see what kind of lord he would be. Raj wanted to howl with frustration.

He looked down at the dark-haired vamp, saw the terror and resignation in his eyes. "Fuck you," he snarled. He pulled back his power and released the vampire, letting him fall to the floor where he coughed and gasped for air.

"Forgive me, my lord," he rasped.

Raj spun away and grabbed Sarah from Yossi, who'd been holding her carefully away from his body, making it clear he was a caretaker and nothing more. "Fuck you, too, Em," Raj snapped as he walked by, hauling Sarah out of the room and down the hallway.

He expected Sarah to struggle, to protest his manhandling, but he hadn't counted on the overload of vampire pheromones or her susceptibility to them. Instead of struggling, she wrapped her arms around his neck and began nuzzling him, rubbing her soft, full breasts against his chest. "Stop it, Sarah," he muttered, embarrassed on her behalf.

"Raj!" she said in delight, as if just realizing who was holding her. "My very favorite vampire!"

"Christ," he muttered. He tightened his hold on her, groaning when she gave a little hop and wrapped her legs around his waist. He could feel the heat between her legs against his hip, could smell the familiar scent of her hair, her perfume. His own body, already riding the high of adrenaline, reacted to her presence and he cursed under his breath. He needed to get them both the hell out of this place.

Kent stepped in front of him, falling to one knee. "Forgive me, my lord, I had no idea she was—" His voice was silenced by the icy grip of Raj's power, choking away his breath without a touch.

"You know now, you bastard," Raj growled and released Kent who sagged nearly to the floor, wheezing harshly. "Em!" Raj roared over his shoulder and stormed out of the house, half carrying Sarah who was now kissing him, soft lips nibbling along his neck, her tongue dipping into his ear and out again.

Striding over to the BMW, he tried to extricate himself from the tangle of her arms and legs without hurting her. She started laughing, as if it was a tremendous game, letting him pull an arm away only to replace it when he moved on to the other one, dropping to her feet obediently when he demanded, and then jumping up again when he reached for the car, forcing him to catch her or let her fall on her ass. He was tempted to do just that, but Emelie and the others had come out of the house and were watching the whole humiliating circus. At least no one else had dared venture outside yet, he thought gratefully.

But while Yossi and Gino were mindful of Raj's earlier rage and kept their faces carefully blank, Em didn't bother to conceal her amusement. "You should at least mark her if you're going to go all caveman like this, my lord," she commented.

"Yeah, Raj," Sarah chimed in. "You should at least—" Her words cut off with a high-pitched yip as Raj picked her up and threw her into his car.

Em stifled a laugh, but Raj was not amused and let her know it. "I'll see you tomorrow night," he said coldly. "At the warehouse."

Em sobered immediately, seeming to realize for the first time how angry he still was. "Raj," she said, touching his arm. "Maybe you should let me . . ."

He looked down at her hand and lifted a cold blue gaze to her face. "Do you think I'll hurt her, Emelie?"

Em jerked her hand back and her mouth tightened briefly. "No," she said.

"Then I'll see you tomorrow."

He slammed into the car, pulling the door shut behind him. "Put on your seatbelt," he ordered Sarah.

"Maybe I don't want—"

"Put on the fucking seatbelt or I'll do it for you, and we both know I can."

Sarah stuck her tongue out at him and shoved the buckle closed, sitting silently, arms crossed, as Raj roared away from the blood house, his tires spitting dirt from the roadside.

Chapter Forty

Raj was going too fast when he pulled into the narrow garage. His tires spun on the slick surface as he hit the brakes and the bumper kissed the far wall. His blood was still boiling, adrenaline still racing through his system. It was hard enough to come down from the rush of a combat high after a confrontation like the one at the blood house, but it was even harder with Sarah's slender hands roaming all over him as he raced through the Buffalo streets.

"Stop it, Sarah," he said for what felt like the hundredth time. Her response was the same, too—a soft, purring laugh that made his cock hard and his fangs ache.

He opened his car door with a snarled oath and marched around to her side. She hadn't moved, hadn't even unbuckled her seat belt. Gritting his teeth against what he knew was going to happen, he reached across and mashed the release on the belt, not evening surprised when he felt her fingers run down his belly and between his legs.

"Ooooooh," she cooed. "Is this for me?"

"Jesus Christ." Raj lifted her out of the car, propped her up long enough to enter his security code, then threw her over his shoulder and shoved roughly through the door. He waited until he heard the lock snap shut behind him, punched in the second code on the interior panel and carried her downstairs, opening the vault door before setting her down inside.

Amazingly, she seemed to have run out of steam at last, leaning against him with a small sigh and resting her head against his chest, her arms draped loosely around his waist beneath his jacket. Raj glanced down at her golden blond head against the black of his sweater, her face hidden behind the fall of her hair. "Sarah?" he said softly.

"Mmmm?"

"You still with me?"

She laughed softly and did a little twisting motion with her hips, reminding him he was still hard as a rock against her belly. He put her aside and activated his daytime security system, turning to find her watching him, her smoky hazel eyes smoldering with emotion, their gold flecks bright in the warm glow of his lamps. She dropped her jacket to the floor and for the first time he noticed what she was wearing. Faded denims clung to her legs and hips like a second skin, showing off firm thighs and that wonderful heart-shaped ass. Her breasts were showcased by a strapless top, red satin against her pale skin, tight enough that the full mounds plumped out invitingly. He wanted to close his eyes against the temptation, but couldn't quite convince himself to do so.

Sarah saw him watching and ran a teasing finger along the top of the red satin, stroking her hand down in a caressing motion until it rested at her waist. She smiled. "At last we meet, Raj."

"Don't, Sarah," he said softly.

"Why not?" she inquired sweetly. "I know you want to. Come on, *sweetheart*. Let's fuck."

His anger returned in a rush. He was furious that she'd put herself in that kind of danger, furious that she'd forced him to show his hand before he was ready. "When I fuck you," he snarled. "It won't be because you're acting like a bitch in heat over the scent of a bunch of mongrel dogs."

Sarah jerked as if he'd slapped her, her eyes filling with tears, hurt written over every inch of her face. "That was cruel," she whispered, "even for you."

It *was* cruel. Cruel and unfair. He knew it, but he'd be damned if he'd apologize, not after she'd played that stupid trick with the blood house. She knew the other women had been taken from blood houses. She'd seen the kind of security he had in place for her protection at the warehouse, and still she'd gone haring off on her own, just to prove that she could.

"I want to go home," she said in a small voice.

"Too bad." She looked up at him in dismay. "It's nearly sunrise," he explained.

"But," she looked around, like a trapped animal seeking escape. "Just open the door. I can—"

"I don't think so," he said dismissively. "You should shower," he said, gesturing toward the bathroom. "I've got some clothes you can put on."

"All right," she said in that tiny voice, like she wanted to disappear. It infuriated him because he knew he was the one who'd made her feel that way. He felt like an asshole as he watched her walk away, watched her kick off her shoes and slip barefoot into the bathroom through the half-open door, closing it behind her with a hitch in her breath.

He had already changed by the time she came out. She was wearing the sweatshirt he'd set inside the door, but not the pants. Her legs were bare, but the shirt hung down to her knees like a nightgown. His clothes. She was wearing *his* clothes. And when she was forced to come closer in order to get to the bed, he could smell *his* soap on her skin. Em was right. If he wanted her, he needed to do something about it. And if not, he needed to let her go.

"You can have the bed," he said gently, trying to make amends. "I'll take the couch."

"It doesn't matter," she said, fresh tears rolling down her cheeks. "I probably won't sleep."

"Sure, you will."

Her look of confusion was the last thing he saw before she fell into his arms. "Sorry, sweetheart," he whispered, "but I can't have you waking up before I do." He carried her to the bed and tucked her in, brushing a lock of golden hair out of her face. "Sleep well."

He lay down on the leather couch, exquisitely aware of Sarah sleeping in his bed only a few feet away. He rolled over once or twice, sat up and shifted to the other end, trying to find a comfortable position. He lay back and gave it up as a lost cause. Once the sun took him, it wouldn't matter anyway.

Chapter Forty-one

Raj awoke hungry and horny, with the solution to both of his problems lying right there in his bed, all toasty warm and flushed with health. He rose to his feet slowly, stretching every muscle, hearing his neck crack after the uncomfortable day on the too-short couch. He crossed the room and stood above her in the near perfect dark of his inner sanctum, watching her sleep. He could hear every beat of her heart, could feel the moisture of every breath, the heat of her body warming the cold sheets of his bed. It had been a mistake to bring her here. An even bigger mistake to do so when he'd gone so long without feeding. He'd meant to stop and feed last night, but then the call had come that Sarah was at the blood house and now . . . here she was.

Memories filled his head—of her dancing with the dark-haired vampire, her body rubbing up against his, his hands all over her. Raj closed his eyes against a fresh swell of rage. When he opened them, she was still there, still sleeping. She was his. Why not take her?

His fangs lengthened eagerly, emerging from between his lips. He opened his mouth to stretch his jaw. As if aware of the danger lurking over her, Sarah murmured in her sleep and rolled over. Her scent drifted up to him, delicate and sweet, laced with the scent of his soap, his clothing. His cock grew hard and heavy, unrestrained in the loose sweatpants he'd put on only because she was with him. He growled softly, aware of a cool, blue glow in the room, the light from his eyes, burning with the heat of two different hungers.

His cell phone rang. A welcome distraction. He crossed the room and checked caller ID. It was Emelie. Of course. She was probably worried about him. Or maybe about Sarah.

Raj didn't answer. Let her think he was in the shower; he would be soon enough. He grabbed up a pair of denims and strode into the bathroom without looking at the bed, closing the door before he could catch another glimpse of the temptation lying there.

* * * *

The shower woke Sarah. At least she thought that's what it must have been. There was no other noise in the room, and while the lights were dim, there was enough that she could see. The bathroom door was closed and she sat up, pulling the covers with her. She didn't remember falling asleep, but she remembered everything else. Her entire body flushed with embarrassment at the memory of Raj storming into the crowded room, coming to rescue her from her own stupidity.

She'd had no idea what the blood house would be like, hadn't even considered there might be such a strong aphrodisiac effect in the air itself. She remembered Raj saying something about it at his club in New York. When she'd had that erotic . . . whatever it had been, right there on the dance floor. But she'd written that off as a reaction to Raj himself. Stupid.

But it wasn't all her fault. What did he think that she was going to do, sit in that stupid warehouse like a good, little dog, waiting for master to come pet her on the head? If he'd just told her what was going on, or better yet, if he'd agreed to visit the blood houses with her like she'd wanted, none of this would have happened.

Honesty forced her to admit she'd been careless, though. She'd realized that from the minute she stepped into the house, beginning with the waiver they made her sign, the appraising looks of the vampires at the door. She'd known right away what everyone assumed she wanted. It was the same thing everyone else there wanted. Sex and blood. Not that she would have minded a little sex and blood herself, it was just that she wanted Raj and only him. But he didn't want her. Or he didn't *want* to want her which was the same thing. Especially when the vampire in question was Mister I'm-in-Control Raj.

The other vampires had seemed to like her well enough. That dark-haired vamp had been all over her. *Oh, be honest, Sarah, you were all over him too.* That's why she rarely drank. It made people stupid. But she'd had a taste last night of what it must feel like to be drunk, and it hadn't been all bad. For once in her life, she hadn't worried about whether she was too short or her breasts too big. Hadn't worried that the nice guy sitting next to her might be a serial rapist or some other sort of freak who only wanted to follow her home and do horrible things to her. It had felt good, or at least it had felt good until Raj showed up and made her feel like a complete whore. A complete *unwanted* whore.

The bathroom door opened, splashing light into the room. She shrank away from the light, growing still as Raj emerged, wearing nothing but pants. They were black denim, hanging low on his hips with the button undone and the zipper halfway open. His chest was bare and still damp and Sarah swallowed a gasp at how beautiful he was. His shoulders were broad and thick with muscle, his chest firm and well-defined, tapering down to a narrow waist and hard, flat belly. His skin glowed golden in the light from the bathroom, and a barely visible down of curly blond hair sprinkled his chest before arrowing straight to the opening of his unbuttoned pants.

Her gaze traveled up to his face and found his icy, blue eyes staring back at her. They were glowing slightly, as they did when he was angry, and she pulled the covers tighter, glad for their flimsy protection. She felt suddenly like a small animal beneath the gaze of a predator, an unhappy image. She frowned and felt her own anger stiffen her determination. She was *not* an animal; she was no one's prey, and she, by God, was not a whore either.

"Raj," she said coolly. It was an acknowledgment of his presence, nothing more.

"Sarah." His voice was low and rumbling, and definitely meant to intimidate. Apparently, he was still pissed at her. Well, too bad.

Summoning her courage and her frostiest voice, Sarah said, "If you're finished, I'd like to use the bathroom."

He blinked. And blinked again. He didn't say anything, but took two steps away from the bathroom door, clearing the way, barely, for her to pass.

Sarah climbed out of the big bed, careful to keep the oversized sweatshirt she was wearing—one of *his*, obviously—from riding up. She had a moment's doubt when she hurried past him, standing there all big and hunky and glowering down at her. But she kept moving and quickly shut the door between them. Once inside, she leaned back against the closed door and blew out a breath of relief. That hadn't been so difficult. So he was a big, bad vampire. His minions might scurry around doing his bidding, even Emelie kowtowed to his moody self, but Sarah didn't have to. He'd made it clear there was nothing between them, so who was he to tell her where she could and couldn't go? If she wanted to drop in at every blood house in the city and dance the night away, it was her business not his. Hell, maybe she'd tell him so. That would be a shock to him, wouldn't it? A human weakling telling him where he could shove his macho bullshit? He should go back to Manhattan and all those beautiful women. They probably fell all over him, lining up to open their veins and their legs, too.

By the time she'd finished a quick shower and found an unopened toothbrush to use—and what was *that* about? Did he bring strange women here all the time that he had to keep a spare toothbrush on hand?— she was ready for the confrontation she knew was coming. He probably expected her to be all apologetic and ashamed. Well, guess again, fang boy.

She found her jeans still hanging on the back of the door from last night. They were somewhat damp having hung there through two showers, but with a few tugs and some chafed skin she finally managed to get them on and zipped. She was still commando beneath them, of course, but it was better than having nothing on at all. She took one look at the too tight, red satin bustier she'd worn, thought about squeezing into it again, and pulled Raj's sweatshirt over her head instead. It was loose enough that she could go braless for the short trip back to her house. There'd be no one to see her but Raj, and he wasn't interested anyway.

She took a deep breath, letting the air slide in and out of her lungs to relieve the stress, and then opened the bathroom door.

* * * *

Raj was standing on the other side of the room, near the closet, when the bathroom door opened and Sarah stomped out. She immediately began searching for something, ignoring him completely. That surprised him. That and her attitude. He'd expected embarrassment, even shame. He'd thought she might slip into the bedroom quietly, so overcome with guilt that she wouldn't even look at him. He could have dealt with that, had even been prepared to make it easy on her and pretend they could forget the whole humiliating evening. But there she was, marching around, yanking the bedclothes aside, muttering under her breath and bending over in those goddamn tight jeans in a way that was very dangerous. To both of them. He was already hanging by a thread where she was concerned.

She located her shoes, standing first on one foot then the other to slip them on her feet. She was instantly several inches taller, and her legs looked a mile longer. He nearly groaned.

She finally looked at him. "I'd like to leave now."

"I'll take you to the warehouse. Em can arrange—" He stopped and stared at her. She was doing something with her hand, holding it toward him and opening and closing her fingers and thumb like a puppet talking or something. "What the fuck is that?" he demanded.

"That, oh great vampire, is *blah, blah, blah*. I need to know where my car is, with my things in it, and then I'm going home. If you don't want to drive me there, you can just open that stupid door and let me out of this dungeon. I'll get a taxi. It may surprise you to learn that I've managed on my own for several years with—"

She stopped mid-word, finally shocked into silence by his abrupt presence only inches away from her, her human senses having failed to see him move.

"Tread lightly, little one," he warned. "You don't want to push me. Not tonight."

Her eyes darkened with anger, narrowing as she met his gaze evenly despite her surprise. "Really? And why is that, Raj? I'm tired of you thinking you have the right to control me. You're not my boyfriend and you're sure as hell not my keeper, so from where I stand, you've got no claim on me whatsoever. Like the song says, you don't want me for yourself so let me find somebody else. It's shit or get off the pot time, Raj. It's now or never. Time to—"

She gave a startled shriek as Raj swung an arm around her waist and lifted her off her feet. He threaded the fingers of one hand through her hair and pulled it aside, freeing the long line of her neck. "Then I choose now," he growled.

Sarah cried out as Raj sank his fangs into the velvet skin of her neck and punctured the fragile wall of her plump jugular. Her cries turned to moans of pleasure and the blood began to flow, warm and sweet, just as he'd known it would be. She wound her arms around him, cradling his head, holding his mouth against her vein. The first orgasm shuddered through her body and she whispered his name over and over, until she was limp in his arms.

He lifted his head away from her neck and licked the wound closed, savoring the bouquet of her blood, the taste of her skin. She nuzzled against him with a contented sigh and he lifted her higher, cupping her ass in both hands and walking toward the bed.

"Don't get too comfortable, sweetheart," he murmured. "I'm nowhere near done with you yet." He lay her down on the bed and stripped away the sweatshirt he'd given her, relishing the sight of every inch of skin as it was revealed to him. He groaned at the sight of her breasts, full and heavy, with nipples and areolas so light a pink that he could barely tell where they ended and her pale skin began. Unable to resist, he lowered his head to taste them, sampling each hard, round nipple, feeling it swell in his mouth like a juicy, ripe fruit. Tracing the outlines of her breasts with his tongue, he moved down her body, unzipping the tight jeans, rolling them off her hips and over her flat stomach.

She arched against his hands as he slid the jeans further down her legs, as the cleft of her sex came into view, smooth and velvety but for a small patch of soft blond curls at the top of her mound. He tugged the pants over her feet and tossed them away, then stood and stripped off his own denims.

"Spread your legs for me, Sarah," he crooned, lowering himself to the bed, sliding his thighs beneath hers. Sarah bit her lip, but spread her thighs enough that her legs straddled his, giving him a bare glimpse of her tender folds. He laughed low in his throat, almost growling as he placed his hands on her knees, running his fingers down the inside of her thighs. "Wider, little one."

She gasped, her entire body blushing with embarrassment as he spread her wide open to his gaze. "Such a pretty pussy." He wet one finger in his mouth, reached out and let it glide through her slit, opening her even further to his inspection. "And so wet for me." He breathed in the sweet scent of her arousal and hummed with pleasure.

"Raj!" she protested, but her body gave her away, her back arched with pleasure, nipples plump and begging for attention. His finger traveled up to the hard button of her clit and lingered, watching her shiver with desire as he circled it over and over again. "Raj," she repeated, but in a whisper this time, full of longing.

Wanting, needing to taste all of her, he buried his face between her legs, his tongue replacing his fingers, her juices flowing, her clit pulsing as he brought her to orgasm after orgasm until she screamed his name, fingers clenched in his hair, jerking spasmodically as if not knowing whether to force him closer or tug him away. His tongue continued to explore her, tasting each new secret valley, while his long, thick fingers teased her from the inside, fucking her, tormenting her, promises of what was to come. She trembled beneath his assault, soaked with the juices of her latest climax, her voice hoarse from crying his name more times than he could count. She moaned suddenly, her head thrashing from side to side. "Raj. Please."

He circled her clit with his tongue once more before raising his head enough to ask, "Please, what, little one?"

She shivered beneath him. "I need you inside me. Please."

He slid up her body, rubbing his chin, his chest, the hard length of his cock against her sensitized clit. "Tell me what you want, Sarah," he demanded.

She stared at him, hazel eyes dark with hunger and filled with tears. "Fuck me, Raj. Please fuck me."

He rewarded her with a slow, satisfied grin, spreading her legs wide around his hips as he sank between her thighs. There was no need for foreplay. She was soaking wet and ready for him. But she was small. And he was not. He slid into her with a long, slow thrust, feeling her body's resistance as it made room for him. She was tight. So tight. She gasped loudly, her fingers tightening against his arms, the muscles of her slick, hot tunnel squeezing his cock in protest at his sudden invasion. He paused for a few seconds, letting her body adjust to his size, and then beginning to move carefully in and out, going deeper with every thrust until her inner muscles softened around him, caressing him in a welcoming embrace.

He thrust hard, sinking himself into her to the hilt as he began fucking her in earnest, driving in and out, holding himself above her with his arms, watching her face, holding her gaze with every thrust of his body. She was murmuring his name, lost in pleasure, her overheated skin gleaming with sweat as she arched upward to meet him. He licked her skin, savoring yet another taste of her, salty and warm. She raised her knees higher and he pushed them against her chest so he could explore even deeper. She cried out and pulled him closer, her nails digging into his back.

He growled his pleasure and drove even harder, her small body lifting with every downward stroke, her breasts shaking, nipples as hard and large as cherries, and flushed as bright a pink. He lowered his head and bit into one, tasting the red juice of her blood, listening to her screams of pleasure as she crested and climaxed one more time.

The feel of her orgasm around his cock was too much for him. It rippled along his length like a thousand fingers, touching everywhere, stroking, massaging, encouraging, begging him to give up his seed. He threw back his head and roared as he crashed over the edge of desire and filled her completely.

Raj collapsed against Sarah, not certain he could move, every breath filled with her scent. He could feel her heart beating beneath him, could smell the scent of her blood. He groaned and rolled over before he crushed her completely, pulling her against him and tucking her under his arm with her head on his chest. He stroked her long hair gently, hearing the rhythm of her breathing grow smooth and even as she slowly relaxed. Her eyes were closed, but she continued to caress him with one hand, starting high on his chest and gliding down over his ribs to his hip and back up again, over and over.

This was a mistake. He knew that. But that didn't explain the bone-deep satisfaction he felt at having her lying sated and hot next to him, her blood already warming him as it coursed through his veins and into his heart. She was his. He'd known it from the moment he saw her, and no matter how much he fought it, no matter how much danger it put her in, he wanted her with him. In his bed, in his life. He sighed deeply, and Sarah's entire body shifted up and down with the movement of his chest.

"If you say you're sorry," she murmured drowsily, "I'm going to stake you while you sleep."

Raj smiled and then laughed, holding her closer. "I'm not sorry," he admitted. "Although this probably wasn't wise."

"Wise be damned. We'd never leave our houses if all we cared about was being wise. I don't want to be wise, I want to *live*."

"Ah."

She sat up and stared down at him sternly, the effect ruined by the tumble of her blond hair, the sway of her gorgeous breasts.

"Gods, you're beautiful," he said softly. "I could stay here and make love to you for days."

Sarah blushed, but gave him a very satisfied smile. "Only days?"

"Well," he began, pulling her closer so he could nuzzle one full mound. He bit her nipple lightly and said, "I have all the food I need right here, but you'll need to eat eventually, too."

"Right," she said, breathlessly, already arching her back to encourage his tongue in its renewed explorations. "Oh, God, Raj!"

He rolled her under him, spreading her legs with his hips and sliding deep into her slippery, wet heat. Her body took him easily this time. She was still open, her walls still pulsing from their earlier lovemaking. He started slowly, thrusting in and out, withdrawing until only the tip of his cock rested against her and then plunging deep once again. She wrapped her legs around his hips, her cries of pleasure urging him to a faster speed. He felt her climax begin to rise, felt her body pulsing around him, sucking him in, caressing his cock until she fell over the edge of ecstasy and screamed wordlessly. Raj threw back his head and howled her name, claiming her to the world. She was his, only his, ever his.

* * * *

Sarah lay beneath the weight of Raj's big body, feeling as if her every bone, every muscle, every tendon had melted, leaving her a puddle of humanlike liquid. A very happy and satisfied liquid to be sure, but certainly not capable of anything so ambitious as movement. He muttered something she didn't catch, then lifted himself on his powerful arms and shifted to one side, one arm reaching out to scoop her in close, as if he feared she'd get away.

She had no intention of going anywhere, but she knew Raj, and the next words out of his mouth were going to be something about keeping her far away from whatever was happening here in town. She was going to have to get used to that, she supposed. Used to having a bossy, arrogant, overly protective, wonderful, handsome lover of a vampire to care about her. Because he did care. He hadn't said it, not in words, but there was something about the way he held her, the way he looked down at her when they made love that said she mattered to him. He considered her *his*. And Sarah thought there were surely worse things in life than to be treasured by someone like Raj.

"I'm surprised you knew that song. *You Keep Me Hangin' On* by the Supremes," he said unexpectedly. "That was before you were born."

Sarah smiled against his chest. *Okay, so maybe the second words out of his mouth*, she thought dreamily. "When I was in that nut house my parents found for me—" He growled softly and she laid a kiss on his chest in thanks. "There was this nighttime orderly. The hospital didn't allow any music; they said it upset the patients, but this guy thought that was cruel and unusual punishment. So he snuck in a radio and we used to sit there listening to music."

Raj made a grunting sound of disapproval. "Is that what you called it?"

She smacked his chest in the very same spot she'd been kissing earlier. "He was way older than I was, old enough to be my grandfather almost, and he liked the oldies so that's what we listened to. Motown mostly; he loved his soul music." She was quiet for a moment, remembering and then she said, "I'm surprised *you* knew the song."

He huffed a dismissive breath. "I was running clubs in New York before you were born, little girl. And they weren't always the hot spots of Manhattan either. We started out with a working class dance club in Brooklyn back in the sixties."

"Huh," she said, as though thinking heavily. "So that means *you're* almost old enough to be my grandfather, too."

Raj laughed. "Great, great grandfather, more likely, but who's counting."

Sarah snuggled closer, happy that he could joke with her and wondering when that *other* subject was going to come up and ruin her evening. Not much longer, it turned out.

"Sarah." He took a deep breath.

Here it comes, she thought.

"You can't be a part of this investigation any longer. Just listen," he added when she sat up and glared at him, stopping her protest before she could draw the breath to voice it. "This has become vampire business, and any humans involved will only get hurt. You'll have to trust me to take care of this, to find Trish and the others." He met her gaze evenly. "You do trust me, don't you?"

She gave him a narrow look. "That's a cheap trick, Raj." He widened his eyes innocently. She blew out a disgusted breath. "Don't even give me that look," she scoffed. She chewed the inside of her lip, then swore softly, "Damn it." She drew her knees up and twisted around, so she was sitting next to him. "What will you do next?"

Raj rested his head on one muscled arm, reaching out with the other to circle her body, cupping her ass with his hand. "I'm going to find out who's doing this and tear him apart."

"It can't be that easy or you would have done it by now."

He grinned. "I know more now than I did a few days ago. I didn't get much from Regina, but I got enough to know where to look. Trust me, sweetheart. This operation is about to be shut down."

Sarah sighed, surrendering. "I can't sit here in the dark waiting for you. I'll go nuts."

He laughed. "Don't worry. I won't leave you in my dungeon."

"I didn't mean it when I said that."

"I know. But I don't think I've ever seen you that angry before. It was . . . impressive."

Sarah snorted. "It got you off your ass, anyway."

"Speaking of asses," he patted hers appreciatively. "But first, I've got to call Em."

Chapter Forty-two

"Raj!" Emelie's voice was as frantic as he'd ever heard it when she answered the phone.

"Is everything all right there, Em?"

"Yes," she said quickly. "It was you I was . . . Is Sarah with you?"

"Yes."

"Is she . . . okay?"

"Yeah, she is." He mock-glared at Sarah when she grinned, obviously having guessed what Em's question had been and probably how she'd asked it too.

"Well, shit," Em swore. "About fucking time, too."

"Listen, Em. I'll be back there before morning with Sarah, and I'll be staying. I want to hit the ground running tomorrow, so lay low tonight. If the guys want to feed from the vein, tell them to hunt the city, not the blood houses, and stay sharp. And I'm sure I don't have to tell you to be discreet."

"My middle name, boss."

"I never knew that."

"Kiss my ass."

"That's kiss my ass, *my lord*, to you." Em's laughter cut off as he hit disconnect. "As for you, little one," he murmured, pulling Sarah close and rolling her beneath him. "I have entirely different plans for *your* ass, although if you ask nicely, I *will* kiss it first."

* * * *

Her ass and every other part of her body was deliciously sore when she stepped into the shower, her muscles like rubber bands that had been stretched too far. She ducked her head under the hot water, letting it soak her hair and run down her back. It felt good, almost as good as the long, hard heat of Raj's body when he stepped into the shower behind her and pulled her against him.

She let him support her as he reached for the soap and began running those wonderful big hands of his all over her body in a halfhearted effort to wash away the hours of sweat-soaked sex. She closed her eyes and leaned into him, half-asleep on her feet. "How long until sunrise," she asked drowsily.

"A couple of hours," he murmured. He wrapped an arm around her waist, letting it slide up until her breasts rested heavily on his smoothly muscled forearm. His other hand slid down over her belly and between her legs, his fingers rocking gently in and out. She gasped as he stroked over her swollen clit, the sensation like an electrical shock starting between her legs and traveling up her to her breasts where her nipples hardened in immediate response. Raj chuckled softly against her ear. "I might just fuck you for days after all."

She shivered as his words triggered memories of the last few hours, hours spent in a state of permanent arousal as the euphorics in his bite roared through her system over and over again until she was too limp to do anything but lie in his arms and tremble. She pressed her ass back against the hard length of his cock, kneading his thighs as she rubbed herself up and down, feeling his erection glide against her soap slicked skin. It was Raj's turn to groan, his arms tightening their hold on her, his hand between her legs pressing harder as he lowered his head to nuzzle her neck and shoulder, biting gently.

Sarah writhed against his assault, wishing he was right, wishing they could stay in his underground hideaway, safe in its soft glow and silken sheets while the world and its stresses went on without them. She heard Raj's breath quicken as he lifted her from behind, trapping her against the wet, tiled wall and spreading her legs with one knee as he slid his full length deep inside her. She shuddered and cried out his name, twisting around as his mouth came down on hers with surprising ferocity, crushing his lips against her teeth so hard that his blood flowed, filling her mouth and throat. She choked and would have pulled away, but he held her steady, not letting go. "Just a sip, little one," he murmured against her skin. "It's important." His cock continued to pound in and out, his fingers playing her clit, overwhelming her with sensation, distracting her so that she drank the warm blood reflexively. "That's my good girl," he whispered, redoubling his efforts until the power of his blood hit her, and he swallowed the scream of her first orgasm. Not stopping, he stroked harder, faster, exploding deep inside her as his fingers brought her over the edge one more time and she joined him in a surging climax that roared through her body, leaving her hanging limp in his arms.

"Sarah."

Her eyes fluttered open. There was water all around and the air was steaming. "Oh, shit," she gasped. Raj laughed and she slapped at him. She'd fallen asleep in the damn shower. "Very funny. This is all your fault, you know."

"If you're suggesting that I've exhausted you with my extraordinary sexual prowess, I am happy to take the blame."

She turned and yawned into his chest. "Am I clean yet?"

"Yes. As clean and sweet as always." He reached over her shoulder and turned off the water. "Come on. Let's get you dry and dressed. We're going to the warehouse for the day."

"You're staying there too?"

"It's either that or we both stay here, and I don't think you want that."

Sarah thought about being locked in Raj's vault-bedroom all day, with him lying all but lifeless on the bed. "No," she said, shaking her head. "But is there room for you over there?"

Raj laughed. "I think they'll make room for their lord and master. Besides, after last night, Krystof knows you're mine, and I don't want you too far away until this thing is done."

Chapter Forty-three

"You see this door?"

Sarah stopped and turned to examine the warehouse door she'd just walked through. She looked up at Raj with a frown of confusion. "Yeah?"

"You don't go past this door until I'm standing next to you."

Sarah gave him a skeptical look. "Yeah, right."

"I'm serious, Sarah. You're perfectly safe as long as you stay here, and I trust my human guards completely. If I didn't, you'd be downstairs with me whether you wanted to be or not."

Sarah opened her mouth to protest his usual high-handed treatment, but he was suddenly right next to her, pulling her against his chest. "I trust them, but I'm trusting you, too, Sarah. Don't make me come looking for you because I will find you. I've tasted your blood and you've tasted mine. You can't hide from me and I *will* be pissed."

Sarah stretched up to put her arms around his neck and tugged his face down for a long, slow kiss. "All right."

"Come on," he said, putting his lips next to her ear. "I'll tuck you in." Her entire body flushed with heat at the suggestion in his words and she glanced at her watch. Raj laughed knowingly. "There's time, sweetheart," he said. "There's always time."

* * * *

Sarah pushed aside the too warm blankets and rolled over. She might have been tired enough to fall asleep standing in the shower, but this bed was too hard and every time she closed her eyes, all she could see was Raj, his blue eyes glowing with satisfaction as she shuddered beneath him, wave after wave of orgasm rolling over her helplessly. She swore softly and sat up, reaching for the bottle of water she'd left on the cheap nightstand. As weird as she'd found the idea of drinking even the smallest amount of Raj's blood, there was only one word for what she'd felt as his blood rolled down her throat and his cock pounded into her body. Ecstasy, utter and complete ecstasy. Just thinking about it had her shivering eagerly, her breasts swelling, nipples hardening, that tight anticipation between her legs. She sighed and checked her watch. Hours to go yet. Raj would be laughing in his sleep if he could see her now.

But at least the little bit of blood she'd consumed had helped with the aches and pains after a long night of sex, especially since she'd been celibate for over a year. What soreness she'd experienced was already beginning to fade, thanks to the healing effect of vampire blood. Clearly, there were definite advantages to having a vampire lover. Apart from the incredible sex, of course. Cyn had dropped hints, more than hints really, of mind-blowing sex. But Sarah hadn't understood until now. And sex with Raj was more than just sex. It was, well, it was that trite old phrase . . . making love. There was more between them than simple sexual attraction. Way more. It seemed impossible that she could love someone after so short a time, but she did. She loved Raj. Absolutely, totally, head-over-heels love. Who would have thought? She laughed out loud and covered her mouth quickly, not wanting anyone to hear.

My God, what would her colleagues at the university think? Proper little Professor Stratton—her thoughts stuttered to a halt. But she wasn't Professor Stratton anymore, was she? That part of her life was gone. The truth was a dark cloud hanging over her happiness, and she shoved it aside along with the blankets. She wasn't going to think about that today.

She swung out of bed. There were hours to kill before sunset. Hours before she could see Raj and he could make her forget all about ruined careers. She sighed and looked around. Well, she might have to stay in the warehouse, but she sure as hell wasn't going to stay in this damn room all day. She needed to work off some energy or she really was going to go nuts.

Peeling off Raj's sweatshirt, she held it to her face, inhaling the warm smell that was eau de Raj. It was the only reason she'd slept in it, not that she'd ever admit that to anyone, least of all him. He wasn't exactly lacking in the arrogance department. *Or any other department*, she thought wickedly. Feeling somewhat smug, she donned a sports bra and underwear and then pulled on a pair of leggings and a t-shirt. She might have to stay inside, but it was a very big warehouse. More than big enough to give her a place to run.

An hour later, Sarah was pounding around the parked SUVs one more time, ducking instinctively as she started along the wall beneath the overhang of the mezzanine balcony. There were empty offices here and she wondered what this warehouse had once been used for. Manufactured goods maybe, from the good old days when Buffalo had been the heart of the steel belt. Now gone to rust like everything else.

She swerved away from the wall to avoid the open grids of the metal stairway and headed toward the living area. Simon was tapping away on his computers. He didn't even look up when she ran past, just as he hadn't on the previous nineteen circuits. She kept going until she hit the stairs again before deciding she'd tormented her body enough for one day and gave up. Besides, it wasn't like she hadn't gotten plenty of exercise the night before. She smiled at the thought and slowed even further, shaking her legs out in a small circle at the foot of the stairs, intending to go directly to her room and into a hot shower.

"Hi."

Sarah jumped about two feet straight up, spinning around to stare at the waiflike young woman sitting about a third of the way up the stairs.

"I'm Nina," the woman said when Sarah blinked at her in confusion. "You must be Sarah."

"Uh, yeah. Sorry, but who're you?"

"Oh, they didn't tell you?

"Tell me what?"

The girl blushed and Sarah felt like an ass. She was a skinny, little thing, barely there in a too summery dress and pink sweater, clutching one of those tiny, pink rhinestone-covered cell phones with fingers that were more bone than flesh. And she was gazing up at Sarah with faded blue eyes in a pale face that seemed too old for her years.

"Sorry," Sarah said again. "You just surprised me, that's all. I didn't know anyone else was here. Well, except for the guards, you know, and Simon."

"Yeah," the girl said vaguely.

"So, who are you again?"

"Nina," she repeated, as if that meant something.

"Are you with one of the human guards?" More likely, Sarah thought privately, this child was with one of the vampires. She certainly looked like she'd been drained of not just blood, but vitality.

"No. I'm with Byron and Serge."

"Are they here too?"

"No," the girl said sadly.

Sarah was beginning to think maybe Nina wasn't playing with a full deck. "Okay. I've got to, uh, go upstairs and, um, shower, so I'll just . . ." She took a step toward the stairs, intending to go over or around the waiflike Nina, but the girl suddenly came alive.

"Do you have any magazines to read?"

Sarah stopped with one foot on the stair and frowned. "I might have something in my car."

Nina brightened. "Is your car here?"

"Well, yeah, but—"

"Maybe you could take me to the store then!"

"Oh. No. I can't do that. I mean I promised—"

"Oh."

The girl seemed so downcast that Sarah felt compelled to add, "But I can look in my car. I probably have something to read. Maybe not a magazine, but I'm sure there's a book or two."

"What kind?" Nina asked uncharitably.

"Romance, I guess. Probably vampires." Sarah knew there were probably a couple of more serious titles in there, too, but figured that wasn't what Nina was looking for.

"Cool. I love those. Can we look?"

"What? Now?"

"Well, yeah."

Sarah sighed. "Okay. Let me get my keys."

The guard wasn't happy. Sarah was fairly certain he'd given in just to make Nina shut up, which was pretty much her own motivation as well. But the truth was she *didn't* think it was a big deal. Sure, she'd promised Raj not to go outside, but he'd meant *outside,* as in a trip to the mall, not a few feet from the door, for God's sake. That whole thing about not crossing the threshold had just been him making a joke out of it. After all, it was full daylight. The bad guys were all vampires and they were tucked away in their dark, little beds just like the ones sleeping downstairs.

The guard opened the inside door and waited while they crowded into the anteroom between the two doors, and then opened the heavier, exterior door, stepping out into the sunshine for a brief moment to look around. He murmured something into his radio, then waved an impatient hand for them to come ahead. Sarah had just started forward when his head suddenly snapped around and she heard the sound of a car engine, revving hard and coming too close too fast.

After that, everything happened in slow motion, seeming to take forever, though it couldn't have been more than a few seconds. The guard staggered backwards to the rattle of gunfire. She heard men shouting and spun around, yanking at the inside door with some vague notion of warning the others, but the security system wouldn't release it as long as the outside door was open. Nina was just standing there, her pale face distorted with panic, only she wasn't looking at the masked men now running toward them, but at the door Sarah was struggling to get open. Sarah finally understood when she felt the other woman's bony fingers grasping her arm, felt the surprising strength as she shoved Sarah toward the black maw of a long, dark car.

As if it was happening to someone else, she heard the battle going on around her, the slam of the heavy door behind her, the cordite smell of gunfire, the burning rubber of squealing tires and above it all the screams of injured men. But then she was being seized by a pair of powerful arms, thrown into the back seat of a car and rolled to the floor. Something rough and smelly was jammed into her mouth and her hands were jerked behind her to be tied with the pinch of plastic binding. A needle stung as it was shoved into her hip and she felt everything fade into unconsciousness. Her last thought was that Raj was really going to be pissed this time.

Chapter Forty-four

Raj came awake with a roar, leaping from the narrow bed and unleashing the full weight of his power for the first time in years. It thundered through the warehouse, shaking the very foundations, as walls trembled and he felt every one of his guards, man and vampire alike, fall to their knees in trepidation.

Sarah! He searched for her, cursing himself for not making the blood link stronger, for not pushing her harder to take more of his blood. There was nothing, and for a moment he knew despair. But close upon it was the certain knowledge that she *was not dead.* She was unconscious, drugged, he didn't know which, but she was alive.

He pulled on his clothes, thinking furiously. He could feel his vampires all around him, their thoughts fearful of his rage, wondering at the cause of it, but still staunch, still holding strong and bracing their power for his use. He'd chosen well in his children. There were no cowards among them, no weaklings. He threw open his door and stormed into the corridor. They waited for him there, on bended knee, heads bowed in fealty and submission.

His gaze found Emelie. She raised her head at his unspoken summons and her eyes were full of knowledge and of fear, but the fear was *for* him, not of him. "No more games, Em. Let's get everyone loaded up and moving. This ends tonight."

Raj watched over Simon's shoulder as the tech wiz played the video of the abduction one more time. He felt Em approaching from behind and he spun around, giving her a cold look. "What the fuck was Nina doing here?"

"I take responsibility, my lord. Byron called last night while you were gone. He said Krystof had heard he was talking to you, that he'd made threats. He asked if Nina could stay with us. He wanted to bring her over and stay, too, but I didn't trust him that far. Abel and I went and picked her up. She must have called someone. I'm sorry. I didn't even know she had a phone."

"I want to talk to the guard who opened the fucking door for them this afternoon."

"He's barely alive, my lord. We've given him enough blood to stabilize him for now, but he's pretty out of it. I got just enough out of him to know what happened, and I confirmed the details with the two guards we had on the roof. They were all three taken down the minute the door opened, before Sarah was even touched."

"Son of a bitch. Where's that asshole Byron?"

"Cervantes and Abel are on their way over to his place. If we're lucky, we'll catch him before he wakes up enough to run. We can only hope Nina was stupid enough to go home to him."

"All right. Let's get everyone loaded up and moving. If Byron's not there, we won't waste time looking for him. He and that bitch of his will pay, but Sarah comes first." He shrugged on his jacket, feeling its weight settle over his shoulders, inhaling the warm scent of the fine leather. He'd lived well as a vampire. As much as he might once have regretted the change, as much as he still despised Krystof for turning him against his will, he had to admit that much. His long life had been far easier than his human life had ever been.

"My lord," Em said tentatively. He looked up and saw the sheen of tears in her eyes.

"Don't cry, Em. We've had a good run."

"Damnit, Raj, don't you dare—"

He gave her a vicious grin. "Don't worry. I have no intention of throwing myself on my sword. Krystof's going down tonight, but I'd be a fool and a lousy Sire if I didn't take precautions."

Em's eyes widened. "I will not—"

"Yes, you will," he said in a hard voice. "I'll take two in with me. I'll even let you pick which ones. But you stay out of it, Em. I need you—"

"You can't do that to me, it's—"

"I can and I will." He took a step closer and in a rare gesture of affection, put a tender hand on her cheek. "You were my first child, Emelie, and you will always be my best. But you're not my only. I have too many here and back home who count on me for protection. If something goes wrong, I need someone outside the kill zone who's strong enough to shelter my people from the backlash. It's bad enough that some will die. I don't want everyone going down with me. You understand? I need *you*, Em. You can save them if I fall."

"You're not going to fall," she whispered fiercely.

"No," he said with another grin "I'm not. I'm going to take down that son of a bitch and anyone else who had anything to do with this. And then I'm going to find Sarah and teach her the price for breaking a promise to her lord and master."

Em choked back something that was part sob and part laugh. "Good luck with that."

"Have a little faith, Emelie."

"I have tons of faith, my lord. If I didn't, you'd have to step over my dead body to get out that damn door."

* * * *

The warehouse was buzzing with energy. Raj stood and absorbed it all—the vicious exhilaration of vampires who knew they would soon be set free, that the bonds of civilization, the confinement of the laws and mores they were forced to live under in this new world of surveillance cameras and DNA, these would be set aside for a night. Tonight was about Vampire, tonight was bloodshed and mayhem, and they were bursting with the joy of it.

He cracked his jaw in an open grin, stretching out his arms as if he could scoop up all that energy and soak it in by great handfuls. He let his own power wash over them, filling them with confidence and the surety of his strength beside them. They would do this together and they would see victory before the night was over. He nodded at Emelie and she grinned back. His vampires howled and began piling into the waiting vehicles. Engines roared to life and the big bay doors rolled open.

He strode toward the open door of the last SUV and slammed to a halt as an awareness of Sarah suddenly flooded his senses. She was awake and alert. He thrust a spear of power outward, struggling to reach her over the weak blood bond, but it wasn't enough. He pounded the roof of the SUV in frustration and settled for a powerful push of reassurance and warmth. She would know he was here, that he was coming. That would have to be enough.

He spun around at the sound of Em's phone ringing. She flipped it up to her ear and listened. Her eyes shifted to him and she mouthed one name—Byron.

"They've got him," she said, disconnecting and shoving the phone back into her pocket.

Raj bared his teeth in a fang-baring snarl. "Then that's our first stop."

Chapter Forty-five

It was cold where she was, and dark and damp. She could smell the moisture creeping down the walls and rising up from beneath the floor to bring an ache to her bones. She rolled over triggering a vicious bout of vertigo that had her grabbing blindly for something solid to ground herself and found the chill rail of a metal bed. She clung to it, feeling the rough craters where flakes of paint had chipped away. She lay there breathing carefully and waited, convinced she was dreaming and would soon wake in her own bed, her own room.

"Hello?" a shaky girl's voice called.

Shock jolted Sarah's eyes open and she woke to her worst nightmare come true. Her heart rate soared, squeezing the air from her lungs and jerking her entire body with every beat.

"Hello? Is someone there?" the girl called again.

Sarah's head swiveled in the direction of the voice and saw a crack of light where the door hadn't completely closed. Her eyes widened and she fisted a hand over her mouth to keep from screaming. She knew this place. The door swung open and she looked up, expecting to see the shadowed form from her nightmares, the one who'd taken Trish and left Regina for dead.

"You're awake." A young woman stood outlined in the light from the hallway, short like Sarah, but thinner and much younger. Trish, Sarah realized. This was Trish Cowens.

"It's all right," Trish was saying. "They're gone for now." She came closer, moving slowly, one hand out as if she was approaching a frightened animal.

Sarah blinked. And felt a swell of fiery rage that started in her heart and raced out to warm every part of her body. It was Raj. She could feel him like a huge, but distant blaze of fury. Memory of his blood warm against her tongue flashed so vividly she could taste it. She hadn't wanted to take any of his blood, had only agreed in order to please him. The idea of more had been disgusting. But now she understood why it had been important. It was the link Cyn had tried to tell her about. She only hoped it was enough for him to find her before it was too late.

"Are you okay?" Trish asked.

Sarah managed a weak smile, but realized the girl might not be able to see it. "Yeah," she said out loud. "Or I will be in a minute." She swallowed her nausea, inhaling deeply, letting the air out slowly and repeating the cycle. She looked up. "You're Trish Cowens, aren't you?"

Trish rushed over to the bed, nearly stumbling in her urgency to get closer. "Are they looking for me? Is my dad—" Her voice cracked and Sarah put out a hand, drawing the girl down to sit next to her. As if the touch was a signal, Trish began to cry, sobbing like a small child. Sarah wrapped her arms around her and let her cry, holding her tight and rocking slightly.

Trish's sobs eventually diminished, but she held on, rubbing her wet face against Sarah's t-shirt. "Are you with the police?" she asked in a small, hopeful voice.

Sarah sighed. If she got out of this alive, Raj was going to kill her. "I'm not with the police, Trish, but my friends know where I am and they'll come for us."

"It's vampires," Trish said dully. "That's who's got us."

"I know," Sarah said and tightened her hold on the frightened young woman.

"They killed Regina."

"No," Sarah said quickly. "We found Regina in time and we saved her."

Trish sat up and stared at her in the faint light. "For real? You're not just saying that to make me feel better?"

"No way, hon. She's alive and so are we, and I intend to stay that way. We're getting out of here, Trish. I don't know how yet, but we are definitely getting out of here alive."

Chapter Forty-six

Byron's house looked much the same as it had four nights ago. Byron, however, did not. He groveled on the floor in front of Raj, naked but for a pair of loose sweatpants, blood running from several deep gashes across his chest and arms.

Raj looked at Cervantes, his brow quirked.

"He tried to escape, my lord," Cervantes deadpanned.

Raj considered the contrast between the spindly Byron and Cervantes and permitted himself a small smile. It didn't last long. He strolled over to Byron and crouched down to meet the weaker vampire's eyes, his forearms on his knees and his hands hanging loosely between them. "You don't look so good, By."

Byron flashed him a look of intense dislike before quickly lowering his head and hiding behind a fall of lanky hair. "I didn't do nuthin," he muttered.

"No? Then maybe it was just Nina. What do you think? Can't have our humans defying us like that, can we? Shall I kill her for you?"

Byron's head came up, sheer panic in his eyes. "Nina didn't do it, Raj. I swear."

"Do what?" Raj asked softly.

Byron blinked quickly, knowing he was caught. "Whatever it is," he insisted, his voice dropping into a plaintive whine. "You send these guys to roust me out, I figure something's going on, but I was sleeping, man. You know that. And Nina, she wouldn't do—"

Raj crooked a finger and Byron screamed, his head thrown back, the tendons in his neck standing out like shards of bone. Raj dropped his hand and Byron fell forward, curling in on himself like the wounded animal he was, his hands wrapped around his head as he wept loudly.

Raj leaned forward to whisper in his ear. "Can you hear Nina's heart beating, By? I can."

The weeping vampire raised his head to stare at Raj in horror.

"How loud do you think you'll have to scream before she comes out of her hiding place? Let's see, shall we?"

"No," Byron whimpered. "No, you can't—" His voice was shredded as he shrieked in agony, blood running from his ears, his eyes, and every pore as Raj closed his fist and squeezed him dry. Blood began to pool beneath him and Cervantes stepped back fastidiously, his eyes gleaming butter yellow with a combination of blood lust and excitement.

Raj raised his head to catch Cervantes's gaze before shifting enough to cast a lazy glance at a section of the cheap, paneled wainscoting lining the dreary room. Cervantes's eyes widened and he studied the paneling carefully, running a thick-fingered hand along the surface until he found what he was looking for. He looked over his shoulder at Raj, who shook his head briefly before returning his attention to the dying Byron.

"What a waste, By," he said with real regret. "I would have protected you." He stood with a slight gesture and watched dispassionately as Byron crumbled to dust at his feet. He brushed his hands together briskly and jerked his chin up in a signal to Cervantes.

The big vampire closed his hand into a fist and smashed it into the wainscoting, eliciting a scream of surprise and fear from Nina who was huddled deep inside her hidey-hole. Cervantes reached in and dragged her out with no more compassion than he'd shown Byron, holding her by the scruff of her neck so that she dangled in front of him. "What shall I do with this, my lord?

Raj's lip curled up in distaste as he touched the weeping woman's mind. Her thoughts were chaotic with fear, scattering before him like leaves in the wind. He caught an image of Sarah and clung to it, wrenching the memory from Nina's brain with no care for the damage he might do. He saw the abductors, saw his human guard fall trying to shove Sarah back to safety, saw her thrown into the back seat as the battle raged all around. But he knew all of this. He searched the muddle that was Nina's brain once more and found what he was looking for. A phone call, the voice on the other end. One that Raj recognized.

He withdrew from Nina's awareness, his power shoving her away like the distasteful piece of meat she was. She fell into the puddle of dust and blood that had been Byron and tried to push herself up, staring at the bloody goop on her hands and shrieking in horror when she realized what it must be. She scrambled away on all fours, leaving red streaks behind as she huddled against the wall, eyes wild as she gibbered madly.

"My lord," Em said from behind him. "Shall I—"

"No," he said sharply. "Leave her as she is."

"But—"

Raj spun and studied his lieutenant with eyes that glowed a deep, frosty blue. Everyone stilled, the only noise the insane mutterings of a madwoman and the sound of Em dropping to one knee.

"Forgive me, my lord."

He let her stay there to the count of three breaths and then strode from the room. "We're going to Krystof's," he said flatly.

His vampires rushed to follow, several cutting ahead of him to serve as a vanguard against any enemies who might have anticipated their moves and lay in wait outside. Raj frowned, but recognized the necessity. It was one he'd have to get used to from now on. Assuming he survived this night.

* * * *

Krystof's house looked the same as it always did. An aging mansion with shuttered windows and a driveway full of late model cars. Raj

stood on the street, his power tamped down once again—there was no
reason to shout out his presence to the vampire lord. Although between
his blowup earlier and his confrontation with Byron, the old man had to
know he was coming, especially once he'd taken Sarah. But it was the
very normalcy of the house that troubled him. He'd expected more
resistance, a frontline of defense, something to give Krystof advance
warning and spend Raj's resources, weakening him before he ever
entered the house.

He felt Em come up behind him. "What's wrong with this picture?"
he asked.

"It's too quiet," she replied immediately. "I'd expect Krystof to set
his frontline far away from his precious self." She nodded at the vampire
lord's house. "I've seen more security than this at a frat house."

Raj smiled tightly. "Been to many of those, Em?"

"A few," she acknowledged. "Those well-fed young men are always
so eager to share."

He snorted in amusement. "I'll take two in with me."

"My lord . . . Raj, I—"

"I need you out here, Em."

She sighed and waved over her shoulder. Cervantes and Yossi
stepped up and took up positions to either side of him. Raj gave Em a
sideways look.

"They drew straws for the honor," she said.

He snorted, thinking that accompanying one's Sire into possible
death was hardly much of an honor. "I do appreciate the thought,
gentlemen."

Cervantes gave him a grin, while Yossi nodded silently. Both eyed
the silent house eagerly, muscles taut with the effort of remaining still,
eyes gleaming in the street lights.

"We'll go in the back again," Raj said coolly. "If my previous visits
are anything to go by . . ." He lifted his head to indicate the house in
front of them with a smirk. ". . . I don't think we'll have a problem. You
can flank me however you want, until . . ." He shifted his gaze, making
eye contact with each of them, marveling that he could earn the staunch
loyalty of such strong, capable vampires. "Until," he repeated, continuing
in a softer voice, "we reach Krystof's inner sanctum. At that point, I
proceed alone."

He saw their uneasy reactions and smiled. "I understand your
concerns," he said and raised his eyes to include Emelie in his words.
"But it must be this way. Emelie?"

"Yes, my lord."

"Remember your promise."

Her eyes filled with pink tears, but she nodded once, sharply. "Yes,
my lord."

He gazed around at the assembled vampires and noted with some
surprise the number of human guards who'd chosen to accompany

them. He hadn't noticed them at Byron's, which meant someone had called them. He glanced over and saw Emelie avoiding his gaze. He shook his head in amazement. She was a rare gem, his Emelie.

He raised his head and let his power flow, reveling in the unparalleled rush of exhilaration as it spun outward into the night, announcing his presence to Krystof and to anyone else in range with the ability to detect such things. He breathed deeply and the air filling his lungs tasted as sweet and pure as any breath he'd ever drawn. His awareness stretched lazily, like a cat rising from an afternoon nap, his senses taking in the night around him. The beating of his vampires' hearts surrounded him like a timpani concerto, those of his human followers weaker but just as true. He closed his eyes against the overload of sensation, the tempting intoxication, and then opened them again with a clear purpose.

"Let's not keep Krystof waiting."

He swept around the house and into the kitchen, surprising three vampires who looked like they'd been caught on a blood run to the refrigerator. They stared at him in shock, only belatedly putting up a weak resistance. Raj brushed them away with a bare wisp of his power, slamming them against the walls and cabinets, draining their power and leaving them lying on the floor in a stupor. This was the price Krystof paid for choosing only the weak and stupid for his minions. Barely slowed by the encounter, Raj strode deeper into the house and down the stairs.

The basement was pandemonium. Warned by his approach through the kitchen, several of Krystof's brutish defenders rushed to the foot of the stairs, full of bristling intent and raging testosterone, but there was no organization to their assault. They seemed directionless, like pinballs in a machine, bouncing back and forth, not knowing whether to charge the intruder or retreat to defend their master's inner sanctum. Between them, Cervantes and Yossi handled the initial assault, and Raj easily overpowered the rest. He stood on the lower step and surveyed the wreckage, wondering once again at the vampire lord's meager resistance. And where was Jozef?

He shook his head. These things no longer mattered. The challenge had been well and truly rung now, and there was no going back. He crossed the room quickly and slammed the door open without ceremony. Krystof was hunched on his elaborate settee, his face buried in the bloodied neck of a young woman. He reared back at Raj's abrupt entry, mouth open in a furious snarl, fangs dripping blood down the lacy, white linen of his shirt. Raj barely registered the vampire lord's anger, his eyes filled instead with the sight of the woman's long, blond hair, her graceful, bare legs hanging limply to the floor, one white arm reaching out, her hand open in entreaty.

He roared, taking the room in two hard strides and tearing the woman from Krystof's grasp. Her hair fell away and he stared at an unfamiliar face. Relief surged through him that this wasn't Sarah lying dead in his arms, followed by guilt that he could find any relief in this woman's senseless death. He lifted his gaze and found the vampire lord who had killed her standing before him, his mouth open in a disgusting parody of laughter.

"You think to unseat me, Rajmund?" he taunted scornfully. His eyes shone like twin flames against his blackened soul as he gave his power free rein, letting it swell until the house groaned with the pressure, furniture flying against the walls and shattering into pieces as if a hurricane had risen fully formed in the center of the small room. But even that wasn't enough. A surge of almost electric power jolted the room as Krystof reached out to his minions, ripping their defenses away and sucking them dry, stealing what strength they had and weaving it into a seemingly impenetrable cocoon of protection for himself.

"You're nothing but a wharf rat," he snarled at Raj. "I was born to rule centuries before you were born, and I will rule for centuries after you've blown away in the wind along with your pitiful collection of *children*." He sneered the last word, flinging it into Raj's face like a gob of spittle.

Raj flexed his will, massing his own power with a sure, smooth elegance. It grew like the first wave of a great storm, raging higher, denser, drawing strength from that impossible place within himself, that reservoir of vampiric power that made the difference between a minion and a lord. He reached out and was aware of Cervantes and Yossi standing untouched just outside the office door, of Emelie on the street above channeling the power of every one of his vampires, both here and in far away Manhattan. She gathered even the meager life force of his human guards, sheltering them all even as she offered a lifeline of power for him to draw upon in need.

He knew his eyes had begun to burn with their cold, blue fire, and he smiled, seeing comprehension dawn on his Sire's face. "Talk is cheap, *my lord.*"

Krystof struck without warning, cracking the defensive cocoon of his power to launch a battering ram of pure energy across the small room. Raj grunted as it hit him, feeling his own strength dip beneath the lethal attack, giving way without breaking, flowing around Krystof's spear of power, consuming it, absorbing it into himself so that it left him stronger than before, not weaker. The vampire lord's eyes widened in shock and he strove viciously to pull back, straining to break free of Raj's might before he found himself sucked as dry as his own minions.

Raj reached out a hand and sliced downward, as if brushing away a clinging bit of flotsam. He felt a jolt of energy as his power closed around him once again, and he saw Krystof reel backwards, staggering slightly against the rubble that had once been his desk. But the old man wasn't finished. He was a vampire lord, not some overreaching slave who could be dismissed with a quick flex of power. He stood straight, arms outstretched, hands fisted as if gathering lightening from the very air. He thundered his challenge, rattling the walls and slamming a solid wall of energy across the room, crashing into Raj like tons of unforgiving stone, driving him back, forcing him to his knees. Raj howled in defiance, furious at his stupidity, his towering pride. He'd been so supremely certain of his own superiority, so swaggering in his arrogance. While he was laughing at the old man's efforts, Krystof had seized the initiative and was battering him with volley after volley of lethal force. He felt himself weakening beneath the unrelenting attack, while Krystof grew stronger, draining more and more of his minions, reaching to the ends of his territory, his very ruthlessness his greatest advantage.

Raj could hear Emelie screaming in his head, demanding he take what she offered, begging him when her demands went unheard. He thought of his vampire children, of Cervantes and Danny, of Yossi and his Angel. Of Emelie. What would happen to them, what vengeance would Krystof exact against his people for their master's arrogance? Unacceptable.

He opened himself to the flow of Emelie's power, drinking from the combined strength of his many children, letting his rage fuel his determination as he surged to his feet with a roar that threatened to bring the house down around them. He pummeled Krystof with blasts of power, one after the other, refusing to permit the vampire lord to dictate the terms of this encounter. He fought back in his own way, attacking from every side, forcing Krystof to defend against volleys from all around. The vampire lord howled, desperately fighting to recreate his impenetrable cocoon even as Raj's power ate away at its very fabric.

Krystof dropped finally to his knees in a last ditch defense, sucking power into himself like a vacuum, giving up any attempt to attack in favor of simple survival. When even that failed, he looked up and met Raj's eyes, his mouth open in a bloody grin, the fires in his eyes dying to faint embers. "I wish you joy of it," he said, and then laughed, howling like a madman as Raj drew his outstretched arms into his body until they were held before him like two fisted pillars of energy. Krystof screamed in agony as a terrible weight crushed him to the floor, every bone in his body cracking beneath the unbearable pressure, joints tearing and lungs bursting, blood seeping from every pore, every orifice, as his body seemed to fold in upon itself. Raj opened one fist wide, his skin whitening with strain, until he snapped the fist closed and Krystof's heart burst into flame within his chest.

The air in the room grew suddenly still, not a whisper of movement, not a speck of dust so much as drifted, and then like a vacuum collapsing in an instant, Krystof's body vaporized and disappeared, becoming no more than a pile of dust and bloody linen on the carpet.

Raj closed himself away from Emelie and fell to his knees, his head falling forward to his chest in exhaustion as he drew a deep breath . . . and screamed in agony. His mind was suddenly filled with thousands of voices as every living vampire in the territory clamored in fear, reaching out to him for sustenance, for protection, for their very lives. He was aware of the office door flying open, of Cervantes and Yossi rushing in to surround him, joining their power in an effort to buffer the overwhelming demands of Raj's new subjects. He rocked slowly back and forth, muscles straining, tendons standing out on his neck as he strove to make sense of what was happening, to bring some semblance of order and reason to the endless cacophony. The wall of power surrounding him grew stronger as Emelie added her own strength, as she channeled the others in carefully, building the wall brick by brick until at last the voices quieted, becoming no more than a steady hum in the background.

Raj remained on his knees, his head hanging forward, chin on his chest. Blood wept from his eyes and welled from his hands where his nails had dug gouges in his palms. He heard voices outside, footsteps pounding down the stairs, and then Emelie was there in the flesh, kneeling next to him.

"My lord?" she said softly. "Raj?" she added urgently, when he didn't respond.

He cracked one eye opened and rasped, "I hate that vampire shit."

She barked a laugh that was more like a sob of relief and called for someone to bring him some blood. More yelling and footsteps, and a bag of warmed blood was thrust into his hand. He ripped it open with his fangs and sucked it down, passing the empty bag and taking another as it was offered until he'd downed six full pints of blood, far more than any single human could have safely provided.

He drew a deep breath and looked at Emelie, his mind clear at last. "Sarah?" he asked her.

"Not in this house, my lord."

Raj swore foully. He'd accessed every filthy corner of Krystof's diseased brain and found nothing there of Sarah's abduction, or of any plot to sell vampire secrets to the drug companies, so where the hell . . .

There was a tumble of footsteps down the basement stairs and more voices arguing. "Damn," he groaned. "What now?"

Emelie remained by his side, but she spun around into a defensive crouch. Raj looked up and saw nothing but the bodies of his vampires forming a defensive wall between him and whatever was coming. He huffed out a laugh, realizing he'd somehow acquired his own wall of meat. He heard Simon's voice raised among the others. Well, at least his wall of meat had a brain. "Let him through, Em."

Simon squeezed between the bulky forms of Raj's guard, dropping into the clear space around him like a glob of toothpaste from a tube. He climbed to his knees and grinned. "My lord."

"Simon," Raj acknowledged. "Was there something you wanted to tell me?"

"Oh! Yes, my lord. You know I monitor all of the cell phone lines, because one never knows—"

"The *point*, Simon." The guy was a technical genius, but got lost in his own explanations sometimes.

"Yes, my lord. Sorry. Well, I noticed one number kept coming into your voice mail. Four calls in less than an hour. Of course, I can't access your voice mail, my lord, that would be—"

"The point?"

"I called the number back and it was Kent from the Amherst blood house. He said to tell you it was Jozef."

Raj froze, staring at his tech expert. "What was his message exactly?" he asked softly.

"He said to tell you he found someone who remembered seeing the girl you were looking for and that she left with Jozef."

"Son of bitch." Raj stood abruptly. It all made sense now. Krystof hadn't been playing a game. The stupid bastard really hadn't known what was going on right under his nose. And that explained why the security chief hadn't been here to defend his master. But did Jozef really believe he could take on Raj? Had he counted on Raj being so weakened by the battle with Krystof that he'd be more easily defeated? "Emelie," he said.

"Already on it, my lord," she replied, busily tapping away at her Blackberry. "He's got a house a couple blocks over, but that's not going to be the place. It's too small. Damn."

"Here, let me." Simon flipped out his own device. "Here it is. There's a house in Clarence, big sucker on three acres. The title's in his wife's maiden name. That's gotta be it." He gestured at Em. "I'm sending the address to you."

"Should we call first?" Em asked. "Make sure—"

Raj held up a hand. "He's there," he growled. They'd forgotten. He'd forgotten himself in all the rush. He was now Lord of the Northeastern Territory and his power had grown exponentially with the assumption of that mantle. Just as he provided life and protection to his vampires, so they lent him a reserve of power he could tap at will. He knew where Jozef was, and he knew Sarah was with him. Raj's blood bond with her had been boosted until he could feel her in his head, just like he could every vampire in the territory. Including Jozef. He could have reached out and snuffed Jozef's life with a thought. But what would be the fun in that?

"Emelie."

"My lord?"

"Leave a reserve here to clear out this mess and dispose of anyone who tries to take advantage of the situation. You're with me."

Chapter Forty-seven

Something was up. Sarah twisted around on the uncomfortable examining table they'd handcuffed her to and watched that bitch Edwards scurrying around the lab like one of her rats. She was backing up computer files like crazy while grabbing every piece of paper she could get her hands on and throwing it all into packing boxes. Like that was going to fool anyone. She had an entire fricking lab down here. Did she think no one would notice? That she'd actually get *away* with this? The stupid woman had spent months working with vampires and she *still* thought she could hide from them? Her life wouldn't be worth two cents if she went public with any of this stuff.

"They'll kill you, you know," Sarah said, conversationally. Edwards ignored her, sitting down at her computer and switching out the flash drives. Clearly there was a lot of data. Sarah wondered just how long this project had been going on. Longer than anyone suspected, that was for sure. "They'll hunt you down and kill you. Probably painfully," she added.

"Shut up, you stupid bitch!"

Sarah smiled. The good doctor was sounding a bit shrill. She hoped that meant help was on the way because she had a feeling these guys wouldn't want to leave any witnesses behind.

The basement windows rattled, as what seemed like a whole convoy of trucks arrived, followed by the sound of several voices. She looked up automatically, but couldn't see anything. The damn windows were completely blacked out. But that didn't stop Edwards from staring up at them in shock, just before she began ripping cables out of the back of her CPU. "Fuck this," the woman swore beneath her breath. "I'll just take the whole damn—"

Whatever she was going to say next was lost as a wave of power picked up the house and shook it like a child's piggybank, shattering the blackened basement windows and sending shards of glass flying. Edwards gave a panicked shriek and dropped under her desk, arms covering her head. When she finally looked up, her face was deathly pale and the wide-eyed gaze she turned on Sarah was full of fear.

Sarah just grinned. "My boyfriend's back."

* * * *

Raj glanced around as he slid out of the backseat of the SUV. He'd wanted to drive, but Em had bullied him into the backseat of the big truck, muttering something about how he'd better get used to it. That and more, apparently. When he started up the driveway toward the two-story colonial where Jozef had set up his little project, he was surrounded by a security cordon that rivaled anything deployed for a world leader. He sighed, wondering if he'd ever get to drive his BMW again.

"Em." She glanced over at him from her position at his left shoulder. "I'll go in fir—" He paused mid-word as she gave him a filthy look. "I have to do this," he said patiently.

Her mouth tightened in irritation. "At least let us go in ahead of you and make sure there's not some sort of booby trap or something. Fucking Jozef has to know he doesn't have a chance in hell in a stand-up fight."

Raj smiled, amused by her assessment of Jozef. His attention was drawn suddenly to the house and his smile fled. The front door opened and Jozef stood there, flanked by Serge and Charles, who were most obviously *not* being held against their will. He couldn't help wondering if Nina realized that Serge hadn't been taken, but had abandoned her to her fate. Not that the bastard would live long enough for anyone to worry about it.

"Move," Raj said. His vampire cordon split, and he strode forward until only a few feet separated him from Jozef and his flunkies.

Raj growled. "Where is she, Jozef? I want Sarah out here now."

"Don't listen to him, Joey!" He heard Jozef's wife's shrill voice just before she shoved her way around the vampires and out onto the porch. Her pointed, little face was twisted in outrage, her kinky hair sticking out wildly, looking as if she'd been recently electrocuted. She stepped to the edge of the short porch and screamed at him, spittle flying. "Who the fuck do you think you are to come here and tell my Joey what to do? Are you the one who put up with that crazy old man all these years, bowing and scraping and getting nothing but leftovers?" she demanded. "Not you, not the great Raj. You flew off to the big city, the big man in Manhattan. Well, not anymore. My Joey's taking over here and we'll say what happens, not you!"

Raj was struck speechless for a full three seconds, and then he laughed. "Are you fucking kidding me, Jozef? You let this human bitch talk you into this? Does she understand *nothing?* Do *you* fucking understand *nothing?*" His voice had risen, growing louder and more furious with every word. "ON YOUR GODDAMNED KNEES, NOW!" he roared.

His command hit the house like a tidal wave, a blast of lethal force that shattered every window and sent a rain of glass showering down in the darkness. The three rebellious vampires were crushed by the power of Raj's command, driven to their knees where they cringed away from the rage on his face. Jozef dared to raise his head, but even he could only stare in open-mouthed shock.

"Did you think Krystof gave me Manhattan because he liked me, Jozef?" Raj demanded in a harsh, low voice. "You of all people should have understood his reasons." He strode forward, taking the steps to the porch to stare down at the defeated trio with utter disgust. "Did you really think you could get away with this? *Are you that fucking stupid?"*

With a high-pitched screech, Celia launched herself at his back, blunt teeth bared, red-tipped fingers curving like claws. Raj didn't bother to turn, repelling her with a punch of power that hit like an invisible battering ram, slamming her off the porch to lie on the glass-covered ground like a pinned insect.

"Celia!" Jozef croaked and would have gone to her, but Raj stopped him with a cold look.

"Don't worry, Jozef. She's not dead yet." Jozef's head swung around, his eyes filled with fear.

"It wasn't her fault, Ra—I mean, my lord. Please, let her live."

Raj stared down at the big vampire, his lip curling in disdain, but all he said was, "Her life is bound to *yours.*" He held out his hand and Emelie slapped a smooth, wooden stake into his palm. He curled his fingers around its cool shaft and said pleasantly, "Go to hell, Jozef."

Jozef found some last shred of pride and snarled, "I'll see you there, you Pollack bastard."

Raj smiled, dipped his head in agreement and said, "Maybe you will." He swung his arm down in a smooth arc, shoving the stake so hard and deep that his fist hit the vampire's thick chest with an audible thud. Jozef fell backward with a gasp, a look of disbelief flashing briefly across his face before he disappeared in a shower of gray dust. Raj heard a long exhaled breath behind him as Celia died along with her mate, their lives wound far too tightly by the long mating bond for her to survive his death.

Serge and Charles fell to their faces, groveling, begging for their lives, in what they had to know was a useless effort. No one involved in this operation could be permitted to live. It violated the most basic tenet of Vampire. Raj didn't even spare them a glance, stepping over the pile of dust and entering the house. Em could take care of these two. He wanted to find Sarah.

Chapter Forty-eight

In the basement, Sarah watched with some amusement as Estelle Edwards tried to jam the desktop computer into a narrow box. The doc was sweating buckets and grunting like a pig with the effort, but it wasn't working. She finally gave up, letting the awkward CPU drop to the floor with a crash. She was swearing viciously, using words Sarah knew existed, but had never actually heard spoken before. Wow.

The door at the end of the corridor thundered open, hitting the wall with more force than usual. Edwards looked up in panic before her mouth tightened into a grim line of determination. This was not a woman who gave up easily. She pulled the keys from the pocket of her white lab coat and quickly uncuffed Sarah from the table, grabbing a fistful of her hair and dragging her backwards across the room to face the door. Sarah stumbled, her bound feet struggling to find purchase, but the woman only tightened her grip, bringing tears to Sarah's eyes. It felt like her hair was being torn out by the roots.

"Don't say a word, bitch," Edwards hissed in Sarah's ear, and she could feel the sharp point of something poking into her back just above her kidney.

She heard footsteps coming down the hall, and then more loud noise as someone kicked in the doors of the three cells. She sucked in a relieved breath, knowing Trish and the others had been found in time, but then blew the breath out quickly when the movement caused Edward's weapon to slice into her skin, drawing blood.

The noise stopped suddenly and she heard a familiar growl that made her smile. Raj was coming.

* * * *

Raj stormed toward the last door in the corridor, the only one standing open. He could smell the night air coming through a broken window, but above that was the scent of blood—Sarah's blood. Emelie would have raced around him, but he held her back with a sharp command, stepping into the doorway himself to find none other than Estelle Edwards, and clutched before her, her head wrenched at a painful angle, was his Sarah.

Raj let his gaze roam over his lover's body, noting the dark bruise on the side of her face, the purpled swelling of bare ankles where someone had bound her feet with plastic ties so tight she could barely stand. He catalogued the injuries, tallying up the damage he would inflict on this human before he killed her. He looked up and met Sarah's eyes, seeing the defiant flash of angry gold despite her predicament. He smiled and said gently, "Sarah."

"Hey, Raj." She managed a grin. "Quite a set up—" She cried out as Edwards jerked her back and Raj smelled the flow of fresh blood.

The woman had a knife. And she was cutting Sarah with it.

His rage was so great, it was nearly paralyzing. He snarled loudly, opening his mouth and baring his fangs. "Emelie."

Emelie came up next to him. "Yes, my lord."

Edwards stiffened, and said, "You let me out of here, or I'll kill—"

That was all she managed to say before everything changed. With movements far too fast for the human eye to see, much less respond to, Raj crossed the room and spun Sarah away from Edwards, throwing the doctor toward Emelie who grabbed her and broke her wrist as an inducement to drop the weapon. Raj's attention was all for Sarah, scooping her up and setting her safely on the examining table before whirling to face the human woman who was screaming in pain, cradling her broken arm.

He crossed the small room in one long step and wrapped his fingers around her throat, cutting off the noise. "I met your husband, Dr. Edwards," he said softly. Her eyes bulged and her face began to purple as she struggled for air, clawing at his fingers with her only functional hand. "He deserves better," Raj said. He dropped Edwards to the floor and Cervantes was there, throwing her limp body over his shoulder. He left the room quickly, footsteps pounding down the hall and up the stairs.

Raj turned back to Sarah who looked up as he approached, her eyes filled with worry as well as relief. Emelie was crouched in front of her, carefully cutting away the plastic ties which were buried in the flesh of her swollen ankles. Raj met Sarah's eyes and smiled grimly. She had a right to be worried. As relieved as he was to find her alive and reasonably well, he was furious that she'd put herself in this position in the first place.

He picked up her bound hands and snapped the metal handcuffs, tossing them across the room. Her eyes filled with tears and she rubbed her wrists carefully, crying out loud when Em finally got the ties off and the blood surged back into her feet.

"Emelie," he said softly, never taking his eyes off Sarah.

He felt more than saw Emelie glance from him to Sarah and back again, and heard her sigh. She leaned in to give Sarah a hug, whispering, "We'll talk later."

Raj scowled at her back as she left the room, and then transferred that scowl to Sarah.

"I know," she said in a resigned voice. He picked her up and moved her farther back onto the table, gently lifting her legs one at a time to soothe away the pain, sending warm drifts of power into the swollen tissue of her feet and ankles. It would have been faster to share blood with her, but he knew she wouldn't want that.

"Raj," she said in a small voice. He glanced up at her. "Are you pissed?"

He released her foot carefully and took her in his arms, holding her against his chest and feeling the steady thud of her heartbeat below his ribs. He kissed the top of her head. "I'm happy to see you alive."

She sighed contentedly and sank into his embrace, scooting forward to wrap her arms around his waist.

"I'm also pissed as hell," he added dryly. Her arms tightened and she rubbed her face against the front of his sweater.

"I'm sorry," she said.

"I'm sure you are."

She slapped him lightly. "Don't be mean. You know what I meant."

He chuckled softly and held her, knowing it couldn't last. His enemies had come close to taking Sarah's life. He couldn't take that risk again, couldn't let Sarah pay for what he was. "We have to get you out of here," he said finally. "Was this the main location?"

"I think so. Edwards pretty much lived in here and I think all the data was kept here. I don't know if she uploaded anything."

"Simon will take care of that. This place, this entire project, will disappear. It never happened."

"I'll need to disappear again too," she said on a tired breath. "Blackwood saw to that before he scuttled out of town."

Raj sighed and pulled away. "Simon can help you," he said. "Anything you need, you can ask him or Emelie. They'll get you a new identity, transportation . . . whatever's necessary."

Sarah looked up at him and he could see the confusion and hurt on her face. "Raj?"

"I can't stay, Sarah, and I can't take you with me. I've got . . . responsibilities. Things I have to do now that—" He cut himself off. She didn't need to hear every bitter detail of his new life as a vampire lord. It would be months before he had the territory under control. Months spent traveling, meeting and defeating challenge after challenge, destroying those who'd grown too independent under Krystof's rule to accept a new lord, gathering in those who needed help, either from neglect or simply the trauma of the transition. Months of exhausting, brutal work followed by a long, long lifetime of rule. It was a burden he'd never sought, but it was *his* burden, not Sarah's. She deserved better.

He took her face in his hands, stroking his thumb over her soft lips, tenderly kissing her swollen temple with its ugly bruise. She closed tear-filled eyes as he bent to kiss her one last time, lingering to savor the sweetness of her mouth. "I'll send Emelie in." He left before she could open her eyes, before he could see the pain he'd just put there.

* * * *

Emelie came around the corner, still scowling after Raj's departing back. She took in Sarah's hurt, bewildered look and crossed to her quickly, shaking her head in disgust. She tsked loudly and said, "Men are such idiots. Makes me glad I'm a lesbian." She looked Sarah up and down, frowning at her injuries. "Didn't he share blood with you?"

Sarah blushed. "No."

"Well, what the hell was he doing in here then? Jesus, I can't believe—"

"It's not his fault," Sarah insisted, jumping to Raj's defense. "It's me. He tried, um, before and I wouldn't, that is, I didn't—" To her horror, she started crying.

"Oh, baby," Emelie breathed. "What will I do with the two of you now?" She held Sarah, letting her cry away all the fear she'd been pushing back since they'd bonked her on the head and thrown her in the backseat of that car, all of the pain from her wretched aching feet and arms, the throbbing in her head. And most of all the pain in her heart at the thought of never seeing Raj again.

"Better now?" Emelie asked.

Sarah nodded, reaching for a tissue from the nearby stand. She blew her nose and threw the used tissue in the trash. "Sorry."

"That's okay. I'm used to it. Raj has that effect on a lot of people."

Sarah laughed and felt her eyes fill with fresh tears. She looked down at her hands so Emelie wouldn't notice and saw the blurry outline of a white card. She frowned and looked up at Em.

"Give him a couple of months," Em said patiently. "It's going to be rough for a while, but after that . . ." She nodded at the card, which Sarah saw had Em's name and cell phone printed on it. Em met her eyes, giving her a steady, meaningful look. "Trust me on this one, babe."

Sarah palmed the card and nodded. "Okay."

"Right," Em said. "Now, let's get you gone. The guys are gonna tear this place apart, and then we'll have Simon get started on your little problem. He's a genius at making people disappear." She grinned wickedly. "In a good way, that is."

Sarah laughed and hoped Em was right. About Simon and everything else.

Chapter Forty-nine

Raj stood on the rooftop high above Manhattan, watching cars moving up and down the street below, the red and white of their lights reflecting off the wet pavement in a blur of color. It had rained again today; the month was shaping up to be one of the wettest in New York history. But for now, the rain had stopped. The air was warm and muggy, but far better than the sterile, processed stuff waiting for him inside, along with yet another marathon session of meetings with his various underlings.

If anyone had told him three months ago that life as a vampire lord was somewhat akin to that of a corporate executive, he'd have laughed. Oh, he'd known there was business involved. After all, he'd been running Krystof's affairs in Manhattan for decades. But this endless nattering about every tiny detail of even the smallest vampire enterprise in the farthest reaches of his territory . . . Christ, there were times he wanted to run as far and as fast as he could go. Find some tropical paradise with warm, velvety nights and soft waves lapping at sun-warmed beaches—just leave all of this crap behind and say *fuck it.*

But there were so many souls he cared about who relied on him— Emelie and the rest of his children. And now a seemingly endless number of others he really didn't care about, but who relied on him just as much, if not more.

And besides, who would spend those velvety nights *with* him? Paradise wouldn't be paradise if he was all alone.

He sighed, straightening away from the railing and turning to survey the many and vigilant vampires who shared the rooftop with him. He was certainly never alone here. Not anymore. His eyes scanned his security team, noting Emelie's absence. Em had seemed to sense his dwindling patience for meetings and suggested he let her clear his calendar for the rest of the night. There were a few hours yet before sunrise, but he'd agreed readily enough, originally thinking about dropping in at one of his clubs, although, he'd quickly discarded that idea as just more business. There were always the trendy human clubs, crowded with beautiful people desperate for attention. But that didn't appeal either. Maybe he'd just spend a quiet few hours at home—some chilled vodka, good music. He shook his head in amusement. He must really be getting old if that was his idea of a good time.

He headed for the stairway that would take him down one flight to the top floor of the building and his penthouse condo. His security team moved with him, anticipating his direction and sending two of their number down the stairwell ahead of him, while the rest formed up around him. Raj stifled another sigh and let them do their job, going the short distance down the stairs, through the fire door and then down the hallway to the double doors of his condo.

They stopped there, waiting while he tapped in his security code, taking up positions to either side of the hallway door while he stepped inside the darkened penthouse alone. That was the one thing he insisted upon, the one thing he and Emelie had fought long and hard over, even though she'd known his will would triumph in the end. He permitted no security inside—this was his home, his inner sanctum. It was the one place where there were no petitioners, no one looking to him for answers or protection. The one place where he could be truly alone.

Except he wasn't alone tonight.

He heard her breathing first, speeding up to match her racing heart. She stood almost directly across from him, one hand touching the back of a chair as if to anchor her in the dark room. He inhaled deeply, closing his eyes as it all came back to him, the feel of her beneath him, around him, her small cries of pleasure as she came over and over until she lay limp in his arms, her pale skin damp with sweat. He exerted his will and candles flared to life around the room, more welcoming than the harsh, artificial light of the modern era.

Her eyes widened, their golden flecks echoing the flames. Finally she looked at him, raising her chin defiantly, as if she expected an argument. He smiled. She'd get no argument from him, not tonight.

"Sarah."

"Raj?" Her voice wavered and he saw the gleam of tears in her eyes.

"Come here, little one."

She ran across the room. He'd intended to let her come to him, but his will failed, his need to touch her too strong, and his heart too weak. He met her halfway, catching her when she jumped into his arms, holding her easily as their mouths met for the first time in what was surely centuries. He crushed her to his chest, their kiss hard at first, a clashing of teeth and tongues, as if their time was limited and they each needed to taste as much of the other as possible in the brief time allotted them. She was whispering his name over and over, tears running down her face. He tasted their saltiness and held her closer, carrying her to his bedroom, kicking open the door and lowering them both to the huge bed where he'd slept alone and hungry for too many months.

His mind was buzzing with questions. How she'd gotten here, where she'd been, but his body had its own plans. He could feel his fangs pressing against the flesh of his gums, his cock straining against its confinement beneath the suit slacks he'd donned for his last meeting an entire lifetime ago. He pulled back and stared down at her, running a finger along the ridge of her pale eyebrows, across her soft cheek and along the crease of her lips. She sucked his finger into her warm little mouth and he laughed. "Hungry, sweetheart?"

"Starving," she said fervently, wrapping her arms around his neck. "You're wearing a suit."

He glanced down at himself. "So I am."

"I think you should take it off," she said. "Now."

"Such a hurry. Maybe we'll take it slow—"

Her clever fingers slid down between their bodies to grip his erection through the cloth of his pants, and he groaned, throwing his head back with a pleasure so great he wanted to howl. He lowered his head and gave her a flat look. "Careful, little one," he growled. "It's been a long time."

She met his gaze evenly. "I missed you, Raj. I missed you so much."

His heart clenched with unfamiliar emotion and he let his hand drop to her neck, sliding beneath the silk of her white blouse, slipping the buttons free until he had bared the valley between her breasts. "I missed you too, Sarah." He bent his head and kissed her softly, tasting her sweet mouth, his tongue exploring, remembering. She made a small, eager noise and his cock jumped in response. He groaned, baring his fangs into their kiss, feeling her tongue glide around them until she nicked an edge and her warm blood flowed into his mouth. The taste drove him over the edge.

He ripped the rest of her blouse away, revealing her full breasts barely concealed by a frothy bit of lace bra. He tore that away as well, sucking hard on her nipples, exploring each one with his tongue until they stood eager and erect, two pretty pink pearls gleaming wet in the candlelight. He renewed his attack, scraping her tender breasts with his fangs and lapping up the slow trickle of blood as she cried out and buried her hands in his hair clutching him closer, arching her back against his mouth.

He moved down her body, ignoring her protests as he left her breasts bare in the cool air of the room. She was wearing a short, tight skirt of some sort. He didn't bother with the zipper, simply slid it up her thighs until it was gathered around her waist. He kissed his way over her abdomen, rubbing his jaw against the soft skin of her belly, tearing the flimsy lace panties away from her mound when they hindered his explorations. Sarah moaned softly, spreading her legs in invitation so that the sweet scent of her arousal drifted up to torment him.

He ran his big hands over her thighs, spreading her legs wider, lowering his mouth to her silken folds and opening her with his tongue. He found her hard, little clit and rasped his tongue over it. She cried out, tugging at his hair frantically and gasping, begging, "Please, Raj. Please."

He didn't know what she was pleading for, but he knew what he wanted. He sucked as hungrily on her clit as he had her nipples, rousing the hot little nub until she was screaming, until he could feel her pussy clenching beneath his mouth as she came hard. He smiled and licked her juices slowly and leisurely as she groaned desperately. "Raj. Baby, my lord, master, whatever you want. Just fuck me, please. Please."

He laughed in pure male satisfaction, standing by the side of the bed and stripping off his suit, watching her hungrily as she writhed beneath his gaze, her little fingers sliding down between her thighs and rubbing frantically, trying to erase the unquenched desire burning there. He stepped out of his underwear and knelt on the bed naked, taking in the sight of her luscious body, her full breasts plump and aching, her pale pink areolas with their deep pink nipples begging for his mouth. His gaze slid down further, past the skirt still gathered at her waist to her hot, little center, all wet and ready for him. He growled low in his chest and her eyes grew wider, raking up and down his body, settling on his jutting cock. Her pink tongue emerged, wetting her lips eagerly. She raised her eyes to meet his and without looking away deliberately spread her legs even wider.

He bared his fangs in a smile and dropped to the bed between her thighs, thrusting his full length deep into her tight sheath in a long, slow stroke. Sarah cried out wordlessly, wrapping her legs around his hips and holding him close, scraping her nails down his back until he felt the warm trickle of blood over his ribs. He drove in and out, eager for the feel of her climax around him, for the rush of his own release. It had been too long. He waited until he felt her begin to tremble beneath him, until her body began squeezing his cock, coaxing it to release his seed. He lowered his head to her neck, rubbing the full length of his fangs along her sweat-soaked skin, before lifting his head slightly and sinking his fangs into the delicious flow of her blood.

She came instantly, screaming, her legs almost spasming around his back, lifting herself even further onto his cock as he joined her in a blazing, uncontrollable freefall of ecstasy.

He collapsed onto her, shifting to one side at the last minute to avoid crushing her. The movement threatened to slide his pulsing cock out of her hot, tight sheath, but she reacted quickly, her legs scissoring sideways to hold him inside her. He chuckled softly and gripped her hip, pulling her more firmly into the curve of his body. He licked her neck lazily, sealing the wound, savoring the delectable flavor of her blood, a flavor that was unique, his Sarah.

"You taste good," he murmured, a rumble from deep in his chest.

She shivered and slid a hand up his back along his ribs, where she'd clawed him open with her nails. Raising fingers red with his blood to her mouth, she sucked them clean and, licking her lips as if savoring the sweetest honey, said, "So do you."

Raj grew still. "Sarah," he said cautiously. "If you—"

"I know," she said firmly. "I'm yours for however long you want me."

"That would be a very long time," he said, kissing her mouth gently. "A very . . ." He kissed her again. ". . very long time."

She curled her arms around his neck and met his gaze. "Okay. But none of this vampire mating shit. I'm not a gorilla. I want a real wedding."

He groaned and rolled his head back in protest, but then lowered his gaze to hers once again and smiled. "It will have to be a nighttime wedding."

Sarah laughed. "I love you, Rajmund."

"Yes, you do," he said smugly. She glared at him until he relented and admitted, "I love you, too."

He kissed her at length, savoring the knowledge that she was his. "I just have one question," he said at last. Her eyes opened wide. "How long have you and Emelie been plotting against me?"

Sarah laughed and began to move against him. "This . . ." She arched her back, sliding herself on and off his hardening cock. ". . . is not a plot, my lord. I think we need to refresh your memory a bit."

Raj growled, rolling them over and forcing her down to the bed, driving himself deep inside her. "I see you need to learn your place, little one. And that is beneath your master."

Sarah slipped her arms around his neck and whispered in his ear. "I love you, master."

Raj smiled as the phone rang. He reached across her to dig his cell out of the pocket of his pants which lay on the floor. He checked the ID. "Emelie," he answered, not waiting for her to say anything. "Clear my schedule for the next three days." Sarah's eyes widened as he began thrusting slowly in and out of her. "And, Em? Thank you."

Epilogue

Malibu, California

Cyn leaned forward, smiling as she read the latest e-mail from Sarah. It tickled her that Sarah and Raj had gotten together. And at the same time, she was delighted to have a friend who truly understood what it meant to be mated to a vampire. Or soon-to-be married, in Sarah's case. Cyn pursed her lips thoughtfully, trying to figure out the best way to convince Raphael they should go to the wedding. Damn vampires were so prickly with one another, especially now that Raj had taken over his Sire's territory.

She pushed back from the computer and picked up a bottle of water, tilting her head back and drinking deeply. With no fresh air, Raphael's underground lair tended to be cool and a little too dry. Still, she preferred to work here during the day, while he slept on the other side of the room. She usually slept with him the first few hours, and then worked awhile, finally ending up back in bed with him before sunset. He liked to have her there when he woke, and she didn't exactly mind, either, since—

She froze, taking the bottle slowly away from her mouth and setting it blindly on the desktop as she turned to stare into the deep shadows over the bed. She'd heard . . . Her mind raced trying to recreate the precise sound and couldn't do it. There shouldn't be any noise at all. Raphael always slept perfectly still. She stood and walked over to the bed, her breath catching in her throat when she heard something again, but this time . . . Was that a groan?

"Raphael?" Her voice cracked with tension, her heart pounding fiercely inside her chest. He groaned louder, a sound of such anguish and pain that she threw herself onto the high bed in a panic, crawling over to him, reaching out blindly in the darkness to touch his face. Her lungs constricted in fear and she scrambled back to the bedside lamp, snapping it up to its brightest setting, before spinning around to examine his face in full light.

It was covered in blood. Cyn screamed, "Raphael!"

To be continued . . .

MAR 2012

CPSIA information can be obtained at www.ICGtesting.com
Printed in the USA
BVOW021316160112

280531BV00003B/11/P